M000214925

DUMBARTON OAKS
MEDIEVAL LIBRARY

Daniel Donoghue, General Editor

THE IBERIAN
APOLLONIUS OF TYRE

DOML 84

DUMBARTON OAKS MEDIEVAL LIBRARY

Daniel Donoghue, General Editor
Josiah Blackmore, Medieval Iberian Editor

Jan M. Ziolkowski, Founding Editor

Medieval Iberian Editorial Board
David Arbesú
Marina Brownlee
E. Michael Gerli
Luis Manuel Girón-Negrón
Dorothy Severin
Ryan Szpiech

The Iberian
Apollonius of Tyre

Edited and Translated by

EMILY C. FRANCOMANO

and

CLARA PASCUAL-ARGENTE

DUMBARTON OAKS
MEDIEVAL LIBRARY

HARVARD UNIVERSITY PRESS
CAMBRIDGE, MASSACHUSETTS
LONDON, ENGLAND
2024

Copyright © 2024 by the President and Fellows of Harvard College
ALL RIGHTS RESERVED
Printed in the United States of America

First Printing

Library of Congress Cataloging-in-Publication Data

Names: Francomano, Emily C., editor, translator. | Pascual-Argente, Clara, editor, translator.

Title: The Iberian Apollonius of Tyre / edited and translated by Emily C. Francomano and Clara Pascual-Argente.

Other titles: Libro de Apollonio. (Francomano and Pascual-Argente) | Dumbarton Oaks medieval library ; 84.

Description: Cambridge, Massachusetts : Harvard University Press, 2024. | Series: Dumbarton Oaks medieval library ; DOML 84 | Includes bibliographical references and index. | Facing-page translation with Spanish on the versos and English on the rectos ; introduction and notes in English.

Identifiers: LCCN 2023035211 | ISBN 9780674291034 (cloth)

Subjects: LCSH: Apollonius, of Tyre (Fictitious character)—Romances. | Romances, Spanish—To 1500. | Spanish poetry—To 1500. | Spanish prose literature—To 1500.

Classification: LCC PA3871.A8 A24 2024 | DDC 883.01—dc23/eng/20231206

LC record available at https://lccn.loc.gov/2023035211

Contents

Introduction

The Legend of Apollonius of Tyre

The tale of King Apollonius of Tyre's adventures is central to the premodern literary imagination. The earliest surviving written version, the prose *Historia Apollonii regis Tyri* (*The Story of King Apollonius of Tyre* = *HART*), which exists in two basic forms, known as Recensions A and B, was composed in Latin in the fifth or the sixth century CE.[1] Throughout the centuries, *HART* was adapted for new audiences, in many forms and languages; the legend remained current until the 1600s, when it hit the boards as Shakespeare's *Pericles*. Even though Ben Jonson called the story "mouldy," it is clear that writers and audiences were delighted to dust off, retell, and retranslate this glittering fiction of a tempest-tossed prince and the trials of his family.[2]

In brief, the story tells how, forced to leave his kingdom when he solves the riddle revealing the king of Antioch's incest, Apollonius saves the city of Tarsus from famine, then loses all his worldly possessions in a shipwreck. Apollonius's good manners earn him a new life and wife in Pentapolis—a wife whom he then loses in childbirth at sea. After leaving his daughter in Tarsus, from whence she is taken by pirates and sold into a brothel in Mytilene, Apollonius sinks into despair until he is at last reunited with his family and seeks

vengeance for all the wrongs done to them, then returns to his kingly duties, including fathering a male heir. He also inherits the throne of Antioch, the incestuous king and his daughter having been struck down by God. No conventional romance or epic hero, Apollonius does quite a bit of sulking when his fortunes turn, and proves his mettle not on the battlefield with horse and sword, but by study, sport, and skillful entertainment of his hosts. The two equally talented heroines of the story, Apollonius's wife and his daughter, embark on parallel adventures before the family's eventual reunion. Through the protagonists' wanderings from one Mediterranean port of call to another—from Tyre to Antioch to Tarsus to Pentapolis to Ephesus to Mytilene and back—the Apollonius legend retraces routes of trade, pilgrimage, and military expansion. The narrative gestures to the genre of Greek romance (or novel) and is also closely related to both folklore and hagiographic legends.

There are medieval versions of the Apollonius story in Old and Middle English, Dutch, German, Danish, Latin, Spanish, Portuguese, Catalan, Polish, Russian, Hungarian, and Greek, all ultimately derived from *HART*. Elizabeth Archibald cataloged one hundred and fourteen Latin manuscripts of the story, to which can be added the recent discovery of yet another witness, a palimpsest located in Saint Catherine's Monastery of the Sinai.[3] Each medieval version takes up the source materials in the manner that the adaptors and translators felt most appropriate for their audiences, some relaying the bare bones of the narrative, others creating elaborate chivalric romances, yet others highlighting the themes of fortune, providence, and patience, and some using prose and others verse. For some, the story of

Apollonius was a tale to be embedded within the framework of exemplary fictions, for others, a historical text on par with the deeds of Alexander the Great. The story of Apollonius of Tyre proved to be particularly popular in the twelfth century, perhaps because of the increased relevance of the eastern Mediterranean—the area where the story is set—to Latin Europe due to the Crusades. Indeed, Apollonius is mentioned in connection with Tyre in crusade chronicles by Fulcher of Chartres, William of Tyre, and Jacques de Vitry.[4]

This volume presents new editions and English translations of the two complete, standalone medieval Iberian versions, the thirteenth-century verse *Libro de Apolonio (The Book of Apollonius)* and the late fifteenth-century prose *Vida e historia del rey Apolonio (The Life and History of King Apollonius)*. Among the many medieval reworkings of the legend, *The Book of Apollonius* is one of the most poetically accomplished vernacular versions, and the only one that has been treated as a canonical work within its own literary tradition. *The Life and History* is a translation from the version of the tale found in the *Gesta Romanorum (The Deeds of the Romans = GR)*, compiled in the late thirteenth or early fourteenth century.

Other Iberian versions of the legend are found incorporated into larger works or have reached us in fragmentary form. Alfonso X of Castile's thirteenth-century *General estoria* announces that the story of Apollonius will be retold at the beginning of the fifth part of his universal chronicle, although this section was either never fully completed or has been lost. Catalan versions of *HART* have recently been uncovered with the identification of partial translations of the work in two fifteenth-century manuscripts, one a songbook

and the other a prose miscellany. Fifteenth-century Portuguese and Castilian translations of Gower's *Confessio Amantis* also include the story of Apollonius as an example of the sin of incest. Lastly, Juan de Timoneda included a prose version in his *Patrañuelo,* a sixteenth-century collection of short stories. Passing references to the figure of the king and his misfortunes also occur in poems and ballads.[5]

THE BOOK OF APOLLONIUS

The Castilian *Book of Apollonius* is part of a tradition of creative rewritings of ancient history in vernacular languages across Latin Europe that began in the period of renewed interest in classical culture often called the "twelfth-century renaissance." A series of Francophone poems known by modern scholars as *romans d'antiquité,* or romances of antiquity, which retell the stories of Alexander the Great, Thebes, Eneas, or Troy, as well as Apollonius (in a *Roman d'Apollonius de Tyr,* of which only a fragment remains), inaugurate the tradition. These romances reshaped the foundational narratives of the ancient past for lay, courtly audiences, using pre-Christian stories as spaces for "intellectual play and ethical inquiry."[6] After this initial wave of vernacular narratives about classical history, new iterations quickly multiplied across languages, adopting verse and prose forms, straddling romance and historiography, and reflecting a variety of local sociopolitical contexts.

The Book of Apollonius, composed around the middle of the thirteenth century, closely follows in the footsteps of the pioneering Castilian *Libro de Alexandre (The Book of Alexander),* the earliest known example of vernacular narrative

about ancient, pagan history composed within the Iberian Peninsula.[7] This monumental poem on the life of Alexander the Great was created in the first third of the thirteenth century, probably by a cleric working for the royal chancery and envisioning the royal court as his initial audience. The *Libro de Alexandre* provides a clericalized alternative to the Francophone romances of antiquity: it employs a Latinizing stanza already associated with religious poetry in French and Italian, the monorhymed alexandrine quatrain (called *cuaderna vía* by scholars of Castilian literature), and introduces explicit Christian moralizing into the story. The alexandrine poem enjoyed an enormous success and became the origin of at least two literary lineages in Castile: clerical works written in the same stanza, sometimes called by scholars *mester de clerecía* (the cleric's craft or task), and narratives about the ancient, pagan past.[8]

The Book of Apollonius fully belongs to both of these lineages. In composing "a romance in the new, learned style" (stanza 1.3), the poem's clerical creator went even further than the *Libro de Alexandre* in the Christianizing of the Gentile past. He carried out a creative and sophisticated rewriting of his source, *HART,* that highlights its hagiographical elements and explicitly casts Apollonius's wanderings as a form of *peregrinatio vitae* (human life as a pilgrimage), whose twists and turns the narrator takes pains to connect to divine providence.[9] A hagiographical interpretation of the story is also reinforced by the history of the *cuaderna vía* stanza: by the time of *The Book of Apollonius's* creation, this metrical form had already been employed as a vehicle to narrate the lives of several local saints by the earliest named Castilian poet, Gonzalo de Berceo. In this way, *The Book of*

Apollonius is a product of both clerical intellectual writing in Castilian and the European tradition of remaking classical history in the vernacular.

Beyond his clerical condition, the identity of the person who composed *The Book of Apollonius* remains a mystery. We can nonetheless surmise that he was part of the intellectual and institutional networks that gave rise to the vernacular clerical poems associated with the *mester de clerecía,* including the *Libro de Alexandre:* a web enabling the circulation of objects, people, and ideas through universities, cathedral schools, ecclesiastical and lay courts and chanceries, and monasteries. The displays of musical and rhetorical knowledge within the poem strongly suggest that its author enjoyed a formal education in the liberal arts. Moreover, the centrality of the concept of courtliness in *The Book of Apollonius* (on which more below) points to a poet who was composing with a courtly, mostly lay audience in mind, perhaps that of the Castilian royal court, which was one of the most active cultural hubs in the kingdom during the mid-thirteenth century.

The only extant copy of *The Book of Apollonius,* in an Aragonese manuscript from the third quarter of the fourteenth century, situates the poem next to a clerical composition focused on female sanctity, the *Vida de Santa María Egipciaca (The Life of Saint Mary of Egypt).*[10] The codex also contains a third clerical text, the *Libre dels tres reys d'orient (Book of the Three Kings of Orient),* a poem recounting some episodes from the early life of Christ. The theme of Apollonius as a *homo viator* (man as pilgrim) takes center stage when the three works—all situated in the eastern Mediterranean and focusing on traveling figures—are read together. The exis-

tence of this manuscript shows that the poem still elicited interest in the 1300s, and it did so beyond the kingdom of Castile. Further evidence of the continued currency of *The Book of Apollonius* is found in the "Cantar del rey don Alonso," a short poem inserted in some versions of the fourteenth-century *Crónica de Alfonso X* and voiced by the Castilian king, who laments his lack of allies against the conflict that opposed him to his son, Sancho (the future Sancho IV), and compares himself to King Apollonius.

The Life and History of King Apollonius

The Life and History is a translation of a late version of the Apollonius story, the one found within the compendium of exemplary tales known as the *Gesta Romanorum (GR)*. The story appears as chapter 153 in the collection and is quite long in comparison to the others. Although it does not end with a Christian allegorization, like the other *exempla* in the collection, its moralizing intentions are made clear in the chapter's title: "Of temporal tribulation, which at the last, will be turned to everlasting joy." The Castilian translator produced a highly literal translation of the text from the *GR,* from the didactic title to the story's conclusion. However, this practice of translational fidelity does not extend to the chapter divisions and titles inserted into *The Life and History,* which are adapted from a German version of the Apollonius tale, the *Hystori des Küniges Appoloni* (ca. 1460), Heinrich Steinhöwel's translation of the story as recounted in Godfrey of Viterbo's *Pantheon.* The Aragonese translator's choice to render the Latin source literally created occasional comprehension problems due to an imperfect under-

standing of the language. The result is Aragonese-inflected Castilian prose that is full of syntactic and lexical Latinisms.[11]

The *Vida e historia del rey Apolonio* was published in Zaragoza by Juan Hurus around 1488; it is a quarto book of forty-six pages (twenty-three folia), densely illustrated by thirty-five woodcuts, one for each chapter of the story.[12] The only known copy of the Spanish prose text, held today at the Hispanic Society of America, seems to have been part of a print volume in which *The Life and History* followed the *Historia de los siete sabios de Roma,* although *The Life and History* is also mentioned on its own in several catalogs, which may point to the existence of another edition, now lost.[13]

Despite its publication in the latter part of the century, *The Life and History*'s version of the Apollonius story is representative of vernacular literary culture's engagement with classical materials throughout the 1400s, and of the movement that dominated the Castilian fifteenth-century: vernacular humanism.[14] Unlike the full-scale transformation and medievalization of its Latin model that characterizes *The Book of Apollonius, The Life and History* follows the well-established tradition, started in Castile around the late fourteenth century, of "service translations," which rendered their sources in a much more literal fashion. Beyond the production of an enormous number of translations, Castilian vernacular literature in the 1400s was also characterized by a deliberate attempt to elevate the register of formal Castilian through the incorporation of Latin syntax and vocabulary, a practice that reached its height in the middle of the century and was still in use at the time *The Life and History* was published.[15] Furthermore, *The Life and History* is also tied to German vernacular humanism through its reliance

on Steinhöwel's *Hystori des Küniges Appoloni,* itself part of a wave of translations making classical, humanist, and other Latin works available in the German language.

The Life and History has also been linked to what scholars of early printing have called the short chivalric tale, an "editorial genre" that drew for the most part from well-known medieval narratives and was relatively easy to produce in print due to the tales' short lengths.[16] In any case, its probable printing alongside the *Historia de los siete sabios de Roma* strongly connects it with other medieval exemplary works set in the classical past. In contrast to the German *Hystori des Küniges Appoloni,* which went through multiple reprintings and saw considerably wide circulation, the Castilian *Life and History* had a relatively narrow readership and influence.

THE IBERIAN APOLLONIUS

If *HART* is, in Archibald's assessment, a "potential romance," *The Book of Apollonius* is very much a full-fledged exemplary romance of antiquity, while *The Life and History of King Apollonius* is an extended exemplum verging on romance.[17] Consequently, the two Iberian texts are representative of how different artists and translators chose distinctive modes of reworking classical material for new audiences over the centuries. Moreover, they show how the Apollonius legend is present at the creation of two major literary and cultural movements in Iberia: vernacular, clerical poetry in the thirteenth century, and the transformation of medieval literature—produced by vernacular humanism and nascent print culture—in the fifteenth century. Both Ibe-

rian reworkings develop the key, interrelated themes inherited from *HART,* which were in large part the narrative ingredients that made the story so popular for so long, namely, incest and the threat of incest, riddling, intellectual heroism, the thematization of written culture, kingship and courtliness, and the vagaries of fortune. The narratives revolve around geminate structures highlighting these central themes.[18] Further, both clearly highlight the exemplary nature of the tale: for medieval Iberian audiences Apollonius's story is a mirror of princes, a spiritual guide, and a story about the pilgrimage of human life.

While *The Book of Apollonius* adds emotional depth to its source material and frequently domesticates as it translates the story for its thirteenth-century audience, *The Life and History* retains more references to the pre-Christian past and displays a broader humor. Although both adaptations are set in what would have been for their Iberian audiences the distant, pagan past, they work to endow the wandering hero and his family with a quasi-saintly status by the end of the narrative. The hagiographic resonances of Apollonius's story are present in *HART* but become all the more salient in the heavily Christianized vernacular versions like *The Book of Apollonius,* where a poor fisherman sermonizes about fortune and providence (stanzas 133–38), and where the poet-narrator concludes the story with an excursus regarding the importance of giving money to the Church rather than leaving it to one's heirs (stanzas 651–54). The tale as a whole is reminiscent of the lives of both Saint Eustace and Saint Clement, and the specific episode of Apollonius's encounter with the poor fisherman is clearly analogous to one in the life of Saint Martin of Tours. Apollonius's travels also pro-

vide multiple examples of guest-host relations, and reflections on the implicit theology of hospitality.[19]

Folklore and erudition meet in the riddles, which not only provide the catalyst for Apollonius's adventures but also attend his betrothal to the princess of Pentapolis and his tearful reunions with his long-lost daughter and wife. Apollonius's first adventure is a failed one: in his attempt to win the hand of the princess of Antioch, he solves a riddle that reveals the incestuous relationship her father has forced upon her and is forced to flee for his life. If at first Antiochus's riddle served as both a ruse to protect him from having to allow another man to marry his daughter and the means of revealing his sin, later riddles serve to secure honorable marriages and to stave off the looming threat of father-daughter incest. This is the case when Archistrates, the king of Pentapolis, tries to figure out who his daughter wants to marry and when Apollonius and his daughter Tarsiana are reunited. With the exception of King Antiochus's riddle, which is a variation on medieval riddles on family relationships and gets somewhat garbled in *The Book of Apollonius,* the riddles in *HART,* the *GR,* and both the Iberian adaptations are variations on riddles found in Symphosius's *Aenigmata,* a late fourth- or early fifth-century anthology of one hundred riddles that circulated widely throughout the Middle Ages.

King Apollonius of Tyre is characterized by his command of the liberal arts, manifested in his unmatched capacity for riddle solving and musical performance, and, in *The Book of Apollonius,* in a desire to expand his knowledge. In this, *The Book of Apollonius* echoes the *Libro de Alexandre,* whose similarly educated protagonist is defined by an unquenchable

thirst for knowledge that is at the root of both his marvel-ous deeds and his eventual fall. Yet if his search for knowl-edge might be one of the causes of Apollonius's misfortunes, it is also his education that allows him to recover from them when he becomes the music teacher, and eventually hus-band, of Luciana (called Cleopatra in *The Life and History*), the king of Pentapolis's daughter, who falls in love with him thanks to his musical abilities. Other characters are also presented as intellectual heroes: the physician's disciple who heals Luciana/Cleopatra, presumed dead after giving birth, and especially Apollonius's studious daughter, Tarsiana, who successfully puts her education in the liberal arts to practi-cal use. When sold into slavery, Tarsiana's rhetorical and mu-sical abilities allow her to escape being prostituted, and later her expert riddling heralds the family's reunion. The stark contrasts between Antiochus's sterile and sinful coupling and the other, freely chosen marriages shows the narratives' investment in marriage by consent.

Both *The Book of Apollonius* and *The Life and History* pay particular attention to written communication. The role of letters and inscriptions, already important in *HART,* is high-lighted in the poem, which often calls attention to charac-ters' literacy and uses the inscriptions on display to guide the audience by pausing and recapitulating the story. The prominence of educated characters and the attention to written culture endow *The Book of Apollonius* with a metanar-rative quality that belies its apparent simplicity and looks to display and celebrate the qualities associated with the cleri-cal class to which the poet belonged.[20] *The Life and History* similarly draws metaliterary attention to its own creation by recalling how Apollonius "wrote down all his deeds and his-

tory in two tomes, placing one in the temple at Ephesus and the other in his own library" (35.2). In the fifteenth-century humanistic context of *The Life and History,* the effect is analogous, stressing the importance of learned study of the ancients.

Yet even if Apollonius has qualities reminiscent of *The Book of Apollonius'*s clerical poet and *The Life and History'*s humanistic translator-scholar, the main character is a king, and courtliness and kingship remain central concerns. The incestuous Antiochus, who destroys not just himself but the future of his line by refusing to marry off his daughter, and the munificent Archistrates are "the extreme points on the scale of good and bad kings," as Archibald points out.[21] Apollonius, for all his learnedness and talent, is often in need of lessons in proper behavior, which he receives from other model princes when he is laid low by the onslaughts of Fortune. Where *HART* and *The Life and History* are short on psychological detail, kingship is tied to emotional regulation in *The Book of Apollonius,* which is filled with expressions of feeling, ranging from joy to despair. For Apollonius—who often acts as an ideal, learned prince should—shame at losing his first intended bride and then intense sadness at the loss of his status, belongings, and family in the shipwrecks that carry him throughout the Mediterranean threaten to strip him of his ability to behave in a courtly and kingly fashion. The poem's function as a mirror of princes extends to modeling the emotional responses to misfortune that befit or dishonor a king. *The Book of Apollonius* employs the language of courtly love, and the banqueting scene in Pentapolis provides audiences with an example of the "joy of the court" in noble conversation and entertainment. The theme

of courtliness in the poem is intimately related to its emphasis on the study of music and the liberal arts, pointing to a learned model of royal power and court culture.

The Book of Apollonius has been the object of modern editions starting with the one published by C. Carroll Marden (1917–1922). Since then, editors have fallen into two camps: Giovanni Battista De Cesare (1974) and Manuel Alvar (1976) have tried to reconstruct the poem's earliest form and therefore intervened extensively in the text, whose metrical form they believe to have been completely regular; while Marden, Carmen Monedero (1987), Dolores Corbella (1992), and Carina Zubillaga (2014, in the context of an edition of the whole codex) have preferred to offer editions of the manuscript that correct only very obvious errors, add modern punctuation, and—in the cases of Monedero and Corbella —stay very close to the codex's spelling.

There are three modern transcriptions of *The Life and History of King Apollonius,* none of which is a critical presentation of the text. In 1964 Homero Serís, who discovered the uncataloged incunable at the Hispanic Society of America, published a transcription as part of his anthology *Nuevo ensayo de una biblioteca española de libros raros y curiosos.* This transcription contains many omissions and errors. Alan Deyermond's *Apollonius of Tyre: Two Fifteenth-Century Spanish Prose Romances* (1973) compares the incunable text to an extract from the Spanish translation of John Gower's *Confessio Amantis.* Manuel Alvar included a transcription and a facsimile reproduction of the text as a companion to his edition of *The Book of Apollonius* (1976).

Our edition offers critical presentations of *The Book of Apollonius*'s manuscript and *The Life and History of King Apollonius*'s incunable (see notes to the text for further details). Our presentation of the texts clarifies potentially ambiguous passages and reflects their phonetic, prosodic, and syntactic features as they are rendered in the manuscript and the incunable, without attempting to regularize metrical form in the case of the poem. For our edition's graphic presentation, we have used the criteria laid out by Pedro Sánchez-Prieto Borja in *Cómo editar los textos medievales: Criterios para su presentación gráfica* (1998) and *La edición de los textos españoles medievales y clásicos: Criterios de presentación gráfica* (2011).

THE TRANSLATIONS

To our knowledge, *The Book of Apollonius* has been translated into English only once, as *The Book of Apollonius* by Raymond L. Grismer and Elizabeth Atkins (1936). Working from Charles Marden's 1917 edition, Grismer and Atkins chose to render the text in verse, using archaic sentence constructions and vocabulary. The result is an inaccurate, if delightful, adaptation of the text. Grismer and Atkins's translation, which does not include the original Spanish poem or notes on the text, is thus a creative work of medievalism, rather than a translation or tool for medieval studies. *The Life and History* has not been translated into English previously.

Our aim in translating *The Book of Apollonius* and *The Life and History of King Apollonius* is to produce clear and idiomatic modern English texts that make the original works accessible for study and teaching. To these ends, we use English-Spanish cognates where possible, and, at times, we find

it necessary to embed explanatory subjects, verb forms, and conjunctions in order to render the meaning of the Spanish clearly. We also seek to convey something of the verbal play and a reflection of the oral performance of the originals. For example, where the poet plays upon the words "sosacar un mal sosacamiento," we echo his repetition by translating "devise an evil device." In our translation of *The Book of Apollonius* we have followed the structure of the *cuaderna vía* verse form, in which the four-line stanza is the basic unit of both content and meaning, with each stanza often further divided into two subunits of two lines each. This division is frequently reflected in the use of semicolons and full stops at the end of the second lines both in the Spanish text and in the translation. Because this structured meaning is fundamental to the medium, we have worked to preserve it in our English text while also producing a coherent modern rendering. Another benefit of retaining the four-line form is that it facilitates reading the Spanish verse alongside the translation.

In the case of *The Life and History of King Apollonius,* we found that it was often necessary to clarify the text's relentless Latinizing structures for the sake of readability in English. Further, the late medieval prose shifts continually between present and past tense. We have opted to maintain the narrative in the past tense for the sake of legibility.

The Iberian Apollonius has been made possible in part by a Scholarly Editions and Translations grant from the National Endowment for the Humanities. Georgetown University and Rhodes College grants and research funding also sup-

ported the project. We would like to express our gratitude to Ricardo Pichel, Patricia E. Grieve, Lydia Spencer, and Mariamnny Contreras for their invaluable insights and assistance in the preparation of this volume. We are also grateful to the librarians at the Royal Library of the Monastery of San Lorenzo de El Escorial and the New York Public Library, who provided access to the *Libro de Apolonio* manuscript and incunables printed by the Hurus brothers.

Notes

1 To date, the most exhaustive study of the Latin textual tradition of *HART* is G. A. A. Kortekaas, *The Story of Apollonius, King of Tyre* (Leiden, 2004), which expands upon his 1984 thesis, *Historia Apollonii regis Tyri: Prolegomena, Text Edition of the Two Principal Latin Recensions, Bibliography, Indices and Appendices* (Groningen).

2 Several scholars have theorized the existence of a now-lost Greek urtext. See Kortekaas, *The Story of Apollonius.* Ben Jonson's comment on *Pericles* is the first of many allusions traced by Elizabeth Archibald in her essential study, *Apollonius of Tyre: Medieval and Renaissance Themes and Variations* (Woodbridge, 1991), 3, which contains the text and an English translation of *HART.*

3 See Michelle P. Brown, "Were Early Medieval Picture Cycles Recycled from Late Antiquity? New Evidence for a Lost Archetype of the *Apollonius pictus*—An Illustrated Classic," in *Illuminating the Middle Ages: Tributes to Prof. John Lowden from His Students, Friends and Colleagues,* ed. Laura Cleaver, Alixe Bovey, and Lucy Donkin (Leiden, 2020), 4–18.

4 Maurice Delbouille, "Apollonius de Tyr et les débuts du roman français," in *Mélanges offerts à Rita Lejeune, professeur à l'Université de Liège,* vol. 2 (Gembloux, 1969), 1171–204; see also Archibald, *Apollonius of Tyre,* chapter 3.

5 On Apollonius in the *General estoria* and poetic allusions, see the editions by Carmen Monedero, *Libro de Apolonio* (Madrid, 1987), 60; and Dolores Corbella, *Libro de Apolonio* (Madrid, 1992), 25–26. On the Catalan translations, see Jaume de Puig i Oliver, "Més textos catalans antics de la

'Biblioteca Capitular y Colombina' de Sevilla," *Arxiu de Textos Catalans Antics* 20 (2001): 453–510; and Rafael Beltrán, "Un nou fragment de traducció del la *Historia Apollonii regis Tyri* identificat dins el *Cançoner Vega-Aguiló:* les endevinalles catalanes," in *"Prenga xascú ço qui millor li és de mon dit." Creació, recepció i representació de la literatura medieval,* ed. Meritxell Simó (San Millán de la Cogolla, 2021), 199–214. On the Portuguese and Castilian versions of the *Confessio Amantis,* see Clara Pascual-Argente, "Iberian Gower," in *The Routledge Research Companion to John Gower,* ed. Ana Saez-Hidalgo, Brian Gastle, and R. F. Yeager (New York, 2017), 210–21. Manuel Alvar studies the Castilian version of Gower's Apollonius and the version reproduced in the *Patrañuelo* in his edition and study of the *Libro de Apolonio* (Madrid, 1976), vol. 1, pp. 247–78.

6 Barbara Nolan, *Chaucer and the Tradition of the Roman Antique* (Cambridge, 1992), 9.

7 Archibald remarks upon the "strong association" linking the stories of Alexander and Apollonius, the one a historical figure and the other fictional, in medieval literature; *HART* is found in many twelfth- and thirteenth-century manuscripts containing accounts of Alexander's life (*Apollonius of Tyre,* 86–87).

8 The term *mester de clerecía* (an expression coined in the nineteenth century from the *Libro de Alexandre*'s second stanza) has sometimes been used to refer to a group of closely related thirteenth-century works composed in monorhymed alexandrine quatrains: *Libro de Alexandre, Libro de Apolonio,* and the epic *Poema de Fernán González,* as well as the hagiographies, *miracula,* and other works focused on religious instruction attributed to Gonzalo de Berceo. It is also employed to designate the wider phenomenon of thirteenth-century clerical writing in Castilian, which includes works composed in a different form, also common in Francophone literature, rhyming couplets.

9 The poet appears to have followed the version of *HART* found in recension A, although there are elements from recension B in the poem as well. See Monedero, *Libro de Apolonio,* 25; and Corbella, *Libro de Apolonio,* 20.

10 MS Escorial K.III.4 (BETA [Bibliografia Española de Textos Antiguos] manid 1407, https://bancroft.berkeley.edu/philobiblon/).

11 Yet another feature of *The Life and History* is the abundant and, for the most part, careful punctuation of the text, a characteristic for which the

Hurus press came to be praised; see Gonzalo García de Santamaría's prologue to the *Catón en latín y en romance,* quoted in María Carmen Marín Pina, "La *Cárcel de amor* zaragozana (1493), una edición desconocida," *Archivo de Filología Aragonesa* 51 (1991): 86.

12 The Hurus brothers, Pablo and Juan, natives of Constance, were successful printers in Zaragoza from around 1476 to 1499. The woodcuts were previously used in the editions of Heinrich Steinhöwel's *Hystori des Küniges Appoloni* printed in Augsburg by Johan Bämler (1475) and Anton Sorg (1479), with the exception of one, which is a roughly made copy of the German woodcut.

13 María Jesús Lacarra, "La *Vida e historia del rey Apolonio* [¿Zaragoza, Juan Hurus, 1488?] y su trayectoria genérica," *Tirant* 19 (2016): 47–56; and "La 'Vida e historia del rey Apolonio' [Zaragoza: Juan Hurus, ca. 1488]: Texto, imágenes y tradición genérica," in *Literatura y ficción: 'Estorias,' aventuras y poesía en la Edad Media,* ed. Marta Haro Cortés (Valencia, 2015), vol. 1, pp. 91–110.

14 On vernacular humanism, see Jeremy Lawrance, "On Fifteenth-Century Spanish Vernacular Humanism," in *Medieval and Renaissance Studies in Honour of Robert Brian Tate,* ed. Ian Michael and Richard Cardwell (Oxford, 1986), 63–79; and "Humanism in the Iberian Peninsula," in *The Impact of Humanism on Western Europe,* ed. Anthony Goodman and Angus Mackay (London, 1990), 220–58.

15 See Lola Pons, "La lengua del Cuatrocientos más allá de las Trescientas," in *Actas del IX Congreso Internacional de Historia de la Lengua Española (Cádiz, 2012),* ed. José María García Martín, vol. 1 (Madrid, 2015), 393–430.

16 Víctor Infantes de Miguel, "El 'género editorial' de la narrativa caballeresca breve," *Voz y Letra: Revista de literatura* 7, no. 2 (1996): 127–32.

17 *Apollonius of Tyre,* 86. On the generic status of *The Book of Apollonius* and *The Life and History,* see Pablo Ancos, "Encuentros y desencuentros de la Antigüedad tardía con la Edad Media en el *Libro de Apolonio,*" *Tirant* 21 (2018): 281–300; and Clara Pascual-Argente, "The Survival of Medieval Antiquity: Fifteenth-Century Transformations of the *Roman Antique* Tradition in Castile and Beyond," in *Early Modern Constructions of Europe,* ed. Florian Kläger and Gerd Bayer (New York, 2016), 71–89.

18 Carolyn Phipps, "El incesto, las adivinanzas y la música: Diseños para la geminación en el *Libro de Apolonio,*" *El Crotalón* 1 (1984): 807–18.

19 On these hagiographic and theological resonances, see Olivier Biag-

gini, "L'hôte malgré lui: la quête de l'identité dans le *Libro de Apolonio,*" in *L'étranger dans la maison. Figures romanesques de l'hôte,* ed. Bernadette Bertrandias (Clermont-Ferrand, 2003), 165–80; Marina Scordilis Brownlee, "Writing and Scripture in the *Libro de Apolonio:* The Conflation of Hagiography and Romance," *Hispanic Review* 51, no. 2 (1983): 159–74; and Patricia Grieve, "Building Christian Narrative: The Rhetoric of Knowledge, Revelation, and Interpretation in *Libro de Apolonio,*" in *The Book and the Magic of Reading in the Middle Ages,* ed. Albrecht Classen (New York, 1998), 149–69.

20 See Pablo Ancos, "Vocalidad y textualidad en el *Libro de Apolonio,*" *Troianalexandrina* 3 (2003): 40–76; and Amaia Arizaleta, "Les vers sur la pierre. Quelques notes sur le *Libro de Alexandre* et le *Libro de Apolonio,*" *Troianalexandrina* 5 (2005): 153–84.

21 *Apollonius of Tyre,* 19.

THE BOOK OF
APOLLONIUS

Libre d'Apolonio

1   En el nombre de Dios   e de Santa María,
     si ellos me guiassen,   estudiar querría,
     componer un romance   de nueva maestría
     del buen rey Apolonio   e de su cortesía.

2   El rey Apolonio,   de Tiro natural,
     que por las aventuras   viscó grant temporal,
     cómo perdió la fija   e la muger capdal,
     cómo las cobró amas,   ca les fue muy leyal.

3   En el rey Antioco   vos quiero començar,
     que pobló Antioca   en el puerto de la mar,
     del su nombre mismo   fízola titolar.
     ¡Si estonce fuesse muerto,   no·l deviera pesar!

4   Ca muriósele la muger   con qui casado era,
     dexole una fija   genta de grant manera,
     no·l sabían en el mundo   de beltat companyera,
     non sabían en su cuerpo   senyal reprendedera.

5   Muchos fijos de reyes   la vinieron pedir,
     mas non pudo en ella   ninguno abenir:

The Book of Apollonius

1   In the name of God and the Virgin Mary,
should they guide me, I wish to endeavor
to compose a romance in the new, learned style,
about good King Apollonius and his courtesy.

2   This is a story about King Apollonius of Tyre
and his adventures, how he survived raging storms at
       sea,
how he lost both his daughter and his queen,
and then found them again, because he loved them so
       well.

3   But I want to begin my story with King Antiochus,
who founded Antioch on the shores of the sea,
giving the city his very own name.
He could have died with no regrets, were that all he
       had done!

4   It so happened that when his lady wife died,
she left him a most lovely daughter,
whose beauty was without compare in all the world;
not a single fault was to be found in her body.

5   Many royal scions came to ask for her hand,
but not a one could ever win her:

ovo en este comedio   tal cosa a contir
que es para en concejo   vergüença de decir.

6   El pecado, que nunca   en paz suele seyer,
tanto pudo el malo   bolver e rebolver
que fiço a Antioco   en ella entender,
tanto que se quería   por su amor perder.

7   Ovo a lo peyor   la cosa a venir:
que ovo su voluntat   en ella a complir,
pero sin grado lo ovo   ella de consentir,
que veyía que tal cosa   non era de sofrir.

8   La duenya por este fecho   fue tan envergonçada
que, por tal que muriese,   non quería comer nada,
mas una ama vieja   que la ovo criada,
fiço·l creyer   que non era culpada.

9   "Fija," dixo, "si vergüença   o quebranto prisiestes,
non avedes culpa,   que vós más non pudiestes,
esto que vós veyedes   en ventura lo oviestes.
¡Alegratvos, senyora,   que vós más non pudiestes!

10   Demás, yo vos consejo,   e vós creyérmelo devedes:
al rey vuestro padre   vós non lo enfamedes.
Maguer grant es la pérdida,   más val que lo calledes
que al rey e a vós   en mal precio echedes."

because at the time something so shameful was going
    on
that I blush to even speak of it in good company.

6   The devil, who is never at rest,
stirred and stoked things up so much
that he made Antiochus burn with desire for his
    daughter—
he would readily condemn his soul for lust.

7   And so, the worst possible thing occurred:
Antiochus had his way with his daughter.
However, he had to force her against her will,
for she was sure that such things were beyond the pale.

8   The lady felt so shamed by the deed
that, hoping for death, she stopped eating.
But an old servant, the nursemaid who had raised her,
convinced the princess that she was not to blame.

9   "My child," she said, "if you feel shamed or defiled,
you are not to blame, for there was nothing you could
    do;
this is what your fate had in store for you.
So, dry your tears, my lady, for there was nothing you
    could do!

10   What is more, here's my advice, and you should heed
    me:
do not spread word about your father's misdeeds.
Though the damage is great, you had best keep silent
lest the king and you both lose your good names."

11 "Ama," dixo la duenya,   "¡jamás, por mal pecado,
    non deve de mí   padre seyer clamado!
    Por llamarme él fija   téngolo por pesado:
    es el nombre derechero   en amos enfogado.

12 Mas, cuando ál no puedo,   desque só violada,
    prendré vuestro consejo,   la mi nodricia ondrada,
    mas bien veo que fui   de Dios desemparada;
    a derechas m'en tengo   de vós aconsejada."

13 Bien sé que tanto fue ell enemigo   en el rey encarnado
    que non avía el poder   de veyer el pecado.
    Mantenía mala vida,   era de Dios airado,
    ca non le facía servicio   don fuese su pagado.

14 Por fincar con su fija,   escusar casamiento,
    que pudiesse con ella   complir su mal taliento,
    ovo a sosacar   un mal sosacamiento,
    mostrógelo el diablo,   un bestión mascoriento.

15 Por fincar sin vergüença,   que non fuese reptado,
    facía una demanda   e un argumente cerrado:
    al que lo adevinase   que gela daría de grado,
    el que no lo adevinase   sería descabeçado.

16 Avían muchos por aquesto   las cabeças cortadas,
    sedían sobre las puertas   de las almenas colgadas.

11   "Nurse," said the princess, "never, not for anything,
      will I ever say 'father' to him again!
      It is unbearable to think he can still call me 'daughter':
      we have both lost the right to those names.

12   Yet, since I am helpless and have been violated,
      I will heed your advice, my dear nursemaid.
      Although I can see that God has abandoned me,
      I believe you have counseled me well."

13   I understand the devil's hold on the king was so strong
      that it blinded him to the sin he committed.
      The king was living an evil life; God's wrath fell upon
            him
      for failing to render pleasing service to him.

14   To keep his daughter with him, and prevent her
            marrying,
      and so he could continue to have his evil way with her,
      the king came to devise an evil device,
      taught to him by that dark beast, the devil.

15   To maintain his honor, and to avoid accusations,
      the king made up a challenge, a cryptic riddle,
      saying he would gladly give his daughter to the man
            who solved it,
      but those who could not solve it would lose their
            heads.

16   In the attempt to win her, many heads were severed
      and were hung from the battlements over the palace
            gates.

¡Las nuevas de la duenya   por mal fueron sonadas,
a mucho buen doncel   avían caras costadas!

17   "La verdura del ramo   escome la raíz,
de carne de mi madre   engruesso mi serviz."
El que adevinase   este vieso qué ditz,
esse avría la fija   del rey, emperadriz.

18   El rey Apolonio,   que en Tiro regnava,
oyó d'aquesta duenya   qu'en grant precio andava;
quería casar con ella,   ca mucho la amava,
la hora del pedir   veyer non la cuidava.

19   Vino a Antioca,   entró en el reyal,
salvó al rey Antioco   e a la corte general,
demandole la fija   por su muger capdal,
que la metrié en arras   en Tiro la cibdat.

20   La corte de Antioca,   firme de grant vertut,
todos ovieron duelo   de la su juventut.
Dicían que non se supo   guardar de mal englut,
por mala de nigromancia   perdió buena salut.

21   Luego de la primera   demetió su raçón:
toda la corte escuchava,   tenía buena saçón.
Puso·l el rey   la sua proposición:
que le daría la cabeça   o la solución.

22   Como era Apolonio   de letras profundado,
por solver argumentos   era bien dotrinado;
entendió la fallença   e el sucio pecado
como si lo oviese   por su ojo provado.

Alas, word of the princess spread far and wide,
and many a worthy young man paid dearly!

17 "The green leaf on the vine consumes its root,
and I grow strong on my mother's flesh."
The man who figured out the meaning of the verse
would have the king's daughter, an empress, for a wife.

18 King Apollonius, who ruled in the city of Tyre,
heard of this princess, whose fame was spreading;
he wanted to marry her, for he was deeply in love,
and he could not wait to ask for her hand.

19 Apollonius entered the royal palace of Antioch,
where he greeted King Antiochus and his court
and asked for his daughter to make her his queen,
promising to give her rich wedding gifts in the city of
  Tyre.

20 The courtiers of Antioch were virtuous at heart,
and they all mourned for the young king.
They said that he could not avoid the evil trap,
and his life would be lost to a wicked dark art.

21 Apollonius announced his intentions then and there:
the entire court listened; he had their full attention.
The king issued Apollonius his challenge:
he must either give his head or the answer to the
  riddle.

22 Now, Apollonius was a very learned man
who had been taught to solve riddles quite well;.
he understood the King's guilt and his foul sin
as if he had seen them with his very own eyes.

9

23   Avía gran repintencia   porque era ý venido,
       entendió bien que era   en fallença caído.
       Mas, por tal que non fuese   por bavieca tenido,
       dio a la pregunta   buen responso complido.

24   Dixo: "¡Non deves, rey,   tal cosa demanar,
       que a todos aduze   vergüença e pesar!
       Esto, si la verdad   non quisieres negar,
       entre tú e tu fija   se debe terminar.

25   Tú eres la raíz,   tu fija el cimal;
       tú pereces por ella,   por pecado mortal,
       ca la fija ereda   la depda carnal,
       la cual tú e su madre   aviedes cominal."

26   Fue de la profecía   el rey muy mal pagado,
       lo que siempre buscava   ya lo avía fallado.
       Metiolo en locura   muebda del pecado,
       aguisole en cabo   cómo fuesse mal porfaçado.

27   Maguer por encobrir   la su iniquitat,
       dixo·l a Apolonio   que·l dixera falsedat,
       que non lo querría fer   por nenguna eredat;
       pero todos asmavan   que dixera verdat.

28   Dixo·l que metría   la cabeça a perder,
       que la adevinança   non podría asolver.
       Aun treínta días   le quiso anyader,
       que por mengua de plaço   non pudiese cayer.

29   Non quiso Apolonio   en la villa quedar:
       tenía que la tardança   podía en mal finar.
       Triste e desmarrido,   pensó de naveyar;
       fasta que fue en Tiro   él non se dio bagar.

23 Apollonius sorely repented having come there,
    and he saw that he had made a fatal mistake.
    But even so, he did not want to be taken for a fool,
    so he gave the full and correct answer to the question.

24 He said, "King, you should not pose such a riddle,
    which truly shames and saddens us all!
    this business — to tell you the truth —
    between you and your daughter must come to an end.

25 You are the root, and your daughter the leaves;
    because of her, you are damned by mortal sin,
    for your daughter has inherited the carnal debt,
    once shared by you and her mother in marriage."

26 This answer greatly displeased Antiochus,
    who had at last gotten what was coming to him.
    The devil had driven him to commit this mad sin,
    and led him to be openly condemned in the end.

27 Nevertheless, to continue to hide his crimes,
    Antiochus told Apollonius that his words were lies,
    and he would never do such a thing, not for any price;
    still, everyone thought that the truth had been told.

28 He said that Apollonius must lose his head,
    because he could not solve the riddle.
    Yet he granted Apollonius thirty days more,
    so that his defeat could not be blamed merely on haste.

29 Apollonius had no desire to remain in Antioch:
    he feared staying there would come to no good.
    Sad and undone, he decided to sail away;
    he did not rest until he reached his home in Tyre.

30 E el pueblo fue alegre   cuando vieron su senyor:
    todos lo querién veyer,   que avién d'él sabor.
    Rendían grandes e chicos   gracias al Criador,
    la villa e los pueblos   todos en derredor.

31 Encerrose Apolonio   en sus cámaras privadas,
    do tenié sus escritos   e sus estorias notadas;
    rezó sus argumentos,   las fazanyas passadas,
    caldeas e latinas,   tres o cuatro vegadas.

32 En cabo, otra cosa   non pudo entender
    que al rey Antioco   pudiese responder.
    Cerró sus argumentos,   dexose de leyer;
    en lacerio sin fruto   non quiso contender.

33 Pero mucho tenía   que era mal fallido,
    en non ganar la duenya   e sallir tan escarnido.
    Cuanto más comidía   qué·l avía contecido,
    tanto más se tenía   por peyor confondido.

34 Dixo que non podía   la vergüença durar,
    mas quería ir perderse   o la ventura mudar.
    De pan e de tresoro   mandó mucho cargar,
    metiose en aventuras   por las ondas del mar.

35 Pocos levó consigo,   que no lo entendieron;
    fuera sus criaçones   otros no lo sopieron.
    Navearon apriessa,   buenos vientos ovieron,
    arribaron en Tarso,   término ý prisieron.

30   The people of Tyre were happy to see their lord:
     everyone had longed to see him, they loved him well.
     Great and small, everyone gave thanks to God,
     throughout the city and all the neighboring towns.

31   Apollonius shut himself away in his private chambers,
     where he kept all his writings and learned books;
     he studied all his texts and all his ancient histories,
     books in Chaldean and Latin too, three or four times
          over.

32   In the end, he still could not find any other answer
     that he could bring back to King Antiochus.
     So, Apollonius closed his books and left off his reading;
     he had no desire to keep laboring in vain.

33   Now, Apollonius felt that he had failed miserably,
     he had not won the lady and had been shamed.
     The more he pondered what had happened to him,
     the more he saw how humiliated he had been.

34   He said to himself that he could not stand the shame,
     he would rather seek out his death or change his
          fortune.
     He ordered his ship loaded with plenty of bread and
          gold
     and set off to sea to meet his fortunes on the waves.

35   He brought few men with him, he did not want to
          spread the news;
     no one but his household knew about his departure.
     They sailed quickly, with good winds at their backs,
     until they ended the journey on the shores of Tarsus.

36   En el rey Antioco   vos queremos tornar,
     non nos deviemos ende   tan aína quitar.
     Avía de Apolonio   ira e grant pesar,
     querríalo de grado,   si lo pudiese, matar.

37   Clamó a Taliarco,   que era su privado,
     el que de sus consejos   era bien segurado—
     avíanlo en su casa   de pequenyo criado—
     acomendó·l que fuese   recapdar un mandado.

38   Dixo el rey: "Bien sepas,   el mio leyal amigo—
     que non diría a otrie   esto que a ti digo—
     que só de Apolonio   capital enemigo,
     quiero fablar por esto   mi consejo contigo.

39   De lo que yo facía   él me á descubierto,
     nunca me fabló ombre   ninguno tan en cierto.
     Mas, si me lo defiende   poblado nin desierto,
     tener me ía por nada   más que un seco ensierto.

40   Yo te daré tresoros   cuantos tú quisieres;
     da contigo en Tiro   cuanto tú más pudieres.
     Por gladio o por yerbas   si matarlo pudieres,
     desde aquí te prometo   cual cosa tú quisieres."

41   Taliarco non quiso   grande plaço prender:
     por amor que ficiesse   a su senyor placer
     priso mortal consejo,   aguisó grant aver,
     fue al rey de Tiro   servicio prometer.

36   And now, let us return to King Antiochus;
        we should not have been so quick to put him aside.
        Apollonius had filled him with rage and sorrow,
        and with the desire to kill him, if only it could be done.

37   Antiochus called Taliarco, who was his favorite,
        a man whose advice he trusted completely—
        he had been brought up in the king's household—
        and the king asked Taliarco to do him a service.

38   The king said, "As you know, my loyal friend—
        and I would never say this to anyone else, only to
            you—
        I hate Apollonius, he is my mortal enemy,
        and I want your advice about what I plan to do.

39   He knows what I was doing, he has found me out,
        no man has ever spoken so truly to me.
        Even so, I must turn over every stone to seize him,
        or I will be taken for nothing more than a withered
            stick.

40   I will give you all the treasure you desire;
        go now to Tyre as fast as you can.
        If you kill Apollonius, by sword or by poison,
        I promise I will pay you whatever you want."

41   Taliarco had no wish to put off the task:
        in his fervor to do what would bring his lord pleasure,
        he decided to commit murder, and filled up his purse,
        and went to promise his service to the king of Tyre.

42 Cuando entró en Tiro,   falló ý grandes llantos,
    los pueblos doloridos,   afiblados los mantos,
    lágrimas e sospiros,   non otros dulces cantos,
    faciendo oraciones   por los logares santos.

43 Vio cosa mal puesta,   ciudat tan denegrida,
    pueblo tan desmayado,   la gente tan dolorida.
    Demandó que esta cuita   por qu'era ý venida,
    por qué toda la gente   andava amortida.

44 Respuso·l un ombre bueno,   bien raçonado era:
    "¡Amigo, bien parece   que eres de carrera!
    Si de la tierra fueses,   cuita avriés llenera,
    dirías que nunca vieras   tal en esta ribera.

45 El rey nuestro senyor,   que nos solía mandar—
    Apolonio le dizen por nombre,   si lo oíste contar—
    fue a Antioco   su fija demandar.
    ¡Nunca podría con ombre   más honrado casar!

46 Puso·l achaque mala,   non la pudo ganar;
    tóvoselo a onta   por sin ella tornar.
    Moviolo de su casa   vergüença e pesar,
    a cuál parte es caído   non lo podemos asmar.

47 Aviemos tal senyor   cual a Dios demandamos;
    si este non avemos,   nunca tal esperamos.

42 When Taliarco arrived in Tyre, he found great
            mourning:
    the people were sorrowful, with their mantles closed
            tight,
    they wept and sighed, they sang no sweet songs,
    they offered up prayers at their holy places.

43 Taliarco saw a city run down, dirty and sad;
    its people were so dejected, everyone so sorrowful.
    He asked them, "What is this trouble that has befallen
            you?
    Why does everyone look like they are at death's door?"

44 A well-spoken citizen of the town responded,
    "Friend, it seems to me you are a stranger here!
    Were you from these lands, you too would be filled
            with grief,
    saying you had never before seen such mourning in
            these parts.

45 The king, our lord, who used to rule us—
    his name is Apollonius, you may have heard of him—
    went to Antiochus to ask to marry his daughter.
    She could never have found a more honorable match!

46 But Antiochus tricked him, there was no way to win
            her;
    Apollonius felt humiliated when he could not have her.
    He has fled from home, driven by shame and sadness;
    we have no idea where he might have gone.

47 We had a lord who was as good as God could give us;
    if we lose him, there is no hope for another like him.

Con cuita non sabemos   cuál consejo prendamos,
¡cuando rey perdemos   nunca bien nos fallamos!"

48   Fue con aquestas nuevas   Taliarco pagado,
tenié que su negocio   avié bien recabado;
tornose al rey Antioco,   que lo avié embiado,
por contarle las nuevas   e dezirle el mandado.

49   Dixo·l que de Apolonio   fuesse bien descuidado,
que era con su miedo   de tierra desterrado.
"¡Non será," diz Antioco,   "en tal logar alçado
que de mí lo defienda   yermo nin poblado!"

50   Puso, aun sin esto,   ley mala e complida:
quiquiere que lo matase   o lo prisiese a vida,
que le darié de sus averes   una buena partida,
al menos cient quintales   de moneda batida.

51   ¡Confonda Dios tal rey,   de tan mala mesura!
Bivía en pecado   e asmava locura:
que querié matar al ombre   que dixera derechura,
que abrió la demanda   que era tan escura.

52   Esto facié el pecado,   que es de tal natura,
ca en otros muchos   en que mucho atura,
a pocos días dobla,   que traye gran abscura.
¡Traye mucho enxemplo   d'esto la Escriptura!

53   Por encobrir   una poca de enemiga
perjúrase ombre,   non comide qué diga;
dell ombre perjurado   es la fe enemiga.
¡Esto que yo vos digo   la ley vos lo pedrica!

In our troubles, we do not know where to turn for
    guidance;
with our king lost, we will never know well-being
    again!"

48   Taliarco was very pleased to hear this news—
he considered his work there was already done;
and he returned to King Antiochus, who had sent him,
to tell him the news and give him the message.

49   Taliarco told Antiochus not to worry about Apollonius,
because the coward had fled from his own land.
"He will," said Antiochus, "never find a place to hide,
he will not be safe, not anywhere, not from me!"

50   The king went on, and issued an evil decree:
whoever killed Apollonius or caught him alive
would be given a large portion of his wealth,
at least one hundred hundredweights of good coin.

51   God curse such an imprudent and undiscerning king!
He lived in sin and his thoughts were crazed:
for he wanted to kill the man who spoke the truth,
the man who unlocked the dark secret of his riddle.

52   This is what the devil does, this is his nature:
he holds many others in his tenacious sway,
sins soon double, and darkness takes hold.
Of this there are many examples in the scriptures!

53   To cover up even the smallest of sins,
a man will perjure himself and not weigh his words;
our faith despises all men who bear false witness.
What I am telling you is what our religion preaches!

54   Esto mismo contece   de todos los pecados,
      los unos con los otros   son todos enlaçados:
      si non fueren aína   los unos emendados,
      otros mucho mayores   son luego ayuntados.

55   De un ermitanyo santo   oyemos retrayer,
      porque·l fiço el pecado   el vino bever
      ovo en adulterio   por ello a cayer,
      depués en omecidio   las manos a meter.

56   Antioco, estando   en tamanya error,
      andava, si pudiese,   por fer otra peyor.
      ¡Del pecado primero   si oviese dolor,
      de demandar tal cosa   non avría sabor!

57   Como dize el proverbio,   que suele retrayer
      que la copdicia mala   saco suele romper,
      fiço la promesa   a muchos fallecer,
      que lo querrían de grado   o matar o prender.

58   Por negra de cobdicia   que por mal fue aparada,
      por ganar tal tresoro,   ganancia tan famada,
      muchos avién cobdicia,   non la tenién celada,
      por matar a Apolonio   por cualquiere entrada.

59   Los que solía tener   por amigos leyales
      tornados se le son   enemigos mortales.
      ¡Dios confonda tal sieglo: por ganar dos mencales
      se trastornan los ombres   por seer desleyales!

54 And this is the way of each and every sin,
  one follows upon the other, all bound together:
  if the first sins are not promptly set straight,
  greater sins will soon be piled upon them.

55 We have all heard the tale of the holy hermit
  who was tricked by the devil into drinking too much
    wine
  and because of his drinking fell into the sin of adultery
  and then committed murder—he had blood on his
    hands.

56 Antiochus, already guilty of a vile crime,
  was now plotting to do something even worse.
  If only he had felt some remorse for his first sin,
  he would not have thirsted for Apollonius's death!

57 As the proverb we hear all the time says,
  "Greedy grasping for all leads to losing it all."
  The promise of bounty made many men sin;
  they would happily bring him in, dead or alive.

58 The wicked greed so evilly inspired by Antiochus,
  the desire to win the treasure, the famous spoils,
  spurred on many men, who did not hide their
    eagerness
  to kill King Apollonius by any means possible.

59 Men who used to be his most loyal friends
  turned against him and became his mortal enemies.
  God curse such a world, where for two gold coins
  men are so fickle and driven to be so disloyal!

60 Mandó labrar Antioco   naves de fuerte madera
    por buscar a Apolonio,   tollerlo de carrera,
    bastirlas de poderes,   de armas e de civera,
    mas aguisó Dios la cosa   en otra manera.

61 Dios, que nunca quiso   la sobervia sofrir,
    destorbó esta cosa,   non se pudo complir:
    no·l pudieron fallar   ni·l pudieron nozir.
    ¡Deviemos atal Senyor   laudar e bendizir!

62 El rey Antioco   vos quiero destajar,
    quiero en Apolonio   la materia tornar.
    En Tarso lo lexamos,   bien nos deve membrar.

63 Cuando llegó a Tarso,   como lazdrado era,
    fizo echar las áncoras   luego por la ribera;
    vio logar adabte,   sabrosa costanera,
    por folgar del lazerio   e de la mala carrera.

64 Mandó comprar conduchos,   encender las fogueras,
    aguisar los comeres,   sartenes e calderas,
    adobar los comeres   de diversas maneras,
    ¡non costavan dinero   manteles ni forteras!

65 Los que sabor an   de su conducho prender,
    dávangelo de grado,   non lo querían vender.

60   King Antiochus ordered stout wooden ships to be
        built,
    to search for Apollonius and stop him dead in his
        tracks;
    he supplied the ships with armed men and viands,
    but God had arranged the matter in a different way.

61   God, who has no patience for inordinate pride,
    intervened and did not grant the search success:
    they could not find Apollonius, nor could they harm
        him.
    We must sing the praises and blessings of our Lord!

62   Now, I want to leave off telling you of King Antiochus,
    and I want to turn my tale back to the story of
        Apollonius.
    As you no doubt remember, we last saw him in Tarsus.

63   When he came to Tarsus, since he was so troubled,
    he ordered the ship to drop anchors immediately
        ashore;
    he saw a fitting spot, a lovely coastal site,
    for resting after their hardship and the rough journey.

64   Apollonius ordered provisions be bought, bonfires be
        lit,
    and dishes be prepared in pans and pots;
    he ordered dishes flavored in many different styles,
    no expense was spared on tablecloths and trenchers!

65   To all those who hungered for the meal,
    they gladly gave food away, they had no wish to sell it.

Avía toda la tierra   con ellos gran plazer,
que era mucho cara   e avíanlo menester.

66   Mala tierra era,   de conducho menguada,
avié gran carastía,   era de gente menguada.
Podrié comer un ninyo   rafez la dinarada,
combrié tres el yuguero   cuando vinise de la arada.

67   Como era Apolonio   ombre bien raçonado,
vinién todos veyerle,   fazíanle aguisado,
non se partié d'él   null ombre despagado.

68   Vino un ombre bueno,   Elánico el cano,
era de buena parte,   de días anciano.
Metió en él mientes,   prísolo por la mano,
apartose con él   en un campiello plano.

69   Dixo·l el ombre bueno,   que avié d'él dolor,
aprisiera las nuevas,   era bien sabidor:
"¡Ay, rey Apolonio,   digno de grant valor,
si el tu mal supieses   deviés aver dolor!

70   Del rey Antioco   eres desafiado:
nin en ciudat ni en burgo   non serás albergado,
quien matar te pudiere   será bien soldado.
¡Si estorcer pudieres   serás bien aventurado!"

This pleased all of the people of Tarsus to no end,
because food was scarce and they were in need.

66 The land was infertile, with little to harvest;
because of a great famine, few people were to be
found.
A child could easily eat a fortune in food there;
a laborer, coming in from the field, three times as
much.

67 Now, Apollonius was an intelligent, well-spoken man,
so everyone came to see him, treating him with
reverence,
and not a single man left his side feeling disappointed.

68 The white-haired Elanico, a good man, came to see
him,
a man of good lineage and advanced in age.
He fixed his eyes on Apollonius, took him by the hand,
and drew him aside, to speak with him in a small
clearing.

69 The good man, who was sorry for Apollonius,
for he had heard the news and knew of his troubles,
said,
"Oh, King Apollonius, most worthy of men,
it would pain you to know the danger you are in!

70 King Antiochus has put a price on your head:
you will not find refuge in any city or town,
the man who kills you will be handsomely rewarded.
It will be a miracle if you manage to escape with your
life!"

71 Respondió Apolonio   como ascalentado:
"Dígasme, ombre bueno,   sí a Dios ayas pagado,
¿por cuál razón Antioco   me anda demandando,
o al quien me matar   cuál don le á atorgado?"

72 "Por esso te copdicia   o matar o prender,
porque lo que es él   tú quisiste seyer.
¡Cient quintales promete   que dará de su aver
al qui la tu cabeça   le pudiere render!"

73 Estonce dixo Apolonio: "¡Non es por el mio tuerto,
ca yo non fice cosa   por que deva seyer muerto!
¡Mas Dios, el mio Senyor,   nos dará buen esfuerço,
el que de los cuitados   es carrera e puerto!

74 Mas, por cuanto la cosa   me feciste entender,
en amor y en grado   te lo devo tener.
Demás, quiero que lieves   tanto del mio aver
cuanto darié Antioco   por a mí confonder.

75 Este puedes en salvo   e sin pecado levar,
que asme tú buscado   placer e non pesar.
Non pierdas tu derecho,   ca me podriés reptar,
¡podría yo por ello   gravemientre pecar!"

71   Apollonius responded, hot with anger,
      "Tell me, my good man, and may God bless you,
      why has king Antiochus put a price on my head,
      and what he has promised to give the man who kills
              me?"

72   "Antiochus wants you taken dead or alive,
      because you wanted to be what he is now.
      He promised one hundred hundredweights of his
              wealth
      to the man who can present him with your severed
              head!"

73   Then Apollonius said, "It is not my fault,
      because I did nothing meriting a death sentence!
      But I know God, my Lord, will give me the strength I
              need,
      he who is the way and the refuge of those who suffer!

74   Nevertheless, for all you have given me to understand,
      I owe you my thanks and gratitude.
      What is more, I want you to take as much of my
              wealth
      as King Antiochus promised to pay for my demise.

75   You can take it in all safety and without sinning,
      for you have given me pleasure and no pain.
      I will not be to blame for the loss of your rightful
              bounty;
      allowing it would be a great mistake on my part!"

76 Fabló el ombre bueno,   dio·l fermosa respuesta:
"¡Mercet, ya rey, e gracias   por la promesa vuestra,
que amiztat vender   non es costumbre nuestra!
Quien bondat da por precio   malamiente se
                                                    denuesta."

77 ¡Dios, a todo cristiano   que su nombre toviere,
tal ombre le depare   cuando mester l'oviere!
¡Demás, ombre nin fembra   que d'este ombre oyere
debe tener su loa   demientre que visquiere!

78 Elánico, de miedo   que serié acusado
porque con Apolonio   facié tan aguisado,
despidiose del rey,   su amor asentado,
tornó para la villa,   su manto afiblando.

79 Fue en esta fazienda   Apolonio asmando:
veyé que se le iva   su cosa mal parando,
sabié que lo andavan   muchos ombres buscando,
tenié que lo matarién   durmiendo o velando.

80 Pensando en esta cosa,   más triste que pagado,
vio un burzés   rico e bien adobado;
Estrángilo le dizen,   ombre era onrado.
Sacolo a consejo   a un lugar apartado.

81 "Quiero," diz Apolonio,   "contigo fablar,
dezirte mi fazienda,   tu consejo tomar.

76 The good man spoke, gave an eloquent response:
    "Thank you, Oh king, I am much obliged by your
            promise,
    but friendship is not for sale in these parts!
    He who trades goodness for a price dishonors himself."

77 God, let all Christians who worship you
    meet with such a man when they are in need!
    Every man and woman who hears about Elanico
    should praise him all the days of their lives!

78 Elanico, fearing he would be accused
    for treating Apollonius with such reverence,
    took his leave of the king, their friendship assured,
    and returned to the town, his mantle wrapped tight.

79 For some time Apollonius considered his situation:
    he understood that it was going from bad to worse,
    he knew many men were searching for him,
    and he thought they would kill him, whether sleeping
            or awake.

80 Mulling all this over, in more sadness than pleasure,
    Apollonius caught sight of a rich and well-dressed
            burgher
    by the name of Stranguillio; he was an honorable man.
    Apollonius took him aside to seek his counsel in
            private.

81 "I want," said Apollonius, "to speak with you,
    to tell you my story, and then to hear your advice.

Ombres de Antioco   me andan por matar,
¡preso seré traído   si me pueden fallar!

82   Si vós me encubriésedes,   por vuestro buen estar,
querría algún tiempo   combusco aquí morar;
si el concejo quisiere   aquesto otorgar,
cuedo a toda Tarso   grant gualardón dar."

83   Estrángilo respuso   —ca bien lo conocía—
"Rey," diz, "¡esta villa   sofrir non te podría!
Grant es la tu nobleza,   grant logar merecía;
esta villa es muy cara,   sofrir non te podría.

84   Pero saber querría   de ti una facienda:
¿con el rey Antioco   por qué oviste contienda?
¡Si en su ira yaces,   non sé quí te defienda,
fuera el Criador   o la su santa comienda!"

85   Recudió·l Apolonio   a lo que·l demanava:
"Porque·l pidié la fija   que él mucho amava
e que·l terminé el viesso   con que nos embargava;
por esso me seguda,   ca esso lo agraviava.

86   En la otra razón   te quiero recodir,
ca dizes que la villa   non me podrié sofrir:
yo vos daré del trigo   que mandé adozir
cient mil moyos por cuenta,   ¡mandatlos medir!

Antiochus has sent men out to find and kill me;
I will be taken prisoner if they can get their hands on
me!

82 If you would be so kind as to hide me from Antiochus,
I would like to stay and live with you here for some
time;
if the town council agrees to grant my request,
I pledge to reward all of Tarsus quite richly."

83 Stranguillio responded—he knew well who Apollonius
was—
"King," he said, "this city could not bear the expense of
protecting you!
Your nobility is great and deserves a suitable place,
but this city is starving and could not bear the expense.

84 But please tell me something about your case:
How did you become King Antiochus's enemy?
If you have incurred his wrath, no one can defend you,
other than God himself or his divine protection!"

85 Apollonius responded, answering the question:
"Because I asked for his much-beloved daughter,
and I solved the riddle that he used to trap me;
that is why he pursues me, because that offended him.

86 And in response to your other concern,
because you say that the city cannot bear the expense:
I will give you, from my stores of wheat,
one hundred thousand bushels; weigh them if you will!

87   Dar vos lo é a compra,   pero de buen mercado,
      como valié en Tiro,   do lo ove comprado.
      Demás, el precio todo,   cuando fuere llegado,
      para la cerca de la villa   quiero que seya dado."

88   Estrángilo fue alegre   e tóvose por guarido,
      besávale las manos   en tierra debatido,
      diz: "¡Ay, rey Apolonio,   en buena ora fuste venido,
      que en tan fiera cuita   nos as tú acorrido!

89   Rey, bien te lo convengo,   quiero que lo tengamos,
      que nos plega contigo   e que te recibamos.
      Cual pleito tú quisieres,   nós tal te le fagamos,
      ¡si menester te fuere,   que contigo muramos!"

90   Estrángilo, por la cosa   más en recabdo poner,
      por buscar a Apolonio   tan estranyo placer,
      entró en la ciudat,   mandó pregón meter
      que se llegassen al concejo,   ca era menester.

91   En poco de rato   fue concejo plegado,
      óvoles a decir   Estrángilo el mandado.
      "¡Seya," dixeron todos,   "puesto e otorgado;
      devié seyer en vida   tal ombre adorado!"

92   Cumplioles Apolonio   lo que les dicho avía:
      guarecié un gran pueblo   que de fambre muría,

87   I will sell the wheat to you, but for a good price,
for what it cost in Tyre, where I bought it.
What is more, once I am paid the full price,
I will donate it all to fortify the city walls."

88   Stranguillio was happy and thought himself saved;
he threw himself to the ground and kissed the king's
      hands,
saying, "Oh, Apollonius, you have arrived at a
      fortunate hour,
you have helped us in our time of desperate need!

89   King, we have an agreement, let us work together,
we are pleased to have you stay with us.
Whatever oaths of fealty you require we will swear,
and if necessary, we are ready to die by your side!"

90   In order to celebrate their pact of loyalty,
and to prepare a rare delight for Apollonius,
Stranguillio went into the city, where it was announced
that the council must convene, as was necessary.

91   The council gathered together quickly,
Stranguillio told them all about the agreement.
"Let us," they all said, "ratify and confirm this pact;
a man like Apollonius should be worshiped as a living
      saint!"

92   Apollonius did everything for them that he had
      promised:
he saved the masses that were dying from starvation,

valié por él la villa   más que nunca valía.
¡Non era fi de nemiga   qui tal cosa facía!

93 El Rey de los Cielos   es de grant providencia,
siempre con los cuitados   á su atenencia,
en valerles a las cuitas   es tota su femencia,
devemos seyer todos   firmes en la su atenencia.

94 Da cuitas a los ombres,   que se faga temer,
non cata a sus pecados,   viénelos acorrer;
sabe maestramientre   sus consejos prender,
trebeja con los ombres   a todo su placer.

95 El rey Apolonio,   de facienda granada,
avía toda la tierra   en su amor tornada:
por cual logar quería   facía su posada,
qui non lo bendicía   non se tenía por nada.

96 Tanto querían las gentes   de onra le buscar,
ficieron en su nombre   un ídolo labrar,
fizieron en un márbor   el escrito notar
del bueno de Apolonio   qué fizo en ese logar.

97 Pusiéronlo drecho   en medio del mercado,
sobre alta columna,   por seyer bien alçado;
fasta la fin del mundo   e el sieglo pasado
el don de Apolonio   non fuese olvidado.

98 Fizo por gran tiempo   en Tarso la morada,
era con él la tierra   alegre e pagada.
Consejó·l un su huéspet,   con qui avía posada,
que fuese a Pentápolin   a tener la ivernada.

and thanks to him, the city prospered more than ever
 before.
These were not the actions of a bad man!

93   In his great providence, the King of Heaven
always gives his protection to those who suffer,
all his power goes to aid us in our suffering,
and we should all be constant in our faith in him.

94   God gives men trials to teach them to fear him;
ignoring all their sins, he comes to the rescue.
In his mastery, God knows what decisions to make
and plays with men's lives according to his pleasure.

95   King Apollonius, man of great deeds,
had won over the entire realm of Tarsus:
he was welcome in any place he wanted to stay,
everyone who was anyone sang his praises.

96   In their great desire to show honor to Apollonius,
the people commissioned a statue in his name,
and along with it a marble plaque bearing the story
of all that good King Apollonius had done for the city.

97   They erected the statue in the center of the market,
atop a tall column, so that it would rise up on high;
until the end of days and the passing of this world,
Apollonius's gift would never be forgotten.

98   Apollonius stayed in Tarsus for a long time,
everyone in the land was happy and content with him.
One of his hosts, with whom he was staying, advised
 him
to go to Pentapolis to pass the winter months there.

99 "Rey," dixo Estrángilo,   "si me quisieres creyer,
   dar t'é buen consejo,   si me·l quisieres prender:
   que fueses a Pentápolin   un ivierno tener,
   sepas que avrán   contigo gran placer.

100 Serán estos roídos   por la tierra sonados,
   contra el rey Antioco   seremos acusados,
   movrá sobre nós huestes,   por malos de pecados,
   ¡seremos en grant cuita   si fuermos cercados!

101 Somos, como tú sabes,   de conduchos menguados,
   para meternos en cerca   somos mal aguisados.
   ¡Si vencernos pudieren,   como venrán irados,
   sin cosiment seremos   todos estragados!

102 Mas cuando entendieren   que tú eres alçado,
   esto serié aína   por las tierras sonado,
   derramarié Antioco   luego su fonsado,
   tornarás tú en Tarso   e bivrás segurado."
   "¡Págome," diz Apolonio,   "que fablas aguisado!"

103 Cargaron las naves   de vino e de cezina,
   e otrosí ficieron   de pan e de farina,
   de buenos marineros   que sabién la marina,
   que conocen los vientos   que se camian aína.

104 Cuando ovo el rey   de Tarso a sallir,
   por entrar en las naves   e en altas mares sobir,

99   "King," said Stranguillio, "If you will kindly believe me,
     I will give you good advice, if you will take it from me:
     if you go to spend the winter in Pentapolis,
     know that everyone there will be happy to host you.

100 The news of your deeds will spread through the land,
     we will be accused by Antiochus of harboring you,
     he will bring an army to attack us, to our great
          misfortune,
     we will be sorely tried if we are besieged by him!

101 There is, as you know, a scarcity of food here,
     and we are ill prepared to face a siege.
     They will come, filled with rage, and if they conquer
          us,
     they will show us no mercy; we will all perish!

102 But if they hear that you are hidden elsewhere,
     and this news soon spreads through the land,
     then Antiochus will choose to disperse his troops,
     and you can return to Tarsus, where you will live in
          safety."
     "Thank you," said Apollonius, "for speaking so wisely!"

103 The ships were loaded with wine and dried meat,
     and also well stocked with plenty of bread and flour;
     Apollonius enlisted many good sailors who knew the
          seas,
     and who knew the winds, which are so quick to
          change.

104 When it was time for the king to leave Tarsus,
     to board the ships and set off on the high seas,

non querían las gentes   ante d'él se partir
fasta que los ovieron   las ondas a partir.

105   Ploravan con él todos,   doliense de su ida,
rogavan que fiziesse   aína la venida,
a todos semejava   amarga la partida.
¡De tal amor me pago,   tan dulce e tan complida!

106   ¡Ovieron en fuerte punto   las naves a partir!
Avién vientos derechos,   facienles bien correr;
non podién los de Tarso   los ojos d'ellos toller
fasta que se fueron yendo   e ovieron a trasponer.

107   El mar, que nunca tovo   leyaltat ni belmez,
cámiase privado   e ensányase rafez,
suele dar mala çaga,   más negra que la pez:
el rey Apolonio   cayó en essa vez.

108   Cuanto tenién dos horas,   abez avían andado,
bolviéronse los vientos,   el mar fue conturbado,
nadavan las arenas,   el cielo levantando,
¡non avié ý marinero   que non fuese conturbado!

109   Non les valién las áncoras,   que non podién travar,
los que eran maestros   non podién governar,
alçávanse las naves,   queríanse trastornar,
tanto que ellos mismos   non se sabién consejar.

the people refused to leave before they lost sight of
    him
when he disappeared beyond the waves of the sea.

105 The people cried for him, saddened by his departure,
and prayed he would make his way back soon,
the parting seemed bitter to them all.
How pleasing is such sweet and complete love!

106 Unfortunately, the ships departed in an ill-favored
    hour!
At first the winds were favorable, and they sailed off at
    speed;
the people of Tarsus on shore could not take their eyes
    off the ships
until they had disappeared well beyond the horizon.

107 The merciless sea is loyal to no one,
it changes quickly and rises to anger easily,
and it can be more of a trickster than the devil himself:
this time, King Apollonius fell into its grasp.

108 When they had been sailing for about two hours,
the winds changed and the sea turned rough,
the sands swam up and churned into the sky,
there was not a single sailor who was not frightened!

109 Their anchors were useless, they could not find
    purchase,
the shipmasters could not steer at the helms,
and the ships tossed on the waves, threatening to
    capsize;
Apollonius and his men did not know what to do.

110 Cuitoles la tempesta   e el mal temporal,
    perdieron el consejo   e el govierno capdal,
    los árboles de medio   todos fueron a mal.
    ¡Guárdenos de tal cuita   el Senyor espirital!

111 Ca como Dios quiso ovo   la cosa de seyer:
    oviéronse las naves   todas a perecer,
    de los ombres nenguno   non pudo estorcer,
    fueras el rey solo,   que quiso Dios valer.

112 Por su buena ventura   quiso·l Dios prestar:
    ovo en un madero chico   las manos a echar.
    Lazdrado e mesquino   de vestir e calçar,
    a tierra de Pentápolin   ovo de arribar.

113 Cuando el mar le ovo   a término echado,
    cayó el ombre bueno   todo desconortado.
    Non fue bien por dos días   en su recuerdo tornado,
    ca maltraído era   e fuera mal espantado.

114 Plogo al Rey de Gloria   e cobró su sentido,
    fallose todo solo,   menguado de vestido.
    Membrole de su facienda,   cómo le avié contecido:
    "¡Mesquino," dixo,   "que por mal fui nacido!

115 Dexé muy buen reino,   do bivía onrado,
    fui buscar contienda,   casamiento famado;
    gané enamiztat,   sallí dende aontado,
    e torné sin la duenya,   de muerte enamiztado.

110   The tempest and the rough weather put them in
        danger,
  they lost their bearings and lost their rudders as well,
  and all their masts were completely destroyed.
  Lord on high, save us all from such danger!

111   And so the tempest worked just as God willed it:
  every single one of the ships was lost,
  and all the men too, not a single one escaped,
  except for King Apollonius, whom God wanted to
        spare.

112   Fortune was with Apollonius; God came to his aid:
  he found a small wooden board to hold onto.
  Wounded and having lost his clothing and shoes,
  Apollonius landed on the shores of Pentapolis.

113   When the sea at last brought him to this destination,
  the good man washed ashore completely devastated.
  For two long days he remained unconscious,
  for he was badly injured and had suffered a great fright.

114   It pleased the King of Heaven to rouse Apollonius,
  who found himself all alone and unclothed.
  Recalling his adventures, and all that had befallen him,
  he said, "Woe is me! I curse the day I was born!

115   I left my good kingdom, where I lived in honor,
  and went looking for a challenge, for a brilliant
        marriage;
  I won myself an enemy, and left for home in shame,
  returning without the lady, and with a price on my
        head.

116   Con toda essa pérdida,   si en paz me soviés,
      que con despecho loco   de Tiro non salliés,
      mal o bien esperando   lo que darme Dios quisiés,
      ninguno non me llorasse   de lo que me abiniés.

117   Desque de Tiro era   sallido e arredrado,
      avíame mi ventura   en tal logar echado,
      si su ermano fuese   o con ellos criado,
      yo seyer non podría   entr'ellos más amado.

118   Moviome el pecado,   fizo·m ende sallir
      por fer de mí escarnio,   su maleza complir;
      diome en el mar salto   por más me desmentir,
      ovo muchas ayudas   por a mí destrovir.

119   Fizo su atenencia   con las ondas del mar,
      viniéronle los vientos   todos a ayudar;
      semejava que Antioco   los enviara rogar
      o se querían ellos   comigo engraciar.

120   Nunca devía ombre   en las mares fiar:
      traen lealtat poca,   saben mal solazar,
      saben al recebir   buena cara mostrar,
      ¡dan con ombre aína   dentro en mal logar!"

121   Estava en tal guisa   su ventura reptando,
      vertiendo de los ojos,   su cuita rencurando,
      vio un ombre bueno   que andava pescando,
      cabo de una pinaça   sus redes adobando.

122   El rey, con gran vergüença   porque tan pobre era,
      fue contra'l pescador,   sallole a la carrera.
      "¡Dios te salve!" le dixo,   luego de la primera;
      el pescador le respuso   de sabrosa manera.

116   Despite all I had lost, had I accepted my lot,
       and had crazed spite not driven me from Tyre,
       leaving my fate, good or evil, in God's hands,
       then no one would have had to shed a tear for my woes.

117   After I had left and traveled far from Tyre,
       Fortune cast me upon such welcoming shores
       that even if had been a brother, born and bred there,
       I could not possibly have been loved more.

118   Then the devil took me away—he made me leave
       to have his fun with me, to work his evil on me;
       he attacked me at sea to hurt me even more,
       he had many helpers in his campaign to destroy me.

119   He made a pact with the waves of the sea,
       all the winds came to the devil's assistance;
       it seemed as if Antiochus had enlisted their aid,
       or as if the winds used me to serve the evil king.

120   No one should ever have faith in the seas,
       they have few loyalties and give cold comfort,
       they know how to welcome you in with a pleasing face,
       and then soon turn against you and bring you down!"

121   As Apollonius was bemoaning his fortune in this way,
       tears streaming from his eyes, lamenting his trials,
       he saw a good man who was a fisherman,
       near a small boat, repairing his nets.

122   The king, with great humility because he was so poor,
       approached the fisherman, crossing his path.
       "God save you!" he said to start the conversation,
       and the fisherman replied with pleasant manners.

123 "Amigo," dixo el rey,   "tú lo puedes veyer,
     pobre só e mesquino,   non trayo null aver;
     sí Dios te benediga,   que te caya en plaçer
     que entiendas mi cuita   e que la quieras saber.

124 Tal pobre cual tú veyes,   desnudo e lazdrado,
     rey só de buen regno,   rico e abondado:
     de la ciudat de Tiro,   do era mucho amado;
     dizienme Apolonio   por nombre senyalado.

125 Bivía en mi reino   vicioso e onrado,
     non sabía de cuita,   bivía bien folgado;
     teníame por torpe   e por menoscabado
     porque por muchas tierras   non avía andado.

126 Fui a Antioca   casamiento buscar,
     non recabé la duenya,   óveme de tornar.
     ¡Si con esso fincase   quito en mio logar,
     non avrié de mí fecho   tal escarnio la mar!

127 Furteme de mis parientes   e fize muy gran locura,
     metime en las naves   con una noche escura;
     oviemos buenos vientos,   guionos la ventura,
     arribamos en Tarso,   tierra dulce e segura.

128 Trobamos buenas gentes,   llenas de caridat,
     fazién contra nós   toda umilitat,
     cuando dende nos partiemos,   por dezirte verdat,
     todos fazién gran duelo   de toda voluntat.

129 Cuando en la mar entramos   fazié tiempo pagado,
     luego que fuemos dentro   el mar fue conturbado.
     Cuanto nunca traía,   allá lo é dexado,
     ¡tal pobre cual tú veyes,   abez só escapado!

123   "My friend," said the king, "as you can see,
       I am poor and wretched, I have no money with me;
       may God bless you, I have a favor to ask of you:
       please hear of my troubles and be willing to listen.

124   You see before you a poor man, naked and afflicted,
       yet I am really the king of a rich and prosperous land:
       the city of Tyre, where I am well loved.
       I am called Apollonius, a name of renown.

125   In my kingdom I lived happily and in honor,
       I knew nothing of cares, I lived quite contentedly;
       but I thought myself uncouth and naïve
       because I had not traveled abroad in many lands.

126   I went to Antioch in search of a wife,
       but I did not win the lady and I had to return.
       If, in spite of this failure, I had stayed at home,
       the sea would not have made such a mockery of me!

127   I left my home and committed something very foolish,
       I set sail in secret, during the dark of night;
       we had good winds, Fortune guided us,
       and we landed on Tarsus's sweet, safe shores.

128   There we found good people, filled with charity,
       who treated us with complete reverence,
       and when we left there, to tell you the truth,
       everyone was heartsick to see us go.

129   When we set sail, the weather was fine at first,
       but suddenly turned rough when we were out to sea.
       Everything I had with me, I have left there;
       I barely escaped, a poor man, with nothing but my life!

130 Mis vasallos que eran   comigo desterrados,
    averes que traía,   tresoros tan granados,
    palafrés e mulas,   cavallos tan preciados,
    ¡todo lo é perdido,   por mis malos pecados!

131 ¡Sábelo Dios del cielo   que en esto no miento!
    Mas non muere el ombre   por gran aquexamiento—
    ¡si yo yogués con ellos   avría gran plazimiento!—
    sino cuando viene   el día del pasamiento.

132 Mas, cuando Dios me quiso   a esto aduzir,
    que las limosnas aya   sin grado a pedir,
    ruégote que, sí puedas   a buena fin venir,
    que me des algún consejo   por ó pueda bevir."

133 Calló el rey en esto   e fabló el pescador,
    recudió·l como ombre   que avía d'él grant dolor:
    "Rey," dixo el ombre bueno,   "d'esto só sabidor,
    en gran cuita te veyes,   non podriés en mayor.

134 El estado d'este mundo   siempre así andido,
    cada día se camia,   nunca quedó estido,
    en toller e en dar   es todo su sentido,
    vestir al despojado   e despojar al vestido.

135 Los que las aventuras   quisieron ensayar,
    a las vezes perder,   a las vezes ganar,
    por muchas de maneras   ovieron de pasar,
    quequier que les abenga   anlo de endurar.

136 Nunca sabrién los ombres   qué eran aventuras
    si no perdiessen pérdidas   o muchas majaduras.

130 All the vassals who had gone into exile with me,
the possessions I carried, my stores of treasure,
my palfreys, mules, and my most prized horses,
I have lost everything, in my great misfortune!

131 God in heaven knows that I am not lying!
Still, a man cannot die from great suffering—
how I wish I were also at the bottom of the sea!—
he dies, rather, when his appointed day comes.

132 Since God has seen fit to reduce me to this state,
I am forced to beg for alms against my will,
and so I beg you, may God save your soul,
please give me some advice to help me survive."

133 Then the king fell silent, and the fisherman spoke,
responding, as one filled with pity for Apollonius,
"King," said the good man, "of this I am sure,
you are in great trouble, it could not be worse.

134 This mortal world always works in this way,
it changes every day and it is never still,
giving and then taking away is its very essence,
clothing the naked and disrobing the clothed.

135 Those who would venture out to seek their fortune,
sometimes they lose and sometimes they win,
they will have to face many ups and downs,
whatever life brings them must be endured.

136 Men could never understand what fortune is
if it were not for losses suffered and blows borne.

Cuando an passado   por muelles e por duras,
después se tornan maestros   e cren las escripturas.

137 El que poder ovo   de pobre te tornar
puédete, si quisiere,   de pobreza sacar.
Non te querrían las fadas,   rey, desmamparar,
¡puedes en poca d'ora   todo tu bien cobrar!

138 Pero tanto te ruego,   sey oy mi combidado,
de lo que yo oviere   servir te é de buen grado.
Un vestido é solo,   flaco e muy delgado,
partir lo é contigo   e tente por mí pagado."

139 Fendió su vestido   luego con su espada,
dio al rey el medio   e levolo a su posada,
dio·l cual cena pudo,   non le ascondió nada.
¡Avía mejor cenado   en alguna vegada!

140 Otro día manyana,   cuando fue levantado,
gradeció al ombre bueno   mucho el ospedado,
prometió·l que, si nunca   cobrasse su estado,
el servicio en duplo   serié gualardonado.

141 "Asme fecho,   huéspet, grant piedat,
mas ruégote encara,   por Dios e tu bondat,
que·m muestres la vía   por ó vaya a la ciudat."
Respúsole el ombre bueno   de buena voluntat.

142 El pescador le dixo: "Senyor, bien es que vayas,
algunos buenos ombres   te darán de sus sayas;

Once we have lived through times of both ease and
    hardship,
then we may become wise and believe the scriptures.

137   The powerful One who turned you into a poor man
may, in his wisdom, decide to pull you up out of
    poverty.
The Fates will not abandon you, O King;
you might soon recover all your lost happiness!

138   But for now I beg you to be my guest today,
I will gladly share with you all that I have.
I have just this one thin and flimsy robe,
but I will share it with you, and you must be content."

139   The fisherman cut his robe in two with his sword;
he gave one half to the king and escorted him home
and shared what little supper he could, hiding nothing.
The king had eaten much better many times before!

140   The next day, upon rising in the morning,
Apollonius thanked the good man for his hospitality
and promised that, if he ever recovered his fortunes,
he would doubly reward the fisherman for his service.

141   "My host, you have shown me great mercy,
and now, I beg you, please, for God's sake,
to show me the road I can take to the city."
The good man then responded most willingly.

142   The fisherman said, "My lord, it is good for you to go
where some good men will surely give you clothes to
    wear,

si consejo non tomas   cual tú menester ayas,
por cuanto yo oviere   tú lazerio non ayas."

143 El benedito huéspet   metiolo en la carrera,
     demóstrole la vía,   ca bien acerca era,
     llegolo a la puerta   que falló más primera;
     pososse, con vergüenza,   fuera, a la carrera.

144 Aún por venir era   la ora de yantar,
     salliense los donzeles   fuera a deportar;
     comenzaron luego   la pellota jugar,
     que solían a ese tiempo   ese juego jugar.

145 Metiose Apolonio,   maguer mal adobado,
     con ellos al trebejo,   su manto afiblado.
     Abinié en el juego,   fazié tan aguisado
     como si fuesse   de pequenyo ý criado.

146 Fazíala ir derecha   cuando le dava del palo,
     cuando la recibié   no·l sallía de la mano.
     Era en el depuerto   sabidor e liviano,
     ¡entendrié quien se quiere   que non era villano!

147 El rey Architartres,   cuerpo de buenas manyas,
     salliese a deportar   con sus buenas companyas;
     todos trayén consigo   sus vergas e sus canyas,
     eguales e bien fechas,   derechas e estranyas.

148 Tovo mientes a todos,   cadaúno cómo jugaba,
     cómo ferié la pella   o cómo la recobrava.

and if you do not find there what you need,
you can have anything of mine to save you from suf-
    fering."

143 The blessed host sent him off on his way,
he showed him the road, which was close by,
and accompanied Apollonius to the first town gate;
struck with shame, the king stopped before entering.

144 It was not yet time for the midday meal;
young men were coming outside to enjoy the fresh air,
and then started up a ball game right away,
for this was their accustomed time to play.

145 Apollonius joined right in, despite his ragged clothes;
he played along with them, his cloak fastened tightly.
The king excelled at the game: he played very well,
so well that it appeared he had learned it as a child.

146 When Apollonius hit the ball, it went straight,
and he always caught passes without fumbling.
He was skilled and light on his feet in the game,
it was clear to everyone that he was no peasant!

147 King Archistrates, a graceful and courteous man,
came out to enjoy the fresh air with his good
        companions;
all the men carried their own sticks and canes,
all of the same size, well made, straight, and quite a
        sight to see.

148 King Archistrates paid close attention to each player,
how each one threw the ball, and how he caught it.

Vio en la rota,   que espessa andaba,
que toda la mejoría   el pobre la levava.

149 Del su continiente   ovo grant pagamiento,
porque toda su cosa   levava con buen tiento.
Semejó·l ombre bueno,   de buen entendimiento,
de deportar con éll   tomó grant taliento.

150 Mandó posar los otros,   quedar toda la rota,
mandó que les dexassen   a amos la pellota.
¡El capdiello de Tiro,   con su mesquindat toda,
bien se alimpiava   los ojos de la gota!

151 Ovo gran pagamiento   Architrastes del juego,
que grant ombre era   entendiógelo luego.
Dixo al pelegrino: "Amigo, yo te ruego
que yantes oy comigo,   ¡non busques otro fuego!"

152 Non quiso Apolonio   atorgar el pedido,
ca non dixo nada,   de vergüença perdido.
Todos lo combidavan,   maguer mal vestido,
ca bien entendién todos   dónde era estorcido.

153 Vino en este comedio   la hora de yantar,
ovo en la villa   el rey a entrar,
derramaron todos,   cadaúno por su lugar;
¡los unos a los otros   non se querién esperar!

154 Apolonio, de miedo   de la corte enojar,
que non tenié vestido   ni adobo de prestar,

He saw that among the many players in the large crowd
the best moves were those made by the destitute
    stranger.

149   He was very impressed with Apollonius's bearing,
because everything he did was done skillfully.
He seemed like a good and knowledgeable man,
and Archistrates keenly wanted to play with him.

150   So the king ordered everyone to stop playing,
and ordered the ball be given to just the two of them.
The leader of Tyre, despite all of his woes,
dried the tears from his streaming eyes!

151   King Archistrates was immensely pleased by the game
and saw right away that Apollonius was an important
    man.
The king said to the stranger, "My friend, I beg you,
dine with me today, please do not sit by any other
    hearth!"

152   Apollonius had no wish to grant the request,
and he did not respond, for he was lost in shame.
Everyone urged him to come, despite his poor attire,
because it was clear that he had survived hardships.

153   Then it was time for the midday meal,
so the king went inside the city walls,
as did all the others, each heading home;
in their hurry, no one waited for anyone else!

154   Apollonius, fearing he would anger the court
because he was not well dressed or suitably attired,

non quiso, de vergüença,   al palacio entrar;
tornose de la puerta,   comenzó de llorar.

155 El rey non tovo mientes   fasta que fue entrado,
luego lo vio menos   cuando fue assentado.
Llamó a un escudero   que era su privado,
preguntó·l por tal ombre,   que dó era parado.

156 Salló ell escudero fuera,   vio cómo seía;
tornó al rey e dixo   que vergüença avía,
ca peligró en la mar,   perdió cuanto traía,
con mengua de vestido   entrar non s'entrevía.

157 Mandó·l el rey vestir luego   de panyos honrados—
los mejores que fueron   en su casa trobados—
mandó que lo metiessen   suso a los sobrados,
do los otros donzeles   estavan asentados.

158 Dixo el rey: "Amigo,   tú escoje tu logar:
tú sabes tu fazienda,   con quién deves posar,
tú cata tu mesura   como deves catar,
ca non te conyoscemos   e podriemos errar."

159 Apolonio non quiso   con ninguno posar,
mandosse en su cabo   un escanyo poner.
De derecho del rey   non se quiso toller,
mandó·l luego el rey   que·l diessen a comer.

refused, out of shame, to enter the hall;
he turned away from the door and began to cry.

155   King Archistrates did not notice until he had entered
but, as soon as he sat down, saw Apollonius was
      missing.
He called a squire to him, one who was in his confi-
      dence,
and asked him about the stranger and where he had
      gone.

156   The squire went out and saw Apollonius in tears,
then told the king that the stranger was ashamed
because he had lost all he had in the tempest at sea
and did not dare to enter the hall dressed so poorly.

157   The king ordered Apollonius be dressed in fine
      clothes—
the best that could be found in all of his household—
and that the stranger be seated at the high table,
where the other young nobles were already seated.

158   Then King Archistrates said, "My friend, choose your
      place:
you know your status, and with whom you should sit;
look to your honor, as befits you to look,
for we do not know you and might be mistaken."

159   Apollonius refused to sit next to anyone,
so he called for a seat placed up on the dais.
He would not leave the honored seat facing the king,
and Archistrates ordered him to be served
      immediately.

160 Todos por el palacio   comién a grant poder,
andavan los servientes   cadaúno con su mester;
non podié Apolonio   las lágrimas tener,
los conduchos que·l davan   non los podié prender.

161 Entendiolo el rey,   començole de fablar:
"Amigo," diz, "¡mal fazes,   non te deviés quexar!
¡Sol que tú quisieres   la cara alegrar,
Dios te daría consejo,   non se te podrié tardar!"

162 El rey Architrastres,   por la corte más pagar,
a su fija Luciana   mandola ý venir.
La duenya vino luego,   non lo quiso tardar,
ca quiso a su padre   obediente estar.

163 Entró por el palacio   la infante bien adobada,
besó al rey manos   como bien ensenyada.
Salvó a los ricos ombres   e a toda su mesnada;
fue la corte d'esta cosa   alegre e pagada.

164 Fincó entre los otros   ojo al pelegrino,
quiso saber quién era   o de cuál parte venido.
"Fija," dixo el rey,   "ombre es de camino.
¡Oy tan bien el juego   ninguno non avino!

165 Sirvióme en el juego,   onde só su pagado;
pero non lo conosco,   ele yo muy gran grado.

160 Everyone in the hall ate most heartily,
the servants walked about, each doing their tasks,
but Apollonius could not contain his tears
and could not touch a bite of the food he was served.

161 The king took notice, and addressed him:
"My friend," he said, "you are behaving badly, you
should not lament so!
If only you would put on a happy face,
God will help you, and he will not make you wait long!"

162 King Archistrates, for the pleasure of his court,
called for his daughter Luciana to come in.
The lady came right away, she did not hesitate,
for she wanted to show obedience to her father.

163 Richly attired, the princess entered the hall
and kissed her father's hands, like the well-bred lady
she was.
Then she greeted all the nobles and all the king's men;
the court was cheered and pleased by her noble
behavior.

164 She saw the pilgrim among all the others
and wanted to know who he was and where he was
from.
"Daughter," said the king, "he's a traveler.
Today, in our ball game, he outplayed them all!

165 I've taken a liking to him, because he played so well for
me;
although I do not know him, I am quite grateful to
him.

    Segunt mi conyoscencia,   del mar es escapado,
    grant danyo á preso,   onde está desmayado.

166 Fija, si vós queredes   buscarme gran placer,
    que vos yo siempre aya   mucho que gradecer,
    sabet de su fazienda   cuanto pudierdes saber,
    contra éll que sepamos   cómo nos captener."

167 Aguisose la duenya   de toda voluntat:
    fue contra Apolonio   con gran simplicitat,
    fue luego diziendo   palabras de amiztat,
    como cosa ensenyada   que amava bondat.

168 "Amigo," dixo ella,   "faces grant covardía,
    non te saber componer   entre tal companyía;
    semeja que non amas   gozo nin alegría,
    tenémostelo todos   a muy gran villanía.

169 Si lo fazes por pérdida   que te es avenida,
    si de linage eres,   tarde se te olvida;
    es tota tu bondat   en fallencia caída:
    poco·l miembra al bueno   de la cosa perdida.

170 Todos dizen que eres   ombre bien ensenyado,
    veyo que es el rey   de ti mucho pagado;
    el tu buen continente   que avías mostrado,
    con esta gran tristeza   todo lo as afollado.

171 Pero que eres   en tan grande dolor,
    quiero que por mí   fagas aqueste amor:
    que digas el tu nombre   al rey mio senyor;
    de saber de tu fazienda   avriemos gran sabor."

From what I understand, he has survived a shipwreck,
he has suffered a great deal, and so he is downhearted.

166 Daughter, if you care for my happiness,
and would like to win my eternal gratitude,
find out all you can about his adventures,
then we will know how best to treat him."

167 The lady readied herself most willingly:
she went over to Apollonius with artless candor
and began speaking with him in a friendly tone;
she was all courteousness and kindness.

168 "My friend," she said, "it is quite cowardly of you
not to pull yourself together, when you are our guest;
you act as if you have no heart for pleasure or
      enjoyment,
and we feel you are gravely insulting us.

169 If you are acting this way because of the loss you have
      suffered,
as a nobleman, you should put it all behind you;
you are doing a disservice to your station:
for a worthy man cares little for what he has lost.

170 Everyone says you are a well-bred man,
and I see that the king is fond of you;
up to now you have behaved in a dignified way,
but you are undoing it all in your great sadness.

171 Even though you are suffering great pain,
for my sake, please do me this honor:
please tell my lord the king your name;
we are all eager to hear about your adventures."

172 Respondió Apolonio,   non lo quiso tardar;
    dixo: "¡Amiga cara,   búscasme grant pesar!
    El nombre que avía   perdilo en la mar,
    el mio linage en Tiro   te lo sabrién contar."

173 Porfiole la duenya,   non lo quiso dexar;
    dixo: "Sí Dios te faga   a tu casa tornar,
    que me digas el nombre   que te suelen llamar,
    sabremos contra ti   cómo devemos far."

174 Començó Apolonio,   de sospiros cargado:
    dixo·l toda su cuita   por ó avía pasado,
    su nombre e su tierra,   e cuál era su regnado;
    bien lo ascuchó la duenya   e óvole gran grado.

175 En cabo, cuando ovo   su cosa bien contada,
    el rey fue más alegre,   la duenya fue pagada.
    Querié tener las lágrimas,   mas no·l valía nada,
    renovósele el duelo   e la ocasión passada.

176 Estonze dixo el rey: "Fija, fe que devedes,
    si Apolonio llora   non vos maravelledes:
    tal ombre a tal cuita   vós venir non sabedes,
    mas vós me pensat d'él   si a mí bien queredes.

177 Fiziésteslo llorar,   avédeslo contristado;
    pensat cómo lo tornedes   alegre e pagado,
    fazetle mucho algo,   que ombre es honrado:
    ¡fija, ren non dubdedes   e fazet aguisado!"

178 Aguisosse la duenya,   fiziéronle logar,
    tempró bien la vihuela   en un son natural,

172 Apollonius did not hesitate to reply;
   he said, "My dear friend, you greatly sadden me!
   The name I once had is lost to the sea;
   in Tyre you would learn all about my family line."

173 The lady insisted, she did not want to let it go;
   she said, "God willing, you will return home,
   but tell me your name, what you are called,
   because we need to know how to treat you."

174 Apollonius, heaving with sighs, began:
   he told her about all the suffering he had endured,
   his name and his origins, and where his kingdom was;
   the lady paid close attention and was grateful to him.

175 Once he had told his story all the way through,
   the king was happier, and the lady was pleased.
   But Apollonius tried in vain to hold back his tears,
   his pain was renewed by the memory of his
         misfortunes.

176 Then the king said, "Daughter, for the love of God,
   if Apollonius weeps, do not be so surprised,
   for you can hardly imagine the great grief of such a
         man,
   but please take care of him, do it for my sake.

177 You made him cry, you have saddened him;
   now find a way to make him happy and content,
   and be very generous to him, for he is a noble man:
   daughter, do not hesitate, and do him honor!"

178 The lady readied herself, a space was cleared for her,
   and she tuned her vielle well, on the natural scale;

dexó cayer el manto,   parose en un brial,
començó una laude   —¡ombre non vio atal!

179 Fazía fermosos sones   e fermosas debailadas,
quedava a sabiendas   la boz a las vegadas,
fazía a la viuela   dezir puntos ortados,
semejava que eran   palabras afirmadas.

180 Los altos e los baxos,   todos d'ella dizién,
la duenya e la viuela   tan bien se abinién
que lo tenién a fazanya   cuantos que lo veyén,
fazía otros depuertos   que mucho más valién.

181 Alabávanla todos,   Apolonio callava;
fue pensando el rey   por qué él non fablava.
Demándole e dixo·l   que se maravellava
que con todos los otros   tan mal se acordava.

182 Recudió Apolonio   como firme varón:
"Rey, de tu fija   non digo si bien non,
mas si prendo la vihuela,   cuido fer un tal son
que entendredes todos   que es más con razón.

183 Tu fija bien entiende   una gran partida,
á comienço bueno   e es bien entendida,
mas aún non se tenga   por maestra complida;
¡si yo dezir quisiere,   téngase por vencida!"

184 "Amigo," dixo ella,   "sí Dios te benediga,
por amor, si la as,   de la tu dulce amiga,

then she let her mantle fall, revealing her rich tunic,
and began to sing a laud—the likes of which had never
    been heard before!

179 She played lovely notes and lovely quarter tones,
she knew well how and when to modulate her voice
and made the vielle sing notes with perfect artistry;
the notes sang out like strong and clear words.

180 Up and down the scale, all spoke as one,
the lady and the vielle were so perfectly attuned
that all who saw the performance were amazed,
and she used other far more remarkable musical
    techniques.

181 While everyone else praised her, Apollonius remained
    silent;
the king was wondering why he had nothing to say.
Archistrates asked, saying that he was surprised
that Apollonius was so out of tune with the others.

182 Apollonius replied, like a man who knew his mind,
"King, I do not want to say anything against your
    daughter,
but if I take up the vielle, I will make such music
that you will soon see what true musical mastery is.

183 Your daughter knows a great deal about music,
she has learned the basics and understands them well,
but she has yet to become a consummate artist;
if I were to perform, she would see herself bested!"

184 "My friend," she said, "God bless you,
if you care for me, your dear friend, at all,

que cantes una laude   en rota o en giga;
¡si no, asme dicho   sobervia e enemiga!"

185 Non quiso Apolonio   la duenya contrastar,
priso una viuela   e sópola bien temprar;
dixo que sin corona   non sabrié violar,
non quería, maguer pobre,   su dignidat baxar.

186 Ovo d'esta palabra   el rey muy gran sabor,
semejole que le iva   amansando la dolor.
Mandó de sus coronas   aduzir la mejor,
diola a Apolonio,   un buen violador.

187 Cuando el rey de Tiro   se vio coronado,
fue de la tristeza   yacuanto amansando,
fue cobrando el seso,   de color mejorando,
pero non que oviesse   el duelo olvidado.

188 Alçó contra la duenya   un poquiello el cejo,
fue ella de vergüenza   presa un poquellejo;
fue trayendo el arco   egual e muy parejo,
¡abés cabié la duenya   de gozo en su pellejo!

189 Fue levantando   unos tan dulces sones:
doblas e debailadas,   temblantes semitones.
A todos alegrava   la boz los corazones,
fue la duenya tocada   de malos aguijones.

190 Todos por una boca   dizién e afirmavan
que Apolo nin Orfeo   mejor non violavan;
el cantar de la duenya,   que mucho alabavan,
contra el de Apolonio   nada non lo preciavan.

sing me a laud and play the cithara or the rebec;
if you do not, you are just a base braggart!"

185 Not wanting to contradict the lady, Apollonius
took up a vielle, and he knew how to tune it well;
but, he said, he could not play without a crown on his
     head,
for, poor as he was, he had no desire to abase himself.

186 The king was well pleased by his guest's words,
for he thought Apollonius's grief was abating.
Calling for his best crown to be brought in,
he gave it to Apollonius, master of the vielle.

187 When the king of Tyre saw himself crowned,
his sadness began to lighten somewhat,
he felt more like himself, the color returned to his face,
but still, he had not forgotten his past sorrows.

188 Apollonius raised an eyebrow at the lady,
and she was caught by a little tremor of shame;
he was plying the bow so steadily and evenly,
that she could hardly contain her pleasure!

189 Apollonius was striking up such sweet notes:
duples and quarter tones, quavering semitones.
His voice brought joy to every heart,
while the lady was pricked with painful longings.

190 Everyone chorused in agreement, saying
that not even Apollo or Orpheus played so well;
although they had much praised the lady's song,
it was worth nothing compared to Apollonius's.

191 El rey Architrastres   non sería más pagado
si ganasse un regno   o un rico condado.
Dixo a altas bozes: "¡Desque yo fui nado
non vi, segunt mio seso,   cuerpo tan acabado!"

192 "Padre," dixo la duenya   al rey su senyor,
"vós me lo condonastes   que yo, por vuestro amor,
que pensasse de Apolonio   cuanto pudiesse mejor;
quiero d'esto que me digades   cómo avedes sabor."

193 "Fija," dixo el rey,   "ya vos l'é mandado,
seya vuestro maestro,   avetlo atorgado.
Dalde, de mi trasoro   que tenedes alçado,
cuanto sabor oviéredes,   que éll seya pagado."

194 E con esto la fija,   qu'el padre segurava,
tornó a Apolonio   alegre e pagada.
"Amigo," diz, "la gracia   de el rey as ganada;
desque só tu dicipla,   quiérote dar soldada.

195 Quiérote dar de buen oro   dozientos quintales,
otros tantos de plata   e muchos serviciales.
Avrás sanos conduchos   e los vinos naturales,
¡tornarás en tu fuerça   con estas cosas atales!"

191   King Archistrates could not have been happier
if he had conquered a kingdom or a rich duchy.
He raised his voice and said, "In all my life,
never have I seen, to my lights, such an accomplished
      man!"

192   "Father," said the lady to the king her lord,
"you requested that I, out of my love for you,
take care of Apollonius, as best I could;
please tell me if you agree with my proposal."

193   "Daughter," said the king, "I have already decided
that Apollonius should be your teacher—take it as
      settled.
Use the stores of my treasure that you have saved,
to pay him as much as you want, make him happy."

194   And the daughter, with her father's promise,
turned with joy and happiness to Apollonius.
"My friend," she said, "you have earned the king's
      grace,
since I will be your pupil, I wish to pay you well.

195   I will give you two hundredweights of gold,
the same amount in silver, and many servants as well.
You will have good food and excellent wines,
you will recover your strength with all these good
      things!"

196 Plogo a Apolonio,   tóvose por pagado
    porque en tanto tiempo   avié bien recabado.
    Pensó bien de la duenya,   ensenyávala de grado.

197 Fue en este comedio   ell estudio siguiendo,
    en el rey Apolonio   fue luego entendiendo:
    tanto fue en ella   el amor encendiendo
    fasta que cayó en el lecho   muy desflaquida.

198 Buscáronle maestros   que le fiziesen metgía,
    que sabién de la física   toda la maestría,
    mas non ý fallaron   ninguna maestría
    nin arte por que pudiesen   purgar la maletía.

199 Todos avían pesar   de la su enfermedat,
    porque non entendían   de aquella la verdat.
    Non tenié Apolonio   más triste su voluntat
    en la mayor cuita   que ovo, por verdat.

200 El rey Architrastres   fieramientre se dolié—
    non avié maravilla,   que fija la avié—
    pero con Apolonio   grant conorte prendié,
    el amor de la fija   en él lo ponié.

201 Ovo sabor un día   el rey de cavalgar,
    andar por el mercado   ribera de la mar;
    fizo a Apolonio,   su amigo, llamar,
    rogole que salliese   con él a deportar.

196 Apollonius was pleased; he considered himself
      content,
  because in such a short time he had come very far.
  He took good care of the lady and was happy to teach
      her.

197 As time passed and her studies progressed,
  the princess soon fell in love with King Apollonius:
  love took flame within her so forcefully
  that she fell very sick, too weak to leave her bed.

198 Doctors were called in to work their medicines;
  they were knowledgeable, great experts in remedies,
  but there was no cure to be found in all their mastery,
  nor any method for purging the princess of her malady.

199 Everyone was saddened by the princess's illness,
  because they did not understand the truth of the
      matter.
  Apollonius's heart had never felt so sad,
  truly, not even during the worst troubles he suffered.

200 King Archistrates was deeply distressed—
  small wonder, for she was his daughter—
  but he took great comfort in Apollonius's company,
  letting his love for his daughter shine on the young
      man.

201 One day, the king wanted to go out riding,
  to go to the market, out by the seashore;
  he had Apollonius, his friend, called in,
  and begged him to come along and enjoy the fresh air.

202 Prísolo por la mano,   non lo quería mal,
vieron por la ribera   mucho buen menestral,
burzeses e burzesas,   mucha buena senyall;
sallieron del mercado   fuera al reyal.

203 Ellos así andando,   uno con otro pagados,
vinieron tres donzeles,   todos bien adobados:
fijos eran de reyes,   ninyos bien ensenyados,
fueron bien recebidos,   como ombres muy honrados.

204 Todos fablaron luego   por lo bien recabdar,
por amor si pudiesen   luego a sus tierras tornar.
Todos vinién al rey   la fija le demandar,
si ganar la pudiesen   por con ella casar.

205 "Rey," dixeron ellos,   "tiempos á pasados
que te pidiemos tu fija   cadaúno con sus regnados;
echéstelo en fabla,   estamos afiuzados,
por oír tu respuesta   somos a ti tornados.

206 Somos entre nós mismos   así acordados:
a cual tú la dieres,   que seyamos pagados.
Estamos en tu fiuza   todos tres enredados,
¡an a ir en cabo   los dos envergonçados!"

207 Respondioles el rey: "¡Amigos, bien fiziestes
que en esti consejo   tan bien vos abiniestes!
Pero por recapdarlo   en mal tiempo viniestes:
la duenya es enferma,   entenderlo pudiestes.

202 He took Apollonius by the hand, as a sign of
        friendship.
    All along the coast, they saw many skilled artisans,
    burghers and burgesses, many signs of prosperity;
    they left the market and went on toward the king's
        dwelling.

203 As they were traveling, happy in each other's company,
    they were approached by three young men, all richly
        attired:
    they were the sons of kings, all well-brought-up youths,
    and they were welcomed as much-honored men.

204 The princes all spoke, each hoping to advance his case
    and desiring to turn back for home all the sooner.
    Each one came before the king to ask for his daughter,
    to see if he could win her hand in marriage.

205 "King," they said, "some time has passed
    since we asked for your daughter, each offering her our
        kingdoms;
    we trust you have been considering our proposals,
    and now we have returned to hear your decision.

206 We have all three agreed among ourselves:
    no matter whom you choose, we will be content.
    The three of us are all hanging on your words,
    although two of us must go away disappointed!"

207 The king replied, "My friends, you have done well
    in having reached such a fitting agreement!
    But you have come at a bad time to resolve the issue:
    the lady is unwell, as you may have heard.

208 Dell estudio que lieva   estando enflaquida,
   que es de la flaqueza   en enfermedat caída.
   ¡Por malos de pecados,   en tanto es venida
   que son desfiuzados   los metges de su vida!

209 Pero non me semeja   que en esto andedes:
   escrevit sendas cartas,   ca escrevir sabedes;
   escrevit vuestros nombres,   qué arras le daredes,
   cual ella escojere,   otorgado lo avredes."

210 Escrivieron sendas cartas,   que eran escrivanos:
   escrivieron sus nombres   con las sus mismas manos,
   sus tierras e sus logares,   los montes e los planos,
   cómo descendían   de parientes loçanos.

211 Sellóyelas el rey   con su mismo aniello,
   non podién seyellarlas   con más primo seyello;
   levolas a Apolonio   un caro mancebiello,
   que fuese a la duenya   con ellas al castiello.

212 Fue luego Apolonio   recabdar el mandado,
   levolas a la duenya   como le fue castigado.
   Ella, cuando lo vio venir   atán escalentado,
   mesturar non lo quiso   lo que avía asmado.

213 "Maestro," dixo ella,   "quiérote demandar:
   ¿qué buscas a tal ora   o qué quieres recabtar?
   Que a tal sazón como esta   tú non sueles aquí entrar,
   nunca lición me sueles   a tal hora pasar."

208 She has been weakened from all her studying,
and from weakness, she has taken to her bed.
It is truly a shame that her condition has worsened
to the point that the doctors fear for her life!

209 However, I do not think it is right to keep you waiting:
each of you must write a letter, for you all know how to
write;
write your names and the wedding gifts you offer her,
then I will give her to whichever man she chooses."

210 Then each prince wrote his letter, they were lettered
men:
they wrote their names, each with his very own hand,
described their lands and towns, mountains and plains,
and their long lines of illustrious ancestors.

211 The king sealed the letters with his very own ring,
they could not have been sealed with a better one;
a noble young page brought the letters to Apollonius,
so that he could take them to the lady in the castle.

212 Apollonius went immediately to fulfill the king's
command,
he brought the letters to the lady as he had been
charged to do.
The lady, when she saw him enter in such a rush,
had no wish to speak openly of her private thoughts.

213 "Master," she said, "I must ask you,
what are you doing here now, what do you want?
You do not usually come to me at this time,
there was never a lesson planned for this hour."

214 Entendió Apolonio   la su entención:
    "Fija," dixo, "non vengo   por pasarvos lición,
    d'esto seyet bien segura   en vuestro corazón,
    mas mensatge vos trayo   por que merecía gran don.

215 El rey, vuestro padre,   sallose a deportar
    fasta que fuesse ora   de venir a yantar;
    vinieron tres infantes   para vos demandar,
    todos muy fermosos,   nobles e de prestar.

216 Sópoles vuestro padre   ricamiente recebir,
    mas non sabié atanto   qué pudiese dezir;
    mandoles sendas cartas   a todos escrevir,
    vos veyet cuál queredes   de todos escogir."

217 Priso ella las cartas,   maguer enferma era,
    abriolas e catolas   fasta la vez tercera.
    Non vio ý el nombre,   en carta ni en cera,
    con cuyo casamiento   ella fuese plazentera.

218 Cató a Apolonio   e dixo con gran sospiro:
    "Dígasme, Apolonio,   el mio buen rey de Tiro,
    en este casamiento   de ti mucho me miro:
    ¡si te plaze o si non,   yo tu voluntat requiro!"

219 Respuso Apolonio,   e fabló con gran cordura:
    "¡Duenya, si me pesasse   faría muy gran locura!
    ¡Lo que al rey ploguiere   e fuere vuestra ventura,
    yo si lo destajasse   faría gran locura!

220 Évos yo bien ensenyada   de lo que yo sabía,
    más vos preciarán todos   por la mi maestría.

214 Apollonius, understanding her meaning, replied:
   "My child," he said, "I have not come to give you a
      lesson;
   rest assured, that is not why I am here.
   Rather, I bring you a message deserving a reward.

215 The king, your father, was out riding,
   enjoying the time before his midday meal;
   three princes came to him to ask for your hand,
   all three handsome, noble, and of good standing.

216 Your father welcomed them with good courtesy,
   but he did not know how to respond to their suits;
   he has ordered each one to write you a letter,
   so that you might choose the one you want."

217 She took the letters, and even though she was weak,
   she opened them and read them three times through.
   But she did not see, on paper or wax,
   the name of the one man she desired to marry.

218 She looked at Apollonius and said, heaving a great sigh,
   "Tell me, Apollonius, my good king of Tyre,
   in this matter of marriage, I look to you for advice:
   Does this please you or not? I must know your mind!"

219 Apollonius replied, and he spoke most wisely:
   "My lady, I would be a fool if it pained me!
   Whatever pleases the king and makes you happy,
   what a fool I would be to stand in your way!

220 I have taught you well from everything I know,
   you will rise in everyone's esteem thanks to my
      knowledge.

¡Desaquí, si casardes   a vuestra mejoría,
avré de vuestra hondra   muy gran plazentería!"

221 "Maestro," dixo ella,   "si amor te tocase,
non querriés que otrie   tu lazerio lograse.
¡Nunca lo creyería   fasta que lo provase,
que del rey de Tiro   desdenyada fincase!"

222 Escrivió una carta   e cerrola con cera,
diola a Apolonio,   que mensajero era,
que la diese al rey,   que estava en la glera.
¡Sabet que fue aína   andada la carrera!

223 Abrió el rey la carta   e fízola catar.
La carta dizía esto   (sópola bien dictar):
que con el pelegrino   quería ella casar
que con el cuerpo solo   estorció de la mar.

224 Fízose d'esta cosa   el rey maravillado,
non podía entender   la fuerça del dictado.
Demandó que cuál era   ell infante venturado
que lidió con las ondas   e con el mar irado.

225 Dixo ell uno de ellos,   e cuidó seyer artero,
Aguilón le dicen   por nombre bien certero:
"¡Rey, yo fui esse,   e fui verdadero,
ca escapé apenas   en poco d'un madero!"

226 Dixo el uno d'ellos: "¡Es mentira provada!
Yo lo sé bien que dizes   cosa desaguisada:

Now, if you were to marry to your advantage,
I would be very happy to see you so honored!"

221 "Master," she said, "if only you knew what love is,
you would not let another take the fruits of your labor.
I would never have believed, until it happened to me,
that I could be rejected by the king of Tyre!"

222 The princess wrote a letter and sealed it with wax,
she gave it to Apollonius, who was the messenger,
to give to the king, who was out by the shore.
To be sure, Apollonius went quickly on his way!

223 The king opened the letter and looked it over.
This is what it said (the princess knew how to write
        well):
that it was the pilgrim whom she wanted to marry,
the man who survived the shipwreck with nothing but
        his life.

224 The princess's letter astonished the king,
he could not make out the meaning of her words.
He asked which of the three princes had suffered that
        fate,
which one had survived the waves and the angry seas.

225 One of the princes, thinking himself very clever,
the one who went by the name of Aguillon,
said, "King, I am that man, truly I am,
because I barely escaped clinging to a plank of wood!"

226 One of the other princes said, "That is a bald-faced lie!
I know well that your words are nonsense:

en uno nos criamos,   non traspassó nada,
¡bien lo sé que nunca tú   prendiste tal espadada!"

227 Mientre ellos estavan   en esta tal entencia,
entendió bien el rey   que dixera fallencia;
asmó entre su cuer   una buena entencia,
ca era de buen seso   e de gran sapiencia.

228 Dio a Apolonio   la carta a leyer,
si podrié por aventura   la cosa entender.
Vio el rey de Tiro   qué avía de seyer,
¡començole la cara   toda a embermejecer!

229 Fue el rey metiendo   mientes en la razón,
fuésele demudando   todo el corazón.
Echó a Apolonio   mano al cabeçón,
apartose con éll,   sin otro null varón.

230 Dixo: "Yo te conjuro,   maestro e amigo,
por ell amor que yo tengo   establecido contigo,
cómo tú lo entiendes   que lo fables comigo.
¡Sinon, por toda tu fazienda   non daría un figo!"

231 Respuso Apolonio: "¡Rey, mucho me embargas,
fuertes paraulas me dizes   e mucho me amargas!
Creyo que de mí traen   estas nuevas tan largas,
¡mas si a ti non plazen,   son para mí amargas!"

232 Recudiole el rey   como leyal varón:
"Non te mintré, maestro,   que sería traiçón:

    we were raised together, and nothing of the kind ever
        happened.
    I know you never suffered any such misfortune!"

227 While the three princes were arguing in this way,
    the king realized that Aguillon was lying
    and, thinking to himself, came up with a good plan,
    because he was a man of good sense and great wisdom.

228 He gave Apollonius the princess's letter to read,
    to see if he could possibly understand it.
    When the king of Tyre saw what the words meant,
    he began to blush—his whole face turned a deep red!

229 When Archistrates understood the message,
    he felt as if his heart was all aflutter.
    He grabbed Apollonius by the collar
    and took him aside, so the two were alone.

230 Archistrates said, "I order you, master and friend,
    for all the love that you and I share,
    what do you think the letter means? Tell me.
    If you do not, I would not give a fig for all your worth!"

231 Apollonius replied, "King, you are upsetting me to no
        end,
    you speak solemn words that make my heart bitter!
    I think I am the man mentioned in this momentous
        letter,
    but if it is not pleasing to you, then it is bitter to me!"

232 The king responded, like the loyal man he was,
    "I will not lie to you, master, that would be a betrayal:

cuando ella lo quiere,   plázeme de corazón.
¡Otorgada la ayas   sin nulla condición!"

233 Destajaron la fabla,   tornaron al consejo.
"Amigos," diz, "non quiero   trayervos en trasecho;
prendet vuestra carrera,   buscat otro consejo,
ca yo vo entendiendo   d'ello un poquellejo."

234 Entraron a la villa,   que ya querién comer,
subieron al castiello   la enferma veyer.
Ella, cuando vido   el rey cerca de sí seyer,
fízose más enferma,   començó de tremer.

235 "Padre," dixo la duenya   con la boz enflaquida,
"¿qué buscastes a tal ora,   cuál fue vuestra venida?
¡De coraçón me pesa   e é rencura sabida
porque vos es la yantar   atán tarde deferida!"

236 "Fija," dixo el padre,   "de mí non vos quexedes,
¡más cuita es lo vuestro,   que tan gran mal avedes!
Quiero vos fablar un poco,   que non vos enojedes,
que verdat me digades   cuál marido queredes."

237 "¡Padre, bien vos lo digo   cuando vós me lo
                                demandades,
que, si de Apolonio   en otro me camiades—

since this is what she wants, it makes me deeply happy.
I will give you her hand without a single condition!"

233   They stopped talking and went back to the group.
"Friends," said Archistrates, "I have no wish to offend
          you,
but you must go your way, seek out another plan,
because I have understood something of the meaning
          of the letter."

234   When the two kings entered the city, hungry for their
          meal,
they went into the castle to see the ailing lady.
When she saw Archistrates come close to her,
she felt even worse, and she began to tremble.

235   "Father," said the lady, her voice weak,
"what do you want, why have you come here now?
My heart is heavy and I am sorely pained
that you have postponed your meal for so long!"

236   "Daughter," said the father, "do not worry about me.
You should worry about yourself, because you are so ill!
I want to speak to you a little, now, do not be
          overwhelmed,
and tell me the truth, which man do you want to
          marry?"

237   "Father, I will happily tell you, since you are the one
          asking:
if you give me any other man instead of Apollonius—

non vos miento d'esto,   bien seguro seyades—
en pie non me veredes   cuantos días bivades!"

238 "Fija," dixo el rey,   "¡gran plazer me ficiestes,
de Dios vos vino esto,   que tan bien escogiestes!
Condonado vos seya   esto que vós pidiestes,
¡bien lo queremos todos   cuando vós lo quisiestes!"

239 Salló, esto partido,   el rey por el corral,
fallose con su yerno   en medio del portal.
Afirmaron la cosa   en recabdo cabdal,
luego fue abaxando   a la duenya el mal.

240 Fueron las bodas fechas,   ricas e abondadas:
fueron muchas de yentes   a ellas combidadas,
duraron muchos días   que non eran pasadas,
por esos grandes tiempos   non fueron olvidadas.

241 Entró entre los novios   muit gran dilección,
el Criador entre ellos   metió su bendición.
¡Nunca varón a fembra   nin fembra a varón
non servió en este mundo   de mejor coraçón!

242 Un día, Apolonio   salló a la ribera,
su esposa con éll,   la su dulce companyera.
Podría aver siete meses   que casado era,
fue luego prenyada,   la semana primera.

I am not lying to you, you can be sure of it—
you will not see me out of the sickbed in all the days of
your life!"

238 "Daughter," said the king, "you make me very happy,
it is truly a godsend that you have chosen so well!
What you have asked for will be given to you,
because your wish is also what we all desire!"

239 Everything settled, the king went out into the
courtyard
and met his son-in-law under the arches.
They confirmed the marriage with solemn oaths,
and the lady quickly recovered from her malady.

240 The wedding celebrations were rich and lavish:
many guests were invited to come join the feasting,
many days passed before they were over and done,
and the wedding was not forgotten for years to come.

241 The newlyweds fell very much in love,
the Creator bestowed his blessings upon them.
Never has so perfect a love existed before in this
world,
no man ever loved a woman so well, nor any woman a
man!

242 One day, Apollonius walked along the shore
along with his wife, his sweet companion.
They had been married for about seven months at the
time,
and she had become pregnant, right away, in the first
week.

243 Ellos así andando,   ya querían fer la tornada,
    vieron una nave,   ya era ancorada;
    semejoles fermosa,   ricamiente adobada.
    Por saber Apolonio   dónde era arribada,

244 demandó el maestro,   el que la gobernava,
    que verdat le dixese   de cuál tierra andava.
    Dixo el marinero,   que en somo estava,
    que todo el mayor tiempo   en Tiro lo morava.

245 Dixo Apolonio: "¡Yo ý fui criado!"
    Dixo el marinero: "¡Sí te veyas logrado!"
    Díxole Apolonio: "Si me ovieres grado,
    dezirte puedo senyales   en que seya provado."

246 Dixo·l el marinero   que avrié gran placer.
    "Tú que tanto me dizes,   quiero de ti saber
    al rey Apolonio   si·l podriés conecer."
    Dixo: "¡Como a mí mismo,   esto devedes creyer!"

247 "Si tú lo conecieses,"   dixo el marinero,
    "o trobar lo pudieses   por algún agorero,
    ganariés tal ganancia   que seriés placentero.
    ¡Nunca mejor la ovo   peyón ni cavallero!

248 Di·l que es Antioco   muerto e soterrado,
    con él murió la fija   que·l dio el pecado;
    destruyolos a amos   un rayo del diablo.
    ¡A él esperan todos   por darle el reinado!"

243 Walking along, the two were about to turn back,
when they saw a ship had come in to anchor;
they thought it was handsome and richly kitted out.
Apollonius wanted to know where it had come from,

244 and he asked the master, who set the ship's course,
to tell him, in truth, where they had come from.
The sailor, calling down from the deck, said
that the ship had come from Tyre, its home port.

245 Apollonius said, "That's where I was born and raised!"
The sailor replied, "What a happy coincidence!"
And Apollonius said to him, "If you will allow me,
I can tell you things that will prove it is true."

246 The sailor said he would be happy to listen.
"You who are telling me so much, tell me now
if by chance you happen to know King Apollonius."
Apollonius said, "Believe you me, I know him as well as
 I know myself!"

247 "If you happen to know him," said the sailor,
"or know where to find him with the help of a seer,
there is a handsome reward to be had—you will be
 pleased.
No peon or knight has ever seen a better prize!

248 Tell him that Antiochus is dead and buried,
and the daughter the devil gave him died with him;
together they were struck down by lightning from hell.
The people of Antioch now await Apollonius as their
 king!"

249 Apolonio, alegre,   tornó a su esposa,
    dixo·l: "¡Non me creyedes   vós a mí esta cosa!
    Non querría que fuese   mi palabra mintrosa;
    bien tenía, sines dubda,   la voluntat sabrosa.

250 Mas cuando tal ganancia   nos da el Criador
    e tan buena bengança   nos da de el traidor,
    quiero ir recebirla   con Dios, nuestro Senyor,
    ¡ca no es Antioca   atán poca honor!"

251 "Senyor," dixo la duenya,   "yo só embargada,
    bien anda en siete meses   o en más que só prenyada,
    para entrar en carrera   estó mal aguisada,
    ca só en gran peligro   fasta que seya librada.

252 Si a Dios quisiere,   só del parto vezina,
    si ventura oviere,   devo parir aína;
    si tú luenye estudieses,   allende de la marina,
    deviés bien venir dende   conortar tu reína.

253 Si atender quisieres   o luego quisieres andar,
    ruégote que me lieves,   ¡non me quieras dexar!
    Si tú aquí me dexas,   recibré gran pesar,
    ¡por el tu grand deseyo   podría peligrar!"

254 Dixo Apolonio: "Reína, bien sepades:
    sol que a vuestro padre   en amor lo metades,

249 Apollonius returned to his wife in happiness,
    saying to her, "You will never believe what I have to
        say!
    I have no wish to speak words that are untrue;
    without a doubt, my heart was completely content.

250 But now, the Creator has given us even greater gifts
    by sending our enemy the just vengeance he deserved;
    I wish to go and accept this boon, by the grace of God,
        our Lord,
    for the city of Antioch is no small honor!"

251 "My lord," said the lady, "I am carrying a child,
    seven months or more of my pregnancy have passed,
    taking such a trip would be ill advised for me,
    because I face great danger until I am delivered of the
        child.

252 God willing, the birth will come soon,
    with good fortune, I will soon be in labor,
    and if you were far off, traveling beyond the seas,
    you would have to come right back to comfort your
        queen.

253 Whether you prefer to wait or leave immediately,
    I beg you to take me with you, do not leave me!
    If you leave me here, I will suffer terribly,
    I will miss you so much that I might die!"

254 Apollonius said, "My queen, know this:
    if you can convince your father to give his consent,

    levar vos é comigo   a las mis eredades,
    ¡meter vos é en arras   que pagada seyades!"

255   Dixo ella al padre: "Senyor, por caridat,
    que me dedes licencia   de buena voluntat,
    que ir quiere Apolonio   veyer su heredat,
    ¡si yo con él non fuere,   perder m'é de verdat!

256   El rey Antioco,   que·l avía irado,
    murió muerte sopitanya,   es del sieglo pasado,
    todos a él esperan   por darle el reinado,
    ¡e si yo con él non fuere,   mi bien es destajado!"

257   "Fija," dixo el padre,   "cosa es derechera,
    si quisiere Apolonio   entrar en la carrera;
    si él levarvos quisiere,   vós seyet su companyera,
    ¡Dios vos guíe, mi fija,   la su potencia vera!"

258   Fueron luego las naves   prestas e aparejadas,
    de bestias e d'averes   e de conducho cargadas,
    por seyer más ligeras   con sevo bien untadas.
    ¡Entró en fuerte punto,   con naves avesadas!

259   Dio el rey a la fija,   por ir más acompanyada,
    Licórides, ell ama   que la avié criada;
    dio·l muchas parteras,   mas una mejorada,
    que en el reino todo   non avía su calanya.

then I will take you with me to see my lands,
where I will give you wedding gifts that will please
    you!"

255 She said to her father, "My lord, for pity's sake,
please give me your permission most willingly,
for Apollonius wants to go see his lands,
and if I cannot go with him, I will surely die!

256 King Antiochus, whom Apollonius had angered,
died a sudden death, he is no longer in this world,
so now all await Apollonius to come be their king,
and if I cannot go with him, my happiness is at an end!"

257 "Daughter," said the father, "it is fitting
that Apollonius desires to set off on this journey,
and if he wants to take you with him, go be his
    helpmate.
May God guide you, my daughter—his power is great!"

258 The ships were made ready and outfitted immediately,
loaded with cattle and riches and provisions for the
    trip
and coated with tallow for smooth sailing.
Alas, Apollonius and his ships set off under a bad sign!

259 To keep her company, the king gave his daughter
Licorides, the nursemaid who had tended her since
    birth,
and many midwives, including one who was excellent:
in all the kingdom, she was unmatched in skill.

260 Bendíxolos a amos   con la su diestra mano,
    rogó al Criador,   que está más en alto,
    que·l guiase la fija   ivierno e verano,
    que·l guardase el yerno   cómo tornase sano.

261 Alçaron las velas   por aína mover,
    mandaron del arena   las áncoras toller;
    començaron los vientos   las velas a bolver
    tanto que las fizieron   de la tierra toller.

262 Cuando vino la hora   que las naves movieron,
    que los unos de los otros   a partirse ovieron,
    muchas fueron las lágrimas   que en tierra cayeron,
    ¡pocos fueron los ojos   que agua non vertieron!

263 Los vientos por las lágrimas   non querían estar,
    acuitaron las naves,   fiziéronlas andar,
    así que las ovieron   atanto de alongar
    que ya non las podían   de tierra devisar.

264 Avién vientos derechos,   cuales a Dios pidién,
    las ondas más pagadas   estar non podién:
    todos a Apolonio   mejorarle querién
    los tuertos e los danyos   que fecho le avién.

265 Atal era el mar   como carrera llana,
    todos eran alegres,   toda su casa sana.
    Alegre Apolonio,   alegre Luciana,
    ¡non sabién que del gozo   cuita es su ermana!

266 Avían de la marina   gran partida andada,
    podién aver aína   la mar atravesada,

260 The king blessed them both with his right hand,
   begging the Creator, who is on high,
   to guide his daughter in all the seasons,
   to protect his son-in-law and bring him back safely.

261 They raised the sails to make a quick departure,
   ordered the anchors be pulled up from the sands;
   then strong winds began to turn the sails,
   pulling the ships away from the shore.

262 When the time came for the ships to depart,
   and for friends to take their leave from one another,
   many were the tears shed upon the ground,
   and few were the eyes that remained dry!

263 The winds paid no heed to all their tears
   and sped on the ships, making them sail,
   carried on the wind so far and fast
   that the ships soon faded from the sight of shore.

264 God answered their prayers for favorable winds,
   the waves could not have been more gentle:
   the winds and the waves were now kind to Apollonius
   after all the cruelty and harm they had dealt him
       before.

265 The sea stretched out like a smooth road before them,
   and all rejoiced, all the company was well.
   Joyful Apollonius, joyful Luciana,
   little did they know that trouble is happiness's twin!

266 When the ships had traveled far
   and were close to halfway across the sea,

tóvoles la ventura   una mala cellada,
cual nunca fue a ombres   otra peyor echada.

267 Ante vos lo oviemos   dicho otra vegada
cómo era la duenya   de gran tiempo prenyada;
que de la luenga muebda   e que de la andada,
era al mes noveno   la cosa allegada.

268 Cuando vino al término   que ovo a parir,
ovo la primeriça   los rayos a sentir.
Cuitáronla dolores   que se quería morir,
¡dizía que nunca fembra   devía concebir!

269 Cuando su sazón vino,   nació una criatura,
una ninya muy fermosa   e de grant apostura.
Mas, como de recabdo   non ovo complidura,
oviéronse a venir   en muy gran estrechura.

270 Como non fue la duenya   en el parto guardada,
cayole la sangre   dentro en la corada,
de las otras cosas   non fue bien alimpiada;
¡cuando mientes metieron,   falláronla pasada!

271 Pero non era muerta,   mas era amortida,
era en muerte falsacia   con el parto caída;
non entendién en ella   ningún signo de vida,
todos eran creyentes   que era transida.

272 Metién todos bozes,   llamando: "¡Ay senyora,
salliemos de Pentápolin   combusco en fuerte hora!
Cuando vós sodes muerta,   ¿qué faremos nós agora?
¡A tan mala sazón   vos perdemos, senyora!"

Fortune set a cruel ambush for them,
the likes of which no man had ever endured.

267 We have already told you once before
about how the lady was in late pregnancy;
after the long journey and all the distance traveled,
the ninth month came quickly upon her.

268 When her time had come, and labor began,
the new mother started feeling the stabs of pain.
In the throes of labor, she hoped for death.
She cried out, "No woman should ever conceive a
      child!"

269 When at last she was delivered of a child,
it was a very lovely girl, of truly noble bearing.
But not all the necessary precautions were observed,
and soon they found themselves in dire straits.

270 Since she had not been properly cared for in the birth,
Luciana's blood festered inside her womb,
and the afterbirth was not fully expelled;
when her attendants noticed the problem, she was
      already gone!

271 But she was not really dead, only unconscious;
she had fallen into a coma caused by her labor.
There was not a single sign of life in her,
and all thought that she had passed away.

272 All lamented, calling out, "Alas, lady,
curse the day we left Pentapolis with you!
Now you are dead, what will we do?
We have lost you, lady, in an evil hour!"

273 Oyó el marinero   estos malos roídos,
    decendió del governio   a pasos tan tendidos;
    dixo a Apolonio: "¿En qué sodes caídos?
    ¡Si defunto tenedes,   todos somos perdidos!

274 ¡Quien se quiere que sía,   echadlo en la mar;
    si non, podriemos todos   aína peligrar!
    ¡Acuitatvos aína,   non querades tardar,
    non es aquesta cosa   para darle gran vagar!"

275 Respuso Apolonio: "¡Calla ya, marinero!
    ¡Dizes estranya cosa,   seméjasme guerrero!
    ¡Reína es honrada,   que non pobre romero!
    ¡Semeja en tus dichas   que eres carnicero!

276 Fizo contra mí ella   cosiment tan granado:
    non dubdó porque era   pobre desemparado,
    sacome de pobreza,   que sería lazdrado.
    ¡Contra varón non fizo   fembra tan aguisado!

277 ¿Cómo me lo podría   el coraçón sofrir
    que yo a tal amiga   pudiese aborrir?
    ¡Sería mayor derecho   yo con ella morir
    que tan aviltadamientre   a ella de mí partir!"

278 Dixo el marinero: "¡En vanidat contiendes!
    ¡Al logar en que estamos   loca razón defiendes!
    Si en eso nos aturas,   más fuego nos enciendes,
    ¡téngote por errado   que tan mal lo entiendes!

279 Ante de poca hora,   si el cuerpo tenemos,
    seremos todos muertos,   estorcer non podemos.

273 The ship's master heard these terrible cries,
    and he came down from the helm with great strides,
    asking Apollonius, "What has befallen you?
    If there is a corpse aboard, then we are all doomed!

274 No matter who it is, throw the body into the sea;
    otherwise, we will all soon be in danger!
    Hurry, do it now, do not wait even for a second,
    this is not the sort of thing that you can put off!"

275 Apollonius retorted, "Be quiet, master!
    You make no sense, and you seem like a heartless killer!
    This is an honored queen, not just any poor pilgrim!
    Your words are those of a cruel villain!

276 This woman showed me such great mercy:
    it did not matter to her that I was poor and forsaken,
    and she rescued me from suffering in poverty.
    Never has a woman been so good to a man!

277 How could my heart ever possibly bear it,
    if I were to treat such a beloved lady so despicably?
    It would be more just for me to die along with her
    than to send her away from me so dishonorably!"

278 The shipmaster said, "Your words are useless!
    It is foolish to try to argue like this when we are at sea!
    Your insistence just fans the flames of the fire.
    You just do not understand how wrong you are!

279 If we keep the body aboard, before we know it,
    we will all be dead, there will be no escape.

¡Si la madre perdemos,   buena fija avemos!
¡Mal fazes, Apolonio,   que en esto seyemos!"

280 Bien veyé Apollonio   que se podrién perder,
mas aún non podié   su corazón vencer;
pero al marinero   óvolo a creyer,
que ya veyén las ondas   que se querién bolver.

281 Balsamaron el cuerpo   como costumbre era,
fiziéronle armario   de liviana madera,
engludaron las tablas   con englut e con cera,
bolviéronlo en ropa   rica de gran manera.

282 Con el cuerpo a bueltas,   el su buen companyero
metió XL pieças   de buen oro en el tablero,
escrivió en un plomo,   con un grafio d'azero,
letras, qui la fallase,   por onde fuese certero.

283 Cuando fue el ministerio   todo acabado,
el ataút bien preso,   el cuerpo bien cerrado,
vertieron muchas lágrimas,   mucho varón rascado,
fue, a pesar de todos,   en las ondas echado.

284 Luego al tercer día,   el sol escalentado,
fue al puerto de Éfeso   el cuerpo arribado;
fue de buen maestro   de física trobado,
ca avié un diciplo   savio e bien letrado.

Though we have lost the mother, we have a good
    daughter!
Apollonius, you're wrong to put us all at risk!"

280 Although Apollonius saw the danger they were in,
he still could not bring his feelings under control;
yet he had to trust the shipmaster's words,
because all could see the waves were turning rough.

281 The body was embalmed, as was their custom,
and they made her a coffin of light wood,
sealed its boards with glue and wax,
and bound the body in rich winding cloths.

282 Her good husband wrapped up with the body
forty pieces of true gold and placed them in the coffin,
then wrote on a lead tablet, with a steel stylus,
a message bearing the truth to whomever might find
    her.

283 Once all the funeral rites were concluded
and the coffin tightly sealed, enclosing the body
    within,
many tears were shed, many a man's face torn in grief;
she was, to the great sorrow of all, thrown upon the
    waves.

284 After three days, when the sun was high in the sky,
the body arrived at the port of Ephesus,
where it was found by a skilled master of medicine,
who happened to have a wise and learned disciple.

285 Por bevir mas vicioso   e seyer más a su sabor,
     como fuera de las ruvas   bive ombre mejor,
     avía todos sos averes   do era morador,
     en ribera del agua,   los montes en derredor.

286 Andaba por la ribera,   a sabor de el viento,
     de buenos escolanos   traíya más de ciento;
     fallaron esta obra   de grant engludimiento,
     que non fizo en ella el agua   null enozimiento.

287 Fízola el maestro   a su casa levar,
     demandó un ferrero   e fízola desplegar;
     fallaron este cuerpo   que oyestes comptar,
     començó el maestro   de duelo a llorar.

288 Fallaron una ninya   de cara bien tajada,
     cuerpo bien asentado,   ricamiente adobada,
     gran tresoro con ella,   casa bien abondada,
     mas de su testamento   non podién saber nada.

289 En cabo del tablero,   en un rencón apartado,
     fallaron ell escrito   en un plomo deboxado.
     Prísolo el maestro   e leyó el dictado;
     dixo: "¡Si non lo cumplo   non me veya logrado!"

290 Quiérovos la materia   del dictado dezir:
     "Yo, rey Apolonio,   embío mercet pedir:
     quiquier que la fallare   fágala sobollir,
     lo que no·l pudiemos   sobre la mar complir.

285 To live in greater tranquility and be more at his ease,
because it is better to live far from the busy city
        streets,
the doctor kept all his belongings and made his home
on the seashore, with a view of the mountains above.

286 He was walking by the shore, taking in the breeze,
accompanied by more than one hundred good
        students,
when they found the tightly sealed box,
which had not been damaged at all by the water.

287 The doctor had the box brought to his home,
he called for a blacksmith and had the box opened,
and when they found the body you have heard about,
the doctor began to cry out in mourning.

288 Inside they found a young woman with a shapely face,
her body, richly attired, was laid out in the coffin,
and great treasure traveled with her in the well-
        provisioned box,
yet there were no clues as to her identity.

289 Then, at one end of the coffin, in a corner set apart,
they found the words etched into the lead tablet.
The master took it up and read its message;
he said, "I will carry this out, or may I never find
        happiness!"

290 Now, I will tell you what the tablet said:
"I, King Apollonius, write to ask this favor:
whoever should find this lady, please bury her,
for we were unable to do so at sea.

291 El medio del tresoro lieve por su lazerio,
  lo ál por la su alma preste al monesterio:
  sallir le an los clérigos mejor al cimenterio,
  rezarán más de grado los ninyos el salterio.

292 Si esto non cumpliere, plega al Criador
  que ni en muerte ni en vida non aya valedor."
  Dixo el metge estonze: "¡Tal seya, o peor,
  si non gelo cumpliere bien así o mejor!"

293 Mandó tomar el cuerpo, ponerlo en un lecho
  que por un grant aver non podrié seyer fecho;
  fízole toda honra como avía derecho.
  ¡Devrié, si ál fiziese, hombre aver despecho!

294 Fecha toda la cosa para'l soterramiento,
  fecha la sepultura con todo cumplimiento,
  entró el buen diciplo, de grant entendimiento,
  llegose al maestro con su abenimiento.

295 "Fijo," dixo el maestro, "grant amor me fiziestes,
  gradézcovoslo mucho porque tal ora viniestes.
  Somos en un ministerio, atal otro non viestes:
  un cuerpo que fallamos, bien cuido que lo oyestes.

296 Desque Dios te aduxo en tan buena sazón,
  finca con tu maestro en esta proceción:

291 Take half the treasure for your troubles,
     give the rest to the Church to pray for her soul,
     so the priests will go more diligently to the cemetery,
     and the choirboys more willingly sing the psalter.

292 If my wishes are not fulfilled, may God
     see you abandoned in life and death."
     The doctor then said, "So be it, or even worse,
     if I do not do all that he asks and more!"

293 The doctor ordered the body be placed in a bed
     so fine that no amount of money could have bought
          one like it;
     he honored the lady, just as was fit and proper.
     Had he acted otherwise, he would have deserved
          contempt!

294 When everything for the burial had been prepared
     and the sepulcher had been readied, finished to
          perfection,
     the good disciple, who was very wise, entered
     and asked for permission to approach his master.

295 "Son," said the master, "you have shown me love;
     I am very grateful that you have come now.
     The task before us is one you have never seen before:
     this body washed ashore here, as you must have heard.

296 Since God has brought you here at just the right
          moment,
     stay here with your master, help me with this process:

ondremos este cuerpo,   ca debdo es e razón,
quiero de la ganancia   que lieves tu quinión.

297 Por tu bondat misma   e por mi amor,
prende en una ampolla   el bálsamo mejor;
aguisa bien el cuerpo,   ca eres sabidor,
¡non aguisarás nunca   tan noble o mejor!"

298 El escolar fue bueno,   un maestro valié;
tollió de sí el manto   que a las cuestas traía,
priso del puro bálsamo,   ca bien lo conecía,
allégose al cuerpo   que en el lecho yazié.

299 Mandó·l toller la ropa   que desuso tenié,
despojole los vestidos   preciosos que vestié;
non lo dava a otrie   lo que él fer podié,
ninguno otro en la cosa   tan bien no abinié.

300 Su cosa aguisada   por fer la unción,
el benedito ombre,   con grant devoción,
puso·l la una mano   sobr'ell su corazón,
entendió un poquiello   de la odicempçón.

301 Fizo alçar el bálsamo   e el cuerpo cobrir,
fue·l catando el polso   si·l quería batir
e otras maestrías   qu'éll sopo comedir;
asmó que por ventura   aún podrié bevir.

302 Tornó a su maestro,   que estava a la puerta:
"¡Senyor, esta reína   que tenemos por muerta—

let us honor this corpse, as duty and propriety
    command us,
and I will give you your rightful part of her treasure.

297 Moved by your own goodness and for my sake,
take a flask and fill it with the finest balsam oil.
Lay out the body well, for you are knowledgeable;
you will never lay out a nobler or better one!"

298 The student worked well, he was as good as a master;
he took off the cloak that he wore on his back,
took up the pure balsam, for he knew its properties
    well,
and approached the body laid out upon the bed.

299 He ordered all the wrappings be removed from her
    body
and took off all the precious garments she wore
    beneath.
He did not let anyone else do what he could do;
no one else could perform this task so well.

300 All was prepared to begin the embalming,
when the blessed man, with great devotion,
placed a hand over the lady's heart
and suddenly felt the slightest palpitation.

301 He had the balsam taken away and the body covered,
then he looked to see if a pulse beat within
and used other methods that he called to mind;
he thought there was a chance she might yet live.

302 He turned to his master, who stood at the door:
"My lord, this queen whom we thought was dead—

creyo que non ternás   la sentencia por tuerta—
cosa veyo en ella   que mucho me conuerta!

303 Yo entendo en ella   espirament de vida,
ca ell alma de su cuerpo   non es encara exida.
Por mengua de recabdo   es la duenya perdida,
¡si tú me lo condonas,   yo te la daré guarida!"

304 "Fijo," dixo el maestro,   "¡dízesme grant amor,
nunca fijo a padre   podrié dezir mejor!
¡Si tú esto fazes,   acabas gran honor,
de cuantos metges oy biven   tú eres el mejor!

305 Nunca morrá tu nombre   si tú esto fizieres,
de mí avrás gran honra   mientre que tú visquieres.
¡En tu vida avrás honra   e, después que murieres,
fablarán de tu seso   varones e mugeres!"

306 Mandó levar el cuerpo   luego a su posada,
por fer más a su guisa   en su casa privada.
Fizo fer grandes fuegos   de lenya trasecada,
que non fiziesen fumo   nin la calor desaguisada.

307 Fizo poner el cuerpo   en el suelo barrido,
en una rica colcha   en un almatraque batido,
puso·l sobre la cara   la manga del vestido,
ca es para la cara   el fuego dessabrido.

308 Con la calor del fuego,   que estava bien bivo,
aguisó un ungüente   caliente e lexativo,

I believe you will not think I speak in error—
I see something in her that gives me great hope!

303   I sense that there is still a breath of life in her,
because her soul has yet to leave her body.
She is in this deathly state due to lack of care,
but with your permission, I will cure her for you!"

304   "Son," said the master, "this is wonderful news,
never could a son have said better to a father!
If you are able to cure her, it will be to your honor,
and you will be the best of all living doctors!

305   Your name will go down in history,
and I will honor you all the days of your life.
In life you will be honored and, after you die,
your wisdom will be praised far and wide!"

306   The student ordered the body be brought to his house,
so that he could work his cure as he wished and in
        privacy.
He had great fires built up with dry wood,
so they would not smoke and he could control the
        heat.

307   He had the body placed upon the clean floor,
laid out on a rich coverlet, on a soft mattress,
and he placed the sleeve of her dress over the lady's
        face,
because the heat of the fire is harsh to the face.

308   By the heat of the fire, which was roaring bright,
he mixed up an ointment that was hot and purgative,

untola con sus manos,   non se fizo esquivo:
respiró un poquiello   el espírito cativo.

309 Fizo, aun sin esto,   ell olio calentar,
mandó los vellozinos   en ello enferventar,
fizo con esta lana   el cuerpo embolcar.
¡Nunca de tal megía   oyó ombre contar!

310 Entrole la melezina   dentro en la corada,
desuyole la sangre   que estava cuajada.
Respiró ell almiella   que estava afogada,
sospiró una vez   la enferma lazdrada.

311 El mege d'esti signo   ovo grant alegría,
entendió que ya iva   obrando la metgía;
començó más a firmes   de fer la maestría,
fizo·l a poca d'ora   mostrar gran mejoría.

312 Cuando vido su ora   que lo podrié pasar,
con otras melezinas   qu'él sopo ý mesclar
engargantó·l el olio,   fízogelo pasar:
ovo de la horrura   la duenya a porgar.

313 Ovo desende a rato   los ojos a abrir;
non sabié dó estava,   non podié ren dezir.
El metge codiciaba   tanto como bevir
en alguna palabra   de su boca oír.

314 Pero cuando Dios quiso   —pasó un gran rato—
metió una boz flaca,   cansada, como gato:

and with no hesitation applied it with his own hands:
a faint breath issued from the tortured soul.

309 In addition to all this, he had oil heated up
and ordered fleeces to be boiled in it,
then he had the body wrapped up in the wool.
Never before has such a cure been heard of!

310 The medicine entered deep into Luciana's womb,
unstopping the blood that had festered there.
The little soul that had been suffocated breathed
    again,
and the afflicted lady heaved a single sigh.

311 The doctor was greatly cheered by this sign,
for he understood that his cure was now working,
so he began to apply his method with more force,
and in no time she showed much improvement.

312 When he saw his patient was ready to drink,
he prepared other medicines that he knew how to mix
and made her swallow them with oil, down her throat:
he successfully purged the lady of all the impurity
    within.

313 After a while, the lady opened her eyes;
she had no idea where she was, nor could she say a
    word.
The doctor wanted, more than his own life,
to hear a single word issue from her lips.

314 When God saw fit—after a long while—
she said, in a weak, tired voice, like a cat's meow,

"¿Dó está Apolonio,   que yo por éll cato?
¡Creyo que non me precia   cuanto a su çapato!"

315 Entró más en recuerdo,   tornó en su sentido,
cató a todas partes   con su ojo vellido,
non vio a sus companyas   nin vio a su marido,
vio ombres extranyos,   logar desconyocido.

316 "Amigo," dixo al metge   que la avié guarida,
"ruégote que me digas dó seyo,   que mal so
                                    desmarrida.
Véyome de mis gentes   e de mi logar partida,
¡si Dios non me valiere   tengo que só perdida!

317 Seméjasme ombre bueno,   non te celaré nada:
fija só de rey   e con rey fui casada;
non sé por cuál manera   só aquí arribada,
¡só en muy gran miedo   de seyer aontada!"

318 Fabló el maestro   a muy gran sabor:
"Senyora, ¡confortadvos,   non ayades pavor!
Tenetvos por guarida   —¡grado al Criador!—
bien seredes,   como nunca mejor.

319 Yoguiésedes folgada,   yo ál non vos rogaría,
yo vos faré servicio   como a madre mía.
Si mucho vos cuitáredes,   faredes recadía,
¡prendrá mala finada   toda nuestra metgía!"

320 Yogó en paz la duenya,   non quiso más fablar,
fue el santo diciplo   su maestro buscar.

"Where is Apollonius, why do I not see him anywhere?
I think he must have thrown me away like a worn-out
    shoe!"

315   As she began to wake and come to her senses,
she looked all around, but her lovely eyes
saw neither her companions nor her husband;
she saw only strangers and a strange place.

316   "Friend," she said to the doctor who had cured her,
"I beg you, tell me where I am, for I am in a bad way.
I see I am far from my people and my home;
without God's help, surely this is the end!

317   You seem to be a good man, I will hide nothing from
    you:
I am the daughter of a king and married to a king;
I have no idea how I have come to be here,
and I am in great fear of being dishonored!"

318   The doctor said with great courtesy,
"My lady, take comfort, do not be afraid!
Understand you are safe—thanks be to the Creator!—
you will recover and feel better than ever.

319   Rest now in comfort, I will ask nothing more of you,
I will serve you as if you were my own mother.
If you worry too much it will only cause you to relapse,
and then all our doctoring will come to no good!"

320   The lady rested peacefully, for she had no more desire
    to speak,
and the blessed student went to find his teacher.

"Maestro," ditz, "albriça   te tengo de demandar:
¡guarida es la duenya,   bien lo puedes provar!"

321 Fuese luego el maestro,   non lo quiso tardar;
falló biva la duenya,   maguer con flaquedat.
Dixo al diciplo,   non por poridat,
que la su maestría   non avié egualdat.

322 Pensaron amos de la duenya   fasta que fue levantada,
¡nunca viyo ombre en el mundo   duenya mejor
                                        guardada!
¡La bondat de los metges   era atán granada,
devié seyer escripta,   en un libro notada!

323 Cuando fue guarida   e del mal alimpiada,
porfijola el metge   que la avía sanada.
Del aver no·l tomaron   cuanto una dinarada,
todo gelo guardaron,   no·l despendieron nada.

324 Por amor que toviese   su castidat mejor,
fiziéronle un monesterio   do visquiese seror;
fasta que Dios quisiere   que venga su senyor,
con otras duenyas de orden   servié al Criador.

325 Dexémosvos la duenya,   guarde su monesterio,
sierva su eglesia   e reze su salterio;
en el rey Apolonio   tornemos el ministerio,
que por las aventuras   levó tan gran lazerio.

326 Desque la muger   en las ondas fue echada,
siempre fue en tristicia   y en vida lazdrada,

"Master," he said, "I bring good news to tell you:
the lady is cured, come and see for yourself!"

321　The master came right away, he did not waste a
　　　　minute;
　　　he found the lady returned to life, although weak.
　　　He said to his disciple, and for all to hear,
　　　that his medical skill was without equal.

322　They both tended to the lady until she was well—
　　　never has a woman in this world been so well cared for!
　　　The virtues of the two doctors were so extraordinary,
　　　they should be put down in writing, in the pages of a
　　　　book!

323　When the lady was cured and purged of evil humors,
　　　she was adopted by the doctor who had cured her.
　　　They had not taken any of the money from her coffin
　　　and had saved it all for her, had not spent a single coin.

324　In order to help her best protect her chastity,
　　　they built her a convent, where she could live as a nun;
　　　until God saw fit to bring her husband back to her,
　　　she served the Creator with other women.

325　Let us now leave the lady to remain in her convent,
　　　serve in her church, and sing her psalter,
　　　as we return our attention to King Apollonius,
　　　who suffered so many great trials at the hands of
　　　　Fortune.

326　Ever since his wife was thrown upon the waves,
　　　Apollonius was saddened and troubled in his life,

siempre trayó de lágrimas   la cara remojada,
non amanecié día   que non fuese llorada.

327 La companya rascada   e el rey descasado,
toieron su carrera,   maldiziendo su fado;
guiyolos Santi Spíritus,   fueles el mar pagado,
arribó en Tarso,   en su logar amado.

328 Tanto era Apolonio   del duelo esmarrido,
non quiso escobrirse   por seyer conocido;
fue para la posada   de su huéspet querido,
Estrángilo, con que ovo   la otra vez manido.

329 Fue cierto a la casa,   ca antes la sabía,
non entró tan alegre   como entrar solía:
salvó duenyas de casa,   mas non se les reyé,
¡espantáronse todos   porque tan triste venié!

330 De los ombres que ovo,   cuando dende fue, levados,
non pareció ninguno,   nin de los sus privados.
Los sus dichos corteses   avíyalos ya olvidados,
¡fazíanse d'esta cosa   mucho maravillados!

331 Trayén la criatura,   ninya rezién nada,
embuelta en sus panyos,   en ropa orfresada;
con ella Licórides,   que era su ama,
la que fue por nodriça   a Luciana dada.

332 Díxole la huéspeda,   que avía gran pesar:
"Apolonio de Tiro,   quiérote preguntar:

his face was incessantly drenched with tears,
not a day dawned without him weeping for his lost
    wife.

327   His company in mourning and the king a widowed
        man,
        they set off on their journey, cursing their fate;
        yet, guided by the Holy Spirit, the sea favored them,
        and Apollonius landed in Tarsus, his beloved land.

328   King Apollonius was so overcome with grief
        that he did not want to make his arrival known,
        so he went straight to the house of his esteemed host,
        Stranguillio, the man with whom he had stayed before.

329   He went directly to the house, for he knew the way,
        but entered less happily than he used to do:
        he greeted the ladies of the house, but without a smile;
        everyone there was taken aback by his great sadness!

330   Of all the men who had left Tarsus in his company,
        not a single one of those friends was seen with him
            now.
        Apollonius had forgotten all of his courtly manners.
        Everyone was quite astounded by the change in him!

331   Then they brought in the newborn baby girl,
        wrapped in swaddling clothes stitched with gold;
        Licorides was with her, her nursemaid,
        who had been Luciana's wet nurse as well.

332   Stranguillio's wife said with great sadness,
        "Apollonius of Tyre, a question I must ask you,

¿qué fue de tus companyas,   mesnadas de prestar?
¡De tantas que leveste   non veyemos uno tornar!

333 De toda tu fazienda   te veyemos camiado,
¡abés te conyocemos,   tanto eres demudado!
Alegrarte non puedes,   andas triste e pesado,
¡por Dios, de tu fazienda   que sepamos mandado!"

334 Recudió·l Apolonio,   entró en la razón,
lorando de los ojos   a una gran mesión;
díxole la estoria   e la tribulación,
cómo perdió en la mar   toda su criazón.

335 Díxoles de cuál guisa   estorció tan lazdrado,
cómo entró en Pentápolin,   cómo fue combidado,
cómo cantó ant'el rey   e cómo fue casado,
cómo salliera dende   tan bien acompanyado.

336 Díxoles de la duenya,   cómo l'avié perdida,
cómo murió de parto   la su muger querida,
cómo fizieron d'ella   depués que fue transida,
cómo esta ninyuela   avié romanecida.

337 Los huéspedes del rey,   cuando esto oyeron,
por poco que con duelo   de seso non sallieron,
fizieron muy gran duelo,   cuanto mayor pudieron,
¡cuando la tenién muerta   mayor non lo fizieron!

what has become of your company, all your worthy
    men?
Of all those you took with you, not a single one has
    returned!

333 It seems that your entire fortune has changed,
we can hardly recognize you as the man we knew
    before!
You are incapable of cheer, filled with sadness and
    sorrow,
for God's sake, tell us what has happened to you!"

334 Apollonius answered them, he began to speak,
weeping continuously and making a great effort;
he told the story of all his tribulations,
how he lost all his men and household in the sea.

335 He told them of how he had escaped in such misery,
had come to Pentapolis and been welcomed to dine
    there,
how he sang before the king and how he had been
    married,
and how he then departed, so well accompanied.

336 He told them of his lady and how he had lost her,
how his beloved wife had died in childbirth,
what they had done with her body after her death,
and how he had been left with this little baby girl.

337 When Apollonius's hosts had heard the story,
they felt they might lose their minds with grief
and wept in mourning, showing the utmost sorrow;
they could not have grieved more for the dead queen!

338 Desque ovieron fecho   su duelo aguisado
     tornó en Apolonio   el huéspet honrado:
     "Rey" dize, "yo te ruego   e pídotelo en donado,
     lo que dezir te quiero   que seya escuchado.

339 El curso d'este mundo   en ti lo as provado,
     non sabe luengamientre   estar en un estado;
     en dar e en toller   es todo su vezado,
     ¡quienquier llore o riya,   él non á ningún cuidado!

340 En ti mismo lo puedes   esto bien entender,
     si corazón ovieses,   devieslo conyocer:
     nunca más sopo ombre   de ganar e perder,
     ¡deviete a la cuita   esto gran pro tener!

341 Non puede a null ombre   la cosa más durar
     si non cuanto el fado   le quiso otorgar;
     non se devié el ombre   por pérdida quexar,
     ca nunca por su quexa   lo puede recobrar.

342 Somos de tu pérdida   nós todos perdidosos,
     todos con tal reína   seriemos muy gozosos.
     Desque seyer non puede,   nin somos venturosos,
     en perdernos por ella   seríamos muy astrosos.

343 Si comprar la pudiésemos   por lanto o por duelo,
     agora finchiriemos   de lágrimas el suelo;
     mas, desque la á presa   la muerte en el lençuelo,
     fagamos nós por ella   lo que fizo ella por su avuelo.

344 Si buena fue la madre,   buena fija avemos;
     en logar de la madre   la fija nós guardemos.

338 After all mourned and paid their due respects,
the honorable host turned to Apollonius and said,
"King, I beg you and ask you as a favor to me,
that what I wish to say to you will be heard.

339 The way of this world, as your life proves,
never runs smoothly for long, is never steady.
This world gives and takes, that is its only constancy;
whoever may cry or laugh, the world does not care!

340 You have seen this in your own experiences.
Examine your conscience and you will see it is true:
no man knows success and loss better that you do;
realizing this should console you in your troubles!

341 No man must endure any misfortune
any longer than fate has decreed for him,
and a m`an should never lament his losses,
for lamenting can never return what is lost.

342 The loss you have suffered is a loss to us all,
and we would all have rejoiced with such a queen.
But since it cannot be, and we are not so fortunate,
we would be wrongheaded if we died in grief for her.

343 If only our weeping and sorrow could bring her back,
then we would flood the ground with our tears;
yet, since death has wrapped her up in its shroud,
we will honor her with our dead and go on.

344 Just as the mother was worthy, so is the daughter;
we will care for the daughter in her mother's place.

¡Aun cuando de todo   algo nós tenemos,
bien podemos contar   que nada non perdemos!"

345 Recudió·l Apolonio   lo que podrié estar:
"Huéspet, desque a Dios   non podemos reptar,
lo que él á puesto   todo deve pasar,
lo que él dar quisiere   todo es de durar.

346 Acomiéndote la fija   e dótela a criar,
con su ama Licórides,   que la sabrá guardar.
¡Non quiero los cabellos   ni las unyas tajar
fasta que casamiento   bueno le pueda dar!

347 Fasta que esto pueda   complir e aguisar,
al reino de Antioco   quiérole dar vagar,
nin quiero en Pentápolin   ni en Tiro entrar;
quiero en Egipto   en tan amientre estar."

348 Dexole la ninyuela,   una cosa querida,
dexole grandes averes,   de ropa grant partida.
Metiose en las naves,   fizo luego la movida,
fasta los XIII anyos   allá tovo su vida.

349 Estrángilo de Tarso,   su muger Dionisa,
criaron esta ninya   de muy alta guisa:
diéronle muchos mantos,   mucha penya vera e grisa,
mucha buena garnacha,   mucha buena camisa.

350 Criaron a gran vicio   los amos la moçuela.
Cuando fue de siete anyos   diéronla al escuela:

What is more, when we have a part of the whole,
we may consider ourselves lucky, as if we had lost
    nothing!"

345 Apollonius answered him, in the only way he could,
"Host, since we cannot possibly challenge God,
everything he decrees must come to pass,
everything he metes out to us must be endured.

346 I am leaving my daughter in your care and keeping,
along with her nursemaid, Licorides, who will care for
    her.
I swear, I will not cut my hair nor will I trim my nails,
until I have arranged a good marriage for her!

347 Until I have arranged and provided this for her,
I will leave my business in Antioch aside,
and I will not go to Pentapolis, nor will I enter Tyre;
in the meantime, I wish to go to Egypt instead."

348 Apollonius left his beloved little baby girl there,
leaving her great riches and much clothing as well.
Then he boarded his ships and set sail immediately,
and he was not to return until thirteen years had
    passed.

349 Stranguillio of Tarsus and his wife, Dionisa,
reared this child in the most noble fashion:
they gave her many mantles of ermine and gris,
many fine fur tunics and many fine shirts.

350 The foster parents spared no expense in her
    upbringing.
When she turned seven, they began her schooling:

apriso bien gramátiga   e bien tocar viuela,
aguzó bien, como fierro   que aguzan a la muela.

351 Amávala el pueblo   de Tarso la cibdat,
ca fizo contra ellos   el padre gran bondat.
Si del nombre queredes   saber certenidat,
dizienle Tarsiana,   esta era verdat.

352 Cuando a XII anyos   fue la duenya venida,
sabía todas las artes,   era maestra complida,
de beltad companyera   non avié conocida,
avié de buenas manyas   toda Tarso vencida.

353 No querié nengún día   su estudio perder,
ca avié voluntat   de algo aprender.
Maguer mucho lazdrava,   cayole en placer,
ca preciávase mucho   e querié algo valer.

354 Cerca podié de tercia   a lo menos estar,
cuando los escolanos   vinién a almorzar,
non quiso Tarsiana   la costumbre pasar:
su lición acordada,   vinié a almorzar.

355 A su ama Licórides,   que la avié criada,
trobola mal enferma,   fuertemiente cuitada;
maguer que era ayuna,   que non era yantada,
en el cabo del lecho   pososse la criada.

356 "Fija," dixo Licórides,   "yo me quiero pasar,
pero ante que me passe   quiérote demandar
cuál tienes por tu tierra   segunt el tu cuidar,
o por padre o por madre   cuáles deves catar."

she learned grammar well and how to play the vielle
    well too;
her wits were well sharpened, just as a file sharpens the
    teeth.

351   The people of the city of Tarsus loved the girl,
for her father had done them a great kindness.
If you would like to know what her name was,
she was called Tarsiana, and that is the truth.

352   By the time the lady had reached the age of twelve,
she knew all the arts and was an accomplished scholar,
she had no rivals where beauty was concerned,
and had conquered all Tarsus with her winning ways.

353   Tarsiana never wanted to miss a day of her studies,
she was so eager to learn as much as she could.
However much she labored, she took pleasure in it,
for she knew her own merit and wanted to be worthy.

354   It was about nine o'clock one morning,
the hour when the students took their breakfast,
and Tarsiana was not one to be left out:
her lesson memorized, she too went to eat.

355   Licorides the nursemaid, who had raised her,
was in bed, struck down with a mortal sickness,
and even though she had yet to break her fast,
the girl sat down beside her on the bed.

356   "My child," said Licorides, "my time has come,
but before I pass away, I want to ask you:
In your mind, where do you think you come from,
whom do you consider your father and mother?"

357 "Ama," dixo la duenya,   "segunt mi conocencia
Tarso es la mi tierra   —yo otra non sabría—
Estrángilo es mi padre,   su muger madre mía.
¡Siempre así lo tove   e terné oy en día!"

358 "Oídme," dize Licórides,   "senyora e criada:
si en eso toviéredes   seredes enganyada,
ca la vuestra fazienda   mucho es más granada,
¡yo vos faré certera   si fuere escuchada!

359 De Pentápolin fuestes   de raíz e de suelo,
al rey Architrastres   oviestes por avuelo,
su fija Luciana,   ementar vos la suelo,
esa fue vuestra madre,   que delexó gran duelo.

360 El rey Apolonio,   un noble cavallero,
senyor era de Tiro,   un recio cabdalero,
ese fue vuestro padre,   agora es palmero,
por tierras de Egipto   anda como romero."

361 Contole la estoria   toda de fundamenta,
en mar cómo entró   en hora carbonenta,
cómo casó con ella   a muy gran sobrevienta,
cómo murió de parto   una cara juventa.

362 Dixo·l cómo su padre   fizo tal sagramento:
fasta qu'éll a la fija   diese buen casamiento—
que todo su linage   oviese pagamiento—
que non se cercenase   por null falagamiento.

363 Cuando esto le ovo   dicho e ensenyado
e lo ovo la ninya   todo bien recordado,

357 "Nurse," said the lady, "as far as I know
Tarsus is my land—I have known no other—
Stranguillio is my father, and his wife is my mother.
That is what I have always believed and what I think
    today!"

358 "Listen," said Licorides, "my lady and my child,
if that is what you think, you are mistaken,
because your true history is much more illustrious
and I will tell you the truth, if you will hear me out!

359 Your roots and land are both in Pentapolis,
your grandfather was King Archistrates,
and his daughter, Luciana, whom I mention often,
she was your mother, and she is much mourned.

360 King Apollonius, a noble knight,
lord of Tyre and a valiant man of honor,
he was your father; now he is a palmer
in the lands of Egypt, where he wanders like a pilgrim."

361 Licorides told the story from its very beginning,
of how Apollonius went to sea at a dark hour,
how his marriage took place, surprising everyone,
and of how Luciana died in childbirth, all too young.

362 She told Tarsiana about how her father had vowed
that until he had arranged a good marriage for his
    child—
one that would please their whole family line—
nothing in the world could induce him to cut his beard.

363 When all this had been told and taught,
and the girl had committed it all to her memory,

fue perdiendo la lengua   e el ora llegando,
despidiose del mundo   e de su gasanyado.

364 Luego que fue Licórides   d'este mundo pasada,
aguisó bien el cuerpo   la su buena criada,
mortajola muy bien,   dio·l sepultura honrada,
mantenié·l cutiano   candela e oblada.

365 La infante Tarsiana,   d'Estrángilo nodrida,
fue salliendo tan buena,   de manyas tan complida,
que del pueblo de Tarso   era tan querida
como serié de su madre   que la ovo parida.

366 Un día de fiesta,   entrante la semana,
pasava Dionisa   por la rúa manyana,
vinié a su costado   la infante Tarsiana,
otra ninya con ella   que era su ermana.

367 Por ó quier que pasavan,   por rúa o por calleja,
de donya Tarsiana   fazían todos conseja:
dizían que Dionisa   nin su companyera
non valién contra ella   una mala erveja.

368 Esta boz Dionisa   óvola a saber,
¡por poco que de embidia   non se querié perder!
Consejo del diablo   óvolo a prender,
todo en cabo ovo   en ella a cayer.

369 Asmava que la fiziese   a escuso matar,
ca nunca la vernié   el padre a buscar;

Licorides's voice became faint, for her hour was
    coming,
and she bid farewell to the world and all its pleasures.

364 When Licorides had passed from this world,
the good child she had nursed prepared her body,
she wound it well in a shroud and gave her an
    honorable burial,
and she made daily offerings of candles and bread.

365 Princess Tarsiana, raised by Stranguillio,
was growing up to be a very accomplished young lady;
she was just as beloved by the people of Tarsus
as she would have been by her own mother.

366 One feast day, early in the week,
Dionisa was out walking in the morning,
and Princess Tarsiana walked by her side,
as did another girl, who was Dionisa's daughter.

367 Wherever they went, through street or alley,
Tarsiana's name was on everyone's lips:
they said that neither Dionisa nor her daughter
could hope to hold a candle to the princess.

368 Dionisa heard the people talking about Tarsiana
and was driven to the verge of madness by envy!
She felt compelled to take the devil's counsel,
though, in the end, she would come to regret it.

369 She planned to have Tarsiana murdered in secret,
because Apollonius was never going to come back for
    her;

el aver que le diera,   poder se lo ié lograr,
non podrié en otra guisa   de la llaga sanar.

370 Dizié entre su cuer   la mala omicida:
"Si esta moça fuese   de carrera tollida,
con estos sus adobos   que la fazen vellida
casaría mi fija,   la que ove parida."

371 Comidiendo la falsa   en esta traición,
entró un ávol ombre   de los de criazón,
ombre de raíz mala,   que yazía en presión,
que faría grant nemiga   por poca de mesión.

372 Su nombre fue Teófilo,   si lo saber queredes,
catatlo en la estoria   si a mí non creyedes.
Asmó la mala fembra   lo que bien entendredes:
que este era ducho   de texer tales redes.

373 Llamolo luego ella   en muy gran poridat,
fízole entender   toda su voluntat;
si gelo acabasse,   prometió·l su verdat,
que le daría gran precio   e toda enguedat.

374 Preguntó·l el mancebo,   todavía dubdando,
cómo podrié seyer   e en cuál lugar o cuándo.
Díxole que manyana   soviese assechando,
cuando sobre Licórides   soviese orando.

375 Por amor, el astroso,   de sallir de lacerio,
madurgó de manyana   e fue para'l ciminterio.

Dionisa would take all the money he had left for
    herself,
she could not think of any other way to salve her
    wounds.

370 The evil murderess then said to herself,
    "If only this young girl were out of my way,
    I could use the ornaments that make her so pretty
    to get my daughter, the one I carried in my womb,
        wed."

371 As the false woman was plotting her betrayal,
    a very base man from her household came in,
    a man born from a bad seed, who was enslaved,
    who would commit great crimes for little recompense.

372 His name was Theophilus, if you want to know—
    look it up in the book, if you do not believe me.
    The evil woman thought, as you will now hear,
    that Theophilus was the right man to set such a trap.

373 She called him right away to meet her in secret
    and told him about all she desired;
    if he would do it, she gave him her word,
    she would reward him well and give him his freedom.

374 The young man asked her, filled with hesitation,
    how he could commit the crime, where and when.
    She told him to lie in wait for Tarsiana in the morning,
    when she would be praying over Licorides's grave.

375 Hoping to escape his misery, the ill-fated brute
    rose with the dawn and went to the cemetery.

Aguzó su cuchiello   por fer mal ministerio,
por matarla rezando   los salmos del salterio.

376 La duenya, gran manyana,   como era su costumbre,
fue para'l ciminterio   con su pan e con su lumbre;
aguisó su incienso   e encendió su lumbre,
començó de rezar   con toda mansedumbre.

377 Mientre la buena duenya   leyé su matinada,
sallió el traidor falso   luego de la celada,
prísola por los cabellos   e sacó su espada;
¡por poco le oviera   la cabeça cortada!

378 "Amigo," dixo ella,   "nunca te fiz pesar,
non te merecí cosa   por que me deves matar,
¡otro precio non puedes   en la mi muerte ganar
fueras atanto que puedes   mortalmientre pecar!

379 Pero si de tu mano   non puedo escapar,
déxame un poquiello   al Criador rogar;
asaz puedes aver   hora e vagar,
non é, por mis pecados,   quién me venga uviar."

380 Fue, maguera, con el ruego   un poco embargado;
dixo: "¡Sí Dios me vala,   que lo faré de grado!"
Pero que aguisasse   cómo livrase privado,
ca non le podría dar   espacio perlongado.

381 Enclinose la duenya,   començó de llorar.
"Senyor," dixo, "que tienes   el sol a tu mandar

There, he readied his knife to carry out the foul deed
and kill Tarsiana as she prayed the psalms of the
  psalter.

376 The lady, as was her custom, early in the morning
came to the cemetery, with her bread and her votives;
she prepared her incense and lit her light
and began to pray with sincere sweetness.

377 As the good lady was chanting her matins,
the false traitor leaped from his hiding place,
grabbed her by the hair, and took out his sword.
He just about cut off her head!

378 "Friend," she said, "I have never harmed you,
nor done anything that gives you the right to kill me,
and you have nothing to gain by my death
other than possibly committing a mortal sin!

379 Yet, if I have no escape from your hand,
let me pray to the Creator for just a little while;
you are in no hurry and have more than enough time,
while I have no one, alas, to come to my rescue."

380 It so happened that Tarsiana's plea stayed the man's
  hand;
he said, "By God, I will do so with pleasure!"
But he told her to not to take too much time,
because he did not have time to waste.

381 The lady knelt down and began to cry.
"Lord," she said, "you who have the sun under your
  power

e fazes a la luna   crecer e empocar,
Senyor, ¡tú me acorre   por tierra o por mar!

382   Só en tierras agenas,   sin parientes criada,
la madre perdida,   del padre non sé nada;
yo, mal non mereciendo,   é a ser martiriada.
Senyor, ¡cuando lo tú sufres   só por ello pagada!

383   Senyor, si la justicia   quisieres bien tener,
si yo non lo merezco   por ell mio merecer,
algún consejo tienes   para a mí acorrer,
¡que aqueste traidor   non me pueda vencer!"

384   Seyendo Tarsiana   en esta oración,
rencurando su cuita   e su tribulación,
ovo Dios de la huérfana   duelo e compasión,
envió·l su acorro   e oyó su petición.

385   Ya pensava Teófilo   del gladio aguisar,
asomaron ladrones   que andavan por la mar;
vieron que el malo   enemiga quería far,
diéronle todos bozes,   fiziéronle dubdar.

386   Coitaron la galea   por amor de uviar,
en aquell traidor falso   mano querién echar;
ovo pavor Teófilo,   non quiso esperar,
fuxo para la villa   cuanto lo pudo far.

387   Fue para Dionisa   todo descolorado,
ca oviera gran miedo,   vinié todo demudado.
"Senyora," dixo luego,   "complí el tu mandado.
¡Piensa cómo me quites   e me fagas pagado!"

and make the moon wax and wane,
Lord, come to my rescue by land or by sea!

382 I am in a strange land, raised without my family,
my mother is dead, I know nothing of my father;
I, having done nothing, am to be martyred.
Lord, if this is your will, I am content!

383 Lord, if you want justice truly served,
and if I have done something to deserve this death,
I know you have some way of coming to my aid
and to prevent this traitor from killing me!"

384 While Tarsiana was saying this prayer,
lamenting her trouble and her tribulation,
God felt pain and compassion for the orphan
and sent her his aid and heard her plea.

385 Just as Theophilus was about to unsheathe his blade,
pirates appeared, who had come by sea;
they saw what the evildoer was about to do,
and they all called out, making him hesitate in fear.

386 The pirates hurried their rowers, rushing to the rescue
and to get their hands on that false traitor;
Theophilus was frightened; he had no wish to stay,
and ran away to the town, as fast as he could go.

387 He went to Dionisa, all pale and wan,
he was frightened beyond all recognition.
"My lady," he said then, "I have carried out your orders.
Consider how you will now free me and satisfy me!"

388 Recudió la duenya,   mas no a su sabor:
"¡Vía," dixo, "d'aquende,   falso e traidor!
¡As fecho omecidio   e muy gran traición,
non te prendré por ello   vergüença nin pavor!

389 Tórnate all aldeya   e piensa de tu lavor;
¡si no, averás luego   la maldición del Criador!
Si más ante mí vienes,   ¡recibrás tal amor
cual tú feziste a Tarsiana   e non otro mejor!"

390 Tóvose el villano   por muy mal enganyado,
querría que no fuese   en el pleito entrado.
Murió en servidumbre,   nunca ende fue quitado.
¡Qui en tal se metiere   non prendrá mejor grado!

391 Corrieron los ladrones   a todo su poder,
cuidaron a Teófilo   alcançar o prender,
mas, cuando a esso non   pudieron acaecer,
ovieron en la duenya   la sanya a verter.

392 Vieron la ninya   de muy gran parecer,
asmaron de levarla   e sacarla a vender;
podrién ganar por ella   mucho de buen aver,
que nunca más pudiesen   en pobreza cayer.

393 Fue la mesquiniella,   en fuerte punto nada,
puesta en la galea   de rimos bien poblada;
rimaron apriesa,   ca se temién de celada,
arribó en Mitalena   la cativa lazdrada.

394 Fue presa la cativa,   al mercado sacada,
el vendedor con ella,   su bolsa aparejada.

388 The lady answered him, but not to his liking:
     "Get out of here," she said, "you false traitor!
     You have committed murder and a great betrayal,
     but I will not be ashamed or frightened because of you!

389 Go back to the village and mind your labors;
     otherwise, the Creator will surely curse you!
     If I ever set eyes on you again, you will get
     just what you gave Tarsiana and nothing better!"

390 The poor wretch felt he had been sorely tricked,
     he wished he had never agreed to the plan.
     He died a slave; in the end, he was never a free man.
     No better thanks are in store if you get involved in
          such deeds!

391 The pirates ran as fast as they could,
     hoping to catch up to and capture Theophilus,
     but, finding they were unable to get him,
     they unleashed their anger on the lady.

392 They saw that the girl was very beautiful
     and decided to take her to the market to sell;
     they thought they could get such a good price for her
     and would never again fall into poverty in all their lives.

393 The poor little girl, born in an evil hour,
     was thrown in the galley ship with its many rowers,
     who rowed quickly, fearing an attack,
     and brought their suffering captive to Mytilene.

394 The captive girl was bound, taken to the market;
     the seller was with her, his purse was ready.

Vinieron compradores   sobre cosa tachada,
que comprar la querién   e por cuánto serié dada.

395   El senyor Antinágora,   que la villa tenié en poder,
vio esta cativa   de muy gran parecer,
ovo tal amor d'ella   que s'en querié perder:
prometioles por ella   diez pesas d'aver.

396   Un hombre malo,   senyor de soldaderas,
asmó ganar con esta   ganancias tan pleneras,
prometió por ella luego   dos tanto de las primeras
por meterla a cambio luego   con las otras coseras.

397   Prometió Antinágora   que·l daría las treinta,
dixo el garçón malo   que·l daría las cuarenta;
luego Antinágora   puyó a las cincuanta,
el malo fidiondo   subió a las sexanta.

398   Dixo mayor paraula   el malo aventurado:
que, de cuanto ninguno   diese por ell mercado,
él enyadrié veyente pesos   de buen oro colado
o, si más lo quisiese,   de aver monedado.

399   Non quiso Antinágora   en esto porfiar;
asmó que la dexase   al traidor comprar,
cuando la oviesse comprada,   que gela irié logar,
podrié por menos precio   su cosa recabdar.

400 Pagógela el malo,   óvola de prender,
¡el que no devié   una muger valer!
Aguisose la ciella   para'l mal menester,
escrivió en la puerta   el precio del aver.

Buyers who deal in such wicked things came,
they wanted to purchase her and to know her price.

395 Lord Athenagoras, who ruled over the city,
saw the beautiful captive girl in the market
and was struck with desire, completely lost his head:
he promised to pay ten weights of gold for her.

396 An evil man, a whoremonger by trade,
thought that he could make a lot of money off the girl,
and he offered to double Athenagoras's price
so he could sell Tarsiana with his other prostitutes.

397 Athenagoras promised more and bid thirty,
and the dissolute man said he would give forty;
then Athenagoras upped his offer to fifty,
and the stinking evildoer raised his bid to sixty.

398 The accursed man made an even better offer:
however much anyone bid for the merchandise,
he would add twenty weights of pure gold,
or, if they would prefer, the same amount in minted
    coins.

399 Athenagoras had no wish to go on with the bidding;
he thought he would let the pimp buy the girl,
and once bought, then he could go and rent her,
and pay much less to get what he wanted all along.

400 The evil pimp paid for her and took her off;
he was a man who could not be trusted with any
    woman!
He prepared a room for his foul business
and wrote the price of his goods on the door.

401 Esto dize el título,   qui lo quiere saber:
"Qui quisiere a Tarsiana   primero conyocer
una livra de oro   avrá ý a poner,
los otros sendas onzas   avrán a ofrecer."

402 Mientre esta cosa   andava rebolviendo,
fue la barata mala   la duenya entendiendo.
Rogó al Criador,   de los ojos vertiendo:
"Senyor," diz, "¡tú me val,   que yo a ti me acomiendo!

403 Senyor, que de Teófilo   me quesiste guardar,
que me quiso el cuerpo   a traición matar,
Senyor, la tu vertud   me deve amparar,
¡que non me puedan el alma   garçones enconar!"

404 En esto, Antinágora,   príncep de la cibdat,
rogó al traidor   de firme voluntat
que le diese el precio   de la virginidat,
que gelo otorgase,   por Dios, en caridat.

405 Ovo esta primicia   el príncep otorgada,
la huérfana mesquina,   sobre gente adobada,
fue con gran procesión   al ostal enviada.
¡Veyer gelo ié quienquiere   qu'ella iva forçada!

406 Salliéronse los otros,   fincó Tarsiana senyera,
romaneció el lobo   solo con la cordera.
Mas, como Dios lo quiso,   ella fue bien artera,
con sus palabras planas   metiolo en la carrera.

407 Cayole a los pies,   començó a dezir:
"¡Senyor, mercet te pido   que me quieras oír,

401 This is what the sign said, for those who wish to know:
"Whoever wants to be the first to know Tarsiana,
a pound of gold is the price he must pay,
and after that, one ounce of gold per man."

402 While the pimp was weaving his evil plot,
the lady realized she was to be damnably trafficked.
She prayed to the Creator, tears streaming from her
      eyes:
"Lord, protect me, I am putting myself in your hands!

403 Lord, you who saved me from Theophilus,
the traitor who wanted to slay my body,
Lord, use your power to defend me now;
do not let my soul be sullied by these ruffians!"

404 Meanwhile, Athenagoras, prince of the city,
had insistently begged the pimp
to take the price of Tarsiana's virginity from him
and to let him be the first, for the love of God.

405 The deflowering was granted to the prince,
so the poor orphaned girl was all dressed up in finery
and brought to the brothel in a grand procession.
It was easy to see that she was forced against her will!

406 The crowd dispersed, leaving Tarsiana all alone,
but the wolf remained with the unprotected lamb.
Yet, because God willed it, Tarsiana was quite clever,
and she set him straight with her plain speaking.

407 She threw herself at his feet and began to say,
"Lord, I beg your mercy, please listen to me,

que me quieras un poco   esperar e sofrir!
¡Aver t'á Dios del cielo   por ello qué gradir!

408 Que tú quieras agora   mis carnes quebrantar,
podemos aquí amos   mortalmientre pecar.
Yo puedo perder mucho,   tú non puedes ganar,
tú puedes en tu nobleça   mucho menoscabar.

409 Yo puedo, por tu fecho,   perder ventura e fado,
cayerás por mal cuerpo   tú en mortal pecado.
Ombre eres de precio,   ¡sí te veyas logrado!
¡Sobre huérfana pobre   non fagas desaguisado!"

410 Contole sus periglos   cuantos avié sofridos:
cómo ovo de chiquiella   sus parientes perdidos;
aviendo de su padre   muchos bienes recebidos,
cómo oviera amos   falsos e descreídos.

411 El príncep Antinágora,   que vinié denodado,
fue con estas paraulas   fieramient amansado.
Tornó contra la duenya,   el coraçón camiado,
recudiole al ruego   e fue bien acordado:

412 "Duenya, bien entiendo   esto que me dezides,
que de linatge sodes,   de buena parte venides.
Esta petición   que vos a mí pedides
véyolo por derecho,   ca bien lo concluídes.

413 Todos somos carnales   e avemos a morir,
todos esta ventura   avemos a seguir.

please be a little patient with me and wait!
You will please God in heaven if you do!

408 Your desire to violate my body now
may cause us both to commit a mortal sin.
I could lose so much, and you have nothing to gain;
you run the risk of besmirching your noble honor.

409 While I, by your deed, will lose my fortune and
happiness,
you will fall for the sake of poor flesh into mortal sin.
You are a man of high esteem, and I wish you only the
best!
Do not do such harm to a poor, orphaned girl!"

410 Then she told him all of the dangers she had survived:
how as a little baby she had lost her parents,
and, having inherited wealth from her father,
how she had been fostered by false and deceitful
people.

411 Prince Athenagoras, who had come in lustful,
found that her words calmed all his desire.
He turned to the lady with a change of heart
and responded to her plea, speaking prudently:

412 "My lady, I understand well all that you have told me:
you are from a noble line, you come from good stock.
This entreaty that you are asking of me,
I see it is right, for you have argued your case well.

413 We are all flesh, and we are all mortal beings;
we all must share this same destiny.

Demás, ell ombre deve comedir
que cual aquí fiziere, tal avrá de padir.

414 Diome Dios una fija, téngola por casar,
a todo mio poder querríala guardar;
porque no la querría veyer en tal logar,
por tal entención vos quiero perdonar.

415 Demás, por ell buen padre de que vós me ementastes
e por la razón buena que tan bien enformastes,
quiérovos dar agora más que vós non demandastes,
que vos venga emiente en cuál logar me viestes.

416 El precio que daría para con vós pecar
quiérovoslo en donado ofrecer e donar,
que, si vós non pudierdes por ruego escapar,
al que a vós entrare datlo para vos quitar.

417 Si vós d'aquesta manya pudierdes estorcer,
mientre lo mío durare, non vos faldrá aver.
¡El Criador vos quiera ayudar e valer,
que vós vuestra fazienda podades bien poner!"

418 Con esto, Antinágora fuesse para su posada,
presto sovo otro para entrar su vegada,
mas tanto fue la duenya savia e adonada
que ganó los dineros e non fue violada.

419 Cuantos ahí vinieron e a ella entraron
todos se convertieron, todos por tal pasaron:

Moreover, every person must consider
that as one does in this life, so will one suffer in the
next.

414 God gave me a daughter who is now of marrying age,
and there is nothing I would not do to keep her safe.
I would never wish to see her in your position,
and that is why I want to grant your petition.

415 Moreover, for the sake of your good father, whom you
mentioned,
and on the strength of the arguments you made so
well,
now I will give you even more than you requested,
so that you will remember where and how we met.

416 The price I was ready to pay to sin with you
I will give to you freely as a gift,
so, if you are not able to escape by pleading your case,
you can pay off the men who come to you.

417 If you can save yourself using this trick,
as long as I have money, you will not lack funds.
May the Creator aid and protect you,
and may you return to your proper place!"

418 This said, Athenagoras left for his home,
and right away another man was at the door for his
turn,
but the lady was so wise and had such a way with words
that she earned her money and was never violated.

419 No matter how many men went in to see Tarsiana,
all were persuaded, all went through the same thing:

nengún danyo no·l fizieron,   los averes lexaron,
¡de cuanto que aduxieron   con nada non tornaron!

420 Cuando vino a la tarde,   el mediodía pasado,
avié la buena duenya   tan gran aver ganado
que serié con lo medio   el traidor pagado.
¡Reyésele el ojo   al malaventurado!

421 Vio a ella alegre,   e fue en ello artera:
cuando él tal la vido,   plogo·l de gran manera,
dixo: "¡Agora tienes,   fija, buena carrera,
cuando alegre vienes   e muestras cara soltera!"

422 Dixo la buena duenya   un sermón tan temprado:
"Senyor, si lo oviesse   de ti condonado,
otro mester sabía   que es más sin pecado,
que es más ganancioso   e es más ondrado.

423 Si tú me lo condonas,   por la tu cortesía,
que meta yo estudio   en essa maestría,
cuanto tú demandases,   yo tanto te daría.
¡Tú avriés gran ganancia   e yo non pecaría!

424 De cual guisa se quiere   que pudiesse seyer
que mayor ganancia   tú pudieses aver,

not a single one did her harm, and each left her his
    money.
No matter how much they brought, they went home
    with nothing!

420 By the later hours of the day, after noon had passed,
the lady had earned quite a large sum,
more than enough to pay off the pimp twice over.
He was overjoyed at the sight of so much money!

421 The pimp saw she looked happy, but Tarsiana was
    crafty:
when he saw her looking so well, he was quite pleased,
and said, "Now, daughter, you know you are on the
    right path
when you come back happy and with a cheerful face!"

422 The good lady replied with a well-thought-out speech:
"Sir, if only you would give me your permission,
I know a different art, one that is without sin,
one that earns more and is also more honorable.

423 If you would allow me, out of your courteousness,
to dedicate myself to the study of this other art,
however much you might ask, that much I would pay
    you.
You will earn a great deal of money and I will not sin!

424 By whatever means there could possibly be
to earn the most money that you could get,

por esso me compreste   e esso deves facer.
¡A tu provecho fablo,   dévesmelo creyer!"

425 El sermón de la duenya   fue tan bien adonado
que fue el coraçón   del garçón amansado.
Diole plaço poco   a día senyalado,
mas que ella catase   qué avié demandado.

426 Luego el otro día,   de buena madurgada,
levantose la duenya,   ricamiente adobada,
priso una viola   buena e bien temprada
e sallió al mercado   violar por soldada.

427 Començó unos viesos   e unos sones tales
que trayén gran dulçor   e eran naturales.
Finchiense de ombres   apriesa los portales,
non les cabién las plaças,   subiense a los poyales.

428 Cuando con su viola   ovo bien solazado,
a sabor de los pueblos   ovo asaz cantado,
tornoles a rezar   un romance bien rimado
de la su razón misma,   por ó avía pasado.

429 Fizo bien a los pueblos   su razón entender,
¡más valié de cient marcos   ese día el loguer!

that is why you bought me, and that is what you should
do.
I am thinking about your interest, you should believe
me!"

425 The lady's speech was so convincing
that the ruffian's heart began to soften.
He gave her a little time, named his date,
and told her not to forget what they had agreed.

426 The very next day, early in the morning,
the lady rose and dressed herself up in fine clothes,
and, carrying a fine and well-tempered vielle,
she went out into the marketplace to fiddle for money.

427 The verses and notes that she began to play
struck up a tune of great sweetness, on the natural
scale.
The market's arcades quickly filled up with listeners;
with no room in the square, people climbed up on the
benches.

428 Once Tarsiana had entertained them well with her
vielle
and had sung many songs for the pleasure of the crowd,
she began to recite a well-rhymed romance:
it was her own story, the tale of all that had befallen
her.

429 She made the people listen attentively to her story.
Her earnings were more than one hundred marks on
that day!

Fuesse el traidor   pagando del menester,
¡ganava por ello   sobejano grant aver!

430 Cogieron con la duenya   todos muy grant amor,
todos de su fazienda   avían grant sabor.
Demás, como sabían   que avía mal senyor,
ayudávanla todos   de voluntat mejor.

431 El príncipe Antinágora   mejor la querié
que si su fija fuese,   más non la amarié;
el día que su boz   o su canto non oyé
conducho que comiese   mala pro le tenié.

432 Tan bien sopo la duenya   su cosa aguisar
que sabía a su amo   la ganancia tornar
reyendo e gabando   con el su buen catar.
¡Sópose, maguer ninya,   de follía quitar!

433 Visco en esta vida   un tiempo porlongado,
fasta que a Dios plogo,   bien quita de pecado.
Mas dexemos a ella   su menester usando,
tornemos en el padre,   que andava lazdrado.

434 A cabo de diez anyos   que la ovo lexada,
recudió Apolonio   con su barba trençada;
cuidó fallar la fija   duenya grant e criada,
mas era la fazienda   otramiente trastornada.

435 Estrángilo, el de Tarso,   cuando lo vio entrar,
perdió toda la sangre   con cuita e con pesar,

The pimp was well pleased with her art,
for he earned a great amount of money from it!

430 Everyone in town grew to love the lady well,
and all took great pleasure in hearing her story.
Moreover, since they knew she had an evil master,
they were all the more willing to help her.

431 Prince Athenagoras loved her most of all,
if she were his daughter, he could not have loved her
    more;
if he went a single day without hearing her voice or her
    song,
any food that passed his lips tasted bitter to him.

432 The lady was so skilled at her business
that she knew to hand over money to her master
while laughing and joking, and putting on a happy face.
Young as she was, she knew how to stay out of trouble!

433 She followed this way of life for quite a long time,
according to God's will and free from sin.
But let us now leave Tarsiana to ply her trade
and return to her father, in his continued suffering.

434 When ten years had passed since he left her,
Apollonius returned, with his long-braided beard;
he thought he would find his daughter grown and well
    brought up,
but the story had taken a very different turn.

435 When Stranguillio of Tarsus saw him arrive,
the blood rushed from his face out of worry and
    shame,

tornó en su encubierta   a la muger a rebtar,
mas cuidávase ella   con mentiras salvar.

436 Salvó el rey sus huéspedes   e fuelos abraçar,
fue d'ellos recebido   como debía estar.
Catava por su fija   que les dio a criar,
non se podié sin ella   reír ni alegrar.

437 "Huéspedes," dixo el rey,   "¿qué puede esto seer?
¡Pésame de mi fija,   que non me viene veyer!
¡Querría d'esta cosa   la verdat entender,
que veyo a vós tristes,   mala color tener!"

438 Recudió·l Dionisia,   dixo·l grant falsedat:
"Rey, de tu fija   esta es la verdat:
al coraçón le priso   mortal enfermedat,
passada es del sieglo,   ¡esta es la verdat!"

439 ¡Por poco Apolonio   qu'el seso non perdió!
Passó bien un gran rato   qu'él non les recudió,
que tan mala colpada   él nunca recibió.
Parosse endurido,   la cabeça primió.

440 Después, bien a la tarde,   recudió el varón.
Demandó a bever   agua, que vino non,
tornó contra la huéspeda   e dixo·l una razón
que devié a la falsa   quebrar el coraçón:

441 "Huéspeda," diz, "querría   más la muerte que la vida,
cuando, por mios pecados,   la fija é perdida.
¡La cuita de la madre   que me era venida,
con esta lo cuidaba   aduzir a medida!

and he took his wife aside to chastise her,
but she thought she could save herself with lies.

436 King Apollonius greeted and embraced his hosts,
and in turn they welcomed him as was fitting.
He looked for the daughter he had left with them to
     raise,
for without her he could neither laugh nor be happy.

437 "Hosts," said the king, "how can this be?
I am sad that my daughter has not come to see me!
I want to know the truth, what is the matter here?
I can see that you are sad, and your faces are pale!"

438 Dionisa responded, she told a great falsehood:
"King, this is the truth about your daughter:
she was struck down by mortal disease of the heart,
and she has passed from this world, this is the truth!"

439 Hearing this, Apollonius nearly lost his mind!
A long time passed before he answered them,
for never before had he received such a blow.
He stood still as a stone, his head lowered.

440 Later, well into the afternoon, Apollonius at last spoke.
He asked for a drink of water but no wine,
then he turned to Dionisa and said something to her
that should have broken the false woman's heart:

441 "Hostess," he said, "I would rather be dead than alive,
knowing that, in my misfortune, I have lost my
     daughter.
After the tragedy of losing her mother befell me,
I thought her company would ease my pain!

442 Cuando cuidé agora   que podría sanar,
que cuidava la llaga   guarir e encerrar,
é preso otro colpe   en esse mismo logar.
¡Non é melezina   que me pueda sanar!

443 Pero las sus abtezas   e los sus ricos vestidos—
poco á que es muerta,   aún non son mollidos—
tener vos lo é a grado   que me sean vendidos,
de que fagamos fatilas   los que somos feridos.

444 Demás, quiero ir luego   veyer la sepultura.
Abraçaré la piedra,   maguer frida e dura,
sobre mi fija Tarsiana   planyeré mi rencura,
¡sabré de su facienda   algo, por aventura!"

445 Cosa endiablada,   la burcesa Dionisa,
ministra del pecado,   fizo grant astrosía:
fizo un monumento   rico a muy gran guisa,
de un mármol tan blanco   como una camisa.

446 Fizo sobre la piedra   las letras escrivir:
"Aquí fizo Estrángilo   a Tarsiana sobollir,
fija de Apolonio,   el buen rey de Tir,
que a los XII anyos   abés pudo sobir."

447 Recibió Apolonio   lo que pudo cobrar,
mandolo a las naves   a los ombres levar;
fue él al monumento   su ventura plorar,
por algunas reliquias   del sepulcro tomar.

448 Cuando en el sepulcro   cayó el buen varón,
quiso facer su duelo   como avié razón;

442 Just when I thought I would find a cure
and I thought my wounds would heal and close,
I received another blow in the very same place.
No medicine can cure me now!

443 However, my daughter's jewels and fine clothing—
since she has only just died, her things are still intact—
I would be most grateful if you would sell them to me,
so I might bind my wounds with them.

444 Also, I want to go and see her tomb now.
I will embrace the stone, even though it is cold and
hard,
I will mourn my loss over my daughter Tarsiana's body,
and perhaps I will learn something more of her
passing!"

445 That fiendish woman, the burgess Dionisa,
minister of sin, had done an atrocious act:
she had erected a fine and beautiful monument
of marble, just as bright and white as a shirt.

446 She ordered these words to be written upon the stone:
"Here Stranguillio entombed Tarsiana,
daughter of Apollonius, good king of Tyre;
she died at only twelve years of age."

447 Apollonius took what was left of Tarsiana's belongings
and ordered his men to take them to the ships;
then he went to the monument to mourn his fate
and to take some relics from the tomb.

448 Yet when the good man fell before the tomb
and attempted to mourn, as he was bound to do,

abaxósele el duelo   e el mal del coraçón:
¡non pudo echar lágrima   por nenguna misión!

449 Tornó contra sí mismo,   començó de asmar:
"Ay, Dios, ¿qué puede   esta cosa estar?
¡Si mi fija Tarsiana   yoguiesse en este logar,
non devién los mios ojos   tan en caro se parar!

450 Asmo que todo aquesto   es mentira provada,
non creyo que mi fija   aquí es soterrada,
mas, o me la an vendida   o en mal logar echada.
¡Seya, muerta o biva,   a Dios acomendada!"

451 Non quiso Apolonio   en Tarso más estar,
ca avié recebido   en ella gran pesar;
tornosse a sus naves,   cansado de llorar,
su cabeça cubierta,   non les quiso fablar.

452 Mandoles que moviesen   e que pensasen de andar,
la carrera de Tiro   pensasen de tomar;
que sus días eran pocos   e querrié allá finar,
que entre sus parientes   se querrié soterrar.

453 Fueron luego las áncoras   a las naves tiradas,
los remos guisados,   las velas enfestadas;
tenién viento bueno,   las ondas bien pagadas,
fueron de la ribera   aína alongadas.

454 Bien la media carrera   o más avién andada,
avían sabrosos vientos,   la mar yazié pagada,

he felt his pain and heartsickness abating:
he found he could not shed a single tear!

449   He stopped, wondered, and thought to himself,
"Oh God, what could possibly be causing this reaction?
If my daughter Tarsiana in truth lies here,
my eyes would not be so easily kept from weeping!

450   I suspect that all this is just a damnable lie—
I do not believe my daughter is really buried here;
they must have either sold her or hidden her body
    away.
Be she dead or alive, may God protect her!"

451   Apollonius had no wish to remain in Tarsus,
because he had felt so much pain there;
he returned to his ships, worn out from crying,
with his head covered, and he spoke to no one.

452   He ordered his men make haste and prepare to sail,
to set a course for Tyre—that is where they should go;
he told them his days were short, and he wished to die
    there,
and then he wanted to be buried there with his family
    line.

453   The anchors were pulled up right away,
the oars readied and the sails raised;
the wind was good and the waves calm,
and soon they had traveled far from the shore.

454   Halfway to Tyre, perhaps even further along,
they had favorable winds and the seas lay calm,

fue, en poco de rato,   toda la cosa camiada,
tollioles la carrera   que tenién començada.

455 De guisa fue rebuelta   e irada la mar
que non avién nengún   consejo de guiar;
el poder del governio   oviéronlo a desemparar,
non cuidaron ningunos   de la muerte escapar.

456 Prísolos la tempesta   e el mal temporal,
sacolos de caminos   el oratge mortal.
Echolos su ventura   e el Rey espirital
en la villa que Tarsiana   pasava mucho mal.

457 Fueron en Mitalena   los romeros arribados,
avían mucho mal passado   e andavan lazdrados.
Prisieron luego lengua,   los vientos ya quedados,
rendían a Dios gracias   porque eran escapados.

458 Ancoraron las naves   en ribera del puerto,
encendieron su fuego,   que se les era muerto,
enxugaron sus panyos,   lasos e de mal puerto;
el rey en todo esto   non tenié null conuerto.

459 El rey Apolonio,   lazdrado cavallero,
naciera en tal día   e era disantero,
mandoles que comprassen   conducho muy llenero
e fiziessen rica fiesta   e ochavario plenero.

but then everything changed in an instant,
and they were thrown from the course they had begun.

455 The sea turned so violent and stormy
that they completely lost their bearings;
the rudder was useless, they had to abandon it,
not a man among them thought he would escape with
his life.

456 The tempest had caught them in the evil storm,
and the deadly wind drove them off course.
They were tossed by fate and the King of Heaven
to the town where Tarsiana was suffering so much.

457 The pilgrims washed ashore in Mytilene
after all their misfortunes and the hardships they suf-
fered.
They learned where they had landed, once the winds
had calmed,
and gave thanks to God for their survival.

458 The ships lowered their anchors at the port's shore;
the sailors relit their fires, which had died out in the
storm,
and tired and dispirited, they wrung out their clothes.
All the while, the king could find no comfort in their
survival.

459 King Apollonius, the long-suffering knight,
had been born on that very day, his saint's day,
so he ordered his men to buy vast amounts of food
and to prepare a rich celebration, lasting a full eight
days.

460 En cabo de la nave,   en un rencón destajado,
    echosse en un lecho   el rey tan deserrado,
    juró que quien le fablasse   serié mal soldado:
    ¡dell uno de los pies   serié estemado!

461 Non quisieron los ombres   sallir de su mandado:
    compraron gran conducho   de cuanto que fue fallado,
    fue ante de medio día   el comer aguisado;
    cualquiere que vinié   non era repoyado.

462 Non osavan ningunos   al senyor dezir nada,
    ca avié dura ley   puesta e confirmada;
    cabdellaron su cosa   como cuerda mesnada,
    pensaron de comer   la companya lazdrada.

463 En esto Antinágora,   por la fiesta passar,
    salló contra el puerto,   queríasse deportar;
    vio en esta nave   tal companya estar,
    entendió que andavan   como ombres de prestar.

464 Ellos, cuando lo vieron   de tal guisa venir,
    levantáronse todos,   fuéronlo recebir;
    gradeciolo él mucho,   non los quiso fallir,
    assentosse con ellos   por non los desdezir.

460 Yet, at one end of the ship, in a lonely corner,
  the wretched king lay down upon his bed,
  swearing that whoever spoke to him would pay a high
    price:
  one of his two feet would be cut right off!

461 Apollonius's men had no wish to disobey his orders:
  they bought great amounts of food, all that was on
    offer,
  and their feast was prepared well before midday;
  there was food for all, no one who came was refused.

462 Not a man dared to speak a word to their lord,
  who had given such a harsh rule and meant what he
    said;
  like the wise men they were, they attended to their
    duties,
  and then the long-suffering company sat down to eat.

463 Meanwhile, Athenagoras, in observance of the feast
    day,
  went out to the port to join in the festivities;
  there he saw the people who had come with the ship,
  whom he could tell were worthy men.

464 When the men saw Athenagoras coming,
  they all rose up and went to greet him;
  he thanked them profusely—he did not want to snub
    them—
  and sat down with them, in a show of respect.

465 Estando a la tabla,   en solaz natural,
     demandoles cuál era   el senyor del reyal.
     "Yaze," dixieron todos,   "enfermo muy mal
     e por derecho duelo   es perdido, non por ál.

466 Menazados nos á   que aquell que li fablare,
     de comer nin de bever   nada le ementare,
     perderá el un pie   de los dos que levare,
     ¡por aventura amos,   si mucho lo porfiare!"

467 Demandó que·l dixiesen   por cuál ocasión
     cayó en tal tristicia   e en tal ocasión;
     contáronle la estoria   e toda la razón,
     que·l dizién Apolonio   de la primera sazón.

468 Díxoles él: "Como yo creyo,   si non só trastornado,
     tal nombre suele Tarsiana   aver mucho usado;
     a lo que me saliere   ferme quiero osado,
     ¡dezir le é que me semeja   villano descoraznado!"

469 Mostráronle los hombres   el logar on yazié,
     que con el ombre bueno   a todos mucho plazié.
     Violo con fiera barba   que los pechos le cobrié,
     ¡tóvolo por façanya   porque atal fazié!

470 Dixo·l: "¡Dios te salve,   Apolonio, amigo!
     Oí fablar de tu fazienda,   vengo fablar contigo;

158

465 Seated at the table, with his accustomed good cheer,
　　Athenagoras inquired after the master of their
　　　　company.
　　"He lies very gravely ill," they all responded,
　　"lost in his mourning, and rightly so.

466 He has ordered us not to speak to him,
　　not even to mention food or drink in his presence;
　　anyone who does so will lose one of his two feet,
　　or possibly both, if he keeps bothering the king!"

467 Athenagoras asked what misfortune had caused
　　their lord to fall into such great sadness and woe,
　　so they told him the whole story and all the details,
　　first revealing their lord's name, Apollonius.

468 Athenagoras cried, "Unless I am mistaken,
　　that is the name that Tarsiana mentioned quite
　　　　frequently;
　　I have an idea that might work, if I dare to try it:
　　I am going to tell him that he is acting like a heartless
　　　　lout!"

469 The men showed him where their leader lay,
　　for they were all impressed by the good man.
　　He saw Apollonius, his long beard flowing over his
　　　　chest:
　　how Athenagoras marveled at the state of the man!

470 He said, "God save you, Apollonius, my friend!
　　I have heard all about you, and I have come to talk
　　　　with you;

si tú me conociesses,   avriés placer comigo,
ca non ando pidiendo   nin só ombre mendigo."

471 Bolviosse Apolonio   un poco en el escanyo;
¡si de los suyos fuesse,   recibría mal danyo!
Mas, cuando de tal guisa   vio ombre estranyo,
non le recudió nada,   enfogó el sossanyo.

472 Afincolo ell otro,   non le quiso dexar;
ombre era de precio,   queríalo esforçar.
Dixo: "Apolonio,   mal te sabes guardar;
¡devieste de otra guisa   contra mí mesurar!

473 Senyor só d'esta villa,   mía es para mandar:
dízenme Antinágora,   si me oíste nombrar.
Cavalgué de la villa   e sallime a deportar,
las naves que yacién   por el puerto a mirar.

474 Cuando toda la ove   la ribera andada,
pagueme d'esta tu nave,   vila bien adobada,
salliéronme a recebir   toda la tu mesnada,
recebí su combido,   yanté en su posada.

475 Vi ombres ensenyados,   companya mesurada,
la cozina bien rica,   la mesa bien abondada;
demandé que cuál era   el senyor de la alvergada,
dixéronme tu nombre   e tu vida lazdrada.

476 Mas, si tú a mí quisieres   escuchar e creyer,
saldriés d'esta tiniebra   la mi cibdat veyer.
¡Veriés por ella cosas   que avriés gran placer,
por que podriés del duelo   gran partida perder!

if you knew who I was, you would welcome me happily,
for I am no beggar coming to you for alms."

471 Apollonius turned a little on his pallet to look;
had it been one of his men, quite an injury would be in
     store!
But when he saw that a stranger was speaking,
he said nothing in return and swallowed his anger.

472 Athenagoras pressed on, he was not going to leave;
he was a valiant man, he wanted to persevere.
He said, "Apollonius, you are behaving badly;
you really should treat me in a more courteous way!

473 I am the lord of this city, it is mine to rule:
my name is Athenagoras, you may have heard of me.
I rode out from the city to enjoy the fresh air
and to see the ships that were anchored in the port.

474 When I was riding all along the shoreline,
your ship pleased me, for I saw it was well kitted out,
and all your company came out to greet me,
so I accepted their invitation and I ate at their table.

475 I met with well-bred men, a courtly company,
rich food, a plentiful and well-laid table;
so I asked who was the lord and host here,
and they told me your name and of your life of
     misfortune.

476 Yet, if only you would listen and trust me,
you would get up out of the dark and come see my city.
You would see things that would gladden you
and would make you leave your mourning behind!

477 Deviés en otra cosa   poner tu voluntat,
que te puede Dios facer   aún gran piedat;
que cobrarás tu pérdida   cuido que será verdat,
¡perderás esta tristicia   e esta crueldat!"

478 Recudió Apolonio   e tornó a él la faz,
dixo·l: "Quienquier que seyas,   amigo, ¡ve en patz!
Gradézcotelo mucho,   fezísteme buen solaz,
entiendo que me dizes   buen consejo asaz.

479 Mas só, por mis pecados,   de tal guisa llagado
que el coraçón me siento   todo atravesado;
desque bevir non puedo   e só de todo desfriado,
de cielo nin de tierra   veyer non é cuidado."

480 Partiose Antinágora   del mal deserrado,
veyé por mal achaque   ombre bueno danyado.
Tornó a la mesnada   fieramiente conturbado,
díxoles que el ombre bueno   fuert era deserrado.

481 Non pudo comedir   nin asmar tal manera,
por cuál guisa pudiés   meterlo en la carrera.
"Só en sobejana cuita,   más que yer non era,
¡nunca en tal fui,   por la creença vera!

482 Pero cuido e asmo   un poco de entrada,
quiero que lo probemos,   que non perdemos nada.
¡Dios mande que nos preste   la su vertut sagrada,
ternía que aviemos   a Jericó ganada!

477 You must turn your mind to other things,
for God is capable of showing you great mercy;
I truly believe you will recover what you have lost,
and you will shake off this sadness and cruelty!"

478 Responding, Apollonius turned to face Athenagoras
and said, "Whoever you may be, friend, go in peace!
I thank you very much, you have brought me good
comfort,
and I understand that your counsel is wise.

479 But, alas, I am so deeply wounded
that my heart feels as if it has been pierced through;
since I can no longer live, and I am indifferent to the
world,
there is nothing in heaven or on earth I care to see."

480 Athenagoras left the sick and wretched king,
seeing how evil affliction had damaged a good man.
He returned to Apollonius's men greatly troubled,
and said to them that their lord was in dire straits.

481 Think as he might, Athenagoras could not find
the way to lead Apollonius out of his plight.
"I am deeply concerned, more than ever before;
by all that is holy, I have never seen a case like this!

482 But I believe a plan is forming in my mind,
which we should put to the test, since we have nothing
to lose.
If God helps us and lends us his sacred powers,
I will consider the city of Jericho conquered!

483 En la cibdat avemos   una tal juglaresa—
    furtada la ovieron—   embiaré por essa;
    ¡si ella non le saca   del coraçón la quexa,
    a null ombre del mundo   no·l fagades promesa!"

484 Embió sus sirvientes   al malo a dezir
    que·l diesen a Tarsiana   que·l viniese servir;
    levarié tal ganancia,   si·l pudiese guarir,
    cual ella se pudiese   de su boca pedir.

485 La duenya fue venida,   sobre gent adobada,
    salvó Antinágora   e a toda su mesnada;
    por la palabra sola,   luego de la entrada,
    fue de los pelegrinos   bien quista e amada.

486 Dixo·l Antinágora: "Tarsiana, la mi querida,
    Dios mande que seyades   en buen punto venida;
    ¡la maestría vuestra,   tan gran e tan complida,
    agora es la ora   de seyer aparecida!

487 Tenemos un buen ombre,   senyor d'estas companyas,
    ombre de gran fazienda,   de raíç e de manyas;
    es perdido con duelo   por pérdidas estranyas,
    ¡por Dios, que·l acorrades   con algunas fazanyas!"

488 Dixo ella: "¡Mostrátmelo,   ca, como yo só creída,
    yo trayo letuarios   e especia tan sabrida
    que, si mortal non fuere,   o que seya de vida,
    yo le tornaré alegre,   tal que a comer pida!"

489 Leváronla al lecho   a Tarsiana la infante.
    Dixo ella: "¡Dios te salve,   romero o merchante,

483 In our city there is a certain songstress —
the one who was a captive — I will call for her,
and if she cannot relieve his heart of sadness,
there is no man in the world who can be helped!"

484 Athenagoras sent his servants to the evil pimp
with a request that Tarsiana should come to serve him;
if she could cure Apollonius, she would earn
as much money as she could possibly want.

485 The lady came, dressed in her finery,
and greeted Athenagoras and all the company;
the very sound of her voice, as soon as she had entered,
won over and warmed the hearts of the pilgrims.

486 Athenagoras said to her, "My dear Tarsiana,
God grant you success in this endeavor.
Use all your arts, so great and honed to perfection;
now is the hour for you to let them shine!

487 We have here a good man, the lord of this company,
a man of high standing, of noble lineage and courtly;
but he is lost in mourning after suffering great losses.
For God's sake, help him with some of your lore!"

488 Tarsiana said, "Show him to me, for I believe
I have such tasty electuaries and spices
that, unless he is at death's door, if there is hope of life,
I will return him to happiness, he will recover his
        appetite!"

489 They took Princess Tarsiana to Apollonius's bedside.
She said, "God save you, pilgrim or merchant!

mucho só de tu cuita,   sábelo Dios, pesante!"
Su estrumente en mano,   parósele delante.

490 "Por mi solaz non tengas   que eres aontado;
si bien me conocieses   tener te iés por pagado,
ca non só juglaresa   de las de buen mercado,
nin lo é por natura,   mas fágolo sin grado.

491 Duenya só de linatge,   de parientes honrados,
mas dezir non lo oso,   por mios graves pecados;
nací entre las ondas,   on nacen los pescados,
amos ove mintrosos   e traidores provados.

492 Ladrones en galeas,   que sobre mar vinieron,
por amor de furtarme   de muerte me estorcieron,
por mi ventura grave   a ombre me vendieron
por que muchas de vírgines   en mal fado cayeron.

493 Pero fasta agora   quísome Dios guardar,
¡non pudo el pecado   nada de mí levar!
Maguer en cuita bivo,   por mejor escapar,
busco menester que pueda   al sieglo enganyar.

494 E tú, si d'esta guisa   te dexares morir,
siempre de tu malicia   avremos qué dezir;
¡camia esta posada   si cobdicias bevir,
yo te daré guarido,   si quisieres ende sallir!"

God knows your troubles give me a heavy heart!"
And she stood before him, with her instrument in her
    hand.

490 "Now, you must not be ashamed if you enjoy my
    performance;
if you knew who I was, you would feel truly fortunate,
for I am not one of those singing girls for sale,
nor am I of low birth—I am a minstrel against my will.

491 I am a lady of noble lineage, of honored parentage,
but unfortunately, I do not dare tell anyone who I am;
I was born amid the waves, where the fish are born,
and I had liars for foster parents, who proved to be
    traitors.

492 Then pirates came in their ships by sea
and saved me from death only in order to kidnap me,
and it was my terrible fate that they sold me to a man
who was the downfall of many virgins.

493 Yet until now God has protected me,
and the devil has not been able to carry me away!
Even though I live under constant threat, to escape
    sin,
I found a trade that lets me fool the world of the flesh.

494 And you, if you allow yourself to die in this way,
we will forever have reason to speak ill of you;
you must leave this place if you have any desire to
    live—
I will find a cure for you, if only you would try!"

495 Cuando le ovo dicho   esto e mucho ál
    movió en su viola   un canto natural,
    coplas bien assentadas,   rimadas a senyal:
    ¡bien entendié el rey   que no lo fazié mal!

496 Cuando ovo bien dicho   e ovo bien deportado,
    dixo el rey: "Amiga,   bien só d'en pagado;
    entiendo bien que vienes   de linatge granado,
    oviste en tu dotrina   maestro bien letrado.

497 Mas, si se me aguisare   e ploguiere al Criador,
    entendriés que de grado   te faría amor:
    si venderte quisiere   aquell tu senyor,
    yo te quitaría   de muy buen amor.

498 Mas, por esto senyero   que me as aquí servido,
    dar te é diez libras   de oro escogido.
    ¡Ve a buena ventura,   que muy mal só ferido,
    que cuantos días biva   nunca seré guarido!"

499 Tornó a Antinágora   Tarsiana muy desmayada,
    dixo·l: "¡Nós non podemos   aquí mejorar nada!
    Mandome dar diez libras   de oro en soldada,
    mas aún por prenderlas   non só yo acordada."

500 "Fazes," diz Antinágora,   "en esto aguisado.
    ¡Non prendas su oro,   ca sería gran pecado!
    Yo te daré dostanto   de lo que te él á mandado,
    ¡non quiero que tu lacerio   vaya en denodado!

501 Mas aún te lo ruego   e en amor te lo pido
    que tornes a éll e mete   ý tu son complido:
    ¡si tú bien entendieres   e yo bien só creído,
    que querrá Dios que seya   por tu son guarido!"

495 When she had spoken thus and said much more,
   she played a song on the natural scale on her vielle,
   with well-composed verses, excellently rhymed:
   the king saw right away that she was not half bad!

496 When she had recited and entertained him well,
   the king said, "Friend, I have been well pleased by you;
   it is easy for me to see that you are from a noble line
   and that you were taught by a very learned master.

497 Now, if only I were able, and it pleased the Creator,
   you know that I would happily do you a favor:
   if the one you call your master wished to sell you,
   I would most gladly buy your freedom from him.

498 However, for just this one service you have done me,
   I will give you ten pounds of the finest gold.
   Go now, in good fortune, for I am badly wounded,
   and I will never be cured in all the days of my life!"

499 Quite dispirited, Tarsiana went back to Athenagoras
   and said, "There is nothing more we can do here!
   He told me to take ten pounds of gold in payment,
   but I have not agreed to take them from him."

500 "You have acted wisely," said Athenagoras.
   "Do not take his gold, that would be a great sin!
   I will give you twice as much as he has promised you,
   for I do not want you to have worked in vain!

501 But still I beg you, and for my sake I ask you
   to go back in to him and play your excellent music:
   if you are as skilled as I believe you to be,
   God willing, the man will be cured by your song!"

502 Tornó al rey Tarsiana   faziendo sus trobetes,
    tocando su viola,   cantando sus vesetes.
    "Ombre bueno," diz, "¡esto   que tú a mí prometes
    téntelo para tú   si en razón non te metes!

503 Unas pocas de demandas   te quiero demandar:
    si tú me las supiesses   a razón terminar,
    levaría la ganancia   que me mandeste dar,
    si non me recudieres,   quiérotela dexar."

504 Ovo el rey dubda   que, si la desdenyasse,
    que asmarién los ombres,   cuando la cosa sonasse,
    que por tal lo fiziera   que su aver cobrasse;
    tornose contra ella,   mandole que preguntase.

505 Dixo: "Dime cuál es la casa,"   preguntó la mallada,
    "que nunca seye queda,   siempre anda lazdrada:
    los huéspedes son mudos,   da bozes la posada.
    ¡Si esto adevinases   sería tu pagada!"

506 "Esto," diz Apolonio,   "yo lo vo asmando:
    el río es la casa   que corre murmujando,
    los peces son los huéspedes   que siempre están
                                            callando."
    "¡Esta es terminada!   Ve otra adevinando:

507 Parienta só de las aguas,   amiga só del río,
    fago fermosas crines,   bien altas las embío,
    del blanco fago negro,   ca es oficio mío;
    ¡esta es más grave,   segunt que yo fío!"

508 "Parienta es de las aguas   mucho la canya vera,
    que cerca ella cría,   esta es la cosa vera;

502   Tarsiana went back to the king with her little tunes,
      playing her vielle and singing her little songs.
      "My good man," she said, "that money you promised
          me,
      you can keep it all, if you do not come to your senses!

503   Now, I have a few riddles for you to guess:
      if you know how to answer them correctly,
      I will take the money you promised me,
      and if you cannot solve them, I will leave it with you."

504   Apollonius was afraid that if he refused the girl,
      people would think, when word got around,
      that he had done so to get out of paying her fee,
      so he turned to her and ordered her to ask away.

505   "Tell me what house," asked the captive girl,
      "is never quiet, but always complaining:
      while its guests are mute, the house cries out.
      If you can guess this, I will be quite content!"

506   "That," said Apollonius, "I can clearly see:
      the river is the house that runs along murmuring;
      the fish are its guests, who are ever silent."
      "That is it!" Tarsiana replied. "Here is another riddle:

507   I am a relative of the waters, a lover of the river,
      I make beautiful tresses and send them aloft,
      I turn white to black, that is my profession;
      this one is more difficult, to my thinking!"

508   "The close relative of the waters is the cane reed,
      which grows close by the stream, and this is true;

á muy fermosas crines,   altas de grant manera,
con ella fazen libros.   ¡Pregunta la tercera!"

509 "Fija só de los montes,   ligera por natura,
rompo e nunca dexo   senyal de la rotura,
guerreyo con los vientos,   nunca ando segura."
"¡Las naves," ditz el rey,   "trayen essa figura!"

510 "Bien," dixo Tarsiana,   "as a esto respondido,
parece bien que eres   clérigo entendido.
Mas por Dios, pues que eres   en responder metido,
¡ruégote que non canses   e tente por guarido!

511 Entre grandes fogueras   que dan gran calentura
yaze cosa desnuda,   huéspet sin vestidura,
ni·l nueze la calor   ni·l cuita la friura.
¡Esta puedes jurar   que es razón escura!"

512 Estonce dixo el rey: "Yo me lo faría
si fuesse tan alegre   como seyer solía,
por entrar en los banyos   yo me lo faría.
¡Fablar en tal vil cosa   semeja bavequía!"

513 "Nin é piedes nin manos   ni otro estentino,
dos dientes é senyeros,   corbos como fozino,
fago al que me traye   fincar en el camino."
"Tú fablas dell áncora,"   dixo el pelegrino.

514 "Nací de madre dura,   só muell como lana,
apésgame el río,   que só por mí liviana,
cuando prenyada seyo   semejo fascas rana."
"Tú fablas de la esponja,"   dixo el rey, "ermana."

it has lovely tresses that grow very tall,
from them books are made. Ask your third riddle!"

509 "I am the daughter of the forest, swift by birth;
when I break ground, I never leave a furrow sign;
I fight with the winds, never sure of my footing."
"Ships!" said the king. "That is what you mean!"

510 "You have," said Tarsiana, "responded quite well;
it is very clear that you are a learned cleric.
Yet I beg you, since you have started the process,
to keep going—do not tire, you will soon be cured!

511 Among raging fires that give off great heat
lies a naked body, an unclothed guest;
he is unharmed by the heat, gives not a care for the
cold.
This is, as you can see, a difficult riddle!"

512 Then the king replied, "That would be me,
if only I were as happy as I used to be.
I would go to the bathhouse, I would be that guest.
Talking about such low things is such nonsense!"

513 "I have neither feet nor hands nor internal organs,
but I do have two teeth curved liked sickles,
I make the man who carries me stand his ground."
"You speak of an anchor," said the pilgrim.

514 "Although I was born of a hard mother, I am soft as
wool;
the river weighs me down, though I myself am light,
and when I am pregnant, I seem just like a frog."
"Sister," said the king, "you speak of a sponge."

515 "Dezir te é," diz Tarsiana,   "ya más alegre seyo,
   ¡a bien verná la cosa,   segunt que yo creyo!
   Dios me dará consejo,   que buenos signos veyo,
   ¡aún, por aventura,   veré lo que desseyo!

516 Tres demandas tengo   que son assaz rafeces,
   por tan poca de cosa,   por Dios, no emperezes;
   si demandar quisieres,   yo te daré las vezes."

517 "¡Nunca," ditz el rey,   "vi cosa tan porfiosa!
   ¡Sí Dios me benediga,   que eres mucho enojosa!
   Si más de tres dixeres,   tener t'é por mintrosa,
   ¡non te esperaría   más por ninguna cosa!"

518 "De dentro só vellosa   e de fuera raída,
   siempre trayo en seno   mi crin bien escondida;
   ando de mano en mano,   tráenme escarnida,
   cuando van a yantar   nengún non me combida."

519 "Cuando en Pentápolin   entré desbaratado,
   si non fuesse por essa   andaría lazdrado;
   fui del rey Architrastres   por ella onrado,
   si no, non me oviera   a yantar combidado."

515   "I will say," said Tarsiana, "I do feel happier now,
     it seems to me that everything will work out!
     God will guide me, all the signs are good,
     I may still, in the end, see the desired effect!

516   I have three more riddles, and very easy ones at that,
     so for God's sake, do not let such a little task unman
        you;
     then, if you want to put riddles to me, I will give you a
        turn."

517   "Never," said the king, "have I met such an insistent
        girl!
     God give me strength, you are trying my patience!
     If you ask me more than three riddles, I will take you
        for a liar,
     and I will not allow you to continue for any reason!"

518   "On the inside I am hairy and on the outside bald;
     I always carry my hair well hidden, close to the chest.
     I'm passed about from hand to hand, manhandled by
        all,
     but when it is time to eat, no one invites me to dine."

519   "When I came to Pentapolis, dispossessed by the
        storm,
     without that riddle's answer I would have been
        wretched;
     thanks to it, however, I was Archistrates's honored
        guest,
     otherwise, he would never have invited me to his
        table."

520 "Nin só negro nin blanco,   nin é color certero,
nin lengua con que fable   un proverbio senyero,
mas sé rendar a todos,   siempre só refertero,
valo en el mercado   apenas un dinero."

521 "Dalo por poco precio   el bufón ell espejo;
nin es ruvio nin negro,   nin blanco nin bermejo.
El que en él se cata   veye su mismo cejo,
a altos e a baxos   riéndelos en parejo."

522 "Cuatro ermanas somos,   so un techo moramos,
corremos en parejo,   siempre nos segudamos,
andamos cada'l día,   nunca nos alcançamos,
yacemos abraçadas,   nunca nos ayuntamos."

523 "¡Rafez es de contar   aquesta tu cuestión!
Que las cuatro ermanas   las cuatro ruedas son;
dos a dos enlazadas,   tíralas un timón,
andan e non se ayuntan   en ninguna sazón."

524 Quiso·l aún otra   pregunta demandar,
¡assaz lo quiso ella   de cuenta enganyar!
Mas sopo cuántos eran   Apolonio contar,
dixo·l que se dexasse   e que estoviés en paz.

525 "Amiga," dixo, "deves   de mí seyer pagada,
de cuanto tú pidiste   bien te é abondada,
e te quiero aún   anyader en soldada;
¡vete luego tu vía,   mas non me digas nada!

520 "I am neither black nor white, I have no true color,
     nor do I have a tongue with which to tell a single tale,
     but I mimic everyone, and I am always talking back;
     I am hardly worth a single coin in the market."

521 "A peddler will sell you a mirror for almost nothing;
     a mirror is neither golden nor black, nor white, nor
          ruby red.
     He who looks in a mirror sees his own reflection:
     tall or short, high or low, the mirror treats them all the
          same."

522 "We are four sisters who live under the same roof,
     we run together, always chasing after each other,
     day in and day out, but we never catch up,
     and though we lie in an embrace, we will never be
          joined."

523 "It is so easy to answer this riddle of yours!
     Clearly, the four sisters are four wheels.
     Hitched two by two, they are drawn by a wagon beam;
     on and on they roll and never come together."

524 She would have liked to ask another riddle,
     she really wanted to sneak one more into the count!
     Yet Apollonius knew well how to keep score
     and told her to leave off and give him some peace.

525 "My friend," he said, "you should be well pleased with
          me
     because I solved each and every one of your riddles,
     and I will pay you even more than I promised before;
     go away now, and please, speak to me no more!

526   Querriesme, bien lo veyo,   tornar en alegría,
      mas por ninguna cosa   non te lo sofriría.
      Ternielo a escarnio   toda mi companyía;
      ¡demás, de mi palabra   por ren non me toldría!"

527   Nunca tanto le pudo   dezir nin predicar
      que en otra leticia   le pudiesse tornar.
      Con grant cuita que ovo,   non sopo qué asmar,
      fuele amos los braços   al cuello a echar.

528   Óvosse ya con esto   el rey a ensanyar,
      ovo con fellonía   el braço a tornar,
      óvole una ferida   en el rostro a dar,
      tanto que las narizes   le ovo ensangrentar.

529   La duenya fue irada,   començó de llorar,
      començó sus rencuras   todas a ementar.
      ¡Bien querrié Antinágora   grant aver a dar
      que non fuesse entrado   en aquella yantar!

530   Dizía: "¡Ay, mesquina,   en mal ora fui nada!
      Siempre fue mi ventura   de andar aontada,
      por las tierras agenas   ando mal sorostrada,
      ¡por bien e por servicio   prendo mala soldada!

531   ¡Ay, madre Luciana,   si mal fado oviste,
      a tu fija Tarsiana   mejor non lo diste!

526 I know you desire to make me happy once again,
     but I could never bear it if you were to do so.
     I would be shamed in the eyes of all my men;
     what is more, nothing can make me go against my
          word!"

527 There was no word Tarsiana could possibly utter
     that would change Apollonius's unhappy mood.
     Greatly troubled, she did the only thing she could
          think of
     and threw her arms around his neck in an embrace.

528 Now, this embrace enraged King Apollonius,
     and he violently twisted her arm away,
     then dealt Tarsiana such a hard blow in the face
     that the blood began to flow from her nose.

529 The lady began to weep with anger,
     and then she began to recount all her troubles one by
          one.
     Athenagoras would have given a king's ransom
     to have never sat down to eat with Apollonius's men!

530 Tarsiana said, "Oh, woe is me, I was born in an evil
          hour!
     It has been my fate to be forever dishonored,
     wandering in strange lands, my virtue under assault,
     and look at the thanks I get for all my attempts to help
          others!

531 Alas, my mother Luciana, if your luck was bad,
     your daughter Tarsiana's is not any better!

Peligreste sobre mar   e de parto moriste,
¡ante que·m pariesses   afogar me deviste!

532   Mi padre Apolonio   non te pudo prestar,
a fonsario sagrado   non te pudo levar,
en ataúd muy rico   echote en la mar,
non sabemos del cuerpo   dó pudo arribar.

533   A mí tovo a vida   por tanto pesar tomar:
diome a Dionisa   de Tarso a criar,
por derecha embidia   quísome fer matar.
¡Si estonce fuesse muerta   non me deviera pesar!

534   Ove, por mis pecados,   la muerte a escusar,
los que me acorrieron   non me quisieron dexar;
vendiéronme a ombre   que non es de prestar,
que me quiso ell alma   e el cuerpo danyar.

535   Por la gracia del cielo,   que me quiso valler,
non me pudo ninguno   fasta aquí vencer,
diéronme ombres buenos   tanto de su aver
por que pague mi amo   de todo mio loguer.

536   Entre las otras cuitas,   esta m'es la peyor:
a ombre que buscava   servicio e amor
áme aontada   a tan gran desonor;
¡devría tan gran sobervia   pesar al Criador!

537   ¡Ay, rey Apolonio,   de ventura pesada,
si sopieses de tu fija,   tan mal es aontada,
pesar avriés e duelo,   e sería bien vengada!
¡Mas cuido que non bives,   onde non só yo buscada!

You faced dangers at sea and died in childbirth—
if only you had killed me before I was born!

532 Apollonius, my father, could not help you;
he could not take you to hallowed ground,
so he threw you into the sea in a fine coffin,
and we do not know where your body came to rest.

533 He kept me alive, if only to suffer great pain:
he gave me to Dionisa of Tarsus to raise,
and she tried to have me murdered out of envy.
If only I had died then, it would have been no loss!

534 It was my fate to escape death at that time,
but my rescuers did not want to leave me in peace;
they sold me to a man—and not a good one—
who wanted to ruin both my soul and my body.

535 By the grace of God in heaven, my protector,
no man until now has been able to conquer me,
and good men have given me enough of their riches,
to pay my master all the money he demands from me.

536 Yet among all my worries, this is the very worst:
a man that I sought to serve with honor and courtesy
has shamed me and caused me great dishonor;
his sinful pride should surely sadden the Creator!

537 Oh, King Apollonius, you ill-fortuned man,
if only you knew the shame your daughter has endured,
you would feel sadness and grief, and I would be
      avenged!
But I fear you are dead and that is why I have been
      abandoned!

538 De padre nin de madre,   por mios graves pecados,
non sabré el ciminterio   do fueron soterrados;
¡tráyenme como a bestia   siempre por los mercados,
de peyores de mí   faziendo sus mandados!"

539 Revisco Apolonio,   plogo·l de coraçón,
entendió las palabras   que vinién por razón.
Tornose contra ella,   demandó·l si mintié o non,
preguntó·l por paraula   de grado el varón:

540 "¡Duenya—sí Dios te dexe   al tu padre veyer—
perdóname el fecho,   dar t'é de mio aver!
¡Erré con fellonía,   puédeslo bien creyer,
ca nunca fiz tal yerro   nin lo cuidé fazer!

541 Demás, si me dixiesses,   ca puédete membrar,
el nombre del ama   que te solié criar,
podriémosnos, por ventura,   amos alegrar:
yo podría la fija,   tú el padre cobrar."

542 Perdonolo la duenya,   perdió el mal taliento,
dio a la demanda   leyal recudimiento:
"La ama," dize, "de que siempre   menguada me siento
dixiéronle Licórides,   sepades que non vos miento."

543 Vio bien Apolonio   que andava carrera,
entendió bien senes falla   que la su fija era;
salló fuera del lecho   luego de la primera,
diziendo: "¡Valme Dios,   que eres vertut vera!"

538 Alas, my father and my mother are lost to me,
   I will never know where their bodies lie buried,
   while I am constantly dragged to market like an animal
   and always serving at the orders of my inferiors!"

539 Apollonius roused up, his heart rejoicing,
   for he heard her words, which were eloquent and true.
   He turned to the girl, and asked if she was lying or not,
   and joyfully inquired, speaking these words:

540 "My lady—may God's will restore your father to you—
   forgive my behavior, and I will give you some money!
   I committed a grave error, of that I am well aware.
   I have never acted in such a way before, nor even
         considered it!

541 What is more, tell me, you must remember,
   the name of the nursemaid who cared for you as a
         child,
   and perhaps we will both have cause to rejoice:
   I might find my daughter, and you, your father."

542 The lady forgave him, forgetting her anger,
   and responded to his question in the spirit it deserved:
   "My nursemaid," she said, "whose loss I still mourn,
   was called Licorides; know that I am not lying."

543 Apollonius knew he was getting to the truth,
   understood that without a doubt this was his daughter;
   he leaped right up out of his bed, as soon as he heard
         her,
   saying, "God help me, you who are goodness itself!"

544 Prísola en sus braços   con muy grant alegría,
diziendo: "¡Ay mi fija,   que yo por vós muría,
agora é perdido   la cuita que avía!
¡Fija, non amaneció   para mí tan buen día!

545 ¡Nunca este día   non lo cuidé veyer,
nunca en los mios braços   yo vos cuidé tener!
Ove por vós tristicia,   agora é placer,
¡siempre avré por ello   a Dios qué gradecer!"

546 Començó a llamar: "¡Venit, los mios vasallos!
¡Sano es Apolonio,   ferit palmas e cantos,
echat las coberturas,   corret vuestros cavallos,
alçad tablados muchos,   pensat de quebrantarlos!

547 Pensat cómo fagades   fiesta grant e complida;
¡cobrada é la fija   que avía perdida!
¡Buena fue la tempesta,   de Dios fue prometida,
por onde nós oviemos   a fer esta venida!"

548 El príncep Antinágora   por ninguna ganancia—
aun si ganase   el imperio de Francia—
non serié más alegre,   e non por alabança,
ca amostró en la cosa   de bien grant abundança.

549 Avielo ya oído,   dizielo la mesnada,
que avié Apolonio   palabra destajada
de barba nin de crines   que non cercenase nada
fasta que a su fija   oviesse bien casada.

550 Por acabar su pleito   e su servicio complir,
asmó a Apolonio   la fija le pedir;

544 He took Tarsiana in his arms with the greatest joy,
saying, "Oh, my daughter, I was dying in mourning for
     you,
and now all the pain I felt has disappeared!
Daughter, a better day has never dawned for me!

545 Never did I think I would see this day come,
never did I think I would have you in my arms again!
My sadness at your loss is now turned to joy,
and I will always be thankful to God for it!"

546 Then Apollonius called out, "Come here, my vassals!
Apollonius is cured, applaud and sing hymns of praise,
bring out your colors and parade your horses,
set up the tourney targets and get ready to joust!

547 Prepare a great feast and a celebration;
I have found the daughter that I had lost!
The tempest was good to us, a gift from God;
without it we would not have come to these shores!"

548 Prince Athenagoras could not have asked for more—
not even if he had won the whole empire of France—
he could not have been happier, and he shook off all
     praise;
rather, he acted with generosity and munificence.

549 He had heard the news, the men had told him,
that Apollonius had given his solemn vow
not to cut a single hair from his beard or from his head
until he had arranged a good marriage for his daughter.

550 To put an end to the wait and to render him a service,
Athenagoras decided to ask for his daughter's hand;

cuando fuesse casada,   que lo farié tundir,
por seyer salva la jura,   e non avría qué dezir.

551 ¡Bien devié Antenágora   en escripto yacer,
que por salvar un cuerpo   tanto pudo facer!
¡Si cristiano fuesse   e sopiesse bien creyer
deviemos por su alma   todos clamor tener!

552 "Rey," dize Antinágora,   "yo mercet te pido
que me des tu fija,   que seya yo su marido:
servicio le é fecho,   non só ende repentido,
¡valerme deve esso   por ganar un pedido!

553 Bien me deves por yerno   recebir e amar,
ca rey só de derecho,   regno é por mandar.
¡Bien te puedes encara,   rey, maravillar,
si mejor la pudieres   oganyo desposar!"

554 Díxole Apolonio: "¡Otorgo tu pedido,
non deve tu bien fecho   cayerte en olvido!
As contra amos estado   muy leyal amigo:
d'ella fuste maestro   e a mí as guarido.

555 Demás, yo é jurado   de non me cercenar,
nin rayer la mi barba,   nin mis unyas tajar
fasta que pudiesse   a Tarsiana desposar.
¡Pues que la é casada,   quiérome afeitar!"

556 Sonaron estas nuevas   luego por la cibdat,
plogo mucho a todos   con esta unidat;

once she was married, Apollonius could tend to his
    hair;
with the oath fulfilled, no one could fault him.

551   Athenagoras deserves to go down in history,
for he was willing to do all this to save a single man!
Had he been a Christian and had he believed in God,
we would be duty bound to pray for his soul!

552   "King," said Athenagoras, "I wish to beg a favor of you,
give me your daughter in marriage, let me be her
    husband:
I have served her well without a single regret,
and for that I deserve to be granted this request!

553   You should accept me as your beloved son-in-law,
for I am by rights a king, with a kingdom to rule.
It would be quite surprising, as well, king,
if a better husband for her is to be found living today!"

554   Apollonius said to him, "I grant your request,
for all your good deeds must not be forgotten!
You have been a loyal friend to us both:
to her you were an adviser, and you cured me.

555   What is more, I swore not to cut my hair,
nor to trim my beard, nor to cut my nails,
until I had arranged a marriage for Tarsiana.
Well, now that I have married her off, I want to trim
    my beard!"

556   Word soon spread throughout the city,
and the marriage indeed delighted everyone.

a chicos e a grandes   plogo de voluntat,
fueras al traidor falso,   que se dolié por verdat.

557   Con todos los roídos,   maguer que se callava,
con este casamiento   a Tarsiana non pesava;
el amor que·l fiziera   cuando en cuita estava,
cuando sallida era   non se le olvidava.

558   Aguisaron las bodas,   prisieron bendiciones;
fazién por ellos todos   preces e oraciones,
fazién tan grandes gozos   e tan grandes missiones
que non podrían contarlas   locuelas ni sermones.

559   Por esto Tarsiana   non era segurada:
non se tenié que era   de la cuita sacada
si el traidor falso   que l'avié comprada
non fuese lapidado   o muerto a espada.

560   Sobr'esto Antinágora   mandó llegar concejo,
fueron luego llegados   a un buen lugarejo.
Dixo éll: "¡Ya varones,   oíd un poquellejo!
Mester es que prendamos   entre todos consejo.

561   El rey Apolonio,   ombre de grant poder,
es aquí acaecido,   quiérevos conocer;
una fija que nunca   la cuidó veyer
ála aquí fallada,   ¡deve a vós placer!

562   Pedila por muger,   só con ella casado;
es rico casamiento,   só con ella pagado:

All, great and small, felt joy in their hearts;
only the faithless pimp was truly pained by the news.

557 Amid all the hubbub, even though she kept silent,
Tarsiana was not displeased with the marriage plans;
all Athenagoras's service and protection during her
      trials
was not forgotten now that she was safe from danger.

558 The wedding celebrations were prepared, blessings
      bestowed;
everyone said prayers and litanies for the couple,
feted them and presented them with such sumptuous
      gifts
that no speeches and sermons could properly describe.

559 Yet there was one thing that still worried Tarsiana:
she felt that she would not be fully out of danger
unless the faithless pimp who had bought her
were stoned to death or put to the sword.

560 Athenagoras called a council to decide the matter,
and they went straight to a good place to confer.
He said, "Listen men, pay some attention now!
We need to come to a decision together.

561 King Apollonius, a very powerful man,
has arrived here, and wishes to meet with you;
his daughter, whom he never thought he would see
      again,
was restored to him here—this should please you all!

562 I asked for her hand, and now I am married to her;
it is a very good match, and I am happy with her:

cuál es vós lo sabedes,   que aquí á morado,
todos vós lo veyedes   cómo ella á provado.

563 Gradécevoslo mucho,   tiénevoslo en amor
que tan bien la guardastes   de cayer en error.
Fuemos ý bien apresos   —¡grado al Criador!—
si non, avriemos ende   grant pesar e dolor.

564 Embíavos un poco   de present prometer:
quinientos mil marcos d'oro,   pensatlos de prender,
en lo que vós querredes   mandatlos despender.
¡En esto lo podedes   cuál ombre es veyer!

565 Pero sobre todo esto,   embíavos rogar
del malo traidor que·l quiso   la fija difamar,
que le dedes derecho   cual gelo devedes dar,
¡que non pueda el malo   d'esto se alabar!"

566 Todos por una boca   dieron esta respuesta:
"¡Dios dé a tan buen rey   vida grant e apuesta!
Cuando él esta vengança   sobre nós la acuesta,
¡cumplamos el su ruego,   non le demos de cuesta!"

567 Non quisieron el ruego   meter en otro plazo,
moviosse el concejo   como que sanyudazo:
fueron al traidor,   echáronle el laço,
matáronlo a piedras,   como a mal rapaço.

you all know her virtues, for she has lived among us,
and you all have seen how she acquitted herself well.

563 Apollonius is very grateful for your service to him,
for having protected Tarsiana from falling into sin.
We were very prudent with her—thanks be to God!—
otherwise, now we would be very sorrowful and
      distressed.

564 He now wants to send you a small gift:
five hundred thousand gold marks; do accept them,
and feel free to spend the money on whatever you
      would like.
This gift shows you what kind of a man he is!

565 However, in addition to this service, he begs you
to punish the evil pimp who tried to dishonor his
      daughter,
because you are duty bound to give the king his
      vengeance.
Do not let this evil man revel in his foul deeds!"

566 The entire council responded in unison:
"God give such a good king a long and prosperous life!
Now that he has asked us to give him this vengeance,
let us grant his request; we will not turn our backs on
      him!"

567 They had no desire to postpone the proceedings,
and the council acted quickly, spurred by their anger:
they went to the villain and tied him up,
then stoned him to death, like an evil thief.

568 Cuando el rey ovieron   de tal guisa vengado—
que fue el malastrugo   todo desmenuzado,
echáronlo a canes   como a descomulgado—
fue el rey de Tiro   del concejo pagado.

569 Tarsiana a las duenyas   que él tenié compradas
dioles buenos maridos,   ayudas muy granadas;
sallieron de pecado,   visquieron muy onradas,
ca seyén las cativas   fieramientre adobadas.

570 Tóvosse el concejo   del rey por adebdado,
ca por verdat avieles   fecho bien aguisado.
Fablaron que·l ficiessen   guallardón senyalado,
por el bien que él fizo   que non fuesse olvidado.

571 Mandaron fer un ídolo   al su mismo estado,
de oro fino era,   de orence labrado;
pusiéronlo derecho   en medio del mercado,
la fija a los piedes   del su padre ondrado.

572 Fizieron en la bassa   una tal escriptura:
"El rey Apolonio,   de grant mesura,
echolo en esta villa   una tempesta dura,
falló aquí su fija   Tarsiana, por grant ventura.

573 Con gozo de la fija   perdió la enfermedat;
diola a Antinágora,   senyor d'esta cibdat,
diole en casamiento,   muy gran solepnidat,
el regno de Antioca,   muy gran eredat.

574 Enriqueció esta villa   mucho por su venida,
a qui tomarlo quiso   dio aver sin medida.

568 When they had avenged the king in this way—
the wretched villain was drawn and quartered
and thrown to the dogs, like a banned reprobate—
the council had given satisfaction to the king of Tyre.

569 Tarsiana gave all the women owned by the pimp
good husbands and very large dowries;
they were all freed from sin and lived very honorably,
because now the poor things were richly endowed.

570 The council felt they were indebted to Apollonius,
for he had truly treated them very well.
They discussed giving him a singular tribute,
so that the good he had done would not be forgotten.

571 They had a life-size statue of Apollonius made,
crafted of the finest gold, wrought by a goldsmith,
and they erected it in the middle of the marketplace,
with the daughter represented at her honored father's
    feet.

572 At the base they placed a plaque with these words:
"King Apollonius, a most courteous man,
was thrown to these shores by a raging tempest,
and in his great good fortune found his daughter
    Tarsiana here.

573 Happiness in finding his daughter cured his sickness;
he gave her hand to Athenagoras, lord of this city,
and gave her as a wedding gift, with all due solemnity,
the city of Antioch, a superb inheritance.

574 His arrival enriched this city very much,
he gave freely of his wealth to whomever would take it.

Cuanto el sieglo dure,   fasta la fin venida,
será en Mitalena   la su fama tenida."

575 El rey Apolonio,   su cuita amansada,
quiso entrar en Tiro   con su barba trençada,
metiosse en las naves,   su barba adobada,
¡non podrié la riqueza   ombre asmar por nada!

576 Yendo por la carrera,   asmaron de torcer,
de requerir a Tarso   sus amigos veyer,
cremar a Dionisa,   su marido prender,
que atán mal sopieron   el amiztat tener.

577 Aviendo esto puesto,   el guión castigado,
vino·l en visión   un ombre blanqueando—
ángel podrié seyer,   ca era aguisado—
llamolo por su nombre,   dixo·l atal mandado:

578 "¡Apolonio, non as   a Tiro qué buscar!
Primero ve a Éfesio,   allá manda guiar;
cuando fueres arribado   e sallido de la mar
yo te diré qué fagas   por en cierto andar.

579 Demanda por el templo   que dizen de Diana,
fuera yaze de la villa   en una buena plana;
duenyas moran en él   que visten panyos de lana,
a la mejor de todas   dízenle Luciana.

As long as the world turns, until the end of days,
his fame will live on and be honored in Mytilene."

575   King Apollonius, now that his troubles had lessened,
desired to return to Tyre with his braided beard,
so he set sail, with his beard dressed for the occasion;
his wealth was absolutely beyond belief!

576   As they were on the way, they decided to turn
and head in the direction of Tarsus, to see their friends,
to burn Dionisa at the stake and imprison her
     husband,
since they had had so little respect for friendship.

577   Having decided on this and set their course,
a ghostly man came to Apollonius in a vision—
he must have been an angel, because he was
     beautiful—
and called the king by name, instructing him in this
     way:

578   "Apollonius, you should not go to Tyre!
First, set your course for Ephesus and go there,
and when you make land and have left the sea,
I will tell you what to do so that you will not be
     mistaken.

579   Ask for the temple that is dedicated to Diana,
which lies outside the town on a goodly plain;
the ladies who live there wear woolen nun's habits,
and the most important of them all is called Luciana.

580 Cuando a la puerta fueres,   si vieres que es hora,
fiere con ell armella   e saldrá la priora;
sabrá qué ombre eres   e irá a la senyora,
saldrán a recebirte   la gente que dentro mora.

581 Verná ell abadessa   muy bien acompanyada:
tú faz tu abenencia,   ca duenya es honrada,
demanda·l que te muestre   el arca consagrada
do yazen las reliquias   en su casa ondrada.

582 Irá ella contigo,   mostrar te á el logar;
luego, a altas bozes,   tú piensa de contar
cuanto nunca sopieres   por tierra e por mar,
¡non dexes una cosa   sola de ementar!

583 Si tú esto fizieres,   ganarás tal ganancia
que más la preciarás   que el regno de França.
Después irás a Tarso   con mejor alabança,
¡perdrás todas las cuitas   que prisiste en infancia!"

584 Razón no alonguemos,   que sería perdición:
despertó Apolonio,   fue en comedición,
entró luego en ello,   cumplió la mandación.
¡Todo lo fue veyendo   segunt la visión!

585 Mientre que él contava   su mal e su lacerio
non pensava Luciana   de reçar el salterio;
entendió la materia   e todo el misterio,
¡non le podié de gozo   caber el monesterio!

580 When you get to the door of the temple, if the time is
        right,
     use the door knocker and the prioress will come out;
     she will see you are a man of worth and will go to her
        lady,
     and the people living within will come out to greet you.

581 The abbess will come with all her companions:
     behave courteously to her, for she is a noble lady,
     and ask her to show you the consecrated ark
     where they keep the relics in her honored house.

582 She will go with you and show you the place;
     then, with a full voice, you must tell her your story,
     all that you have experienced on land and sea—
     do not leave a single detail out of your account!

583 If you do this, you will obtain riches
     worth more to you than the entire kingdom of France.
     Then you will go to Tarsus in a far better state,
     you will have shaken off all the troubles of your youth!"

584 I will not be long-winded now, that would be a shame:
     Apollonius awoke and contemplated his situation,
     decided to act immediately, and followed the angel's
        orders.
     Then everything came to pass, just as he had been told
        in the vision!

585 While he was recounting all his trials and tribulations,
     Luciana forgot all about singing her psalms;
     she understood his story and all its hidden meanings—
     truly, all the monastery could not contain her joy!

586 Cayó al rey a piedes   e dixo a altas bozes:
"¡Ay, rey Apolonio,   creyo que me non conoces!
Non te cuidé veyer   nunca en estas alfoces,
¡cuando me conocieres   non creyo que te non gozes!

587 ¡Yo só la tu muger,   la que era perdida,
la que en la mar echeste,   que tienes por transida!
Del rey Architrastres   fija fui muy querida,
Luciana é por nombre,   ¡biva só e guarida!

588 ¡Yo só la que tú sabes   cómo te ove amado!
Yaziendo mal enferma   venísteme con mandado,
de tres que me pidién   tú me aduxiste el dictado,
yo te di el escripto,   cual tú sabes, notado."

589 "¡Entiendo," dize Apolonio,   "toda esta estoria!"
¡Por poco que con gozo   non perdió la memoria!
Amos, uno con otro,   viéronse en gran gloria,
car avieles Dios dado   grant gracia e grant victoria.

590 Contáronse uno a otro   por lo que avién passado,
qué avié cadaúno   perdido o ganado;
¡Apolonio del metge   era mucho pagado,
avié·l Antinágora   e Tarsiana grant grado!

591 A Tarsiana con todo esto   nin marido nin padre
non la podién sacar   de braços de su madre;

586 She fell at the king's feet and cried out:
"Oh, King Apollonius, I think you do not recognize
    me!
I never thought to see you in these lands;
when you see me for who I am, I do not think you will
    be unhappy!

587 I am your wife, the one who was lost,
the one you threw in the sea, the one you think is dead!
I was the most beloved daughter of King Archistrates,
Luciana is my name, I am alive and well!

588 Remember, I am the one who loved you to no end!
When I lay sick in my bed, you brought me word
from three suitors, you brought me their letters,
and I gave you my response in writing, as you recall."

589 "Of course," said Apollonius, "I remember every-
    thing!"
And then he almost fainted away in rapturous joy!
The two found themselves together in utmost
    happiness,
for God had given them immense grace and triumph.

590 They told each other the stories of their
    misadventures,
what each had lost and what each had gained;
Apollonius felt very much obliged to the doctor,
Athenagoras and Tarsiana were also very grateful to
    him!

591 Reunited with her mother, neither husband nor father
could make Tarsiana leave Luciana's arms;

de gozo Antinágora,   el cabosso confradre,
lorava de los ojos   como si fuesse su fradre.

592 Non se tenié el metge   del fecho por repiso,
porque en Luciana   tan gran femencia miso;
diéronle presentes   cuantos él quiso,
mas, por ganar buen precio,   él prender nada non
quiso.

593 Por la cibdat de Éfesio   corrié grant alegría,
avién con esta cosa   todos plazentería;
mas lloravan las duenyas   dentro en la mongía,
ca se temién de la senyora   que se quería ir su vía.

594 Moraron ý un tiempo,   cuanto sabor ovieron,
fizieron abadessa   a la que mejor vieron,
dexaron los averes   cuantos prender quisieron,
cuando el rey e la reína   partir se quisieron.

595 Entraron en las naves   por passar la marina,
doliendo a los de Éfessio   de la buena vezina.
En el puerto de Tarso   arribaron aína,
alegres e gozosos,   el rey e la reína.

596 Antes que de las naves   oviessen a sallir,
sópolo el concejo,   fuelos a recebir.
¡Nunca non pudo ombre   nin veyer nin oír
ombres a una cosa   tan de gozo sallir!

in his joy, Athenagoras, that most prudent man,
cried unceasingly, as if he were their brother.

592 The doctor saw he had nothing to regret
in having put all his effort into saving Luciana;
they offered to give him whatever gifts he could wish
    for,
but mindful of his good name, the doctor would accept
    no payment.

593 A great happiness ran throughout the city of Ephesus,
where the family's reunion brought joy to all;
yet inside the convent all the nuns were in tears,
because they feared that their lady wished to leave
    them.

594 The family lived happily there for some time,
then they named the best of the nuns as the new
    abbess,
gave the convent as many riches as it could hold,
and the king and queen at last took their leave.

595 They boarded their ships for the sea crossing,
to the dismay of the Ephesians who were losing their
    good lady.
Then they soon struck land in the port of Tarsus,
to the great joy and happiness of the king and queen.

596 Before the company could disembark from the ships,
the council learned of their arrival and went to
    welcome them.
Never before had the world ever seen or heard
of people so happy to go out to greet a ship!

597 Recibieron al rey   como a su senyor,
cantando los responsos   de libro e de cor,
bien les vinié emiente   del antigo amor;
mas avié Dionisa   con ellos mal sabor.

598 Ante que a la villa   oviessen a entrar
fincó el pueblo todo,   non se quiso mudar.
Entró el rey en medio,   començó de fablar:

599 "¡Oítme, concejo,   sí Dios vos benediga,
non me vos rebolvades   fasta que mi razón diga!
Si fiz mal a alguno   cuanto val una figa,
aquí ante vós todos   quiero que me lo diga."

600 Dixieron luego todos: "Esto te respondemos:
¡por tú fincamos bivos,   bien te lo conocemos!
De lo que te prometiemos   non te nos camiaremos,
¡quequiere que tú mandes,   nós en ello seremos!"

601 "Cuando vine aquí morar   la segunda vegada—
de la otra primera   non vos emiento nada—
aduxe mi fija,   ninya rezient nada,
ca avía la madre   por muerta dexada.

602 A los falsos mis huéspedes   do solía posar,
con muy grandes averes   dígela a criar;

597 They welcomed the king as if he were their lord,
singing anthems from choir books and from memory,
and recalling how much love was between them;
however, Dionisa was upset by this turn of events.

598 Just before they were about to enter the city,
everyone stopped dead in their tracks.
Apollonius stood in the center of the crowd and began
    to speak,

599 "Listen to me, councilmen, God save you!
Do not turn away from me until I have spoken my
    piece!
If I have ever wronged anyone here, even in the
    slightest,
let him declare it to me now, before all here
    assembled."

600 All immediately replied: "This we say to you:
we owe our lives to you, and we thank you for it!
We will not go back on what we promised you;
whatever you ask of us, that we will do!"

601 "When I came to stay here for the second time—
I have nothing bad to say about my first visit—
I brought you my daughter, a newborn baby,
because I had left her mother behind, thinking she was
    dead.

602 I gave those liars, the ones who used to be my hosts,
my child to foster and raise, and great riches as well;

los falsos, con embidia,   mandáronla matar,
mas, mal grado a ellos,   ovo a escapar.

603 Cuando torné por ella,   que sería ya criada,
dixiéronme que era   muerta e soterrada;
agora, por mi ventura,   ela biva fallada,
mas en este comedio   grant cuita é passada.

604 Si d'esto non me feches   justicia e derecho,
non entraré en Tarso,   en corrall nin so techo,
¡avriedes desgradecido   todo vuestro bienfecho!"

605 Fue de fiera manera   rebuelto el concejo,
non davan de grant cuita   uno a otro consejo;
dizién que Dionisa   fiziera mal sobejo,
¡mecerié recebir   por ello mal trebejo!

606 Fue presa Dionisa   e preso el marido,
metidos en cadenas,   ell aver destruído;
fueron ant'éll con ellos   al concejo venido,
fue en poco de rato   esto todo bolvido.

607 Como non sabié Dionisa   que Tarsiana ý vinié,
tovo en su porfía   como antes tenié,
dizié que muerta fuera   e por verdat lo provarié,
do al padre dixiera,   en esse logar yacié.

608 Fue luego la mentira   en concejo provada,
ca levantosse Tarsiana   do estava assentada;

filled with envy, those liars ordered her to be
    murdered,
but she, much to their dismay, escaped death.

603 When I came back for my fully grown child,
    they told me that she was dead and buried;
    now, my good fortune has led me to find her still living,
    yet, in the meantime, I have suffered mightily.

604 If you do not give me the justice I rightly deserve,
    I will never set foot in any square or under any roof in
        Tarsus,
    and you will be ingrates, after all I have done for you!"

605 The council was extremely upset by Apollonius's
        words;
    troubled, they did not know what to say to one
        another,
    but all agreed that Dionisa had committed an evil
        crime
    and deserved to receive harsh punishment for it!

606 Dionisa was taken prisoner, as was her husband;
    both were put in chains and their goods destroyed.
    They were brought before Apollonius and the council,
    and the case was decided in short order.

607 Since Dionisa did not know that Tarsiana was present,
    she told the same lies that she had told before,
    saying that Tarsiana was dead and she could prove it,
    that her body was buried where she had told her father.

608 The lie was soon revealed to the council,
    when Tarsiana rose from where she was seated,

como era maestra   e muy bien razonada,
dixo todas las cuitas   por ó era passada.

609 Por provar bien la cosa,   la verdat escobrir,
mandaron a Teófilo   al concejo venir,
que ant'el rey de miedo   non osarié mentir,
avrié ante todos   la verdat a dezir.

610 Fue ant'el concejo   la verdat mesturada:
cómo la mandó matar   e sobre cuál soldada,
cómo le dieron por ella   cosa destajada;
¡con esto, Dionisa   fue mucho embargada!

611 Non alongaron plazo   nin le dieron vagar:
fue luego Dionisa   levada a quemar,
levaron al marido   desende a enforcar.
¡Todo fue ante fecho   que fuessen a yantar!

612 Dieron a Teófilo   mejorada ración
porque le dio espacio   de fer oración;
dexáronlo a vida   e fue buen gualardón:
¡de cativo que era,   diéronle quitación!

613 El rey, esto fecho,   entró en la cibdat,
fizieron con él todos   muy grant solepnitat.
Moraron ý un tiempo,   segunt su voluntat,
dende dieron tornada   para su eredat.

and, availing herself of her many talents and verbal
    skills,
she recounted all the trials that she had suffered.

609 To better prove her case and reveal the truth,
Theophilus was brought before the council,
for before the king, he would not dare to lie
and would tell the truth in the presence of all.

610 Theophilus made the truth clear to the whole council:
how he was ordered to kill Tarsiana, and for what price,
and how they thought the deed had been done:
with all this evidence, Dionisa was well and truly
    caught!

611 The council did not delay nor put the sentence off:
Dionisa was immediately taken to be burned at the
    stake,
and her husband was taken off to be hanged
    straightaway.
It all was done before they went to eat the midday
    meal!

612 Theophilus received a better portion
because he had given Tarsiana the opportunity to pray;
they let him live and gave him a goodly reward:
he had been a slave, and they freed him!

613 The case settled, King Apollonius entered the city,
where he was received with great ceremony by all.
They decided to live there for some time,
and, in the end, they set off for Apollonius's lands.

614 Fueron para Antioca,   esto fue muy privado,
    ca ovieron buen viento,   el tiempo fue pagado.
    Como lo esperavan   e era desseyado,
    fue el pueblo con el rey   alegre e pagado.

615 Diéronle el emperio   e todas las fortalezas,
    tenienle sobrepuestas   muy grandes riquezas,
    diéronle los varones   muchas de sus altezas;
    ¡mal grado a Antioco   con todas sus malezas!

616 Prísoles omenatges   e toda segurança,
    fue senyor dell emperio,   una buena pitança.
    ¡Non ganó poca cosa   en su adevinança,
    mucho era camiado   de la otra malandança!

617 Desque fue en el regno   senyor apoderado
    e vio que todo el pueblo   estava bien pagado,
    fízoles entender   el rey aventurado
    cómo avié el regno   a su yerno mandado.

618 Fue con este senyorío   el pueblo bien pagado,
    que veyén ombre bueno   e de sen bien esforçado;
    recibiéronlo luego   de sabor e de grado.
    ¡Ya veyé Antinágora   que no era mal casado!

614　They went to Antioch, the trip went very quickly,
　　　for the winds were favorable and the weather was
　　　　　pleasant.
　　　Since the people were awaiting him and wanted
　　　　　Apollonius,
　　　they were happy and well pleased with their king.

615　The people of Antioch gave him the empire and all its
　　　　　castles,
　　　they had great stores of wealth waiting for him,
　　　and the nobles gave him many of their treasures.
　　　How little this would have pleased evil King
　　　　　Antiochus!

616　Apollonius received their oaths of fealty and peace,
　　　and thus became the lord of the empire, nothing to
　　　　　scoff at.
　　　Indeed, this was not a bad return on solving the riddle,
　　　a complete reversal from his early misfortunes!

617　Once Apollonius had established his power
　　　and assured himself that his kingdom was well
　　　　　contented,
　　　the fortunate king announced to the people
　　　that he had given Antioch to his son-in-law to rule.

618　The people were well pleased with their new lord,
　　　whom they could see was a noble and intelligent man;
　　　they readily welcomed him with happiness and plea-
　　　　　sure.
　　　Athenagoras could see that he had truly married well!

619 Cuando ovo su cosa   puesta e bien recabdada,
salló de Antioca,   su tierra aconsejada,
tornó en Pentápolin   con su buena mesnada,
con muger e con yerno   e con su fija casada.

620 Del rey Architrastres   fueron bien recebidos,
ca cuidavan que eran   muertos o perecidos,
car bien eran al menos   los xv anyos complidos,
como ellos asmavan,   que eran ende sallidos.

621 El pueblo e la villa   ovo grant alegría,
todos andavan alegres,   diziendo "¡Tan buen día!"
Cantavan las palabras   todos con alegría,
colgavan por las carreras   ropa de grant valía.

622 El rey avían viejo,   de días anciano,
nin les dexava fijo   nin fincava ermano,
por onde era el pueblo   en duelo sobejano,
que senyor non fincava   a quien besasen la mano.

623 Por ende, eran alegres,   ca derecho fazién,
porque de la natura   del senyor non saldrién;
a guisa de leyales   vassallos comidién
las cosas en que cayén,   todas las conyocién.

624 De la su alegría,   ¿quién vos podrié contar?
Todos se renovaron   de vestir e de calçar,

619   Once all his affairs had been put in good order,
       Apollonius left Antioch, his well-administered realm,
       and set off for Pentapolis, along with all his men,
       with his wife, son-in-law, and his well-married
              daughter.

620   They received a warm welcome from King
              Archistrates,
       for everyone thought they had been killed or perished,
       because at least fifteen long years had passed,
       by their reckoning, since the family had left Pentapolis.

621   The people of Pentapolis were filled with happiness:
       all were joyful, crying out, "What a great day!"
       They went about singing words of jubilation
       and decked the streets with precious hanging cloths.

622   Their king was growing old, nearing the end of his
              days;
       he had left them no heir, nor had he a brother,
       and for this reason, the people were sorely mournful,
       for they feared they would be left without a lord's hand
              to kiss.

623   So, by rights they were very happy when Apollonius
              arrived,
       because the natural line of their king would not be
              broken;
       in the manner of loyal vassals, they knew well
       all of the many dangers they would have faced.

624   Who could possibly describe the joy they all felt?
       Everyone put on new clothing and new shoes,

entravan en los banyos   por la color cobrar,
avían los alfagemes   priessa de cercenar.

625 Fumeyavan las casas,   fazían grandes cozinas,
trayén grant abundancia   de carnes montesinas,
de tocinos e de vacas,   rezientes e cecinas,
¡non costavan dinero   capones ni gallinas!

626 Fazía el pueblo todo   cada día oración
que al rey Apolonio   naciese criazón.
Plogo a Dios del cielo   e a su devoción,
concibió Luciana   e parió fijo varón.

627 El pueblo, con el ninyo   que Dios les avié dado,
andava mucho alegre   e mucho assegurado;
mas a pocos de días   fue el gozo torbado,
ca murió Architrastres,   un rey muy acabado.

628 Del duelo que fizieron   ementar non lo queremos,
a los que lo passaron,   a essos lo dexemos;
nuestro curso sigamos   e razón acabemos,
¡si non, dirán algunos   que nada non sabemos!

629 Cuando el rey fue   d'este sieglo passado,
como él lo merecié   fue noblemiente soterrado;
el governio del rey   e todo el dictado
fincó en Apolonio,   ca era aguisado.

630 Por todos los trabajos   que·l avían venido
non olvidó el pleito   que avié prometido;

went to the bathhouses to refresh their complexions,
and the barbers were overwhelmed with beards to
trim.

625 Cooking fires were lit, huge meals prepared,
an abundance of game was brought forth,
and bacon and beef, both fresh and cured—
no money was spared on capons and chickens!

626 Each day the people offered up their prayers
that King Apollonius would have a successor.
Their devotions were pleasing to God in heaven,
and Luciana conceived and gave birth to a son.

627 The son God had given to the people of Pentapolis
brought them great joy and assured their future;
sadly, just a few days later their happiness was troubled
when Archistrates, that most revered king, died.

628 I do not wish to describe how they mourned the
king—
let us leave the mourning to those who grieved.
Now I must follow the course of our tale to its end,
for if I do not, some might say that I know nothing at
all!

629 When King Archistrates left this mortal world,
he was nobly entombed, as he well deserved,
and his kingdom, government, and all his power
passed into Apollonius's hands, as was fitting.

630 Throughout all the trials that he had suffered,
Apollonius had not forgotten the promise he had
made;

membrole del pescador   que·l avié acogido,
el que ovo con él   el mantiello partido.

631 Fue buscarlo él mismo,   que sabié dó morava,
fincó el ojo bien luenye   e violo dó andava;
embió que·l dixiesen   qu'el rey le demandava
que viniesse ant'él,   que él lo esperava.

632 Vino el pescador   con su pobre vestido,
ca más de lo que fuera   non era enriquecido;
¡fue de tan alta guisa   del rey bien recebido
que para un rico conde   sería amor complido!

633 Mandó·l luego dar   honradas vestiduras,
servientes e servientas   e buenas cavalgaduras,
de campos e de vinyas   muchas grandes anchuras,
montanyas e ganados   e muy grandes pasturas.

634 Diole grandes averes   e casas en que morase,
una villa entera   en la cual eredase,
que nunca a null hombre   servicio non tornase,
nin éll nin su natura,   sino cuando se pagasse.

635 ¡Dios, que bive e regna,   tres e uno llamado,
depare atal huéspet   a tot ombre cuitado!
¡Bien aya atal huéspet,   cuerpo tan acordado,
que tan buen gualardón   da a un ospedado!

he remembered the fisherman who had taken him in,
the one who had given him half of his poor mantle.

631   The king knew where he lived and went to find him;
looking into the distance, he saw where the fisherman
          was
and sent word that the king wished to see him:
he should come before his lord, who was awaiting him.

632   The fisherman arrived, wearing his humble robe,
for he was no richer than he had been before,
and he was treated to such a courtly welcome by the
          king
that even a rich count would have felt flattered!

633   Apollonius ordered sumptuous clothing for the
          fisherman
and gave him male and female servants, beasts of
          burden,
fields and vineyards that stretched far and wide,
mountains, flocks, and very large pastures.

634   He gave him great stores of treasure and houses to live
          in,
as well as an entire city to pass on to his descendants,
so that he would never have to serve another man,
not he nor any of his line, unless they so desired.

635   God, who lives and reigns, called three in one,
provide such a good guest to all afflicted men!
Blessed be the guest, such a grateful man,
who knows how to reward his host with such gifts!

636 Fizieron omenatge   las gentes al moçuelo,
pusiéronle el nombre   que avía su avuelo,
diéronle muy grant guarda,   como a buen majuelo,
metieron en él mientes,   olvidaron el duelo.

637 El rey Apolonio,   cuerpo aventurado,
avié a sus faziendas   buen fundamento dado,
ca buscó a la fija   casamiento ondrado,
era como oyestes   el fijo aconsejado.

638 ¡Acomiéndolos a todos   al Rey espirital,
déxolos a la gracia   del Senyor celestial!
Él con su reína,   un servicio tan leyal,
tornosse para Tiro,   donde era naturall.

639 Todos los de Tiro,   desque a éll perdieron,
duraron en tristicia,   siempre en duelo visquieron;
non por cosa que ellos   assaz non entendieron,
mas, como Dios non quiso,   fablar non le pudieron.

640 Cuando el rey vieron,   ovieron tal plazer
como ombres que pudieron   de cárcell estorcer;
veyenlo con los ojos,   non lo podién creyer,
mas aún dubdavan   de cerca non lo tener.

636 The people of Pentapolis paid homage to the baby
and gave him the name that belonged to his
  grandfather.
He was as well tended as a tender new grapevine,
the people's thoughts turned to him, and grieving was
  forgotten.

637 King Apollonius, most fortunate man,
had created a solid foundation for his line and lands,
for he had married off his daughter well,
and his son, as you have heard, was in good hands.

638 I commend them all to the divine King
and leave them in the grace of the Lord of Heaven!
Apollonius, with his queen, his most loyal wife,
then returned to Tyre, the land of his birth.

639 Ever since the people of Tyre had lost their king,
they had lived in deep sadness and in constant
  mourning.
They not had heard anything of his misfortunes;
indeed, since God wished it, they had had no news of
  him at all.

640 When they saw their king, the people were so
  overjoyed,
they felt like condemned men set free from prison.
Though they saw him, they could scarce believe their
  eyes;
even seeing him up close, they doubted it could be
  true.

641 Plogo a éll con ellos   e a ellos con éll
como si les viniesse   ell ángel Gabriel.
¡Sabet que el pueblo   derecho era e fiell,
non avién, bien sepades,   de aver rey novell!

642 Falló todas sus cosas   assaz bien aguisadas:
los pueblos sin querella,   las villas bien pobladas,
sus lavores bien fechas,   sus arcas bien cerradas,
las que dexó moçuelas   fallávalas casadas.

643 Mandó llegar sus pueblos   en Tiro la cibdat,
llegosse ý mucho buen ombre   e mucha rica potestat.
Contoles su fazienda,   por cuál necessitat
avía tanto tardado,   como era verdat.

644 Pesoles con las cuitas   por que avía passado,
que por mar e por tierra   tanto avié lazdrado;
mas, deque tan bien era   de todo escapado,
non dava ninguna cosa   por todo lo passado.

645 "Senyor," dixeron todos,   "mucho as perdido,
buscando aventuras   mucho mal as sofrido;
pero todos devemos   echarlo en olvido,
ca eres en grant gracia   e grant prez caído.

641 Apollonius was delighted with his people and they
         with him,
    as happy as if the angel Gabriel had appeared among
         them.
    You should know that the people were upright and
         loyal;
    it is quite clear that they had no desire for another
         king!

642 He found all the affairs of the kingdom in good order:
    the people were at peace, the towns well populated,
    labor on the land well managed, the coffers well shut,
    and the maidens he had left were now married women.

643 He ordered his subjects to come to the city of Tyre,
    and many good citizens and powerful magnates
         arrived.
    He told them the whole story, all the reasons why
    he had stayed away for so long; he told them the truth.

644 The people were saddened to hear of all he had suf-
         fered,
    of all the trials he had endured at sea and on land;
    yet, since he had come through it all so well,
    Apollonius did not give a fig for all his misfortunes.

645 "Lord," they all said, "you have endured great losses,
    it has been your fate to suffer much hardship and pain;
    however, we all should let it slip from memory,
    for now you have reached a high state of grace and
         honor.

646 El poder de Antioco,   que te era contrario,
     a tú se es rendido   e a tú es tributario;
     ordeneste en Pentápolin   a tu fijo por vicario,
     Tarso e Mitalena   tuyas son sin famario.

647 Desdende, lo que más vale,   aduxiste tal reína
     cual saben los de Tarso,   do fue mucho vezina,
     onde es nuestra creyença   e el cuer nos lo devina
     que la vuestra provincia   nunca será mesquina.

648 Por tu ventura buena   asaz aviés andado,
     por las tierras agenas   assaz aviés lazdrado;
     ¡desque as tu cosa   puesta en buen estado,
     senyor, desaquí deves   folgar assegurado!"

649 Respondioles el rey: "Téngovoslo en grado,
     téngome por vós   muy bien aconsejado;
     por verdat vos dezir,   siéntome muy cansado,
     ¡desaquí adelante lograr quiero   lo que tengo ganado!"

650 Fincó el ombre bueno   mientre le dio Dios vida,
     visco con su muger   vida dulce e sabrida.
     Cuando por ir deste sieglo   la hora fue venida,
     finó como buen rey,   en buena fin complida.

651 Muerto es Apolonio,   nós a morir avemos,
     por cuanto nós amamos,   la fin non olvidemos;
     cual aquí fiziéremos,   allá tal recibremos,
     allá iremos todos,   nuncá acá saldremos.

646 All of King Antiochus's power was against you,
and now it is in your hands, and it pays you tribute;
you have installed your son as viceroy in Pentapolis,
and Tarsus and Mytilene are also yours, it is true.

647 More importantly, you have brought home a queen
known for her virtue in Tarsus, where she lived for a
long time,
and so, it is our belief and we know it in our hearts,
that poverty will never trouble your realms.

648 In your good fortune you have traveled far,
through foreign lands where you have undergone many
travails;
now that your life and family are all in order,
from now on, lord, you can live happily without
worry!"

649 King Apollonius responded, "I am grateful to you,
and I believe you have counseled me very well;
to tell you the truth, I am feeling very tired,
and from now on, I want to enjoy what I have earned!"

650 The good man stayed in Tyre for as long as God gave
him life,
living a sweet and easy life with his wife.
When the hour had come for him to pass from this
world,
he died a good and honorable death, like a good king.

651 Apollonius is dead, as we all must die,
for all that we love in life, let us not forget our end;
all that we do in this world will seal our fate in the next,
where we will all go, never again to return.

652 Lo que aquí dexamos   otrie lo logrará,
   lo que nós escusáremos   por nós non lo dará,
   lo que por nós fiziéremos,   esso nos uviará,
   ca lo que fará otro   tarde nos prestará.

653 Lo que por nuestras almas   dar no enduramos
   bien lo querrán alçar   los que bivos dexamos;
   nós por los que son muertos   raciones damos,
   non darán más por nós   desque muertos seyamos.

654 Los hombres con embidia   perdemos los sentidos,
   echamos el bienfecho   tras cuestas, en olvidos;
   guardamos para otrie,   non nos serán gradidos,
   ell aver avrá otrie,   nós iremos escarnidos.

655 Destajemos palabra,   razón non allonguemos:
   pocos serán los días   que aquí moraremos,
   cuando d'aquí saldremos,   ¿qué vestido levaremos
   al convivio de Dios,   de aquell en que creyemos?

656 El Senyor, que los vientos   e la mar á por mandar,
   él nos dé la su gracia   e él nos denye guiar;
   él nos dexe tales cosas   comedir e obrar,
   que por la su merced   podamos escapar.

   El que oviere seso responda e diga "amén."

   Amen Deus

652 Whatever we leave behind here will belong to another,
whatever we neglect to give will not be given for us,
whatever we do for our souls, that will help us,
for others' deeds are of no use to us.

653 All that we are not willing to give for our souls
will be snatched up by those who live on after us;
we who give alms for the souls of the dead
cannot hope more will be given for our souls after
death.

654 Envy can make us mortals lose our minds,
and we are quick to forget good deeds once done;
if we save up our wealth for others, they will not thank
us.
They will take our money, and we will be cheated.

655 I will cease talking now, I will not draw out my tale:
our days living here on earth will be few,
and when we leave this place, what clothes will we wear
to sit at God's table, in whom we all believe?

656 The Lord, who rules the winds and the sea,
let him give us his grace and let him see fit to guide us;
let him allow us to think and act correctly,
so that we may be saved through his mercy.

Let the man of sound mind who hears this respond and
say "amen."

Amen, God

THE LIFE AND HISTORY
OF KING APOLLONIUS

I

Aquí comiença la vida e historia del rey Apolonio,
la cual contiene cómo la tribulación temporal se muda
en fin en gozo perdurable.

El rey Antíoco regñó en la cibdad de Antioquía, del cual
ella tomó este nombre. Esse rey hovo de su muger una fija
muy fermosa. E como ella llegasse a edad legítima e flore-
ciesse de fermosura e belleza—allende de ser fija de rey, do-
tada e morigerada de otras muchas perfeciones—muchos
grandes e famosos príncipes la pidían por muger, ofrecientes
cada uno muy grande e inestimable cantidad de dote e arras.

2   Mas el rey su padre, ante que deliberasse a quién la mejor
otorgasse en matrimonio, por malvada concupiscencia e
non menos con flama de crueldad, se encendió en desorde-
nado amor de su fija, de manera que començó a l'amar más
que pertenecía a padre; el cual, como lidiasse con el furor o
pugnasse con la vergüença, fue vencido del amor.

I

Here begins the life and the history of King Apollonius,
in which earthly tribulations turn into happiness
in the hereafter.

King Antiochus ruled over the city of Antioch, which is how the city came to be so named. Antiochus's queen had given him a very beautiful daughter. When she came of age, her loveliness and beauty came into full flower: not only was she a princess, she was also endowed with every perfection and accomplishment. Many wealthy and honorable princes asked for her hand, each one offering untold riches for her bride gift and dowry.

Yet before Antiochus could begin his deliberations over 2 which prince would be the best match for his daughter, the flames of evil lust kindled within him and he burned not only with disordered desire for his daughter, but with the fire of cruelty. He began to love her more than was seemly for a father and, try as he might to overpower his passion or fight against his shameful desires, he was conquered by love.

2

De cómo entró el padre en la cambra de la fija
e la forçó ende contra su voluntad.

E assí, un día él se llegó a la cama de su fija, mandando a todos arredrarse lexos, como que quería fablar en secreto con la fija, encendido con carnal apetito e furor. Por grand espacio la fija repugnante cuanto pudo, finalmente él la corrompió e defloró.

2   E como la donzella estuviesse pensando qué faría de sí, súbitamente entró a ella su ama, la cual, viéndola con cara llorosa, dízele: "¿Por qué tu ánima se aflige d'essa manera?" Responde la fija: "¡Oh, muy amada mi ama, la causa es por cuanto agora, en esta cama, dos nobles nombres han perecido!" Dize la nudriza: "Senyora, ¿por qué dizes esso?" Ella declara: "¡Porque ante de mi matrimonio muy escelerada e malamente soy corrompida!"

3   La ama, como oyesse e entendiesse esto, casi tornada loca, dize: "¿E cuál diablo ha osado violar el lecho de la reina?" Responde la donzella: "¡La crueldad ha causado este pecado!" Dize la nudriça: "¿Por qué no fazes saber al padre?" La fija dixo: "¡Si tú entiendes el fecho, perecerá el nombre de 'padre' en mí, e a mí no plaze otra cosa sino el remedio de la muerte!"

4   La ama, oyendo que ella quería el remedio de morir, por palabras dulces la amonestó que del tal propósito tan aborrecible se apartasse, e assí la revocó.

2

How the father entered his daughter's chamber
and raped her.

And so, one day, burning with carnal appetites and passions, the king approached his daughter's bed and sent all the attendants away, as if he wanted to speak with her privately. She fought him off for as long as she could, but finally he defiled and deflowered her.

While the damsel was wondering what would become of 2 her, her nursemaid rushed in, and, seeing the princess's tear-stained face, asked, "Why are you so upset?" The daughter replied: "Oh, my dear nurse, because just now, in this very bed, two noble names have perished!" The nursemaid asked, "Whatever do you mean, my lady?" She declared, "Because I have been most criminally and evilly defiled before marriage!"

Upon hearing these words, the nurse turned half mad and 3 asked, "What devil has dared to violate the queen's bed?" The damsel replied, "This sin comes from cruelty!" The nursemaid said, "Why don't you tell your father?" The daughter said, "If you must know, I will never utter the name 'father' again! There is no hope for me now but death!"

Hearing that the princess was ready to kill herself, the 4 nurse spoke gently to convince her to forget such a horrifying course of action, and brought the princess back to her senses.

3

En qué manera el rey mandó poner editos que
contenían que cualquier que quisiesse casar con su fija
havía de soltar la cuestión del rey propuesta,
e si no la soltava que fuesse degollado.

Entre estas el rey, su padre cruel, mostrándose a los de su
regño por piadoso padre, gozávase en ser marido de su fija
en su casa. E por que siempre usasse impiadosamente de su
fija, para excluir los que gela demandavan por muger, nueva
manera de maldad inventó, proponiendo una cuestión e di-
ziendo que si alguno soltasse aquella cuestión, aquel havría
su fija en muger, e si no soltare será degollado.

2 Oído esto, muchos reyes e príncipes e otros grandes om-
bres de muchas partes, por la grand e increíble fama de fer-
mosura e lindeza de la donzella, vinieron allí a provar e ver
si la soltura de la cuestión podrían por ciencia de letras al-
cançar. E el que respondía a la cuestión, casi que no dixiesse
nada, era degollado e su cabeça colgavan sobre la puerta del
palacio, por que los que viniessen, viendo las cabeças de los
muertos, se turbassen de manera que no osassen a ponerse
en tal peligro. E todo esto fazía por él mesmo permanecer en
aquel incesto nefario con su fija.

3

How the king sent out edicts announcing that
any man who wanted to marry the princess had to solve
the king's riddle, and if he could not solve it,
his head would be cut off.

All the while the king, cruel father that he was, was outwardly behaving as if he were a good, devout father and taking pleasure in being his daughter's husband behind closed doors. In order to continue sinfully using his daughter and to reject all her suitors, the king thought up a new kind of evil plan: he set a riddle and said, "If any man can solve this riddle, he can marry my daughter, but anyone who gives the wrong answer will be decapitated."

Hearing this news and inspired by the damsel's unmatched reputation for incredible loveliness and grace, many kings and princes and other great men from far-off lands came to Antioch to try and see if they could solve the riddle with their erudition. And each one had barely uttered a word before he was decapitated and his head hung above the palace gates as a warning: all those who came would see the severed heads of the dead men and be so frightened that they would not dare to risk their own lives. Now, the king did all this in the service of prolonging his own nefarious incest with his daughter.

4

Aquí pidió Apolonio la fija del rey porque
havía soltada la cuestión.

E el Antíoco tales crueldades usante, passado algund poco
de tiempo, un joven de Tiro, príncipe de su tierra muy rico,
que havía nombre Apolonio, bien sabio en letras, llegó en
Antioquía por mar. E entrando al rey, fízole reverencia. E
él respondió: "Salvos sean el padre e madre de ti, que vienes
a casar." Dize el Apolonio: "Alto rey, yo demando tu fija
por muger." El cual, oyendo lo que no quería oír, mirando
al mancebo díxole: "¿Sabes la condición de las bodas?"
Responde Apolonio: "Conocí e aun a la puerta vi." El rey con
saña dize: "Pues oye la cuestión: 'Por la maldad soy traído, la
carne de la madre como, busco mi hermano, marido de mi
madre, ni lo fallo.'"

2   El Apolonio, tomada la cuestión, apartose un poco del
rey, e como estudiasse per la ciencia, mediante Dios, falló la
solución de la cuestión. E tornando al rey, dize: "Excelente
rey, pues pusiste la cuestión, oi la solución. En cuanto dixiste
'por la maldad soy traído,' no has mentido: a ti mismo mira.
E en cuanto dizes 'la carne de la madre como,' mira a tu fija."
El rey, como oyesse el joven haver fallado la solución de la
cuestión, temiendo que no pareciesse su pecado, con cara

4

In which Apollonius asked for the princess's hand because
he had solved the riddle.

After Antiochus had been living in this cruel manner for a short time, Apollonius, the rich and young prince of the kingdom of Tyre, who was well learned in letters, sailed to Antioch. He came before the king and bowed to him. The king responded: "Blessings upon your father and mother, you who come seeking to marry." Apollonius said: "Great king, I ask for your daughter's hand in marriage." The king, hearing just what he least wanted to hear, looked at the young man and asked him, "Do you know the price of the wedding?" Apollonius responded, "Yes, I know, and I have even seen the palace gates." The king said angrily, "Well then, hear my riddle: 'Evil brings me to eat my mother's flesh; I seek my brother, my mother's husband, but I cannot find him.'"

After listening to the riddle, Apollonius drew himself 2 aside, a little ways away from the king, and pondered the question using his knowledge, and by the grace of God, he solved the riddle. Turning back to the king, he said, "Excellent king, since you set the riddle, now hear the solution: when you said 'I am spurred by evil,' you were not lying: that means you. And when you said 'I eat my mother's flesh,' that means your daughter." When the king heard that the young man had indeed solved the riddle, he feared that his sin

irosa mirándolo, dixo: "Lexos eres, mancebo, de la solución de la cuestión; ¡no has dicho cosa de verdad, e assí, mereces ser degollado! Mas aún avrás xxx días de espacio. E en tanto, piensa bien, tórnate a tu tierra e, si fallares la solución de la cuestión, tomarás a mi fija por muger. E si no, serás degollado."

5

Cómo Apolonio se fue por mar a su tierra
por miedo del rey que lo mandó matar
e cómo el rey procurava su muerte.

El Apolonio, turbado, tomando su compaña entró en el navío, e assí fue para Tiro, su tierra. Mas después de su partida, el rey llamó a Taliarco, su despensero, al cual dixo: "Taliarco, muy fiel ministro de mis secretos, sepas que Apolonio ha fallado la solución de mi cuestión. Por ende, cumple que luego embarques e vayas a perseguir a él e, como serás en Tiro, búscalo e con fierro o ponçoña mátalo. E assí torna, e recibirás grand merced de mí." Taliarco tomó armas e pecunias e fuese a la tierra de Tiro.

2   Mas Apolonio primero vino e entró en su casa, e en estudio apto vio e rebolvió todos sus libros, pero no pudo fallar

would be discovered, so he said, his face filled with ire, "You are very far from solving the riddle, young man; you have not said a single word of truth, and so you have earned your decapitation! However, I will give you thirty days of grace. During this time, think it over well, return to your lands and, if you solve the riddle, come back to marry my daughter. If you do not, you will be decapitated."

5

How Apollonius sailed off to his lands,
fearing the king would have him killed
and how the king ordered Apollonius's death.

Troubled, Apollonius gathered his company, returned to his ship, and set sail for his homeland of Tyre. Following his departure, King Antiochus called his steward, Taliarco, and said, "Taliarco, most loyal keeper of my secrets, I must tell you that Apollonius has solved my riddle. You must go now quickly in pursuit and when you get to Tyre, find Apollonius and kill him by sword or by poison. When you return, I will richly reward you." Taliarco prepared his weapons and money and set off for Tyre.

In the meantime, Apollonius had arrived home and devoted himself to rigorous studies, going through all of his books, but he was unable to find any other solution to the

otra cosa sino lo que dixo al rey. E dixo entre sí: "¡Por cierto, si no me engaño, el rey Antíoco por amor ilícito ama su fija!" e, tornando a pensar, dize entre sí: "¿Qué fazes, Apolonio? La cuestión suya soltaste, mas la fija no tomaste. Por ende, eres diferido de Dios por que no mueras." E allí luego mandó aparejar los navíos e cargar en ellos cient mill moyos de trigo con mucho oro, plata e vestiduras preciosas, con pocos compañeros muy fieles que tomó. E a la hora tercia de noche entró en la nao e començó navigar.

3   En el día seguiente, los de su regño buscándolo e no lo fallando, muy grand lloro fue entre ellos porque aquel muy amado príncipe no parecía en la tierra, por lo cual fue grandíssimo planto en la ciudad. E por el grand amor que havían a él, mucho tiempo cessaron los barberos de afeitar, fueron quitados los públicos juegos o espetáculos, e cerrados los baños, templos e tabernas de manera que alguno no entrasse en ellos.

riddle other than the one he had already given the king. Apollonius said to himself, "Surely, if I am not mistaken, King Antiochus loves his daughter with illicit desire," and, thinking it over some more, he said to himself, "What are you doing, Apollonius? You solved his riddle, but you did not take his daughter. Surely God intervened to spare your life." And so, Apollonius ordered his ships be prepared and provisioned with one hundred thousand bushels of wheat and a great deal of gold, silver, and precious garments. He took a few of his most loyal men as well. They boarded the ship and sailed away at the third hour of the night.

The next day, when Apollonius's subjects looked for their 3 beloved prince and could not find him, they began to weep because he was nowhere to be seen. A great mourning ensued. For love of their lost ruler, the city's barbers stopped their shaving, public gaming and entertainments were banned, and the baths, temples, and taverns were shuttered so no one could enter them for a long time.

6

Cómo Taliarco vino en Tiro, donde preguntava por
Apolonio, que havía fuído, e, como supo que
ende no era, tornó al Antíoco e gelo denunció,
el cual mandó grandes dones
al que lo fallasse o matasse.

Estas cosas assí passando, sobrevino allí Taliarco, el cual
fue embiado por el rey Antíoco a matar Apolonio, e viente
tal mudança e estar todas las tiendas cerradas, con grand
tristeza que todos mostravan, dixo a un moço: "Demués-
trame, si quieres vivir, ¿por cuál causa esta cibdad está assí en
luto e tristeza?" Responde el ninyo: "Oh, muy amado, ¿no
sabes tú la causa? ¿O por qué preguntas? Esta cibdad ha to-
mado luto porque Apolonio, príncipe de tierra, tornado del
rey Antíoco nunca ha parecido."

2   Taliarco, como esto oyó, lleno de muy grand gozo se
buelve a la nao e tornó para Antioquía. E entrado al rey dize:
"Rey mi señor, ¡alégrese vuestra excelencia, ca Apolonio por
miedo de vós ha fuído e no parece en su regño!" Entonces
dixo el rey: "¡Fuir podrá él, mas no escapar!" E luego mandó
poner un edicto d'esta manera: "Cualquier que me traxiere
a Apolonio Tiro, menospreciador de mi regño, recibirá de
mí cincuenta marcos de oro; e el que su cabeça me dará
havrá cient marcos de oro." Fecho esto assí, no solamente
los enemigos, mas aun los amigos, movidos por cubdicia, se
aparejavan a perseguir a Apolonio. De los cuales con grand

6

How Taliarco arrived in Tyre, where he looked for
Apollonius, who had fled, and, upon learning of Apollonius's
absence, how he returned to Antiochus with the news.
The king promised a handsome reward for
whoever killed or captured Apollonius.

Meanwhile, Taliarco, who had been sent by King Antio-
chus to kill Apollonius, arrived in Tyre, where he saw how
changed things were and how all the storefronts were shut
up and the sadness on all the people's faces. He asked a boy,
"Tell me, on your life, why is the city in this state of mourn-
ing and sadness?" The boy responded, "My dear sir, have you
not heard why? Why are you asking? The city is in mourning
because Apollonius, our prince, never returned home from
his visit to King Antiochus."

When Taliarco heard this news, he was filled with joy and 2
headed back to Antioch. He came before the king and said,
"My lord king, be happy, because Apollonius has fled, fear-
ing you, and is not to be seen in his realms!" Then the king
said, "He can run, but he cannot escape!" The king immedi-
ately published the following edict: "I will reward whoever
brings me Apollonius of Tyre, that insulter of my authority,
with fifty marks of gold; and one hundred marks of gold to
the man who brings me his head." With this edict, not only
his enemies, but even Apollonius's friends were moved by
greed to pursue him. They all strove to find Apollonius,

diligencia era buscado Apolonio por mar e por tierra, montes e valles, por todos modos e maneras, empero non se fallava. Estonces el rey mandó aparejar flotas o armadas de navíos para buscar e perseguir al Apolonio.

7

De cómo Apolonio vino en Tarsia e libró a los moradores
d'ella de la fambre, e cómo Elímito lo amonestó fielmente.

Mas retardando los que regían e aparejavan las flotas e armadas, Apolonio vino a Tarsia; el cual, andando cerca de la ribera, fue conocido de un siervo suyo que havía nombre Elímito, que vino a essa hora ende e, llegando a él, fízole reverencia, nombrándolo por su nombre. Apolonio, saludado de aquel, no curó d'él, segund que costumbran los potentes.

2   Entonces aquel siervo, que era viejo, indignado fue muy mucho d'este menosprecio e tornó otra vegada a lo saludar, diziente: "¡Dios te ensalce, rey Apolonio! Resalúdame e no quieras menospreciar la pobreza decorada de honestas virtudes; ca si tú sabes lo que yo sé, proveerás sobre ti, e te guardarás." Apolonio le dize: "Si plaze, dime qué cosa sea." El viejo le dixo: "Escripto eres por edito." Dize él: "¿E quién escrive en edicto al príncipe de la tierra?" Elímito responde: "El rey Antíoco." Pregunta Apolonio: "¿E por cuál causa?"

searching by sea and by land, mountains and valleys, in every place and every way possible, but he was not to be found. Then the king ordered an entire armada of ships to be readied, to go out in search of Apollonius.

7

Of Apollonius's arrival in Tarsus and how he saved the
population from famine and Elimito loyally advised him.

While Antiochus's ships were still being fitted out by his men, Apollonius arrived in Tarsus. As he was walking along the shore, one of his own servants, named Elimito, who had only just arrived there, came up to him and, with a bow, greeted him by name, but Apollonius ignored him, as is the way of powerful men.

This behavior offended the old servant, who felt severely 2 insulted and addressed him once more, saying, "God bless you, King Apollonius! Acknowledge my greeting and do not look down upon poverty when it is adorned by honest virtues; for if you knew what I do, you would be watchful and take care." Apollonius said "Please tell me what you mean." The old man replied, "There is a price upon your head." Apollonius then asked, "And who has put a price on the head of the prince of this land?" Elimito responded, "King Antiochus." Apollonius asked, "For what reason?" Elimito said,

Elímito dize: "Porque lo que el padre es tú quisiste seer."
Pescuda Apolonio: "¿Cuánto precio ha mandado por mí?"
Responde el siervo: "A cualquier que te levare vivo a él
ha prometido cincuenta marcos de oro, e al que levare tu
cabeça cient marcos de oro. Por ende, te amonesto que te
dispongas a fuir."

3   E dichas estas palabras, Elímito se partió d'él, mas Apolo-
nio le rogó que llegasse a él e le daría cient marcos de oro, e
dize: "Toma tanto de mi pobreza, porque lo mereciste, e quí-
tame la cabeça e preséntala al rey, e entonces havrá grand
alegría. E cata que havrás cient marcos de oro, e serás sin
culpa, pues lo farás por mi consentimiento e presentarás
gozo al rey." Responde el viejo: "Señor, ¡no quiera Dios que
yo tal faga ni reciba yo por tal causa merced, ca cerca los
buenos la amistad no es de comparar con precio ni merced!"
E assí se despidió d'él.

8

Cómo Apolonio fue recibido honradamente de los
cibdadanos de Tarsia, a los cuales vendió el trigo
e después les tornó el dinero que por él recibió.

Después d'esto, vio Apolonio en este mesmo lugar pas-
seando venir un ombre llamado Estranguilio, doliente e con

"Because you wanted to take the place of the princess's father." Apollonius inquired further, "How much is the price on my head?" The servant responded, "Antiochus has promised fifty gold marks to whoever can bring you in alive, and one hundred marks to the man who can bring him your head. So, I urge you to flee."

Having spoken these words, Elimito turned to take his leave, yet Apollonius begged him come closer and gave him one hundred marks of gold, saying, "Take this much of my poverty, because you have earned it, and cut off my head and give it to the king—then he will be overjoyed. And look, you will have one hundred marks of gold, guilt free, because you will do it with my consent and you will please the king." The old man responded, "God forbid I should ever do such a thing or be paid for such a service, for among good men, friendship cannot be bought and sold!" And with that, he took his leave. 3

8

*How Apollonius was received honorably by the
citizens of Tarsus, and how he sold them wheat
but then gave back all the money they had paid him.*

Afterward, as Apollonius was walking along the same shores, he saw a sorrowful man with a sad face coming

cara triste, e llegose a él luego. E Apolonio lo saludó. Estran-
guilio responde: "¡Dios te salve, rey Apolonio!" E dízele:
"¿Cómo en estos lugares con voluntad turbada andas?" Dixo
Apolonio: "Porque, como dixe la verdad, la fija del rey pidí
por muger, assí que pidila, si puede ser fecho, e en nuestra
tierra no me quiero asconder." Estranguilio dize: "Señor,
esta nuestra cibdad es muy pobre e no podría sostener tu
nobleza. Ítem, dura fambre e muy grand mengua padecemos
de pan e cevada, de manera que aun los cibdadanos non han
otra esperança sino la muy cruel muerte que todos tenemos
ante los ojos." Dízele Apolonio: "Fazed gracias a Dios, el
cual vos ha embiado a mí fuido a vuestra tierra, ca yo daré a
vuestra cibdad cient mill moyos de trigo, si solamente me
encubrís en vuestra cibdad." Estranguilio, como esto oyó,
echose a los pies d'él, diziéndole: "¡Senyor Apolonio, si tú
socorres a esta cibdad fambrienta, no solamente te encubri-
remos, mas aun, si necessario fuere, por tu salud pelearé-
mos!"

2   Apolonio, entrado en la ciudad, subió en el mercado, en el
tribunal del juizio presentes todos, e dixo allí: "¡Ciudadanos
de Tarsia, que estáis turbados e opremidos por mengua de
pan e viandas! Yo, Apolonio Tiro, me ofrezco a vos relevar
d'esta fambre e de vos dar pan en abundancia. E creo que
vosotros seréis tales que me encubriréis mi fuida. Ca sabed
por cierto que no soy fuido por malicia del rey Antíoco, mas
antes por mi viaje prósperamente soy aquí llegado. Por ende,
yo vos daré cient mill moyos de trigo en el precio mesmo
que he comprado en la tierra, es a saber, a ocho sueldos cada

toward him, who was called Stranguillio. He came up to Apollonius, who greeted him. "God save you, King Apollonius!" said Stranguillio, and he asked, "What brings you here with such a troubled heart?" Apollonius said, "I told the truth, so I asked for the hand of the king's daughter in marriage. Having sought her, now I am seeking asylum, because I do not wish to hide in my own country." Stranguillio replied, "My lord, this city of ours is very poor and could not offer hospitality to a man of your rank. In fact, we are suffering a terrible famine and a great shortage of bread and barley. The situation is so dire that our citizens' only hope for the future is the cruel death we all see before us." Apollonius said to him, "Give thanks to God, who has sent me fleeing to your land, because I will give your city one hundred bushels of wheat, if only you will give me safe harbor in your city." When Stranguillio heard this, he threw himself at Apollonius's feet, saying, "My lord Apollonius, if you help this starving city, not only will we shelter you, we will fight for your life, if necessary!"

When Apollonius had entered the city, he mounted the tribunal platform in the marketplace and addressed all of the people: "Citizens of Tarsus, who are troubled and oppressed by your want of bread and food! I, Apollonius of Tyre, offer my services to you to relieve you of this famine and to give you bread in abundance. In return, I know you will be the ones to give me safe harbor. Truly, you will come to see that my arrival was not caused by my flight from King Antiochus's malice; rather, I was brought here by the hand of Providence. So, I will give you one hundred thousand bushels of wheat for the same price that I bought it for in my land, that is, for just eight pence a bushel." The citizens, 2

moyo." Los ciudadanos, oyentes que por ocho sueldos pudiessen comprar el moyo, fueron muy alegres, e faziéndole gracias luego começaron tomar del trigo.

3   Empero, Apolonio, temiendo que, en esto quitada la dignidad real, no tomasse nombre de mercader más que de donador e rey, todo el precio del trigo a las utilidades de la mesma ciudad otorgó e dio. Los ciudadanos, como vieron tan grandes beneficios, pusieron en el auditorio una biga, en la cual estante con la mano derecha los panes e con el sinistro pie los ollasse. E escrivieron en la mesura: "A la ciudad de Tarsia Tiro Apolonio dio don, el cual libró la ciudad de la muerte cruel."

9

En qué manera Apolonio fue amonestado fielmente
de su huésped, llamado Estranguilio, que se partiesse de allí,
e cómo sus naos perecieron por fortuna.

Dende passados pocos días, por amonestamiento de Estranguilio e de Dionisia, de su mujer, propuso de navegar a la ciudad de Pentápolin de los tirones por que allí se ascondiesse, porque los beneficios con gran opulencia e sossiego se fazían ende. E assí con excelente honor fue acompanyado fasta la mar, e regraciándose a todos entró en la nao.

hearing that they could buy a bushel of wheat for eight pence, were overjoyed, thanked Apollonius, and immediately began to buy his wheat.

However, Apollonius, fearing that this deal was damaging 3 to his royal dignity, for he must not be known as a merchant, but rather as a benefactor and king, gave all the profits of the sale back to the city for their use. In honor of Apollonius's great generosity, the citizens of Tarsus erected a statue of him on a pedestal in the middle of the forum; in its right hand the statue held loaves of bread, and with its left foot it trod upon more loaves. At the base of the statue, they wrote: "Apollonius of Tyre gave a gift to the city and saved it from a cruel death."

9

How Apollonius was loyally advised by
Stranguillio, his host, to leave Tarsus
and how his ships were wrecked in a storm.

After a few days had passed, on the advice of Stranguillio and his wife Dionysias, Apollonius decided to sail to the city of Pentapolis in Tyre, where he could remain safely hidden while enjoying the life of comfort and leisure on offer there. And so he was escorted to the port with all honors, where he gave thanks to all and boarded his ship.

2   Mas él después que navegó en tres días con vientos prós-
peros, súbitamente se mudó el tiempo después que la ribera
de Tarsia passó. E a pocas horas, con vientos aquilionales e
contrarios, con gran fortuna la companya de Tiro Apolonio
fue corregida por tempestad, e la nave quebrada e rompida
en tanto grado que granizo e obscuridad e inmensos vientos
fuertemente los perturbavan, en manera que cada uno
d'ellos se ayudava lo mejor que podía. Finalmente todos
perecieron.

10

Cómo Apolonio, perdida toda su companya,
escapó solo.

Mas Apolonio, por beneficio de una tabla, Dios me-
diante fue lançado en la ribera de una gran ciudad nombrada
Pentápolis. E assí estando en la ribera, mirando la mar mansa
e tranquila, dixo assí: "¡Oh, fe de la mar, antes me caeré en las
manos del muy cruel rey que entre ende! ¿Dónde iré, qué
tierra pidiré, cuál conocido a mí, no conocido, ayudará?"

However, the weather suddenly turned rough soon after 2 they had left the shores of Tarsus after three days of smooth sailing. In a few hours, the violent north winds stirred up a storm that battered Apollonius of Tyre and all his company until the ship was broken into tiny pieces, utterly destroyed. In the darkness, as the ferocious winds attacked them, each man desperately tried to save himself. But, in the end, they all perished.

IO

How Apollonius alone survived, when all his men
had perished.

Only Apollonius, thanks to a plank of wood and God's mercy, washed up on the shores of the great city of Pentapolis. And as he was standing there on the shore, gazing at the calm and tranquil sea, he said, "Oh faithless sea, I would rather fall into cruel Antiochus's hands than into your care! Where can I go? What lands can I seek? What friend do I, friendless, have to help me?"

II

De cómo un pobre pescador, haviendo compassión de
Apolonio, lo recibió e lo vestió.

Como estas cosas fablasse Apolonio, vio un mancebo ro-
busto, pescador, venir contra sí, cubierto con un saco no lim-
pio. E con la gran necesidad, él se echó a sus pies e, llorando
de sus ojos, dixo assí: "¡Have misericordia, cualquier que tú
seas, de mí, que soy escapado del naufragio e peligro de la
mar, nacido de padre e madre no baxos, mas nobles! E por-
que sepas a quién te apiades, yo soy Tiro Apolonio, príncipe
de mi tierra. ¡A ti ruego e pido socorro de mi vida!"

2   El pescador, como vio la fermosura del mancebo, movido
de misericordia lo alçó e lo levó a casa, e le dio de comer
d'essas viandas que pudo haver e, por mas piadad mostrarle,
desnudándose su vestidura, partiola en II partes e la una
parte dio a él, la otra reteniendo en sí, diziéndole: "Toma
d'esto que tengo."

II

How a poor fisherman took pity on
Apollonius and gave him shelter and clothing.

Just as Apollonius was speaking, he saw a robust young fisherman wearing a dirty cloak coming toward him. And, out of his great necessity, Apollonius threw himself down at the fisherman's feet and said, sobbing, "Take pity on me, whoever you are, for I have survived a shipwreck and perils at sea, and I am born of a father and mother of no low station; rather, they were nobles! So that you know who you have taken pity on, I am Apollonius of Tyre, prince of my lands. I beg of you to help me, to save my life!"

The fisherman, seeing the other young man's beauty, was moved to compassion, so he helped Apollonius up and took him to his home, where he shared what little food he had and, in a show of even greater generosity, took off his cloak, cut it in two pieces, and gave one half to Apollonius, keeping the other for himself, saying, "What is mine is yours." 2

12

Cómo lo pescador le mostró
la ciudad de Pentápoli.

Esto fecho, mostrole lo camino a la ciudad, diziendo: "Vete a la ciudad, donde por ventura fallarás quien haya misericordia de ti; empero, si no fallares, buélvete acá e partiré contigo de la pobreza cuanto bastare, e pescaremos en uno. Esto solamente te ruego: que, si a tu dignidad fueres restituido, no menosprecies la mi pobreza." Apolonio dize: "¡Si no me acordare de ti, aun otra vegada padesca peligro e no falle otro semejante a ti!" E dichas estas palabras, e mostrada a él la vía de la ciudad, él entró por las puertas d'ella.

12

How the fisherman showed Apollonius
the way to Pentapolis.

Then the fisherman showed Apollonius the way to Pentapolis, saying, "Go to the city, where with luck you will find someone who will take pity on you, but if you cannot find anyone, come back here and I will share with you whatever my poverty allows, and we will fish together. I only ask that, if you are returned to your former dignity, you do not look down upon me." Apollonius said, "If I forget you, may I again suffer perils and never find another like you!" After they exchanged these words and the fisherman showed him the way to the city, Apollonius entered the gates of Pentapolis.

13

Cómo Apolonio vino en la ciudad de Pentápolin e entró en
el banyo, donde sirvió diligentemente al rey Archistrate,
de lo cual ganó gran loor.

Como pensasse dónde buscaría el socorro de la vida, vio
en la plaça un ninyo desnudo corriente, untada la cabeça de
olio, ciñido de una sábana, llamante con gran voz e diziente:
"¡Oíd todos, assí peregrinos como siervos: quien quiere la-
varse, vaya al banyo!" Oído esto, Apolonio, desnudando su
vestidura, entró en el banyo, e se lavó e usó del licor e, como
mirasse a todos, busca su par e no lo falla. E él estante assí,
súbito entró Archistrado, rey de todo el regñado, con su
companya en el banyo.

2   E començando exercitar con sus familiares el rey el juego
de la espera, Apolonio se llegó al rey, e fizo quedar la espera
corriente, e sotilmente la soltó e la remetió al rey jugante. E
entonces dize el rey a los criados: "¡Apartadvos! Por cierto
este mancebo, segund sospecho, es de comparar a Apolo-
nio." El cual, como oyó que lo alavava el rey, constantemente
se llegó a él e, tomando de la agua del banyo con mano des-
trada, lavó a él con sotileza; dende en el estrado muy agra-
dable lo recreó. E assí saliente él del oficio, se partió.

13

How Apollonius came to the city of Pentapolis and entered
the baths, where he diligently served King Archistrates,
thus earning great praise.

While Apollonius was wondering where he might turn
for aid and sustenance, he saw a naked boy whose head was
slathered in oil and whose waist was cinched by a towel
go running through the plaza, calling out in a loud voice,
"Hear ye, one and all, pilgrims and laborers, whoever wishes
to wash, come to the baths!" Hearing this, Apollonius took
off his clothes and entered the bath, where he washed and
oiled himself, and then he looked among the other bathers
for someone of his own rank, and found no one. But just
then, while Apollonius looked, King Archistrates, ruler of
the land, suddenly entered the baths, accompanied by his
retinue.

Archistrates began to play ball with his companions, and 2
Apollonius approached, trapped the rolling ball, and deftly
threw it back to the king. And then the king said to his men,
"Move aside! For surely, this young man, if I am not mis-
taken, resembles Apollonius." When Apollonius heard the
king singing his praises, he went directly up to him and, tak-
ing water from the bath with a skilled hand, deftly began to
wash him and then entertained Archistrates most agreeably
on the dais. Once Apollonius had fulfilled his duties, he took
his leave of the king.

3 Dixo el rey a sus amigos después que se apartó el mancebo: "Júrovos que nunca mejor me soy lavado que oy por servicio de un mancebo; no sé quién es." E dixo a uno de sus familiares: "Mira quién es aquel mancebo que me lavó." El cual, seguiéndole, violo vestido de ropa no limpia e, tornando al rey, dize: "Aquel mancebo es escapado de algún navío que ha perecido." El rey le pregunta: "¿Dónde sabes?" Él dize: "El hábito muestra la causa, aunque él calla." Dende, el rey le manda venir a cena.

14

De cómo Apolonio vino al palacio del rey,
el cual lo mandó vestir,
e del modo que assentó en la mesa.

Apolonio, como oyó, obedeció e con el mensajero vino al rey. El criado entrando, dize al rey: "He aquí el naúfrago, mas por la vileza del hábito ha vergüença de entrar." E assí, mandó el rey que lo vestiessen de ropas dignas e que entrasse a cenar.

2 Entrado Apolonio a la sala del rey, en lugar senyalado en derecho del rey se assentó. Traxieron viandas e en

After the young man left, Archistrates said to his friends, 3
"I swear to you that I have never before been bathed so well
by a young man in my service, and I do not know who he
was." Then king said to one of his company, "Find out who
that young man who bathed me is." The king's man, follow-
ing Apollonius, saw that he was dressed in dirty clothes, and
went back to Archistrates, saying, "That young man has sur-
vived a shipwreck." "How do you know?" asked the king.
"His clothes tell the tale, even if he does not." Upon hearing
the news, Archistrates ordered that the young man be
brought to dine with him.

14

Of Apollonius's arrival at the king's palace,
where the king ordered he be dressed,
and how Apollonius sat down to dine.

As soon as Apollonius heard, he obeyed and went with
the messenger to the king. The servant went in before him
and said to the king: "I have here the shipwrecked man, but
he is too ashamed of his tattered clothing to enter." So, the
king ordered that Apollonius be dressed in fine clothing and
then be brought in to supper.

Apollonius entered the king's hall and sat down in the 2
seat of honor in front of the king. Viands were served and

conseguiente la cena real. E Apolonio, aunque los otros cenassen, no comía nada, mas llorando por gran espacio, el oro e la plata de la vaxilla del rey mirava. Entonces uno de los assentantes dixo al rey: "¡Si no soy engañado, este mancebo ha invidia a la fortuna del rey!" Dixo el rey: "No sospechas bien, ca este non ha invidia de mis bienes, mas antes muestra él haver perdido más cosas." Dende, mirando con cara alegre a Apolonio, dize el rey: "¡Joven, come con nós e espera de Dios reparo!"

15

De cómo la fija del rey vino e
fabló con Apolonio.

E en tanto que el rey confortasse al mancebo, entró súbitamente la fija del rey, virgen ya de edad legítima, la cual dio paz al padre e dende a todos los assentantes. Dada la paz, tornándose al padre, dízele: "Señor padre, ¿quién es este mancebo, el cual ante ti tiene tan honrado lugar e tiene gran lástima e pesar?" El rey dize: "Dulce fija, este hombre es escapado de la tormenta de la mar. Hame servido muy graciosamente, por lo cual yo lo convidé a cenar. Mas quién él sea, no sé. Empero, si quieres saber, pregúntalo. Ca a ti está bien saber todas las cosas e, por ventura, como conocerás, havrás piedad d'él."

then the royal dinner. Yet while the others ate, Apollonius did not touch his food. Rather, for a long while, he cried as he gazed upon the king's gold and silver tableware, causing one of the king's attendants to say, "If I am not mistaken, the young man is envious of the king's good fortune!" The king responded, "You are misguided, for this young man is not envious of my wealth, he is weeping from having lost his own." And the king turned a smiling face to Apollonius saying, "Young man, eat with us and be hopeful that God will restore your fortunes!"

15

Of the king's daughter, who came and
spoke with Apollonius.

While the king was comforting the young man, his daughter, a young virgin of marrying age, rushed in and kissed her father and each of his guests in greeting. She then turned to her father and asked, "My lord father, who is this young man seated in honor before you and who is so sad and woeful?" The king said, "Sweet daughter, this man has survived the raging seas. He served me most graciously, and so I invited him to dine. Yet I do not know who he might be. If you wish to find out, ask him. For it is fitting that you know such things and, if you find out about him, then perhaps you will take pity on him."

2   Oyente estas cosas, la donzella allegose al mancebo, e
dízele: "Tu naturaleza mostra nobleza; si no lo has por enojo,
dime tu nombre e tus fortunas e casos." Él responde: "Si el
nombre quieres, en la mar lo perdí; si la nobleza, en Tiro la
dexé." Dize la donzella: "Más claramente me fabla por que lo
entienda." Entonces Apolonio le declara su nombre e todas
sus fortunas e acaecimientos. Acabadas las palabras, derra-
mar començó lágrimas. Al cual como el rey vio llorar, dixo a
la fija: "Dulce mi fija, ¡pecaste en preguntarle el nombre e sus
fortunas al mancebo, porque en ello renovaste sus passados
dolores! Pues, mi amada fija, ya sabes la verdad, justa cosa es
que la tu liberalidad como reina muestres a él." La donzella,
como vio la voluntad del padre, mirando al mancebo dize:
"¡Nuestro es, Apolonio! Quita el lloro e de mi padre serás
rico." Entonces Apolonio, con gemido e vergüença, fizo gra-
cias a la donzella.

3   Dende, el rey dize a la donzella: "¡Trae la viyuela por que
con cantar alegres el combite!" La donzella mandó traer el
instrumento e empeçó con mucha dulçor tanyer, donde to-
dos començaron alavarla e dezir: "¡No se puede cosa mejor
ni más dulce ser oída!" Entre los cuales todos Apolonio calló.
Dize el rey a Apolonio: "¡Cosa fea cometes! Todos alavan a
mi fija en la arte de música e tú solo vituperas." Responde él:
"¡Alto rey, si me das licencia diré lo que siento! La tu fija fue a
aprender la arte de música, mas aún no la aprendió. Por
ende, mándame ser dada la viyuela e luego sabrás lo que no
supiste." El rey dize a Apolonio: "¡Yo te veo ensenyado en

Hearing these words, the damsel approached the young   2
man, saying to him, "Your looks and bearing are those of a
nobleman; if it does not upset you, tell me your name, your
fortunes, and how you came to be here." Apollonius re-
sponded, "If you want to know my name, I lost it in the sea;
as to my nobility, I left it in Tyre." The damsel replied,
"Speak more clearly, because I do not understand." Then
Apollonius told her his name and the story of all his misfor-
tunes. Once he had finished speaking, tears began to flow.
When the king saw that Apollonius was crying, he said,
"Sweet daughter of mine, you were wrong to ask the young
man to tell you his name and his story, because you have
made him relive all his past pains! Now that you know the
truth, my dear daughter, you must show him the generosity
of a queen." When the damsel understood her father's
wishes, she looked at the young man and said, "You are one
of us now, Apollonius! Leave your mourning aside, and my
father will make you a rich man." Apollonius, moaning with
grief, humbly thanked the damsel.

Then the king said to the damsel, "Bring out the vielle to   3
cheer our guests with your songs!" The damsel sent for her
instrument and began to play very sweetly upon it. Every-
one was praising her and saying, "Never has anything better
or sweeter been heard!" Yet among them all Apollonius kept
silent. The king said to him, "You are very rude! Everyone is
praising my daughter's playing and you alone criticize her."
Apollonius responded, "Great king, if you would permit me,
I will say what I feel! Your daughter has studied the art of
music, but she has yet to learn it. Therefore, have the vielle
be passed to me and then you will savor music like you have
not before." The king said to Apollonius, "I see you are a

todas las cosas!" E mandó que le fuesse dado el instrumento e, salido fuera, lo decoró con la corona de su cabeça. E assí, entró en la cámara e tanyía ante el rey con tan gran dulçor, de manera que todos pensassen que no fuesse Apolonio, mas Apolo. E los que estavan con el rey dixieron que nunca havían visto ni oído cosa mejor.

4   La fija del rey, oyendo estas cosas e mirando al mancebo, fue presa de su amor. E dize a su padre: "Excelente rey, ¡desme licencia que dé al mancebo lo que me plaze!" Responde el padre: "Faz lo que te plazerá." Ella mirante al joven, dize: "Maestro Apolonio, toma de licencia de mi padre dozientos marcos de oro, e cuatrocientas libras de plata, e vestiduras en abundancia, con xx siervos e x siervas." A los cuales dize: "¡Traedle aquello que le he prometido!" E presentes los amigos, por mandato de la reina fueron traídas todas estas cosas en la sala.

man well educated in all things!" The king called for the instrument to be brought to Apollonius and, leaving the room, he placed the crown from his own head upon the young man's. Thus attired, Apollonius entered the chamber and played before the king so sweetly that everyone thought he was not Apollonius, but rather Apollo. And the king's companions said they had never seen or heard anything better before.

The king's daughter, hearing all this and looking upon the young man, was struck by love for him. So, she said to her father, "Excellent king, allow me to decide how to reward the young man as I please!" Her father responded, "Do as you wish." Looking at the youth, she said, "Master Apollonius, take with my father's permission two hundred marks of gold, and four hundred pounds of silver, and rich garments, along with twenty serving men and ten serving women." She said to Apollonius's new servants, "Bring him all that I have promised!" And so, in the presence of the king's friends, all these things were brought into the hall at the queen's command. 4

16

Cómo la fija del rey fizo rogar al padre que diesse
lugar convenible de morar en el palacio a Apolonio
por que oyesse e aprendiesse d'él la música.

Fecho esto, levantáronse todos e se fueron regraciando. E
dize Apolonio: "Buen rey, misericordioso de los menguados,
e tú, reina amadora de estudios e de filosofía, ¡de Dios seáis
enxalçados!" E assí licenciándose d'ellos, dixo a los siervos
que la reina le havía dado: "Tomad, servidores, estas cosas
que me son dadas e vamos a buscar posada." La donzella, te-
miente que perdiesse su amado, fue triste. E mirando al pa-
dre dize: "Alto rey e muy bueno, ¡no plega a ti que Apolonio,
que es oy de ti enrequecido, se parta, por que lo que le have-
mos donado no le sea tomado de algunos malos!" Entonces
el rey mandó luego serle dado un palacio donde honesta-
mente pudiesse folgar.

2   Mas la donzella, encendida en amor, passó la noche sin
folgura. E a la mañana, ella se va a la cámara del padre. La
cual como vio el padre, díxole: "¿Qué cosa es que assí has
contra tu costumbre madrugado?" Dize la donzella: "Fol-
gança alguna yo no puedo haver. Por ende, muy amado pa-
dre, suplícote que me deis al mancebo por maestro para que
me ensenye la arte de música e las otras cosas que me cum-
plen." El rey, oyendo estas cosas, huvo placer en ello, e
mandó llamar al Apolonio e dize: "Mi fija cubdicia mucho

16

How the king's daughter begged her father to give
Apollonius good rooms in the palace,
so she could listen to him play and learn music from him.

When all this had been done, everyone rose and bid farewell. And Apollonius said, "Good king, who takes pity on the misfortunate, and you, queen, who loves learning and philosophy, may God favor you!" And taking his leave, he said to the servants the queen had given him, "Take all these gifts I have received, my servants, and we will go seek out lodgings." The damsel was saddened, fearing that she would lose the man she loved. Looking to her father, she said, "Most high and good king, it cannot please you that Apollonius, whom you have just made a rich man, leave us, to be robbed of all we have given him by evildoers!" So the king immediately ordered that Apollonius be given chambers where he might be honorably housed.

Yet the damsel, burning with love, spent a sleepless night. In the morning, she went to her father's chamber. When he saw her, he asked, "What is it that has caused you to get up so early this morning?" The damsel replied, "I was unable to sleep at all. So, my beloved father, I beg you to give me the young man as a teacher, so he might teach me the art of music and other fitting things." Hearing these words pleased the king, so he had Apollonius brought before him and said, "My daughter has a deep desire to learn your art, so I beg

aprender tu arte, por que te ruego que la ensenyes todas las artes que sabes e yo te daré el gualardón que merecerás." Responde el Apolonio: "Yo soy presto a cumplir todo lo que mandares." E assí, amostró a la donzella como él aprendió.

17

Cómo la fija del rey, vencida del amor carnal de
Apolonio, no quiso otro marido alguno sino a Apolonio.

Después d'esto, la donzella, por el grand amor de Apolonio, fue enferma. El rey, como vio su fija haver caído en enfermedad, luego llamó los médicos, los cuales tocaron e vieron todas las venas e partes del cuerpo, e no fallavan en ella enfermedad alguna.

2   Después de pocos días, tres jóvenes muy nobles, los cuales havía grand tiempo que huvieran pidido aquella donzella por muger, juntamente saludaron al rey. Los cuales mirante el rey, pregúntales la causa de su venida; ellos dizen: "Porque muchas vezes nos prometistes dar a uno de nós la vuestra fija en matrimonio, por esta causa venimos oy todos tres en uno. Nós somos de tu regño, ricos e descendientes de nobles generaciones. Por ende, escoge de todos tres a cuál quieres haver en yerno." Responde el rey: "¡No me demandáis en tiempo convenible! La mi fija entiende en estudios, e por causa del estudio yaze enferma. Pero, por que no paresca

you to teach her all the skills you know and I will reward you according to your merits." Apollonius responded, "Your wish is my command." And then he taught the damsel just as he himself had learned.

17

How the king's daughter, overcome with carnal love for
Apollonius, wanted no other husband.

The damsel was so passionately in love with Apollonius that she became sick with it after studying with him. The king, seeing how his daughter had fallen ill, called for the doctors, who palpated and examined all her veins and the parts of her body, but were unable to find any disease.

A few days later, three youths of high nobility, who had long been asking to marry the damsel, arrived and jointly greeted the king. Looking at them, the king asked them why they had come, and they responded, "We three have come today because you have promised to give one of us your daughter in marriage many times. We are from your kingdom, and we are the wealthy scions of noble lineages. So, choose from among us three the one you want as a son-in-law." The king responded, "You have come to ask me at an inconvenient time! My daughter has been working so hard at her studies that she has fallen ill. But because I do not

que quiero mucho dilatar, escrivid en vuestras cartas vuestros nombres e la cantidad de la dote e yo las embiaré a mi fija por que escoja a quien querrá." Ellos fizieron todo esto. El rey recibió la escriptura, leyó, signó e dio a Apolonio, diziente: "Toma, maestro, estas escripturas e dalas a tu discípula."

3   Apolonio tomó las escripturas e diolas a la donzella. Ella, como vio a quien amava, dize: "¿Qué es esto, maestro, que entraste solo en mi estrado e cama?" Dize Apolonio: "Toma estas letras que te embía tu padre e léelas." La donzella abrió las letras e leyó en ellas tres nombres de los pididores e, lançadas las letras, mirando a Apolonio dize: "Maestro Apolonio, ¿no te pesa que a otro devo ser dada en matrimonio?" E dize él: "No, porque toda cosa que a ti sea honrosa será mi provecho." Dize la donzella: "Maestro, ¡si tú amasses, pesaríate!" Estas cosas diziente, tornó a escribir, e signó las letras e diolas a Apolonio que las levasse al rey. E lo que en ellas escribía era esto: "Rey e padre muy bueno, por cuanto tu piadad me permitió que te rescriviesse, rescrívote que aquel naúfrago escapado de la mar quiero haver por marido."

4   El rey, como leyesse la voluntad de la fija, no sabiendo por cuál náufrago dixiesse, mirando a los mancebos dize: "¿Cuál de vós ha padecido peligro de la mar?" Uno d'ellos, que havía nombre Ardonio, dixo: "¡Yo he padecido grand tormenta de mar!" Respondiole otro d'ellos: "¡Landre te consuma, de manera que ni salvo ni sano seas! Yo te conosco desde ninyo, e de una edad somos. ¡Nunca saliste de la puerta de la cibdad! ¿E dónde padeciste naufragio?" El rey, como no fallasse que

want you to think that I am unnecessarily delaying this matter, each of you write out a letter with your name and your dowry amount, and I will send them to my daughter, so that she may choose the man she wants." The young nobles did as he requested. Then the king took the letters, read them, sealed them, and gave them to Apollonius, saying, "Master, take these letters and give them to your pupil."

Apollonius took the letters and gave them to the damsel. 3 When she saw the man she loved, she said, "Master, what is this? Why have you entered into my bedchamber alone?" Apollonius said, "Take these letters sent by your father, and read them." And when she read the three names of her suitors, she threw down the letters and looked at Apollonius, saying, "Master Apollonius, does it not upset you to think I would be given to another man in matrimony?" And he replied, "No, because everything that honors you is also good for me." The damsel said, "Master, if you loved me, it would upset you!" Saying these words, she began to write, sealed her letter, and gave it to Apollonius to take back to the king. And this is what she wrote: "King and good father, since in your mercy you permitted me to write back to you, I write back that I want the shipwrecked man who survived the sea as a husband."

When the king read his daughter's wishes, he did not 4 know which shipwrecked man she meant, and looking at the young men he asked, "Which of you has suffered dangers at sea?" One of the suitors, who was named Ardonius, said, "I have suffered a great storm at sea!" One of the others replied, "Curse you! I hope you die! I have known you since you were a boy—we are of the same age. You never left the city gates! Where were you ever shipwrecked?" When the

alguno d'ellos padecido huviesse naufragio, miró a Apolo-
nio, diziente: "Toma las letras e lee, porque podrá ser que lo
que yo no conosco tú entiendas, el cual fuiste presente."
Apolonio, tomadas las letras, corrió prestamente e, como
sentió que era amado, huvo vergüença. Al cual dize el rey:
"Apolonio, ¿fallaste al que padeció el naufragio?" Mas él, por
vergüença, pocas cosas dixo. E el rey, como entendió que
la su fija lo amava, dixo a los otros: "Como será tiempo, yo
veniré a vos." E assí aquellos regraciando se partieron.

18

Cómo el rey casó su fija con Apolonio e
le fizo grandes bodas.

El rey solo entró a su fija e le dixo: "¿A cuál escogiste por
marido?" Ella, caída ante él con lágrimas, dixo: "¡Muy caro
padre, al naúfago Apolonio pido!" El rey, como viesse las lá-
grimas de su fija, alçola de tierra e assí la fabla, diziendo: "Mi
amada fija, no seas pensosa de alguna cosa, porque tal has
desseado cual yo mesmo, porque assí como vi que amando
soy fecho padre. ¡Yo soy alegre de te casar con él sin tar-
dança!"

king realized that none of the three suitors had been ship-wrecked, he turned to Apollonius and said, "Take this letter and read it, for it could be that I do not understand, but you, who were present when she wrote these words, will." Apol-lonius, having taken the letter, read it through quickly and, seeing that he was loved, blushed. The king asked him, "Apollonius, have you found out who the shipwrecked man is?" Yet, in his embarrassment, he could say little. The king, at last, understood that his daughter loved Apollonius and said to the other three, "In good time, I will come to you." And so, the suitors bid farewell and took their leave.

18

How the king married his daughter to Apollonius and
the splendid wedding celebrations he gave her.

The king went by himself to his daughter's chambers and asked, "Which man did you choose as a husband?" She fell before him weeping, saying, "My dear father, I ask for Apol-lonius the shipwrecked!" The king, seeing his daughter's tears, lifted her up from the ground and said, "My beloved daughter, do not be troubled by anything at all, for the man you have chosen is the same one I chose for you, because as soon as I saw him, I loved him like a father. I am happy to marry you to him right away!"

2   E assí, otro día siguiente fueron llamados los amigos de las ciudades cercanas para el rey, a los cuales dize: "Mis muy amados amigos, la mi fija se quiere casar con Apolonio su maestro. Pídovos a todos que lo hayáis en plazer, porque mi fija a hombre prudente se ayunta." Estas cosas dichas, con alegría de todos señaló día cierto para las bodas, las cuales celebradas, ella concebió en breve.

19

Cómo el rey Antíoco murió mala muerte e
fue buscado Apolonio para que sucediesse en su regño,
el cual fue con su muger para Antioquía.

Estando ella prenyada, como anduviesse con Apolonio su marido cerca de la ribera de la mar, acaeció que vio una nave muy fermosa, cual conoció Apolonio que fuesse de su tierra. E buelto al maestro de la nao, preguntole: "¿Dónde vienes?" Él responde: "De Tiro." Dize Apolonio: "¡Mi tierra nombraste!" El otro respondió: "¿Pues Tiro eres tú?" Él dize: "Como dizes, es." El maestro le pregunta: "¿Conociste alguno príncipe de aquella tierra llamado Apolonio? Ruégote que, dondequiera que lo vieres, digas que se alegre, que el rey

So, the very next day the king's friends from nearby cities   2
were summoned, and he said to them: "My beloved friends,
my daughter wishes to marry Apollonius, her schoolmaster.
I ask you all for your good wishes, because my daughter is
betrothed to a prudent man." These words were spoken to
everyone's delight and the king set the date for the wedding
celebrations, after which his daughter soon conceived a
child.

19

How King Antiochus died an evil death and
Apollonius, as his successor to the throne,
set out with his wife for Antioch.

It so happened that one day, while she was pregnant and
walking with her husband Apollonius along the seashore,
Cleopatra saw a beautiful ship, which Apollonius recog-
nized came from his homeland. And he went to the ship's
captain and asked, "Where do you come from?" The captain
responded, "From Tyre." Apollonius said, "You have named
my homeland!" The other man said, "You are from Tyre, you
say?" He said, "It is as you say." The ship's captain asked, "Do
you happen to know a prince from that land called Apollo-
nius? I beg you to tell him, wherever you might see him, to
rejoice, because King Antiochus and his daughter were

Antíoco e su fija son muertos, feridos del rayo, e las riquezas del regño de Antioquía son reservadas a Apolonio."

2   Como esto oyó, Apolonio, lleno de gozo, dize a su muger: "Demándote licencia que me dexes ir a recibir el regño." Ella, como esto oyó, con muchas lágrimas dize: "¡Oh, señor, e si fuesses aun en apartada tierra, devrías venir para el tiempo de mi parto! ¿Cómo quieres agora partirte, siendo cerca de mí? Mas si assí quieres, vamos entreambos." E veniendo al padre, dize: "¡Oh, muy piadoso padre, gózate y alégrate, ca el muy cruel rey Antíoco, con su fija, por juicio de Dios es ferido del rayo, e sus regños e riquezas son a nós reservados! Por ende, dame licencia para navegar con mi marido." El rey, muy alegre por estas nuevas, manda que sean aparejadas las naves en la ribera, e inchirlas de todos los bienes de la tierra. E mandó que con ella fuesse una dueña, por nombre Ligórides, para criar, e assimesmo la partera. E assí juntamente començaron navegar, después que fue el rey con todos los principales de su regño a la ribera e con su licencia.

struck down and killed by lightning, and all the riches of the kingdom of Antioch await Apollonius."

When Apollonius heard this news, he was filled with joy 2 and said to his wife, "Please give me your leave to go and take possession of my kingdom." However, when she heard his request, she said tearfully, "Oh, my lord, if you were in a far-off land now, you would have to come back in time for my birthing! Now, when you are beside me, how is it that you could wish to leave me? If you want to go, let us leave together." She went to her father and said, "Oh most merciful father, be happy and rejoice, because the most cruel King Antiochus, together with his daughter, has been struck by lightning in God's judgment, and his kingdom and riches are all now come down to us! Please give me your permission to set sail with my husband." The king was very pleased by this news and ordered that ships be made ready at the shore, and filled with all sorts of goods from his land. He ordered that a maidservant named Licorides, as well as a midwife, go with his daughter. Then the king, with all the nobles of his reign, went to the shore to give his blessing as they set sail.

20

Cómo la reina, muger de Apolonio, parió en la mar,
e murió en el parto, e fue echada en un ataúd en la mar.

Mas, como por algunos días fuessen en la mar, levantose
grand tempestad. E la reina en tanto se enfermó pariendo
una fija que fue fecha casi muerta, lo cual viendo la familia,
llamava con grand boz e lloro. Oyendo esto, Apolonio corrió
e vio su muger casi muerta yaziente, segund a él parecía. E
rompiendo sus vestidos, con muchas lágrimas se echó sobre
el cuerpo d'ella, diziendo assí: "¡Oh, amada mi muger, fija del
rey Archistrato, ¿qué responderé a tu padre por ti?"

2   E como estas cosas dixiesse, díxole el governador: "¡El
cuerpo muerto no se puede soportar en el navío! Por ende,
mándalo echar en la mar por que nós podamos escapar."
Dize Apolonio: "¿Qué dizes, muy malvado? ¿Plázete que
este cuerpo lance en la mar, el cual me recibió por marido
pobre e desbaratado?" E llamando los siervos, dízeles:
"Fazed un ataúd e fazed linir con bitumen los forados, e
poned carta de plomo dentro e assí sea cerrado." Acabado el
ataúd, apuéstanlo con ornamentos reales, e assí ponen la
reina dentro con xx marcos de oro a su cabeça. E Apolonio,
besándola con muchas lágrimas, mandó la ninya ser criada
diligentemente para que, en lugar de la fija, la nieta mos-
trasse al rey. E mandó el ataúd lançar en la mar con grand
lloro.

20

How the queen, Apollonius's wife, died giving birth at sea
and was thrown into the sea in a coffin.

A few days after they had set sail, a huge storm rose up. In the midst of the storm, the queen gave birth to a daughter and became deathly ill. When her family saw that she was dying, they cried out and wept. Hearing their voices, Apollonius ran in and saw his wife, lying almost dead, it seemed to him. Tearing at his clothes and sobbing, he threw himself upon her body, saying, "Oh, my beloved wife, daughter of King Archistrates, what will I ever say to your father?"

No sooner had he said these words than the ship's helmsman replied, "The ship cannot carry a dead body! You must order it be thrown into the sea, so we will not be cursed." Apollonius said, "What are you saying, you villain? You want me to throw this body into the sea? This body, of the lady who took me as a husband when I was a poor and broken man?" And calling the servants, he said, "Make a coffin and seal all its holes with tar, put a lead tablet inside, and let it be closed up." Once the coffin was finished, they adorned it with royal finery, and put the queen inside with twenty gold marks beneath her head. Sobbing and kissing his wife, Apollonius ordered that the baby girl be well cared for, so that he could give a granddaughter to the king, in his daughter's place. Then, weeping in mourning, he ordered that the coffin be cast into the sea.

21

Cómo la reina fue echada de el agua en la ribera de Éfeso,
donde tornó a vida e assí fue puesta en un monesterio.

Mas, el tercero día, la onda de la mar echó el ataúd a la
ribera de los efesios, lexos de la casa de un médico que havía
nombre Cerimonis, el cual esse día con los discípulos a la
ribera andava e vio el ataúd, que estava lançado de las ondas,
e dixo a sus siervos: "¡Tomad este ataúd con toda diligencia e
traedlo a la villa!" El cual como fiziessen, el médico abrió e
vio dentro una donzella apostada e ornada de ornamentos
reales, muy fermosa, yaziente casi muerta. E espantado,
dize: "Oh, buena donzella, ¿por qué sois assí desamparada?"
E vio debaxo de su cabeça puesta copia de oro e, debaxo
de la pecunia, una carta escripta, e dize: "¡Sepamos qué
contiene la carta!" La cual como abriesse, falló un título
escripto: "Cualquier que este ataúd fallare, pido que haya los
diez marcos de oro e los otros diez dé para la sepultura, ca
este cuerpo muchas lágrimas ha dexado a sus parientes, e
amargos dolores. E si otra cosa fiziere que el dolor demanda,
caya en el postremero día e no sea quien su cuerpo sotierre."
E leídas las cartas, dize a sus siervos: "El postremo dolor que
manda al cuerpo. ¡Júrovos, por la esperança de la mi vida,
que yo gaste en en este enterramiento más que el dolor
manda!"

2 Luego mandó fazer fuego, mas, como se quitava el
cuerpo, sobrevino un discípulo del médico, joven de edad,

21

How the queen washed ashore in Ephesus,
where she came back to life and then entered a convent.

Now, on the third day, the sea's waves cast the coffin onto the shores of Ephesus, a ways away from the house of a doctor named Cerimonis, who was out walking on the shore that day with his disciples and saw the coffin as it was being tossed upon the waves and said to his servants, "Go get that coffin and take it carefully to my house!" Once this was done, the doctor opened it, and he saw a beautiful damsel inside, dressed and ornamented in regal finery, lying as if dead. Taken aback, he said, "Oh, good damsel, why have you been abandoned in this way?" Then he saw the great quantity of gold beneath her head and, beneath the coins, a letter, so he said, "Let us see what this letter says!" Opening the letter, he found that it said, "To whomever may find this coffin, I beg you to keep ten gold marks, and to use the other ten for the burial, for this body has caused many tears and bitter sorrows for its family. If you do anything less than proper mourning requires, may you have no one to bury you on your dying day." Having read those words, the doctor said to his servants, "The body requires its last rites. I vow, on my life, to spend more on this burial than mourning rituals require!"

Then he ordered a pyre be built up, and just as the body was being removed from the coffin, one of the doctor's

279

mas cuanto al ingenio viejo. Aqueste, como viesse el cuerpo fermoso puesto sobre el fuego, mirando a él el maestro dízele: "¡Bien seas venido! Esta hora esperava a ti. Toma la ampolla del ungüento e encima del cuerpo muerto derrama a la sepultura." Vino el mancebo al cuerpo, e quitó las vestiduras del pecho e derramó el ungüento con la mano por todo el cuerpo, e siéntelo en las entrañas vivir, por lo cual, marabillado, el mancebo palpa las venas e las narizes e prueba los labros con sus labros. E assí, sintió la vida en ella luchante con la muerte, e dize a los siervos: "Poned debaxo por cuatro partes cuatro azes lene e temperadamente." E assí aquella sangre que era coajada fue regalada. Lo cual como vio el joven, dixo al maestro: "¡La moça que dizes muerta, vive! E por que más ligeramente me creas, por experiencia satisfaré." Dichas aquestas cosas, tomó la donzella e púsola en su cama. Sobre el pecho de la cual puso la lana mojada en azeite caliente e por todo el cuerpo, de manera que la sangre d'ella que era coajada dentro se descoajó por tiempo, e assí, començó el espíritu por las médulas descender, e assimesmo abiertas las venas, abrió los ojos. E tomando el espíritu, dize: "¿Quién eres tú? ¡No me toques en otra manera que convenga, ca fija soy de rey e muger de rey!"

3   El mancebo, oídas estas cosas, lleno de gozo entró al maestro e dize: "¡Cata, maestro, que vive la moça!" El cual responde: "¡Pruebo la ciencia, la arte alavo, de la prudencia soy maravillado! Oye diligencia de la disciplina, no quieras ser ingrato de tu arte, toma el gualardón, ca esta donzella

disciples, who was young in years but mature in wisdom, arrived. This young man watched as the beautiful body was put on the pyre, and his master looked at him and said, "You have come at a good time! Your time has come. Take this flask of unguent and pour it over the dead body as a burial offering." The young man approached the body, removed the clothes from its chest and spread the unguent with his hands all over the body, and he felt a sign of life stir deep within, which caused him to marvel and check the pulse points and nostrils and touch his lips to the body's lips. Since he could feel the life fighting against death within her, he said to the servants, "Put four torches below the four corners of the body, burning low and gently." The effect was that all the blood that had clotted in the body was softened. When the young man saw what was happening, he said to his master, "The maid you thought was dead is alive! I will show you, so you will have no trouble believing me." Having said these words, he lifted up the maiden and placed her upon the bed. Then he covered her chest and the rest of her body with wool soaked in hot oil, so that all the clotted blood in her body soon began to flow again and the spirit began to move in her marrow and open up her veins, and then she opened her eyes. Coming to, she said, "Who are you? Do not touch me improperly, for I am the daughter of a king and the wife of a king!"

When the young man heard her words, he was filled with joy and went to his master and said, "Look, master, the maid is alive!" His master responded, "I approve of your skills, I applaud your art, I am amazed by your prudence! Look at the results of your diligent study, do not be ungrateful, and accept these gifts for your art, for this damsel carried

mucha pecunia traxo consigo." E assí, mandó aquella con vestiduras e viandas saludables ser recreada e reparada. Después de pocos días, conociendo que ella fuesse fija de rey, llamados sus amigos la adoptó por fija. E ella lo rogava con lágrimas que no se dexasse tocar de alguno, a la cual puso entre los sacerdotes de Diana con las mugeres sagradas por que fuesse guardada sin corrupción.

22

Cómo Apolonio traxo a su fija en Tarsia e
allí la encomendó a su huéspede Estranguilion.

Entre estas, navegando Apolonio con grand luto, por governación divina aplicó a Tarso. E saliendo del navío, pidió la casa de Estranguilion e de su muger, a los cuales, después que saludó, todas sus fortunas les recontó, diziénteles con dolor: "Muerta es mi mujer; empero, su fija queda, de que me gozo. E por ende, assí como en vós confío, el regño perdido, el cual me es guardado, quiero recibir, ni me bolveré al suegro, pues perdí su fija en la mar, mas antes faré obras de mercader. A vós encomiendo mi fija, que con vuestra fija Filomancia sea criada, e que mi fija sea llamada Tarsia. Ítem, la ama de mi muger, que ha nombre Ligóriden, quiero que haya cura de la guarda de mi fija."

splendid riches with her." And then the doctor ordered that she be cured and brought back to health with good clothing and foods. A few days later, in the knowledge that she was the daughter of a king, with all his friends there to witness, the doctor adopted her as a daughter and she begged never to be touched by any man. Rather, she wished to live among the priests of Diana with the holy women, where she would be protected from sin.

22

How Apollonius brought his daughter to Tarsus and
left her there to be raised by his host Stranguillio.

Meanwhile, Apollonius sailed the seas in deep mourning; with God at the helm he landed in Tarsus. When he disembarked, he asked the way to Stranguillio and his wife's home, where, after greeting them, he dolefully recounted all his misfortunes, saying, "My wife is dead, but the daughter that she gave me brings me joy. Therefore, I am putting my trust in you, for I wish to reclaim the kingdom I have lost, but I cannot go back to my father-in-law because I lost his daughter in the sea—I would much rather become a merchant! I entrust my daughter Tarsia to you, please raise her along with your daughter Philomancia. I will also leave my wife's maid Licorides with you, and I want her to be my daughter's nursemaid."

2   Dichas estas cosas, dio la fija a Estranguilion e diole oro, plata e preciosas vestiduras, e juró que nunca faría la barba ni cortaría los cabellos ni unyas fasta que diesse su fija en matrimonio. E aquellos, marabilléntesse del juramento tan grave, tornaron a le prometer de criar con gran diligencia a su fija. E assí, Apolonio, subiente en el navío, se partió para luengas tierras.

23

Cómo a Tarsia pusieron en estudio e después su ama, que la
crió, en su fin reveló la generación e nacimiento de la fija.

Entre tanto, la infanta Tarsia, complidos los v anyos, fue puesta en estudio de las artes liberales en uno con Filomancia, fija d'ellos. E como llegasse a los xiiii anyos, tornando del estudio, falló a su nudriza caída en enfermedad subitánea. E assentántese cerca d'ella, pregunta las causas de su enfermedad, a la cual la ama dize: "¡Oye, fija, mis palabras, e guárdalas en tu coraçón! ¿A quién tienes tú por padre o madre, o de qué tierra piensas que seas?" Dize la infanta: "La tierra es Tarsia; padre, Estranguilio; la madre, Dionisiaden." La ama gemió e dize: "¡Oye, fija, el origen e nacimiento de

Having said these things, Apollonius gave his daughter to 2
Stranguillio, and gave him gold, silver, precious clothes, and
then swore that he would never trim his beard, nor cut his
hair and nails, until he had given his daughter in marriage.
Stranguillio and his wife marveled at such a solemn oath and
promised Apollonius that they would raise his daughter
with the utmost care. And so, Apollonius boarded his ship
and set off for faraway lands.

23

How Tarsia was sent to study, and how her nursemaid
revealed her parentage and birth on her deathbed.

As soon as princess Tarsia had reached the age of five, she
was sent to study the liberal arts along with Philomancia,
the daughter of her foster parents. One day, when she was
fourteen years old, she came home from her studies to find
her nursemaid had suddenly fallen ill. She sat at her bedside
and asked her the cause of her illness, to which the nurse
said, "Listen, child, to my words, and hold them in your
heart! Who do you think is your father or your mother?
What country do you think you are from?" The princess re-
plied, "My country is Tarsus, my father is Stranguillio, my
mother is Dionysias." The nursemaid moaned and said,
"Listen, child, to the origins and birth of your parents, and

tus parientes, e tierra, por que sepas cómo te hayas de haver después de mi muerte! Tu padre se llama Apolonio, e la madre Cleopatra, fija del rey Archistrato, la cual, como parió a ti, luego fue muerta. Tu padre, Apolonio, en un ataúd con aparatos reales la echó en la mar. E grand suma de oro puso debaxo de la cabeça d'ella por que, dondequiera que fuesse echada, aquel oro fuesse en su ayuda. Otrossí, el navío con vientos contrarios, con tu padre lutuoso e tú en la cuna puesta, llegó a esta ciudad, e assí a estos huéspedes, Estranguilion e Dionissiaden, en uno comigo te encomendó Tiro Apolonio, tu padre. E fizo voto de nunca se fazer la barba ni cortar cabellos ni uñas ante que te casasse. E assí, te amonesto que, si después de la mi muerte estos huéspedes que llamas padre e madre alguna injuria por ventura te fizieren, que subas al mercado e ende fallarás la estatua de tu padre estante. E toma aquella e llama que eres fija de aquel cúya es esta estatua, e los ciudadanos, acordándose de los beneficios de tu padre, vengarán la tu injuria." Responde Tarsia: "¡A Dios dó por testigo que, si estas cosas no me huviesses dicho, no supiera en ninguna manera dónde era!"

2   E ellas assí fablando, la ama dio su espíritu, e Tarsia, después que soterró el cuerpo de su ama, por todo el año llorava su muerte. Mas después vestió la primera dignidad e tornó a los estudios liberales. E como de las escuelas se tornasse, no tomava primero vianda ante que el monumento de la ama entrasse, donde entrava trayente una ampolla de vino e, ende estando, llamava a sus padre e madre.

your country, so you will know how to behave after I am dead! Your father is called Apollonius, and your mother Cleopatra, daughter of King Archistrates; she died when you were born. Your father, Apollonius, put her in a coffin adorned with royal finery and cast her into the sea. He also put a large quantity of gold beneath her head so that, wherever she might land, the gold would protect her. After that, while your father mourned and you were in your crib, harsh winds forced the ship to this city, where your father Apollonius put you into Stranguillio and Dionysias's care, leaving me with you. At that time, he vowed never to trim his beard nor cut his hair and his nails until he had married you off. And so, this is my advice to you: if, after my death, your hosts, whom you call father and mother, for some reason do you any harm, go to the marketplace and there you will find the statue of your father. Take hold of it and announce that you are the daughter of the man whose likeness is there, and the citizens will remember all the good things your father did for them and will avenge you." Tarsia responded, "With God as my witness, if you had not told me these things, I would never have known where I came from!"

While the two were speaking of these things, the nurse- 2 maid gave up her spirit, and Tarsia, after having her buried, mourned for a full year. Afterward, Tarsia once again dressed according to her station, and went back to her studies of the liberal arts. Whenever she returned from school, she never touched a bite to eat without first visiting her nursemaid's tomb, where she entered bearing a flask of wine and would honor her father and mother.

24

Cómo Dionisiades con su fija Filomancia
e con Tarsia passava por el mercado,
donde su fija fue motejada de fea.

E passando esto assí, un día passava con Filomancia su fija
por el mercado Dionisiades. E vientes todos los ciudadanos
la fermosura de Tarsia e su ornamento, dixieron: "¡Bienaven-
turado es el padre cuya fija es Tarsia! ¡Mas aquella otra que va
con ella, torpe e fea es!" Dionisiades, como oyó alavar a Tar-
sia e vituperar su fija, buelta en sanya e ira, estando sola
pensó entre sí: "xɪɪɪɪ anyos ha que su padre se fue de aquí e
nunca es venido a la recibir ni ha embiado letras por ella.
¡Pienso que sea muerto! Su ama muerta es, no hay quien pro-
cure por ella; ¡yo mataré a esta, e con sus vestiduras e orna-
mientos decoraré e ornaré a mi fija!"

2   E como ella huviesse pensado esto, vino de la villa un
siervo llamado Teófilo, al cual llamando dize: "Si quieres pe-
cunias, mata a Tarsia." Dize el villano: "¿Qué pecó la virgen
inocente?" Dixo ella: "Es muy mala e, por ende, no me deves
denegar esto. E si no lo fazes, ¡mal te venga por ello!" Dize él:
"¡Dime, senyora, ¿cómo puede ser fecho esto?" Dize ella:
"Su costumbre es, luego que viene de las escuelas, de no
tomar primero vianda ante que entre en el monumento de

24

How Dionysias, her daughter Philomancia,
and Tarsia walked through the market,
where Philomancia was called ugly.

One day, Dionysias was walking through the marketplace with her daughter, Philomancia. All of the citizens looked upon Tarsia's beauty and refinement, saying, "Blessed is the man who is Tarsia's father! But that other girl out walking with her is awkward and ugly!" Dionysias became outraged when she heard how the people were praising Tarsia and insulting her daughter. So, when she was alone, she thought to herself, "It's been fourteen years since Tarsia's father left her here, and he has never come back for her or sent word about her. I think he must be dead! Her nursemaid is dead, Tarsia has no one to defend her, so I will kill her and dress my daughter up in all her clothes and finery!"

With all this in mind, Dionysias called a servant named Theophilus, who had come from the countryside, and said, "If you would like to earn some money, kill Tarsia." The low-born country man asked, "What crime did the innocent virgin commit?" Dionysias said, "She is so evil that you must not deny this request. If you do not do this you will be punished!" He replied, "Tell me, my lady, how can this be done?" She explained, "It is Tarsia's custom to go straight to her nursemaid's tomb when she leaves the schoolroom, without taking any refreshment first; wait for her there with this

su ama, donde le espera con un ponyal e, tomándola de los crines, degüéllala e échala en la mar. E tú recibirás de mí la libertad con grand gualardón."

3   El vílico tomó el punyal, mas gemiendo e plorando iva al monumento, e dixo entre sí: "¡Guay de mí, que no merecí la libertad, salvo por derramamiento de la sangre inocente de la virgen!" La moça, tornante de las escuelas, entró en el monumento con la ampolla del vino, como otras vezes solía. El vílico moviose contra ella e, tomándola de los cabellos, echola en tierra. E queriéndola ferir, dize a él Tarsia: "Oh, Teófile, ¿qué pequé yo contra ti o contra otro alguno por que muera?" Dize el vílico: "Tú no has pecado, mas tu padre, que te dexó con muchos dineros e ornamentos reales." Al cual dize la donzella: "¡Pídote, senyor, de gracia que, si no puedo escapar en alguna manera, que a lo menos me dexes que faga a Dios mi oración!" Dize el aldeano: "¡Faz tu oración, ca esse mesmo Dios sabe que por fuerça te mato!"

dagger, grab her by the hair and slit her throat, then throw her body into the sea. I will reward you with your freedom and a generous sum."

So, the servant took the dagger and went to the tomb, 3 but he was moaning and weeping as he went, and said to himself, "Woe is me! Spilling innocent blood is the price of my freedom!" Just then, the maiden entered the tomb on her way back from her studies, carrying her flask of wine, as she had so many times before. The serving man leaped upon her, grabbed her by the hair, and threw her to the ground. As he was about to strike her, Tarsia said, "Oh, Theophilus, what have I ever done to you or to anyone else? Why should I deserve to die?" The servant said, "You have done nothing, but your father left you with great riches and regal finery." The damsel responded, "I beg of you sir, if there is no escape for me, please at least let me say my prayers to God!" The rustic said, "Say your prayers. God himself knows that I am killing you out of necessity!"

25

Cómo los marineros libraron a Tarsia del poder de Teófilo,
e Estranguilion e su muger creyeron que fuesse muerta,
por que los ciudadanos le fizieron gran planto e
preciosa sepultura.

E como ella estuviesse en oración, venieron unos cossa-
rios; vientes la donzella estar debaxo del yugo de la muerte e
al hombre armado queriente ferir a ella, dixieron llamán-
dolo: "¡Oh, muy cruel bárbaro, perdónala, ca ella es nuestro
robo e no tu vitoria!" El vílico, como esto oyó, escondiose
tras el monumento, fuyendo por la ribera, mas los cossarios
tomaron la virgen e entraron en la mar.

2   El vílico tornó a la señora e dixo: "¡Lo que me mandaste
fecho es! Por ende, me parece que te deves vestir de luto, e
yo contigo, e derramemos lágrimas falsas en el acatamiento
del pueblo, e digamos que es muerta por grave enfermedad."
Como Estranguilion oyó, temor e espanto lo tomó, e dixo:
"Pues dame también vestidura de luto para que llore, porque
de tal maldad soy embuelto. ¡Guay de mí! ¿Qué faré? El pa-
dre de la donzella libró a esta ciudad del peligro de la muerte,
e por causa d'esta ciudad padeció gran peligro en la mar e
sufrió pobreza. ¡Agora el mal le es tornado por el bien! Ca su
fija, que nos encomendó para criar, esta malvada cruel ha
muerto, por lo cual yo soy cegado e no cessaré de llorar
la inocente, e conosco que soy ayuntado a ponçonyosa

25

How the sailors freed Tarsia from Theophilus,
and how Stranguillio and his wife believed she was dead,
causing all the citizens of Tarsus to mourn her and
honor her with a splendid tomb.

Just as Tarsia was praying, a group of corsairs arrived, and seeing that the damsel was about to be slain by the armed man who wanted to stab her, they cried out, "Oh cruel, barbarous man, spare her! Let her be our bounty and not your prize!" No sooner had the servant heard these words than he stole behind the tomb and ran off toward the shore, allowing the corsairs to grab the damsel and set off to sea.

The servant went back to his lady and reported, "I have 2 carried out your orders! Now I think you should dress in mourning, as should I along with you, and we should cry false tears in front of your people; let us tell them that Tarsia died of a grave sickness." Overhearing these plans, Stranguillio became worried and fearful, and said, "Give me mourning clothes as well, because I am implicated in this evilness too. Woe is me! What will I do? The damsel's father saved our city from starving to death and, for the sake of our city, he faced great dangers at sea and suffered poverty. Now we pay him back with evil for all his goodness! He entrusted his daughter to us to raise, and this cruel, evil woman has killed her; I was blind, and now I will never cease weeping for the innocent girl, and I know that I am joined to a

serpiente." E alçando los ojos al cielo, dize: "¡Tú sabes, Senyor Dios, que soy limpio de la sangre de esta Tarsia! ¡Demándala de mi cruel mujer malvada!" E mirante a ella, dize: "¿Cómo afogaste la fija del rey, enemiga de Dios e denuesto de los hombres?"

3   Mas ella e su fija vestiéronse vestiduras de luto e derramaron falsas lágrimas ante los ciudadanos, diziendo: "¡Oh, muy amados ciudadanos, la causa de nuestro clamor es porque Tarsia, esperança de nuestros ojos que vós vistes, súbitamente es muerta, de manera que nos ha dexado tormentos e amargos lloros! La cual con gran lástima havemos enterrado." Entonces fuéronse los ciudadanos donde era figurado el padre e, por los merecimientos del padre e por sus beneficios, ende un sepulcro de arambre le fizieron fabricar.

26

Cómo Tarsia fue vendida a un rufián para el burdel
en la ciudad de Militena.

Mas los ladrones que robaron la donzella vinieron con ella a la ciudad de Militena, donde la ponen a vender entre otras esclavas. Un rufián muy infame e no puro començó de trabajar por la comprar. E assimesmo Atanágora, príncipe de aquella ciudad, viéntela noble e fermosa e sabia, dava por

poisonous snake." Raising his eyes to the heavens, he continued, "You, Lord God, know that I am not stained with Tarsia's blood! Blame it all on my cruel, evil wife!" And, looking at her, he said, "How could you kill the king's daughter, you heretic and insult to humanity?"

Nevertheless, Dionysias and her daughter dressed themselves up in mourning closes and shed false tears in front of the citizens of Tarsus, saying, "Oh most beloved citizens, the cause of our grief is that our dear Tarsia, whom you all knew, has died suddenly, leaving us in bitter torment and sorrow! In our great lamentation, we have buried her." All the citizens then went to where the statue of Tarsia's father stood and, grateful for all the good he had done, they erected a bronze tomb in her memory. 3

26

How Tarsia was sold to a pimp for the brothel
in the city of Mytilene.

Meanwhile, the thieves who stole the damsel came with her to the city of Mytilene, where they put her up for sale with other enslaved women. A disreputable and immoral pimp set out to buy her. However, Athenagoras, the prince of the city, seeing that she was noble, beautiful, and wise,

ella diez pieças de oro. El rufián dixo: "¡Yo daré xx!" Atanágora dize: "¡Yo xxx!" El rufián pújala en xl, Atanágora la sube en l. E assí, de grado en grado subieron fasta que el rufián prometió c sistercias de oro, anyadiendo más: que si alguno más ofrecía, él daría x pieças allende del que más dava. Viendo esto, dixo Atanágora: "Si yo profío contender e profiar con el rufián, por que haya una sierva havré de vender muchas. Dexar lo he que la compre, e como la pusiere al burdel, entraré primero a ella e gozaré de la flor de su virginidad. E tanto me valerá como si yo la huviesse comprado."

2 ¿Qué más? Como la huvo comprado, el rufián levola al templo, donde tenían al dios Príapo ornado de oro e de gemas, e dízele: "¡Moça, adora a este!" E dize ella: "¿E por ventura tú eres lapsadano?" El rufián dize: "¿Por qué lo dizes?" "Por cuanto los lapsadanos adoran al dios Príapo." El rufián dize: "¿No sabes tú, mezquina, que hayas caído en casa de rufián avariento?" La donzella, como oyó esto, echada a sus pies comiença dezir: "¡Oh, senyor, have merced de mi virginidad e no pongas este mi cuerpo en tan torpe título!" Responde el rufián: "¿No sabes tú que cerca el cruel rufián ni ruegos ni lágrimas valen?"

also bid ten gold coins for her. The pimp said, "I'll give twenty!" Athenagoras said, "I bid thirty!" The pimp upped the bid to forty, and Athenagoras raised it to fifty. And so, they went on raising their bids until the pimp had promised one hundred gold coins, and then he added even more: however much anyone bid, he would give ten more gold coins. At this, Athenagoras said to himself, "If I keep competing and bidding against the pimp, I will have to sell many serving girls in order to have just this one. I'll let him buy her, and once he's put her in the brothel, I will be the first to go to her and enjoy the flower of her virginity. I will profit from her just as much as if I had bought her myself."

What more can I say? The pimp bought Tarsia and 2 brought her to the temple, where a golden image of the Priapus stood, covered with gemstones, and he ordered the maiden, "Worship him!" She replied, "Are you, by chance, from Lampsacus?" "Why do you ask?" said the pimp. "Because the Lampsacans worship the god Priapus." The pimp said, "Don't you see, wretched girl, you have landed in the house of a greedy pimp?" When she heard his response, the damsel threw herself at his feet and spoke these words, "Oh, my lord, have mercy on my virginity and do not condemn my body to such ill repute!" The pimp replied, "Don't you know that neither begging nor tears can move a cruel pimp?"

27

Cómo Tarsia escapó sin ser corrompida de
Atanágora e de todo el pueblo.

Entonces llamó al huésped e vílico de las moças e dízele:
"Esta moça sea ornada de vestiduras preciosas e séale escrito
tal título: 'Cualquier que a Tarsia deflorare, media libra dará,
e después a sueldo estará.'" El vílico fizo como le fue man-
dado. La donzella al tercero día, con instrumentos e juglares
diversos, compañada de gran gente fue levada al burdel,
donde Atanágora, cubierta la cabeça, entra a ella primero.

2   Tarsia, viéndose en tanta vergüença, cae a los pies d'él e
dize assí: "¡Senyor, have piadad de mí, por Dios nuestro se-
ñor, por el cual te requiro que no me quieras violar! E resiste
a tu ilícito apetito, e oime mis fortunas, desaventuras, e la
generación donde desciendo considera diligentemente." Al
cual como todos sus casos huviesse contado, el príncipe,
confundido e movido de piedad, dize: "Yo he una fija seme-
jante a ti, de la cual temo otros tales actos e casos. Por ende,
soy contento de te non ofender." E diole xx dineros de oro,
diziendo: "¿Qué tienes, más que la estima fecha de tu virgi-
nidad? Fabla a los que a ti vendrán como a mí e serás librada."
La donzella con lágrimas dize: "¡Yo agradezco a tu piedad e
pido que no cuentes a alguno lo que de mí oíste!" Atanágora
dixo: "¡No recontaré sino a mi fija, por que se escarmiente
e se guarde!" E assí partió d'ella llorando, al cual dende

27

How Tarsia escaped corruption at the hands of
Athenagoras and the whole city.

The pimp called for the brothel keeper and manager of
his girls and said to him "Dress this girl up in fine clothing
and advertise her with these words: 'Whoever wants to de-
flower Tarsia must pay half a pound of gold; after that, her
price will be one gold coin.'" The brothel keeper obeyed.
Three days later, the damsel was paraded to the brothel,
accompanied by music, many jugglers, and a large crowd.
Athenagoras, his head covered, was the first to enter.

Tarsia, seeing herself in such a shameful position, fell at   2
his feet and said, "My lord, for God's sake, have pity on me, I
beg of you, do not rape me! Resist your sinful appetites, and
listen to the story of my misadventures and carefully con-
sider my noble birth." When she had recounted the tale of
her misfortunes, the prince was overcome with compassion
and said, "I have a daughter just like you. Since I would not
want anything like this to happen to her, I am happy to leave
you untouched." He gave her twenty gold coins, saying,
"What else do you have, other than the honor of your vir-
ginity? Speak to the other men who come to you in the same
way you did to me, and you will be safe." The damsel cried,
"I thank you for your mercy and I beg you not to tell anyone
my story!" Athenagoras said, "I will tell no one but my
daughter, to teach her a lesson and to keep her safe!" As he

saliente encontró otro, e dízele: "¿Cómo te ha contecido con la moça?" Responde el príncipe: "¡No puede ser mejor!" E él era triste.

3 Entró el otro mancebo, e la moça cerró la puerta, a la cual pregunta el mancebo: "¿Cuánto te dio el príncipe?" Respondió la moça: "XL dineros de oro." E aquel dize: "¡Toma libra entera de oro!" El príncipe oyendo esto, dize: "¡Cuanto más le darás, tanto más llorará!" La moça tomó los dineros e, echándose en tierra, le començó contar sus casos e fortunas. El mancebo, turbado, dízele: "¡Levántate, senyora! Hombres somos, e todos sometidos a casos e venturas." E dichas estas cosas salió, e vio Atanágora riendo, e dízele: "Grande hombre eres, ¿no tienes a quién derrames lágrimas sino a mí?" E assí entravan, por que estas palavras a alguno no fuessen manifestadas, e començaron esperar a otros que venían. E entravan muchos, e todos salían llorando. Después ofreció el dinero al rufián, diziente: "¡He aquí el precio de la mi virginidad!" Dize el rufián: "Cata que, de aquí adelante, cada día me has de responder con tanto."

4 Otro día, oyendo que aún estava virgen, con sanya llama al huéspede d'ellas, diziendo: "¡Tráela para ti e tú mesmo corrómpela!" A la cual dize el vílico: "Dime si eres virgen." Responde ella: "En tanto que Dios quiere, virgen soy." Pregúntala el amo: "¿Pues dónde has havido tanto dinero?" La moça dixo: "Con muchas lágrimas rogué a los que a mí entravan, declarándoles las mis fortunas e casos, que huviessen misericordia de mi virginidad." E assimesmo, echándose a sus pies, dízele: "¡Have merced de mí, señor, e socorre a mí,

was leaving her, with tears in his eyes, he met another man, who asked, "How did it go with the girl?" The prince replied, "It couldn't have been better!" Yet he was downcast.

The other young man entered, and when the maiden 3 closed the door, he asked, "How much did the prince pay you?" The maiden responded, "Forty gold coins." He said, "Take a whole pound of gold!" Overhearing this, the prince said, "The more you give her the more she will weep!" The maiden took the money, threw herself to the floor, and began to tell the young man of her misfortunes and adventures. The young man was troubled and said to her, "Get up, my lady! Like all mankind, we are all subject to chance and misfortunes." And, having said these words, he left her. He then saw Athenagoras laughing, and said to him, "You are a great man—don't you have anyone else to tell your troubles to?" And the two hid together so that their conversation would not be overheard as they waited for other men to enter. Many men entered and they all left in tears. Afterward, Tarsia gave the money to the pimp, saying, "Here is the price of my virginity!" The pimp said, "Look now, from now on, you must give me the same amount every day."

The next day, however, the pimp learned that Tarsia was 4 still a virgin, and he angrily called the brothel keeper and said, "Take her yourself and defile her!" The brothel keeper said to Tarsia, "Tell me if you are a virgin." She responded, "I will be a virgin for as long as God grants it." The keeper asked, "Then how have you earned so much money?" The maiden answered, "Weeping, I begged the men who came to me to have mercy on my virginity and told them the history of my misfortunes." And in just the same way, she threw herself at the brothel keeper's feet and said, "Have mercy on

que soy fija de rey e captiva, e no me quieras corromper!"
Dize él: "El rufián es avariento, no sé si podrás escapar virgen." E ella torna: "Yo soy enseñada en estudios de las artes liberales, e no menos sé tañer e cantar por música. Liévame al mercado e ende podrás oír mi saber. Propónganme cuestiones ante el pueblo e yo las soltaré. E en esta arte podré ganar dineros de cada día." Responde el vílico: "¡A mí bien me plaze esso!"

5   E assí, la levó a la plaça, donde todo el pueblo se ayuntó a ver la donzella, la cual comiença entrar en las elocuencias de los estudios e demanda serle puestas cuestiones, e las asuelve clara e elegantemente; e assí, por esta manera mucha pecunia recibió del pueblo. E d'esta manera Atanágora la guardó en su virginidad, e dende le donó muchas cosas e la encomendó como fija.

28

Cómo Apolonio vino en Tarsia por su fija e,
sabida la muerte d'ella, cómo de gran pesar
e angustia descendió baxo del trillado
de la nao, donde no quería salir.

En este tiempo vino Apolonio su padre, passado el año XIIII, e aplicó en la ciudad de Tarso, e preguntó por la casa

me, my lord, and help me! I am the daughter of a king and a captive, please do not defile me!" He said, "The pimp is greedy, I don't know if you will be able to remain a virgin." She responded, "I am well educated in the study of the liberal arts, and no less in playing music and singing. Take me to the marketplace, and there you will hear how talented I am. Set questions to me in front of the crowds, and I will solve them. That's how I can earn money every day." The brothel keeper said, "It would be my pleasure!"

And so, the brothel keeper took the damsel to the town square, where all the people gathered to see her perform all her knowledge eloquently, and solve the questions put to her clearly and elegantly, earning a great deal of money from the crowds in the process. Athenagoras watched over her and protected her virginity, all the while showering her with gifts as if she were his own daughter. 5

28

How Apollonius returned to Tarsus for his daughter,
and how, after learning of her death, filled with great pain
and anguish, he took refuge in the lower hold
of his ship and refused to leave.

Meanwhile, Tarsia's father Apollonius returned to the city of Tarsus after his fourteen-year absence, and asked for

de Estranguilion. Al cual como vio su huéspede, vase para su muger aquexosamente e comiénçale dezir: "¡Dixísteme que Apolonio era muerto! ¡Sepas que es vivo e viene a levar su fija! Por tanto, piensa qué razón daremos de la donzella." La Dionisiades dize: "Cumple que tú e yo tomemos vestiduras de luto e lloraremos ante él. E sé que seremos creídos que su fija sea muerta por su muerte natural."

2   Dende a poco viene Apolonio a su casa e, como los vio vestidos de luto e llorantes, pregúntales: "¿Por qué en mi recibimiento derramáis lágrimas? Yo creo," dize, "que estas lágrimas non son vuestras, mas mías." Responde la muger: "¡Quisiera que otro e no yo ni mi marido te huviera dicho esto que te quiero dezir! Tarsia tu fija es defunta súbitamente." Apolonio oyente esto, todo su cuerpo començó a tremer, de manera que por grand tiempo estuvo desmayado. Finalmente, mirando la muger, dize: "Oh, huéspede, si mi fija, como tú dizes, es defunta, ¿por ventura la pecunia e las vestiduras no menos perecieron?" Respondió la muger: "Algunas quedaron e muchas son gastadas. ¡Créenos que creímos que tu fija fallasses viva! E por que sepas que te dezimos verdad, testimonio tenemos, ca los cibdadanos de la cibdad, acordándose de tus beneficios recibidos, en la ribera cercana fizieron a tu fija monumento de arambre, el cual puedes veer."

3   Apolonio, creyendo que ella fuesse muerta, dize a los criados: "Tomad estas cosas que quedaron a la nao. Yo quiero andar a ver el sepulcro de mi fija." Leyó el título, assí como suso es dicho; dende, estando casi fuera de sí, maldiziendo

Stranguillio's house. When Stranguillio saw him coming, he worriedly approached his wife and said, "You told me Apollonius was dead! Well, you should know that he is alive and has come back for his daughter! You must think up some story we can tell him about the damsel." Dionysias said, "All we need to do is put on our mourning clothes and weep when he comes. I know he will believe us when we say that his daughter died of natural causes."

Apollonius soon arrived at their house, and when he saw 2 Stranguillio and Dionysias dressed in mourning and crying, he asked, "Why does my arrival cause your tears to flow? I believe," he said, "these tears are not yours but my own." Dionysias responded, "If only someone else, and not I or my husband, could tell you what I must say! Your daughter Tarsia died suddenly." When Apollonius heard the news, his whole body began to tremble and he fell into a swoon for a long time. At last, looking at the woman, he said, "Oh, hostess, if, as you say, my daughter is dead, by chance have her wealth and finery perished as well?" The woman responded, "Some of her things are left, but many are gone. Trust us, we thought you would return to find your daughter alive and well! As evidence of the truth of all we say, you can see how the citizens of our city, recalling all of the good you did for them, erected a bronze monument to your daughter by the seashore."

Apollonius, in his belief that Tarsia was dead, said to his 3 servants, "Take her things that are left and stow them in the ship. I want to go to see my daughter's tomb." Upon reading the abovementioned words written upon the tomb, Apollonius was beside himself. Damning his own eyes, he said,

sus ojos propios, dixo assí: "¡Oh, ojos crueles! ¿No pudistes derramar lágrimas sobre mi fija?" E dichas estas cosas, fuese al navío e dize a sus familiares: "¡Lançadme, ruego, en la fondura de la mar, ca deseo en las ondas dar mi espíritu!"

4   E navegando para Tiro con prosperidad, súbitamente se mudó el tiempo e començaron los navíos con la grand tormenta peligrar. Mas, todos rogantes a Dios, a la ciudad de Mitilena, donde estava su fija, aportaron. El governador de las naves, como se vio fuera del peligro, mandó fazer grandes alegrías. E dize Apolonio: "¿Qué son de alegría ha tocado mis orejas?" Respondió el maestre: "¡Alégrate, señor, ca oy este día se celebrarán nuestras fiestas del nacimiento!" Apolonio dixo: "Todos celebren fiesta salvo yo, ca la mi pena e dolor vasta. A mis criados mándoles dar diez áureos, e compren lo que querrán e fagan fiesta. E cualquier que llamare a mí o fiziere alegría, yo le quebrantaré las piernas." E assí, el despensero traxo las cosas necessarias a la nao, mas como la nave de Apolonio fuesse más honrada de todas, con grand convite, mejor que los otros, celebran la fiesta los marineros de Apolonio.

5   Acaeció que este mesmo día vino Atanágora, que amava a Tarsia, a ver los navíos. E dize a los amigos, viendo la nao de Apolonio: "Este navío me plaze más que otro porque lo veo muy bien e conveniblemente ornado e atabiado." Los marineros, como oyeron alavar su navío, dixiéronle: "¡Señor, suplicámosvos queráis subir en la nuestra nao!" Él responde: "¡A mí plaze!" E, con coraçón alegre, subió e se assentó entre ellos, e puso diez áureos en la mesa, e dixo: "He aquí por que no convidéis de gracia." Ellos dixeron: "¡Señor, muchas gracias te damos!" E como el príncipe viesse todos los del navío

"Oh, cruel eyes! Why can you not shed a tear for my daughter?" Having said these words, he returned to his ship and said to his company, "Throw me into the depths of the sea, because I wish to commend my spirit to the waves!"

As they were sailing with good winds back to Tyre, the sea 4 suddenly changed and a rough storm endangered the ships. However, thanks to all of their prayers, they were delivered to Mytilene, where Apollonius's daughter was. Seeing they were out of danger, the ships' governor ordered a great celebration. Apollonius said, "What sounds of happiness have reached my ears?" The shipmaster responded, "Be glad, my lord, because today we celebrate a feast day!" Apollonius said, "Let everyone else celebrate, but my pain and sorrow are enough for me. As for my servants, I will give them ten gold coins, so they may buy what they want and celebrate the feast. But I will break the legs of whoever calls me or tries to make merry with me." The ship's bursar brought all the necessary things to the ship, and since Apollonius's ship was the grandest of all, the feast celebrated by his sailors was better than all the rest.

It so happened that that very day Athenagoras, who was 5 in love with Tarsia, went to see the ships. When he saw Apollonius's ship, he said to his friends, "I like this ship better than all the others because I can see it is well made and fittingly decorated and ornamented." The sailors, hearing their ship praised, said to Athenagoras, "My lord, we beg you to come aboard our ship!" He responded, "I would be delighted!" And, with a happy heart, he alighted and sat among the sailors, placed ten gold coins on the table, and said, "Take this, so you do not have to host me for free." They said, "My lord, we are very grateful!" Since the prince saw

assentantes, dize: "¿Quién es de vosotros el señor del navío?" Respóndele el governador: "El señor con luto está, baxo yaze, e pensamos que él morirá de pesar porque ha perdido en el mar la muger e la fija en tierra ajena."

6   Atanágora dize a un siervo que havía nombre Ardalio: "Por que abaxes al señor del navío e le digas que el príncipe de la ciudad le ruega que salga de las tiniebras a la luz, quiero te dar dos sueldos." Dixo el siervo: "No puedo con tus dineros las piernas reparar; por ende, busca otro. Ca él mandó que a cualquier que lo llamasse le serían quebrantadas las piernas." Dixo Atanágora: "Esta ley sobre vosotros puso e no a mí, e yo me descenderé. Solamente me dezid cómo se llama." Dízenle: "Apolonio se llama." Oído este nombre, dize entre sí: "E Tarsia llamó a su padre Apolonio."

7   E assí, descendió a él, al cual como vio con barba larga, dizo con boz baxa: "Dios te salve, Apolonio." Él, como oyó su nombre, pensando que alguno de los suyos lo llamava, mirándolo con cara turbada, vio hombre no conocido, honesto e fermoso; e assí, se refrenó. E dízele el príncipe: "Sé que te marabillas por yo, no conocido, te llame por tu nombre. Sépasme ser príncipe d'esta cibdad, llamado Atanágora. Descendía la ribera por mirar las naves; entre todas he visto este tu navío adreçado e ornado. E assí, desseándote veer, subí en él convidado de los marineros e pregunté por el señor. Respondieron que eras en grand tristeza e luto; por esto he descendido, por sacarte de tiniebras a luz, esperando que Dios te dará, después del luto e tristeza, alegría." Apolonio alçó la cabeça, e dize: "¿Quién eres tú, señor? Sube arriba, e

them all seated there, he asked, "Which one of you is the lord of this ship?" The helmsman replied, "The lord lies below in mourning and we think he might die from sorrow, because he has lost his wife to the sea and his daughter to a strange land."

Athenagoras said to a servant named Ardalius, "Why 6 don't you go down to the lord of the ship and beg him to come out of the shadows and into the light? I will give you two coins." The servant said, "I cannot fix my legs with your two coins, so ask someone else. The lord forbade anyone to speak with him, or else their legs would be broken." Athenagoras said, "This rule applies to you all but not to me, so I will go down. Just tell me his name." They said, "He is called Apollonius." Hearing this name, Athenagoras said to himself, "Tarsia called her father Apollonius."

So, Athenagoras went down into the hold and said in a 7 low voice to the long-bearded man he saw there, "God save you, Apollonius." Apollonius, thinking it was one of his men calling his name, looked up in anger, but saw an honorable and good-looking man that was unknown to him, so he curbed himself. The prince said, "I know you are surprised to hear a stranger call you by your name. I am the prince of this city; my name is Athenagoras. I came down to the shore to look at the ships, and saw how yours was so well outfitted and ornamented. Wishing to see you, I was invited aboard by your sailors and asked for the lord of the ship. They told me that you were suffering great sadness and mourning, and that is why I have come down to take you out of the shadows and into the light, in the hopes that God will give you happiness after your mourning and sadness." Apollonius raised his head and said, "Whoever you are, my lord, go back

alégrate, e vete en paz, ca yo no soy digno de comer ni ale-
grar, mas antes no quiero más vivir." Atanágora, confundido,
subió a la compaña, diziente: "¡No puedo con vuestro señor
que salga a la luz!"

29

Cómo Atanágora fizo llamar a Tarsia e le prometió
muchos dones si a Apolonio provocasse a alegría.

E pensando qué fiziesse para que revocasse su propósito
de muerte, llamó uno de sus moços, diziéndole: "Vete al ru-
fián e dile que me envíe a Tarsia; porque ella ha saber e fabla
amorosa, por ventura podrá estorvar que tal hombre no
muera." Venida Tarsia a la mar, dixo Atanágora: "Ven acá
agora, Tarsia, e piensa en la arte de tus estudios para que
consueles el señor del navío, que está en teniebras e tristeza
por la muerte de su muger e fija. E procura por le fazer salir a
luz, por que, mediante tú, Dios por ventura bolverá su tris-
teza en gozo. E si esto acabas, yo te mando xxx libras de oro
e otras tantas de plata; e más, dentro de xxx días yo te redi-
miré del rufián."

2   La doncella oyente esto, con grand constancia descendió
para él, e con boz húmil lo saludó, diziendo: "Dios te salve,
quienquier que seas, e alégrate, ca sepas que una virgen que

up, be happy, go in peace, for I am not worthy of feasting or rejoicing; I would rather die." Athenagoras, bewildered, went back up to the company, saying, "I cannot convince your lord to come into the light!"

29

How Athenagoras called for Tarsia and promised
to reward her richly if she could make Apollonius happy.

Athenagoras, pondering how to convince Apollonius to abandon his plans to die, called one of his servants and ordered, "Go to the pimp's house and tell him to send Tarsia to me; since she is wise and speaks sweetly, she might be able to prevent the death of such a man." When Tarsia arrived at the port, Athenagoras said, "Come here now, Tarsia, and consider how you might use all your learning to console the lord of this ship, who is overcome by the shadows and sorrows caused by the deaths of his wife and daughter. Make sure you bring him into the light; perhaps God will use you to turn his sadness to joy. If you can cure him, I will give you thirty pounds of gold and another thirty of silver, and what is more, in thirty days, I will free you from the pimp."

When the damsel heard this, she went to Apollonius 2 straightaway, and, speaking modestly, greeted him: "God save you, whoever you may be, and be happy, because a

su virginidad entre grandes peligros ha guardado te saluda."
E dende començó con boz suave e honesta por metros can-
tar, con tan grand dulçor que Apolonio se marabillava. E
dixo cantando estos metros que se siguen:

3   "Morando entre vilezas, no me tocan algunas,
     ca no sabe la rosa violarse de espinas.
     Cayera el robador e ferido de alguno,
     levada soy al lenón no corrupta de ninguno.
     Las llagas me dexarían e de llorar cessasse
     si por vía alguna mis padres conociesse.
     Fija de rey e reina e sola só yo nombrada,
     confío por alto Dios sea por tiempo reparada.
     Por que dexes, suplico, el lloro con la tristura,
     e salirte a luz convides, quitada la rencura,
     ca Dios omnipotente, criador e governador,
     no dexará tus lágrimas assí passar sin honor."

4   A estas cosas Apolonio alçó los ojos e, como vio la don-
     cella, gemió e dixo: "¡Huay de mí, mezquino! ¿En cuánto
     lucharé? Gracias fago a tu prudencia e nobleza. Esta palabra
     te dó, que yo me acordaré de ti cuando me convenirá alegrar
     e fuere alçado en las fuerças de mi regño. Por ventura, como
     dizes, eres descendiente de linaje real e serás a los nacimien-
     tos de tus progenitores representada. Por agora, toma cient
     pieças e vete en paz. E no me infestes, ca de nuevo luto e
     miseria renovada me desfaga."

5   La donzella, recebidos los dineros, comiença ir, e dize a
     ella Atanágora: "¿Dónde, Tarsia, sin efecto has trabajado?

virgin who has preserved her virginity in the face of great dangers has come to greet you." And then she began to sing in a soft and measured voice, verses of such sweetness that Apollonius was struck with wonder. Singing, she intoned the following verses:

> "I live among base crimes, but none touch me, 3
> because the rose cannot be violated by her thorns.
> The thief fell, struck down by another;
> I was given to a pimp, but corrupted by no one.
> My wounds would heal and my tears cease,
> if only I could somehow know my parents.
> I am called the only daughter of a king and a queen;
> I trust that in time God on high will restore me.
> Why do you not end your sorrowful crying? I beseech
> you
> and bid you come into the light with all your rancor
> gone;
> for omnipotent God, creator and governor,
> will not allow your tears to flow without honor."

Apollonius looked up in response and, seeing the girl, 4 sobbed, "Alas, woe is me! How much longer must I suffer? I thank you for your prudence and nobility. I give you my word, I will remember you when my happiness returns, and I am once again lifted up to my proper station in my kingdom. If you are, as you say, descended from a royal line, you will be recognized as their heir. For now, take these hundred coins and go in peace. Do not plague me anymore, because I am once again undone by grief and misery."

Having received the money, the damsel took her leave, 5 and Athenagoras said to her, "How is it, Tarsia, that all your

¿No pudiste fazer misericordia e socorrer al hombre que se quiere matar?" Responde Tarsia: "Todo cuanto pudi fize, mas dándome cient libras me rogó que lo dexasse." Dixo Atanágora: "Yo te daré dozientas; e vuelve, e tórnale lo que te ha dado. E dile 'Salud tuya busco yo, non tu pecunia.'"

6   Descendiente Tarsia, assentose cerca d'él; dízele: "Si assí quieres que passe, a lo menos déxame disputar contigo, e si tú soltares mis cuestiones, iré. E si no, dexar te he tu dinero." Estonces Apolonio, por no tornar a tomar la pecunia que havía dado, e non menos por no negar de oír las palabras e cuestiones de la donzella prudente, dize: "Maguer en mis males ninguna cura de remedio espere salvo llorar e plañir, mas por que no caresca del ornamento de tus palabras, dime lo que quieres preguntar, e apártate. E pídote que me des espacio para llorar."

7   Dize Tarsia: "Oídme, señor, esta cuestión:

Casa es en tierras, a nós suena cerrada.
El huéspede, sonante ella, no murmura nada;
ambos corren, él e ella, juntos una vegada."

E dize: "Si rey eres, como dizes, conviénete ser más prudente que yo; por ende, suelta la cuestión." Dize Apolonio: "Por que sepas que no miento: la casa que en la tierra suena la onda es; el huéspede callado es el pez, el cual con su casa corre."

8   "Ítem," dize ella, "respóndeme a esta otra problema:

work was in vain? Why were you unable to do him a kindness and help the man who would die?" Tarsia responded, "I did everything within my power, but he gave me one hundred pounds of gold and begged me to leave him be." Athenagoras said, "I will give you two hundred; now go back and give him back what he gave you. Tell him, 'I want your well-being, not your money.'"

Tarsia went back to Apollonius and sat down by his side,   6 saying, "If you insist on behaving in this way, at least let me talk with you, and if you can solve my riddles, I will go away. If you cannot, I will give you back your money." Then Apollonius, not wanting to take back the money he had given her, and no less because he did not want to refuse to listen to the wise damsel's words and riddles, said, "Even though I can only hope for the remedy of tears and mourning for my troubles, I want to hear your eloquent words, so ask me your riddles, and then leave me be. I beg you to leave me in peace to mourn."

Tarsia said, "Listen, my lord, to this riddle: 7

There is a house in the land, which resounds; it is closed
   to us.
Its guest keeps silent, while the house sings,
but they both run together, side by side."

She continued, "If you are a king, as you say, you should be wiser than I am, so solve the riddle." Apollonius said, "To prove to you that I am no liar: the house that sings in the land is the waves; the silent guest is a fish, that runs along with its house."

"Here is another one," she said. "Solve this enigma: 8

Fija soy de la foresta, fermosa e ligera,
levada, de caterva estipada, por la ribera,
corro en muchos viajes, mas no dexo carrera."

Dize Apolonio: "Si me fuesse lícito, yo te mostraría muchas cosas que no sabes. Como responderé a tus cuestiones, de una cosa me marabillo: como seas en tierna edad, ¿de qué manera eres así enseñada de prudencia marabillosa? Ca el árbol estipado de catervas, corriente muchas carreras e vías, no dexante pisadas algunas, es la nave."

9   "Ítem," añade la donzella, "otra cuestión assí":

"Por ruedas e por casas aquel passa ileso,
al cual ninguno quita natural calor incluso,
más aptamente que casa vacuo huéspede pienso.
Si el planto no mudas, arderías inculpuso."

Dixo el Apolonio: "Entra en el baño, donde de una parte e de otra se levantan las tablas. La casa desnuda, en la cual no hay cosa alguna, es el huéspede desnudo, e desnudo sudará."

10   E como estas e otras semejantes cosas fablassen, la donzella començó a abraçar Apolonio, diziente: "¡Señor, oye la boz de la rogante, mira a la virgen, ca tal hombre morir, cosa desaguisada e inhumana es! Si la muger la cual desseas Dios por su gracia te restituyesse e la fija que dizes que es defunta fallasses, por el grand gozo convernía que viviesses." Apolonio, oyendo estas palabras, fue buelto en saña, e assí, levantántese, ferió la donzella con el pie, la cual cayó del golpe e, rompidas las maxillas, començóle salir sangre. E turbada,

I am the daughter of the forest, lovely and light;
I am borne along the shore filled with multitudes,
I travel many roads, but leave no trace."

Apollonius replied, "If only it were fitting, I would teach you many things you do not know. Even though I will answer your riddles, one thing surprises me: how is it one so young could be so filled with marvelous wisdom? The tree filled with multitudes, that travels many roads and byways without leaving a single footprint, is a ship."

"Here is another riddle," the damsel continued: 9

"It passes unharmed through rounds and houses,
and no one can steal its natural heat;
it is more fitting for the guest than the house to be
    empty.
If you do not stop your mourning, you will burn in
    innocence."

Apollonius replied: "Enter a bathhouse, where on each side the boards are raised to allow the heat to pass through. The empty house, where there is nothing at all, is the naked guest who, naked, will sweat in the bath."

When they had exchanged more riddles and answers, and   10
talked of similar things, the damsel went to embrace Apollonius, saying, "My lord, listen to my beseeching voice, look at this virgin, for it is senseless and inhuman for a man like you to die! You should live, if only for the chance of great joy, that God might bring back the wife you love and the daughter you say is dead." Hearing these words, Apollonius grew angry, rose up, and kicked the damsel, who fell to the floor and began to bleed from the cuts on her cheeks. Upset, she

començó llorar, diziendo assí: "¡Oh, Dios, criador de los cielos, vee la mi aflición! Yo fui nacida en la fortuna e tempestad de la mar: dentro, mi madre fue defunta de dolores del parto, e fuele negada la sepultura en tierra; en un ataúd con ornamento real con xx marcos de oro fue lançada en la mar. Yo, mezquina, fui de mi padre encomendada a Estranguilion e a su muger, con mucha pecunia e honradas e reales vestiduras, e fui mandada matar del esclavo d'ellos. Finalmente, pidí de gracia para rogar a Dios ante que me matasse, e estando en esto, de los ladrones cossarios sobrevenientes fui presa, e aquel que me quería matar fuyó. E agora soy traída e vendida en este lugar, de donde soy venida aquí. ¡Dios cuando le plazerá me torne a mi padre Apolonio!"

30

En qué manera Apolonio conoció su fija en
la narración que fizo de sus nacimiento e fechos,
e cómo la abraçó con gozo.

Oídas todas estas palabras e señales muy ciertas, llamó Apolonio con grand boz, e dixo: "¡Oh, Señor misericordioso, el cual miras el cielo e el abismo, e todos los secretos manifiestas, bendito sea el tu nombre!" E assí, se echó sobre su

broke into tears, saying "Oh God, creator of the heavens, see how I suffer! I was born in a stormy tempest at sea: my mother, aboard the ship, was killed by the birth pains, and was denied a burial on land; she was thrown into the sea in a coffin bearing the royal seal and twenty gold marks. And I, in my misfortune, was left by my father, along with a great deal of money as well as rich and regal clothing, in Stranguillio and his wife's care, and they ordered their slave to kill me. In the end, I asked him to let me pray before killing me, and while I was praying, corsair thieves came and kidnapped me, and the slave who wanted to kill me ran away. And then I was brought to this place and sold, and that is why I am here with you today. God, let it be your will to return me to my father Apollonius!"

30

How Apollonius recognized his daughter in
the story she told of her birth and deeds,
and how he joyfully embraced her.

Once Apollonius had heard Tarsia's words and the clear evidence of her identity, he cried out in a booming voice, "Oh, merciful lord God, who looks over heaven and hell, and makes all secret things known, blessed be your name!" Then, in his great happiness, he threw himself into his

fija, abraçando e besándola de grand alegría, llorando de
gozo. E dize: "¡Oh, muy dulce mi fija, sola meitad de mi
ánima! ¡No muera yo por amor de ti, por la cual quería mo-
rir!" E dende llamó a sus amigos e familiares, diziendo:
"¡Agora han havido remedio mis dolores e lloros, porque he
fallado la que havía perdido, es a saber, a mi fija muy amada!"

2   Oyendo este clamor, corrieron para él sus criados e ami-
gos, e fue entre ellos Atanágora príncipe. E, descendientes
a él, falláronlo llorante por grand plazer, echado sobre el
cuello de su fija, diziente: "¡He aquí mi fija, la cual llorava!
¡Ya, mis amigos amados, quiero vivir!" E todos començaron
de llorar de goço con él. Entonces Apolonio, levantántese,
quitadas las vestiduras de luto, vestiose de otras limpias e
decentes. E dizíanle todos: "¡Oh, senyor, cómo te semeja
mucho tu fija! ¡Aunque otra experiencia no fuesse, la seme-
jança sola bastaría para provar que ella sea tu fija!" Entonces
la fija, por muchas vezes besando al padre, dixo: "¡Oh, padre
muy amado, alavado sea Dios, que me dio gracia que te pu-
diesse veer, e vivir e morir contigo!" E dende le recontó
cómo fue comprada del rufián, puesta en el burdel, e de qué
manera Dios su virginidad conservó.

3   Oyente esto todo, Atanágora, por que no diesse aquella
fija a otro en matrimonio, suplicó con grand reverencia a
Apolonio, diziendo: "¡Por parte de Dios vivo te requiro, el
cual te ha restituído a la fija, que no la des a otro en muger
sino a mí! Ca yo soy príncipe d'esta cibdad, con mi ayuda ha
guardado su virginidad, e por mí mediante ha conocido a ti,
su padre." Entonces Apolonio dize: "¡No puedo ser a ti con-
trario, ca muchas cosas por mi fija fiziste! Por ende, a mí

daughter's arms and kissed her, shedding happy tears. He said, "Oh, my sweet only daughter, you are half of my soul! Now I will not die for the love of you, when I thought I would die!" He called to his friends and company, saying, "My sorrows and tears are now remedied, because I have found what I had lost, my beloved daughter!"

All his servants and friends, along with Athenagoras, 2 came running down into the hold of the ship when they heard the clamor. They found Apollonius crying with happiness, embracing his daughter, saying, "This is the daughter that I was mourning! Now, dear friends, I want to live again!" Everyone began to weep tears of joy as well. Apollonius stood up, took off his mourning clothes, and dressed in clean, fitting ones. Everyone remarked, "Oh lord, your daughter looks so much like you! Even without the other evidence, the likeness would suffice to prove that she is your daughter!" Then Tarsia, kissing her father without ceasing, said, "Oh beloved father, God be praised for giving me the blessing of seeing you, and being able to live and die with you!" Then she recounted how she had been bought by the pimp and put in the brothel, and how God had protected her virginity.

Athenagoras, listening to the story, did not want Tarsia to 3 be given in marriage to any other man. So, he reverently appealed to Apollonius, "For the sake of the living God who has restored your daughter to you, I beg you not to give her as a wife to any man but me! For I am the prince of this city, and with my assistance she has kept her virginity, and thanks to my mediation she has found you, her father." Apollonius said, in response, "I cannot refuse you, for you have done many things for my daughter! So, it pleases me that she be

plaze que ella sea tu muger. E agora resta que me vengue de aquel cruel rufián."

4   Atanágora entró en la cibdad e, ayuntados los cibdadanos, díxoles: "Por que la cibdad no sea destruida por un malvado, sabed Apolonio rey, padre de Tarsia, aver venido aquí. Veed las flotas de naves, se llegan con grand gente d'armas para destruir la cibdad por causa del rufián, el cual su fija Tarsia puso en el burdel." Sabidas estas nuevas, ayuntose toda la cibdad, de manera que no quedó hombre nin muger que no veniesse a ver al rey Apolonio e pidir d'él misericordia. Dixo Atanágora: "Conséjovos, por que la ciudad non sea destruida, que sea levado el rufián al rey." Luego, conseguiendo su consejo, fue preso el rufián e, atadas las manos atrás, levado a él.

5   Apolonio, vestido con vestiduras reales, fecha la barba, puesta su corona en la cabeça, subió en el tribunal con la fija e cibdadanos. E dize d'esta guisa: "Ya vos es manifiesto cómo hoy es conocida la virgen Tarsia de su padre, la cual, en cuanto en él fue, el muy avariento rufián procuró de corromper, que ni por amistad ni ruego ni precio quería desistir de su mal propósito. Pues assí es, ¡fazed vengança d'él a mi fija!" Todos por una voz dixieron: "¡Señor, el rufián sea quemado vivo, e sus bienes a la donzella sean dados!" E assí, luego fue traído el rufián, e ante todos fue quemado en fuego.

6   Tarsia dize al huéspede del burdel: "Yo te dono libertad, ca por tu consejo e beneficio quedé con mi virginidad." E encima de lo fazer libre, le dio dozientas pieças de oro. E assimesmo dio libertad a todas las moças que ante ella se

your wife. Now all that remains is for me to get vengeance on that pimp."

Athenagoras entered the city and said to the people gath- 4
ered around, "Know that King Apollonius, Tarsia's father, has come here so that our city will not be destroyed by one evil man. See all the ships coming, filled with armed men ready to destroy the city, all because of the pimp who put his daughter Tarsia in the brothel." With this news afoot, everyone in the city came together as one: there was not a single man or woman who did not appear before Apollonius to beg his mercy. Athenagoras said, "I advise—so the city will not be destroyed—that the pimp be brought before the king." The people followed his advice and quickly took the pimp prisoner, and brought him, hands bound behind his back, before Apollonius.

In all his regalia, his beard trimmed, his crown upon his 5
head, Apollonius ascended the tribunal platform with his daughter. He addressed the citizens in the following way: "You already know how the virgin Tarsia is now reunited with her father, and how the avaricious pimp tried to corrupt her, how neither friendship nor pleading nor money could sway him from his evil designs. Since this is the case, avenge my daughter!" All the people said as one, "Lord, let the pimp be burned alive and all his goods be given to the damsel!" And so the pimp was brought before everyone and burned on the pyre without delay.

Tarsia said to the brothel keeper, "I will grant you your 6
freedom, because thanks to your advice and help I kept my virginity." In addition to his freedom, she gave him two hundred pieces of gold. Moreover, she freed all of the brothel

presentaron, diziendo: "Porque con vuestros cuerpos fasta agora servistes, d'aquí adelante sed libres."

7 Dende Apolonio, fablando al pueblo, dize: "Gracias muchas riendo a vós por los beneficios fechos a mí e a mi fija, por lo cual agora vos dó cincuenta libras de oro." Ellos le fizieron reverencia, tornándoles muchas gracias. E assí, los cibdadanos la estatua de Apolonio pusieron en medio de la cibdad e escribieron en el epitafio: "A Tiro Apolonio, restaurador de nuestras casas, e Tarsia, su fija virgen."

31

De cómo Tarsia fue desposada con Atanágora.

Dende a pocos días, Apolonio dio su fija en matrimonio a Atanágora, con gran alegría de toda la ciudad. E con el yerno e fija queriendo por Tarso passar para su tierra, en suenyos fue amonestado por el ángel que fuesse a Éfeso e entrasse en el templo con la fija e yerno suyo, e declarasse ende todos sus casos e fortunas que había passado desde su juventud, e después veniesse a Tarso e vengasse la su fija.

2 Apolonio despertado, todas las cosas que le fueron reveladas manifestó a su yerno e fija. Ellos le repondieron: "¡Faz,

girls, saying, "Until now, you have served with your bodies; from now on, you are free."

Then Apollonius addressed the people and said, "I am 7 very grateful to you for all the kindness you have shown me and my daughter; in return, I now give you fifty pounds of gold." The people all bowed to Apollonius and gave him their thanks. And so it was that the citizens erected a statue of Apollonius in the city center, with an epitaph that read: "In honor of Apollonius of Tyre, restorer of our homes and of his daughter Tarsia, the virgin."

31

Of Tarsia's marriage to Athenagoras.

A few days later, Apollonius gave his daughter in marriage to Athenagoras, to the great joy of the whole city. As he was traveling to his home country by way of Tarsus with his son-in-law and daughter, Apollonius was visited by an angel in his dreams, who told him he must go to Ephesus and enter the temple with his daughter and son-in-law, and there recount his entire history and misfortunes from the time of his youth, and then go to Tarsus and avenge his daughter.

When he awoke from the dream, Apollonius told every- 2 thing that had been revealed to his son-in-law and his daughter. They said in response, "Do as you think best,

señor, lo que te parecerá bueno!" Entonces mandó al piloto que guiasse las naos para Éfeso.

32

Cómo Apolonio con su fija e Atanágora
su marido vino en Éfeso, donde falló su muger,
que creía que era muerta.

El cual como descendiesse de la nao, pidió el templo donde su muger vivía santamente, donde rogó que le fuesse abierto el templo, lo cual fuele cumplido. E oyendo su muger que un rey venía con su yerno e fija, adornose con gemas e piedras preciosas, e vestiose de púrpura, e con honesta compañía entró en el templo. E ella era muy fermosa e, por el grand amor de la castidad que havía, todas afirmavan que aquella era la más graciosa virgen. La cual mirando, Apolonio en cosa ninguna la pudo conocer, e echose a los pies d'ella con su yerno e fija. E tanto resplandor procedía de su fermosura que los que la miravan pensavan que aquella fuesse Diana.

2   Ofrecidos en el templo muchos preciosos dones, començó recontar Apolonio, como el ángel le havía revelado: "Yo, Apolonio, rey desde mi adolescencia, natural de Tiro, como llegasse a saber e entender toda manera de ciencia,

lord!" So, Apollonius ordered the ship's pilot to plot a course for Ephesus.

32

How Apollonius went to Ephesus with his daughter
and Athenagoras, where he found his wife,
whom he thought was dead.

When Apollonius disembarked in Ephesus, he went to the temple where his wife was living a saintly life, begged to be allowed in, and was granted entrance. His wife, hearing that a king had come with his son-in-law and daughter, adorned herself with gems and precious stones. Then, dressed in royal purple, she entered the temple, attended by honorable companions. She was quite beautiful, and due to her special devotion to chastity, everyone agreed that she was the loveliest virgin alive. Gazing at her, Apollonius did not recognize her at all, and threw himself at her feet, along with his son-in-law and his daughter. His wife's beauty shone with such brilliance that they thought she must be Diana herself.

After he had made many splendid offerings in the temple, 2 Apollonius began to retell his story, just as the angel had revealed he must do: "I am Apollonius, king from a young age, of Tyre, where I was born. Thanks to my learning and

solté la cuestión del mal rey Antíoco, por que recibiesse a su fija por muger. Mas él, como perverso e cruel defloró aquella e continuamente la tuvo, cometiendo crimen de incesto; por lo cual él me queriendo matar, yo fui delante su faz e, andando por la mar, todo cuanto tenía perdí. Mas después del rey Archistrato fui recebido muy graciosamente, e en tanto grado caí en su benivolencia que me dio a su fija en matrimonio. Dende, muerto el Antíoco, tomé e traxe a mi muger para recibir el regño. En la mar parió la reina, mi muger, a esta mi fija, la cual murió de su parto. Yo con xx marcos de oro en un ataúd cerrado la eché en la mar, por que, fallada, dignamente fuesse sepultada. Después encomendé esta mi fija a unos marido e mujer muy malvados a criar e, assí, yo me fui a las partes superiores de Egipto. Dende al xiiii anyo tornando para tomar e casar mi fija, dixiéronme que ella era defunta. E creído esto por mí, tomé vestiduras de luto e, en lloro e planto morante, me fue restituida la fija."

33

En qué manera Cleopatra conoció a su marido Apolonio.

Como estas e otras muchas fortunas contasse Apolonio, la fija del rey Archistrato, su muger, levantose e començó lo

mastery of all the sciences, I solved the evil King Antiochus's riddle, in the hopes of winning his daughter's hand. However, that perverse and cruel father deflowered his daughter and lived with her in incest, so he wanted to kill me, and I fled from his sight and lost all that I had at sea. But then, King Archistrates graciously took me in and showed me so much kindness that he gave me his daughter in marriage. After that, once Antiochus died, I went with my wife to take possession of his kingdom. My wife, the queen, gave birth at sea to my daughter, who you see here, but she died from the birth. I put twenty gold coins in her sealed coffin and cast it into the sea, hoping she would find a worthy burial. Then, I entrusted my daughter to be raised by an evil man and his wife and I left for the north of Egypt. After fourteen years I returned for my daughter so I could arrange a marriage for her, and they told me she was dead. Believing them, I put on mourning clothes, and while I was grieving and sorrowing her death, my daughter was restored to me."

33

How Cleopatra recognized her husband Apollonius.

When she heard Apollonius retell his many misfortunes and adventures, the daughter of King Archistrates rose to

abraçar, queriéndolo besar. Mas el rey Apolonio la arriedra de sí con sanya, pensando que ella fuesse muger sagrada e non la que era conjunta con él matrimonialmente. E ella dezía: "Oh, senyor mío, ¿por qué assí fazes?" E llorando de sus ojos, llamávalo: "¡Tú eres medio de mi ánima, ca yo soy tu muger, fija del rey Archistrato, e tú eres el rey Apolonio, mi marido amado e mi señor e maestro que me ensenyaste! ¡E tú eres aquel naúfrago al cual yo amé, no por amor de luxuria, mas de la sapiencia!"

2   Apolonio, oyendo estas senyales tan ciertas, cayó sobre su cuello d'ella con gozo ingente, deziendo assí: "¡Bendito sea el muy alto Dios, que me ha restituído a mi fija con mi senyora amada muger!" E pregunta ella: "¿Dónde es mi fija?" La cual luego le fue mostrada, llamándola por nombre Tarsia, e la recibió besántela con gran alegría. E assí, fue luego por toda ciudad e comarcas divulgado con grandes plazeres cómo el rey Apolonio havía fallado a su muger en el templo.

34

Cómo Apolonio, tomando a su muger,
yerno, fija, bolvió para su tierra, e de la justicia que
fue fecha en la ciudad de Tarsia de sus huéspedes.

Dende Apolonio, tomando a su mujer con el yerno e fija, entró en la mar para bolver a su tierra. E d'esta forma,

embrace and tried to kiss him. But Apollonius pushed her away angrily, thinking that she was a holy woman and not the woman who was joined to him in matrimony. She said, "Oh, my lord, why are you behaving in this way?" Her eyes streaming with tears, she went on, "You are the other half of my soul! I am your wife, daughter of King Archistrates, and you are King Apollonius, my beloved husband and my lord, and the master who taught me! You are also the shipwrecked man I fell in love with, not out of lust, but for your wisdom!"

Hearing these evident truths, Apollonius rushed to embrace her, overwhelmed by joy, and said, "Blessed be God on high, who has restored my daughter and my beloved lady wife to me!" She asked him, "Where is my daughter?" Tarsia was immediately introduced to her mother, who met her with happy kisses. The news of how King Apollonius had found his wife in the temple soon spread throughout the city and surrounding lands, to the great pleasure of all. 2

34

How Apollonius returned to his homeland with his wife,
son-in-law, and daughter, and how judgment was
passed on his hosts in the city of Tarsus.

Then, Apollonius set sail for his homeland, taking his wife, son-in-law, and daughter with him. First, he went to

veniente Apolonio, recibió el regño de Antioquía a él reservado e, yendo a Tiro, en su lugar estableció a su yerno Atanágora. Conseguientemente, veniendo con su muger, yerno e fija, con gran cavallería, a Tarsia, mandó que fuessen presos Estranguilion e Dionisiade su muger, e ser traídos ante él. E assí, dixo ante todos los ciudadanos: "Mis amados amigos, pregunto si a alguno de vós haya seído ingrato." Todos respondieron: "¡Senyor, no, antes todos havemos recibido grandes beneficios de vós! Por ende, conoced que estamos prestos e aparejados de vos servir fasta la muerte. Esta estatua fizimos aquí poner en memoria de cómo vós nos librastes de la muerte."

2   Dízeles Apolonio: "Encomendé a mi fija a Estranguilion e a su muger, e no me la quisieron bolver." La malvada Dionisiade dize: "¡Senyor bueno, tú mesmo leíste el título de su monumento!" Apolonio mandó que su fija veniesse ende en presencia de todos, e Tarsia maldixo a la muger, deziendo: "¡Aquella que es tornada de los infiernos te saluda!" La desventurada de la muger, viendo aquella, toda se tremió. Los ciudadanos, veyentes a Tarsia, gozávanse, marabillados. E mandó Tarsia venir al esclavo que la quería degollar e dízele: "Teófilo, tú conociste abiertamente; por ende, respóndeme: ¿Quién te mandó que me degollasses?" Afirmó el siervo que su senyora Dionisiade le havía mandado matarla. Entonces, los ciudadanos rabataron luego a Dionisiade e su marido Estranguilion e, sacánteslos fuera de la ciudad, los apedrearon. E no menos querían matar a Teófilo, sino que Tarsia lo libró, diziendo: "Si no me huviesse dado espacio para orar e rogar a Dios, no le havría agora defendido de la muerte."

3   Apolonio aún tornó a dar muchos dones a la ciudad para su reparo, e moró entre ellos por III meses, e después navegó

take possession of the kingdom awaiting him in Antioch, and then he went to Tyre, which he gave his son-in-law Athenagoras to rule. Next, accompanied by a large army, he went with his wife, son-in-law, and daughter to Tarsus, where he ordered that Stranguillio and Dionysias, his wife, be taken prisoners and brought to him. Apollonius then addressed all the citizens gathered before him: "My dear friends, I wonder if I have been ungrateful to any of you." They all assured him, "Lord, no; rather, we all have received great kindnesses from you! In return, know that we are ready and willing to serve you to the death. We erected this statue here in memory of how you saved our lives."

Apollonius said to them, "I entrusted my daughter to 2 Stranguillio and his wife, and they took her from me." Evil Dionysias said, "Good lord, you yourself read the epitaph on her tomb!" Apollonius ordered his daughter to appear in the sight of all present, and Tarsia cursed the woman, saying, "The child come back from the grave salutes you!" Seeing Tarsia, the doomed woman began to tremble. The citizens of Tarsus marveled in delight. Tarsia called the slave who had tried to slit her throat forward and said to him, "Theophilus, you know who I am, so answer me this: Who ordered you to cut my throat?" The servant declared that his lady Dionysias had ordered the killing. The citizens immediately seized Dionysias and her husband Stranguillio, took them outside the city, and stoned them to death. They wanted to kill Theophilus as well, but Tarsia spared him, saying, "If he had not given me time to pray and call on God, I would not now be defending him."

Apollonius gave many gifts for the improvement of the 3 city and lived among them for three months, afterward

dende para la ciudad de Pentápolin a la corte del rey Archistrato con gran alegría, donde fueron recibidos excelentemente del rey su suegro, ya viejo. El cual viendo su fija e nieta en uno con sus maridos, fue recreado marabillosamente. E los tuvo consigo por un anyo entero con grandes plazeres e gozos. E dende a tiempo murió el rey Archistrato, e dexoles el regño a Apolonio e a su muger a medias.

35

Cómo Apolonio dio grandes dones al pescador e
a Elímito.

Passadas todas estas cosas, un día andando Apolonio en la ribera de la mar vio aquel pescador que lo recibió cuando salió desnudo e desbaratado de la mar. E mandó que lo tomassen e fuesse traído a su palacio. El pescador, viéntese tomar de los cavalleros, pensó que lo querían matar. Entrando en una cámara, mandó Apolonio que entrasse allí el pescador, diziente: "Este es mi huéspede, el cual cuando salí del naufragio el primero socorro e ayuda me dio, e me consejó que viniesse a la ciudad." E díxole: "Yo soy Tiro Apolonio," e mandole dar CC marcos de oro e siervos e siervas, e fízole su

sailing happily to Pentapolis, to the court of King Archistrates, where they received an excellent welcome from the king, his father-in-law, who was now advanced in age. Seeing his daughter and granddaughter, together with their husbands, was a marvelous remedy for Archistrates's old age. They stayed with him for an entire year of splendid celebrations and delights. And, in time, King Archistrates died, leaving the kingdom to Apollonius and his wife.

35

How Apollonius gave Elimito and the fisherman
splendid gifts.

After all these things had come to pass, one day Apollonius was walking along the seashore when he saw the fisherman who had taken him in when he first washed up from the waves, naked and beaten by the sea. He ordered that the fisherman be seized and brought to the palace. The fisherman, seeing himself taken by the guards, thought he was going to be killed. But Apollonius entered a room in the palace and had the fisherman brought in, saying, "This man is my host, the one who first aided me when I survived a shipwreck. He helped me and gave me directions to the city." He said to the fisherman, "I am Apollonius of Tyre," and gave him two hundred gold coins, serving men and women, and

conde mientra que vivió. Elímito, viente esto, echándose a
sus pies, suplícale, diziendo assí: "¡Acuérdate, senyor, de Elí-
mito tu servidor, que te denunció la muerte del rey Antíoco!"
Apolonio, tomándolo de la mano, lo alçó, e lo fizo rico e
conde.

2   Después de todo esto, Apolonio engendró un fijo en su
muger, al cual estableció por rey en lugar de su abuelo Ar-
chistrato. E vivió Apolonio con su muger LXXXIIII años e
tuvo el regño de Antioquía e de Tiro. E folgadamente, con
gran felicidad, escrivió todos sus fechos e casos en dos volú-
mines: el uno puso en el templo de Éfeso e el otro en su li-
brería colocó e puso. E assí acabó bienaventuradamente sus
días e fue para la vida perdurable, a la cual nos lieve Dios por
su piedad. Amén.

AQUÍ SE ACABA EL *APOLONIO*.

DEO GRACIAS.

made him a count for his lifetime. Elimito saw all this and threw himself at Apollonius's feet, begging him, "Remember, my lord, Elimito, your servant! It was I who told you about King Antiochus's death!" Taking him by the hand, Apollonius brought him to his feet, and made him a rich count.

After all this, Apollonius fathered a son with his wife, 2 whom he named king in place of his grandfather, Archistrates. Apollonius lived with his wife for eighty-four years, ruling over Antioch and Tyre. In his leisure and happiness, he wrote down all his deeds and history in two tomes, placing one in the temple at Ephesus and the other in his own library. And thus, he ended his days in blessedness and now he is in heaven. May God in his mercy send us all there. Amen.

HERE ENDS THE *HISTORY OF APOLLONIUS.*

THANKS BE TO GOD.

Abbreviations

GR = *Gesta Romanorum,* ed. Hermann Oesterley (Berlin, 1872); English trans. Christopher Stace (Manchester, 2016)

HART = *Historia Apolonii regis Tyri,* ed. Elizabeth Archibald, in *Apollonius of Tyre: Medieval and Renaissance Themes and Variations* (Woodbridge, 1991)

Note on the Texts

The texts of *The Book of Apollonius* and *The Life and History of King Apollonius* offer critical presentations of the single witnesses for each of the two works: manuscript Escorial K.III.4, copied in Aragon in the third quarter of the fourteenth century, for the poem; and the incunable printed by Juan Hurus in Zaragoza in around 1488, whose only exemplar is held today by the Hispanic Society of America in New York City. We have emended those texts only in cases of evident mistakes (for example, in the case of rhyme words for *The Book of Apollonius*), when the correct solution was very clear and there were not several available options, or when not correcting would have made the text incomprehensible. We have consulted all earlier editions of both texts, discussed in the Introduction, and have often adopted the emendation proposals of earlier editors. A detailed list of such proposals for *The Book of Apollonius* can be consulted in the edition by Carina Zubillaga, *Poesía narrativa clerical en su contexto manuscrito. Estudio y edición del Ms. Esc. K-III-4 ("Libro de Apolonio," "Vida de Santa María Egipciaca," "Libro de los tres reyes de Oriente")* (Buenos Aires, 2014). Meanwhile, previous emendations to *The Life and History* have been included in Alan D. Deyermond, *Apollonius of Tyre: Two Fifteenth-Century Spanish Prose Romances* (Exeter, 1973). In the Notes to

the Texts, we have recorded our emendations, followed by the single witness's reading, leaving out only some purely graphic corrections (such as missing *cedillas*).

For the text's graphic presentation, we have used spelling and punctuation to convey our understanding of the phonetic, prosodic, and syntactic features of the texts. To this end, we have followed the principles outlined by Pedro Sánchez-Prieto Borja in *Cómo editar los textos medievales: Criterios para su presentación gráfica* (Madrid, 1998) and *La edición de los textos españoles medievales y clásicos: Criterios de presentación gráfica* (San Millán de la Cogolla, 2011). In *The Book of Apollonius,* the spacing between each of the two halves of each line reflects the metrical pause, or caesura, which remains an important feature of this type of verse.

Notes to the Texts

83.1	conocía: conoscie
88.4	en: ay
92.3	por él: por
92.3	valía: valio
93.1	providencia: prouença
94.1	se: se les
97.4	olvidado: oluido
99.3	ivierno tener: yuiero tenjr
101.1	menguados: mengados
101.4	cosiment seremos: consentimiente sermos
102.2	*This line is probably an interpolation.*
103.3	sabién: sabien bien
116.4	abiniés: abienes
132.3	venir: nir. *An ink blot has made the first part of the word illegible.*
137.3	rey: y. *An ink blot has made the first part of the word illegible.*
139.4	cenado: cenada
140.4	en: sin
	serié: te sera
144.4	juego jugar: Jugar
151.1	juego: luego
159.1	*The rhyme scheme makes clear that* posar *is a scribal mistake.*
161.3	quisieres: qusieres
162.2	*The rhyme scheme makes clear that* venir *is a scribal mistake.*
168.1	componer: coponer
168.3	alegría: algria
175.1	contada: contado
176.1	Fija, fe que devedes: fija que deuedes
179.1	fermosas debailadas: fermosos debailados
180.1	dizién: dizian
183.4	si yo: Sio
184.3	giga: gigua
190.2	Apolo nin Orfeo mejor non violavan: Que apolonjo *["*F*" crossed out]* Ceteo mejor non violaua
197.2	entendiendo: entiendo
197.4	*There is a mistake in the last word, since the rhyme calls for a word that ends in* -endo.

202.4	del: al
204.1	bien: vynien
211.3	a Apolonio: apolonyo
221.2	que otrie tu lazerio lograse: que tu lazerio otrie lograse
222.2	a Apolonio: Apolonyo
228.3	començole: Conmeçole
229.2	corazón: corzon
233.4	poquellejo: poquellio
235.4	deferida: ferjda
264.3	mejorar le: meior lo
271.4	era: eran
280.1	se podrién perder: perder se podrjen
285.1	sabor: plazer.
289.1	tablero: tabllero
292.4	si non: si assí non
299.1	tenié: tenya
300.4	odicempcón. *This word is a hapax.*
311.3	maestría: maestrio
316.3	Véyome de mis gentes: Veyo demj gentes
321.2	maguer con flaquedat: con flaquedat maguer
323.2	porfijola: Porfiola
331.1	nada: nasçida
339.3	vezado: vegado
342.3	venturosos: venturos
347.3	nin quiero en Pentápolin ni en Tiro entrar: Nin quiero en pentapolin entrar Ni en tiro otro que tal
349.3	penya: pena
350.3	viuela: viula
356.4	cuáles: queles
368.1	Esta boz Dionisa óvola a saber. *In the manuscript, this line comes at the end of the stanza, likely because the scribe or one of their predecessors forgot to copy it, realized their mistake after finishing the quatrain, and then added it at the end.*
373.4	enguedat: eguedat
383.3	a mí: mj
390.1	enganyado: enganado

395.4	diez pesas: ueynte pesar. *The subsequent bids for Tarsiana make clear that the initial number must be ten, not twenty.*
398.3–4	*We have reversed the manuscript's ordering of the last two lines in the stanza, which do not make sense otherwise.*
400.3	ciella: siella
401.4	avrán a ofrecer: ha ofreçer
405.3	ostal: Apostol
414.2	querríala: qrria la
425.2	amansado: Amansando
426.1	madurgada: madurguada
427.4	cabién: cabie en
442.2	llaga: llagua
444.2	frida: fidra
449.4	parar: partir
453.4	alongadas: alongados
458.3	de: del
469.1	yazié: Jazia
469.2	con: com
484.1	sirvientes: sirujetes
489.3	cuita: cuytada
489.4	su: Sue
490.2	conoscieses: conscieses
505.1	casa: cosa
510.3	por Dios: por dios te rruego
515.1	diz Tarsiana: tarssiana
520.1	negro nin blanco: negro
522.1	so un techo moramos: sso vn techo
526.1–2	*These two lines appear to have been switched in the manuscript, since the meaning of the stanza becomes much clearer in this order.*
553.1	deves: deuos
557.2	casamiento: casmjento
559.3	si el traidor falso que l'avié: Nin el traydor falsso quela
572.1	bassa: balssa
598	*A line is missing from this stanza, probably the second one, in which Apollonius would have refused to enter the city (see stanza 604).*
605.2	grant cuita: grant. *There is clearly a missing word in this line;* cuita *is the likeliest option, as it is used in similar contexts in 47.3 and 527.3.*

622.1	viejo: vieijo
631.2	demandava: demandua
633.2	servientes: sieruentes
634.4	cuando: quado
646.2	tributario: trjbutado
655.4	al convivio de Dios: sinon el convivio de Dios

THE LIFE AND HISTORY OF KING APOLLONIUS

5.1	tomando: tomado
5.2	cargar en ellos: cargar en ellas
8.1	encubrís: encubriys
8.3	utilidades: utilitades
9.1	Pentápolin de los tirones: methapolin delos thirones. *The reading is* Pentapolim Tyrenorum *in the GR.*
13	ciudad de Pentápolin: ciudad Pentapolin
14.2	a la sala: la sala
15.2	verdad: verdado
15.3	instrumento: instrumeuto
	Dize el rey a Apolonio: Dize el rey apolonio
	tanyía: tanya
20.1	desbaratado: desbaratato
22.2	diligencia a su fija: diligenci a su fija
23.1	tornando: tornado
24.3	Dize: Dixe
26.1	contender: condender
27.1	como le fue mandado: como le mandado
28.2	desmayado: desmasiado
28.5	subir en la nuestra nao: subir la nuestra nao
29.8	problema: poblema
	estipada: stirpada
30.4	manera: manenera
32.2	Antíoco: anchioco
35.1	cámara: cama. *This same mistake may also be present in 2.1 and 17.3.*

Notes to the Translations

1.3   *compose a romance in the new, learned style*: In this stanza the poet announces the horizons of expectation for the work. By using the term *romance,* the poet refers to the vernacular language, but in this context may also be referring to narrative genre as well. The term *nueva maestría,* which we have translated "new, learned style," is a metapoetic reference to the metrical form of *cuaderna vía,* or alexandrine monorhymed quatrains, which had recently been introduced in Castilian poetry by the *Libro de Alexandre,* another romance of antiquity, in the first third of the thirteenth century.

1.4   *courtesy*: Courtesy, or courtliness, which will be a central preoccupation of the poem, is the ensemble of personal qualities and social skills that can be learned at and are crucial to success in a court.

2.1   *Tyre*: The Phoenician port city of Tyre, located in what is now southern Lebanon, was the legendary birthplace of both Europa and Dido.

2.2   *adventures*: The poet plays here upon the concept of adventure, key to medieval romance, and fortune *(ventura),* which carried the further meaning in medieval Castilian of a storm at sea.

3.1   *King Antiochus*: King Antiochus of the Apollonius of Tyre legend is possibly identifiable as one of several historical figures, including Antiochus I, son of the founder of the city of Antioch and of the Seleucid dynasty in the third century BCE. According to legend, Antiochus I fell in love with and married his

stepmother, Stratonice. Ancient Antioch was located on the banks of the Orontes river; Elizabeth Archibald, *Apollonius of Tyre: Medieval and Renaissance Themes and Variations* (Woodbridge, 1991), 38–44.

17.3   *the meaning of the verse*: Riddles provide the catalyst for Apollonius's adventures and later attend his reunion with his daughter in most versions of the story. Here, the riddle regarding King Antiochus's incestuous behavior is particularly cryptic, whether by design or because of the poet's veering away from the Latin riddle in the *Historia Apolonii regis Tyri*: "Scelere vehor, maternam carnem vescor, quaero fratrem meum, meae matris virum, uxoris meae filium: non invenio" (I am borne on crime; I eat my mother's flesh; I seek my brother, my mother's husband, my wife's son: I do not find him); ed. and trans. Archibald, *Apollonius of Tyre*, 114–15.

18.2   *heard of this princess, whose fame was spreading*: Apollonius's ability to fall in love by hearsay—the *topos* of the *amor de lohn* is common in medieval lyric and romance—is an addition of the Castilian poet's and one of many early indications of the protagonist's nobility and courtliness.

42.2   *the people were sorrowful, with their mantles closed tight*: The tightly closed cloak was a sign of mourning or anger; Carmen Monedero, ed., *Libro de Apolonio* (Madrid, 1987), 108n.

62.1–3 *Now, I want to leave off telling you of King Antiochus*: This is one of five three-line stanzas in the poem (62, 67, 196, 516, 598, and 604). These changes in form are due to dropped lines rather than poetic intentions. The inclusion of one stanza that is five lines long (102) is likely due to scribal activity as well.

98.4   *Pentapolis*: In the ancient world, there were several groups of five cities that were known as Pentapolis. According to Monedero, there is no way to know exactly which Pentapolis *The Book of Apollonius* poet has in mind (*Libro de Apolonio*, 126n). However, Archibald equates Pentapolis with Cyrene, located in what is today the northeast of Libya (*Apollonius of Tyre*, 123). The ancient port of Cyrene was called, interestingly, Apolonia.

139.1   *The fisherman cut his robe in two with his sword*: Medieval audi-

ences would have recognized the similarities between this scene and one from the life of Saint Martin of Tours, who shared his cloak with a poor man. As Dolores Corbella points out, other intertexual references in this scene are readily apparent as well, including Ovid's *Metamorphoses,* Apuleius's *Golden Ass,* and the twelfth-century German *Kaiserkronik;* Corbella, *Libro de Apolonio* (Madrid, 1992), 119n.

144.1   *It was not yet time for the midday meal*: This is the beginning of a major departure from the poet's source, *HART.* See the note to *Life and History of King Apollonius* 13.3.

150.4   *dried the tears from his streaming eyes*: The poet says that Apollonius "cleaned the drops from his eyes," so it is also possible that Apollonius is brushing the sweat from his brow. We agree with Monedero that the sense of wiping the tears from his eyes is metaphorical: Apollonius is forgetting his sorrows thanks to the game. The ball game is one of the many courtly activities that provide relief from care—if only temporary—in the poem.

162.1   *King Archistrates, for the pleasure of his court*: Throughout this scene, King Archistrates behaves as a model head of the court (in contrast to Antiochus): he takes great care to ascertain the status of his mysterious guest so that he can honor him, a sentiment that will be echoed by his daughter, Luciana. This is one of the episodes that most clearly establishes the poem as a mirror of princes.

164.1   *pilgrim*: Apollonius is often characterized as a pilgrim throughout the poem, reflecting the poet's choice to portray the hero as an *homo viator* (man on a journey) and develop the Christian metaphor of human life as a pilgrimage.

168.3   *enjoyment*: *Alegría* was a courtly and political virtue (here opposed to *villanía,* or "baseness," the quality typical of a *villano,* that is, of a "commoner"). The word *alegría* was used at the time to refer both to the feeling that allows a king or noble person to regulate their emotional state when confronted with troubles, providing consolation, and to the kind of activities that may be used to create such a feeling: hunting, playing

board games, listening to stories, or, as later in this scene, play-
ing and listening to music. Around the time of the creation of
The Book of Apollonius, a reflection and prescriptions on *alegría*
(in both senses) can be found in works on courtly behavior by
King Alfonso X of Castile, especially the second of his *Siete
partidas,* concerning the comportment of kings and knights,
and the *Libro de ajedrez* (Book of Chess).

178.1   *The lady readied herself*: This abrupt transition suggests that
there is a lacuna in the manuscript's text. Chapter 15 of the
prose *Life and History of King Apollonius* provides the missing
plot details.

178.2   *she tuned her vielle well, on the natural scale*: The vielle is a bowed
string instrument and the ancestor of the modern fiddle. In
the Latin sources, the princess plays a lyre. This section of the
poem introduces and showcases one of the signature charac-
teristics of the Castilian poet's adaptation of the story, the em-
phasis on musical performance and musical ability in relation
to courtliness. The poet's wide musical vocabulary suggests his
own familiarity with both musical performance and theory; see
Daniel Devoto, "Dos notas sobre el *Libro de Apolonio,*" *Bulletin
Hispanique* 74, nos. 3–4 (1972): 291–330; and Ross W. Duffin, *A
Performer's Guide to Medieval Music* (Bloomington, 2000), 545–
62. The "natural scale" refers to the diatonic scale.

178.4   *laud*: Although a *laude* generally refers to liturgical music, in the
thirteenth century the term was also used to describe secular
compositions.

179.1   *quarter tones*: The *debailadas,* here translated as "quarter tones" to
maintain parallelism below in stanza 189, have been the subject
of some debate among scholars. The poet may also have been
referring to *portamentos,* or slides from one note to another on
stringed instruments. A quarter tone, also known as a micro-
tone, is an interval equal to half a semitone, or a half step, and
was common in pre-Renaissance tuning. It is at this point that
one of *The Book of Apollonius*'s signal motifs comes into play:
meloterapia, that is, music and its effect on the emotions. On
meloterapia and the relations between music, love, and love-

sickness in *The Book of Apollonius,* see María Jesús Lacarra, "Amor, música y melancolía en el *Libro de Apolonio,*" in *Actas del I Congreso de la Asociación Hispánica de Literatura Medieval,* ed. Vicenç Beltran (Barcelona, 1988), 369–79.

180.1   *Up and down the scale*: This expression, literally, "the highs and the lows," is a pun that refers simultaneously to ranks of everyone in the court (the people of higher and lower social status, and even those who are tall and short) and to the way in which the vielle's high and low musical notes harmonize (Devoto, "Dos notas," 307–8).

184.3   *cithara or the rebec*: Two additional stringed instruments. The cithara is plucked with the fingers or a plectrum, and the rebec, like the vielle, is bowed.

185.3   *he could not play without a crown*: Apollonius asks for a crown because he does not want to be mistaken for a simple performer. Contemporary sources encourage kings to listen to music but suggest that royal dignity may be compromised by musical or other kinds of performance (Devoto, "Dos notas," 317–30). Archibald explains that the reference to a crown derives from classical tradition, "the garland worn in classical times for feasting and recitation" (*Apollonius of Tyre,* 77). In *HART,* Apollonius also acts and mimes, activities that would have been far beneath the dignity of a thirteenth-century Iberian king.

189.2   *duples . . . quarter tones . . . semitones*: In medieval music, the term *dobla* (duple or dupla, from the Latin *duplus*), could refer to several aspects of performance, including an increase in tempo, or, in early polyphony, to a melody sung above a continuo line, or to two notes played together.

192   *"Father," said the lady to the king her lord:* There is a lacuna in the manuscript's presentation of the narrative suggesting a missing stanza or stanzas before 192. As the prose version explains and the next stanza makes clear, the princess asks her father to make Apollonius her teacher.

270.1   *Since she had not been properly cared for in the birth*: The description of Luciana's labor and postpartum illness (and eventual cure) provides the poet with another opportunity to display his eru-

dition, in this case medical. The birthing scene is also a good example of how the poet adds material and emotional details to his sources as a mode of amplification.

277.2   *such a beloved lady*: Here and elsewhere, the Castilian poet uses vocabulary familiar from Occitan and Galician-Portuguese poetic terminology for *fin'amors* (*cosiment,* "mercy"; *amiga,* "beloved woman") when Apollonius describes his relationship with Luciana, as part of his project of imbuing *HART* with courtly values.

284.2   *at the port of Ephesus*: Ephesus was an ancient Greek and Roman port city, located on the Aegean coast of what is now Turkey. Ephesus was an important pilgrimage site in the Greek, Roman, Christian, and Muslim traditions, due to the temple of Artemis located there—one of the "Seven Wonders" of the ancient world, described in Pliny the Elder's *Natural History* 36.97—and the fifth-century Christian House of the Virgin Mary. It was also revered as the site were Saint Paul cured the sick in Acts 19:11–12; see Amaia Arizaleta, "La transmisión del saber médico: *Libro de Alexandre* y *Libro de Apolonio*," in *Actas del VIII Congreso Internacional de la Asociación Hispánica de Literatura Medieval,* ed. Silvia Iriso and Margarita Freixas (Santander, 2000), 230.

300.4   *and suddenly felt the slightest palpitation*: The Castilian text contains a hapax in this line, *odicempón,* which has been interpreted by various editors as a reference to palpitations, auscultation, and evidence of Luciana's recently having given birth .

343.4   *we will honor her with our dead and go on*: The literal translation of the Spanish is, "we will do as she did for her grandfather." As Monedero explains, the meaning here is that the people will mourn the queen's death, but then they will get on with their lives as before (*Libro de Apolonio,* 199–200n).

348.4   *thirteen years*: There is some discrepancy in the poet's timekeeping. Later, in stanza 434, he says that Apollonius has been away for ten years.

350.4   *her wits were well sharpened, just as a file sharpens the teeth*: This is a reference to the commonplace medieval image of Lady Gram-

mar shaping her students' teeth with a metal file to correct their pronunciation. For this image, see Katie Walter, *Middle English Mouths: Late Medieval Medical, Religious, and Literary Traditions* (Cambridge, 2018), 156–57.

360.3–4 *now he is a palmer . . . a pilgrim*: Medieval Castilian has three synonyms for "pilgrim," each relating to the destination of the traveler: the *palmero* traveled to Jerusalem; the *romero,* to Rome; and the *peregino,* to Santiago de Compostela. In this stanza, the *Apolonio* poet uses both *palmero* and *romero,* so we have opted for the antiquated English "palmer" in the first instance in order to reflect the poet's variation.

366.4 *Dionisa's daughter*: The Spanish text literally says, "who was her sister," meaning that Tarsiana was brought up with Dionisa and Stranguillio's daughter as her sister.

391.1 *The pirates ran as fast as they could*: According to Monedero, there's a lacuna in the poem's text prior to this stanza, where Dionisa recounts the murder she plotted to Stranguillio (*Libro de Apolonio,* 214n).

426.3–4 *carrying a fine and well-tempered vielle . . . for money*: The Castilian poet is undoubtedly punning on the terms *violada* (deflowered, raped, violated), *soldadera* (prostitute), and *violar por soldada* (to fiddle for money) in this episode, in which Tarsiana escapes being violated in exchange for money by playing music in the open market. Like her father, who had to distinguish himself as a king from a mere minstrel when he played the vielle in Archistrates's court, Tarsiana is in danger of her nobility being confused with baser social categories.

427.2 *on the natural scale*: See note on 178.2.

428.3–4 *she began to recite . . . all that had befallen her*: Here, Tarsiana becomes a figure for the poet: her performance is a recap of the romance the poet promised to tell in the first stanzas of the work.

434.1 *ten years*: The poet's references to the number of years between Apollonius's visits to Tarsus conflict. We later hear that Tarsiana "died" at the age of twelve (stanza 446). See also 348.4.

459.2 *had been born on that very day*: In *HART* and the *GR* the feast of

Neptune is being celebrated in Mytilene (the feast day that Athenagoras celebrates in stanza 463), and Apollonius gives his men money to celebrate but insists that he will not participate and threatens to break the legs of anyone who interrupts his grieving. The substitution of Apollonius's saint's day for the pagan festival is yet another instance of the thirteenth-century poet's anachronistic Christianization of the hero.

482.4   *Jericho*: A reference to the battle of Jericho in Joshua 6:1–27, the first battle fought by the Israelites in the conquest of Canaan.

488.2   *electuary*: Electuaries appear in medieval texts as both candies and medicines. They were confections made by mixing honey and other sweet ingredients with spices as well as with substances thought to have curative properties.

505.1   *Tell me what house*: This riddle and the ones that follow, like the riddles in this episode in *HART,* the *GR,* and the anonymous Spanish prose version of the Apollonius story also included in this volume, all derive from the *Aenigmata* of Symphosius, a collection of one hundred Latin riddles, thought to have been composed in the late fourth or early fifth century, that circulated widely throughout the Middle Ages. Tarsiana's first riddle is a rendering of Symphosius's *Aenigma* 12: "Est domus in terris, clara quae voce resultat. / Ipsa domus resonat, tacitus sed non sonat hospes. / Ambo tamen currunt, hospes simul et domus una." (There is a house in the earth which reechoes with a clear voice. The house itself resounds, but the silent guest makes no sound. Nevertheless, both guest and house run together at the same time.) T. J. Leary, ed. and trans., *Symphosius, the Aenigmata: An Introduction, Text and Commentary* (London, 2014), 41 and 84.

508.1   *The close relative of the waters*: This riddle, Symphosius's *Aenigma* 2, with the solution of reed pen *(harundo),* becomes somewhat confused in the *Libro de Apolonio.* "Dulcis amica dei, ripae vicina profundae, / suave canens Musis, nigro perfusa colore / nuntia sum linguae digitis signata magistris." (Sweet mistress of a god, neighbor of the infernal bank, singing sweetly for the Muses, steeped in the color black, I am the tongue's messenger, having been distinguished by a master's fingers.) Leary, *Symphosius,* 39 and 66.

509.   *I am the daughter of the forest*: This is *Aenigma* 13 (*navis*, "ship") and
        a fairly close rendering of the Latin: "Longa feror velox formo-
        sae filia silvae, / innumeris pariter comitum stipante cater-
        vis, / curro vias multas, vestigia nulla relinquens." (Long, fast,
        daughter of a handsome wood, I am carried, pressed at the
        same time by numberless crowds of companions. I run along
        many courses leaving behind no footprints.) Leary, *Symphosius*,
        41 and 87.

511.1   *Among raging fires*: *Aenigma* 89 (*balneum*, "bath"): "Per totas aedes
        innoxius introit ignis. / Est calor in medio magnus, quem nemo
        veretur. / Non est nuda domus, sed nudus convenit hospes." (A
        harmless fire goes in through the whole establishment. In the
        middle there is a great heat which no one fears. The house is
        not naked but, naked, the guest assembles.) Leary, *Symphosius*,
        50 and 222.

513.1   *I have neither feet nor hands*: *Aenigma* 61 (*anchora*, "anchor"): "Mu-
        cro mihi geminus ferro coniungitur uno. / Cum vento luctor,
        cum gurgite pugno profundo, / scrutor aquas medias, ipsas
        quoque mordeo terras." (My twin point is joined in a single
        piece of iron. I strive with the wind, I fight with the ocean
        deep. I search through the midst of the waters and I also bite
        the very earth.) Leary, *Symphosius*, 47 and 173.

514.1   *Although I was born of a hard mother*: *Aenigma* 63 (*spongia*,
        "sponge"): "Ipsa gravis non sum, sed aqua mihi pondus inhae-
        ret. / Viscera tota tument patulis diffusa cavernis. / Intus lym-
        pha latet, sed non se sponte profundit." (I myself am not heavy,
        but the weight of water clings to me. All my innards swell, dis-
        tended with outspread chambers. Water lies hidden, and it
        does not pour forth of its own accord.) Leary, *Symphosius*, 47
        and 176.

518.1   *On the inside I am hairy*: *Aenigma* 53 (*pila*, "ball"): "Non sum compta
        comis et non sum nuda capillis; / intus enim crines mihi sunt,
        quos non videt ullus. / Meque manus mittunt manibusque re-
        mitter in auras." (I am not dressed with hair and I am not de-
        void of tresses; for my hair is inside, which nobody sees; and
        hands send me forth and by hands I am sent back into the air.)
        Leary, *Symphosius*, 46 and 169.

521.1   *A peddler will sell you a mirror*: A decidedly moralistic and eco-
nomic take on Symphosius's *Aenigma* 69 (*speculum,* "mirror"):
"Nulla mihi certa est, nulla est peregrina figura / fulgor inest
intus radiant luce coruscus, / qui nihil ostendit nisi si quid
viridit ante." (No shape is fixed for me, none is foreign. There
is within a brightness flashing with beaming light which shows
nothing unless it has seen something earlier.) Leary, *Symphosius,*
49 and 187.

546.4   *tourney targets*: The *tablado* was a wooden structure, often made
in the shape of a castle, that knights would try to break apart
with their lances in chivalric games. What is most important
to note here is that the "joy of the court" has been restored.

598.2   *everyone stopped dead in their tracks*: The missing line in this stanza
is probably the second one, because it is Apollonius who ap-
pears to be the one that refuses to enter the city, judging from
what he says later.

612.4   *he had been a slave, and they freed him*: The poet announced in
stanza 390 that Theophilus "died a slave; in the end, he was
never a free man," yet here Theophilus does actually become a
free man, precisely because he failed to carry out Dionisa's or-
ders.

651.1   *Apollonius is dead, as we all must die*: According to C. Carroll
Marden, the stanzas from here to the end are a late addition to
the poem, perhaps the invention of the fourteenth-century
copyist; see Marden, ed., *Libro de Apolonio: An Old Spanish Poem,*
vol. 2, *Grammar, Notes, and Commentary* (Princeton and Paris,
1922), 65.

The Life and History of King Apollonius

8.1   *I told the truth*: Apollonius is referring to having solved the rid-
dle. The Spanish translator seems to have had some difficulty
with the Latin text here, which says, "Quia filiam regis, ut
veram dixeram, conjugem et in matrimonium petivi: petivi
itaque, si fieri potest, in patria nostra nolo latere" (*GR,* 513). In
his English translation of the *GR,* Christopher Stace renders
this confusing sentence: "Because I sought the hand of a king's

daughter, who was in truth his wife, and wanted to marry her. So I have been seeking asylum, if it can be had" (*Gesta Romanorum. A New Translation,* Manchester, 2016), 383.

9.1   *Pentapolis*: See above, the note to *The Book of Apollonius* 98.4.

13.1   *Archistrates*: The Spanish chapter heading gives the king's name as *Archistrate,* while the body of the text reads *Archistrado* or *Archistrato.* Throughout the translation, we regularize the name.

13.2   *this young man . . . resembles Apollonius*: As will become clear, it does not make sense here that Archistrates would recognize Apollonius at this point in the story. As Stace explains in his translation of the *GR,* there appears to be an error in the Latin source, which reads "mihi comparandus est Appollonius" (Apollonius is comparable to me), but probably should read simply "mihi comparandus est" (he is a match for me); *GR,* 515, trans. Stace, 385.

    dais: The Latin source has the king sitting *in solis* (on the throne). But here we see an instance of translational domestication by the Spanish translator, who places the king, and perhaps Apollonius as well, on an *estrado,* a raised dais, generally covered with rugs and pillows, where Iberian nobles placed their thrones, sat, or reclined.

13.3   *that young man who bathed me is*: In *HART,* Apollonius massages as well as bathes King Archistrates. *The Book of Apollonius,* perhaps in an attempt to avoid any tinge of eroticism, omits the bathing scene altogether and depicts a ball game on the beach.

15.3   *the crown from his own head*: This scene and the importance of wearing the crown while entertaining the banqueters are highlighted much more in *The Book of Apollonius.* See stanzas 185–87.

15.4   *at the queen's command*: The Spanish text uses *reina* (queen) when the story means *princesa* (princess). The term *regina* was used for princesses and other high-ranking noblewomen in late medieval Latin, but our translator is a stickler and translates *regina* as "queen." The literal translation adds to the general air of incest that hangs over the entire narrative.

18.1   *as soon as I saw him, I loved him like a father*: This is one of the instances in the Spanish text where the translator has followed the Latin so literally that the result barely makes sense. As

Stace explains, the Latin text, "ut eum vidi, quia et amando factus sum pater" could be interpreted as "as soon as I saw him, through my love for him I became (as) his father" (*GR,* 518, trans. Stace, 389). Although Stace decided to render the line to mean that Archistrates chose Apollonius as a son-in-law the moment he saw him, the alternate reading seems to make better sense to us in the context of the story.

19.1   *Cleopatra*: Apollonius's new wife is called Cleopatra in this version of the story, in contrast to *The Book of Apollonius,* where she is Luciana.

21.1   *a ways away from the house:* The Latin text reads *a longe a domo;* Stace renders this "not far from the house," which seems logical, given the plot (*GR,* 519, trans. Stace, 391). However, the Spanish text correctly translates *a longe a domo* as "lexos de la casa," which we have respected in our translation to English.

21.1   *The body requires its last rites*: The Spanish translator seems to have misread *prestemus* (let us lend) for *postremus* (the last) or perhaps had a copy with an error. Our English translation is a compromise between the Spanish, "el postremo dolor que manda al cuerpo" (the last pain sent to the body) and the meaning of the Latin source, "Prestemus corpori, quod dolor exposcit," or "Let us bury the body as compassion requires" (*GR,* 519, trans. Stace, 391).

21.3   *Diana*: In the Roman pantheon, Diana is the virgin goddess of the hunt.

26.2   *Priapus*: In the Greek pantheon, the god Priapus was a god of fertility, represented as a small man with an enormous phallus. His cult was related to the region around the ancient Greek city of Lampsacus, now in Turkey. The statue and Tarsia's knowledge of the cult are not included in *The Book of Apollonius.* Archibald notes that while *HART*'s audiences may well have been familiar with the cult, the effect of the scene is to highlight Tarsia's learnedness (*Apollonius of Tyre,* 78).

27.5   *Athenagoras watched over her*: The Spanish translator has skipped over a word in the Latin text here, which makes clear that

Athenagoras gave the brothel keeper gifts so that he would take good care of Tarsia (*GR*, 524).

28.3 *Why can you not shed a tear for my daughter*: As *The Book of Apollonius* explains, Apollonius cannot weep at the tomb of his daughter because somehow his body senses that the monument is false. See stanzas 448–51.

29.4 *you will be recognized as their heir*: The Latin source reads "natalibus parentum tuorum representaberis," which Stace translates as "you will be reunited with your parents" (*GR*, 527, trans. Stace, 401). As G. A. A. Kortekaas explains, *represento* has here the rare meaning of "restoring," which would account for the Spanish translator's confusion; G. A. A. Kortekaas, *Commentary on the "Historia Apollonii regis Tyri"* (Leiden, 2007), 697.

29.7 *There is a house in the land*: The riddles in this episode in *HART*, the *GR*, and both the verse *Book of Apollonius* and this prose version are variations on riddles found in Symphosius's *Aenigmata*, a late fourth- or early fifth-century anthology of one hundred riddles that circulated widely throughout the Middle Ages. This riddle corresponds to *Aenigma* 12; see above, the note to *The Book of Apollonius* 505.1.

29.8 *I am the daughter of the forest*: *Aenigma* 13; see the note to *The Book of Apollonius* 509.1.

29.9 *It passes unharmed through rounds*: The Spanish translation of this riddle is incomprehensible. The prose translator and/or subsequently the incunable's typesetter may have both misread their source texts. For the Latin riddle, Symphosius's *Aenigma* 89, see the note to *The Book of Apollonius* 511.1.

35.1 *I who told you about King Antiochus's death*: In chapter 7, Elimito actually told Apollonius that there was a price on his head.

Bibliography

EDITIONS AND TRANSLATIONS

Alvar, Manuel, ed. *Libro de Apolonio*. 3 vols. Madrid, 1976.

Corbella, Dolores, ed. *Libro de Apolonio*. Madrid, 1992.

De Cesare, Giovanni Battista, ed. *Libro de Apolonio*. Milan, 1974.

Deyermond, Alan, ed. *Apollonius of Tyre: Two Fifteenth-Century Spanish Prose Romances*. Exeter, 1973.

Grismer, Raymond L., and Elizabeth Atkins, trans. *The Book of Apollonius*. Minneapolis, 1936.

Marden, C. Carroll, ed. *Libro de Apolonio: An Old Spanish Poem*. 2 vols. Princeton and Paris, 1917–1922.

Monedero, Carmen, ed. *Libro de Apolonio*. Madrid, 1987.

Pérez Gómez, Antonio, ed. *La vida e hystoria del rey Apolonio (Zaragoza? 1488?)*. Valencia, 1966.

Serís, Homero. *Nuevo ensayo de una biblioteca española de libros raros y curiosos*. New York, 1964.

Zubillaga, Carina. *Poesía narrativa clerical en su contexto manuscrito. Estudio y edición del Ms. Esc. K-III-4 ("Libro de Apolonio," "Vida de Santa María Egipciaca," "Libro de los tres reyes de Oriente")*. Buenos Aires, 2014.

FURTHER READING

Ancos, Pablo. "Encuentros y desencuentros de la Antigüedad tardía con la Edad Media en el *Libro de Apolonio*." *Tirant* 21 (2018): 281–300.

Archibald, Elizabeth. *Apollonius of Tyre: Medieval and Renaissance Themes and Variations*. Woodbridge, 1991.

Arizaleta, Amaia. "Los comienzos de la aventura moral de Apolonio en

textos medievales y renacentistas *(Libro de Apolonio, Confisyón del amante, Historia de Apolonio, El Patrañuelo)."* In *Le commencement . . . en perspective: L'analyse de l'incipit et des oeuvres pionnières dans la littérature du Moyen Âge et du Siècle d'or,* edited by Pierre Darnis, 9–30. Toulouse, 2010.

Brownlee, Marina Scordilis. "Writing and Scripture in the *Libro de Apolonio:* The Conflation of Hagiography and Romance." *Hispanic Review* 51, no. 2 (1983): 159–74.

Desing, Matthew V. "Women on the Edge of Glory: Tarsiana, Oria, and Liminality." *La corónica* 42, no. 1 (2013): 229–58.

Deyermond, Alan D. "Motivos folklóricos y técnica estructural en el *Libro de Apolonio."* *Filología* 13 (1968–1969): 121–49.

Francomano, Emily C. "The Riddle of Incest in Medieval Iberia." *La corónica* 35, no. 2 (2007): 5–14.

Grieve, Patricia E. "Building Christian Narrative: The Rhetoric of Knowledge, Revelation, and Interpretation in *Libro de Apolonio."* In *The Book and the Magic of Reading in the Middle Ages,* edited by Albrecht Classen, 149–69. New York, 1998.

Hazbun, Geraldine. "Memory as *Mester* in the *Libro de Alexandre* and *Libro de Apolonio."* In *Medieval Hispanic Studies in Memory of Alan Deyermond,* edited by Andrew M. Beresford, Louise M. Haywood, and Julian Weiss, 91–119. Woodbridge, 2013.

Kortekaas, G. A. A. *Commentary on the "Historia Apollonii regis Tyri."* Leiden, 2007.

Lacarra, María Jesús. "La *Vida e historia del rey Apolonio* [¿Zaragoza, Juan Hurus, 1488?] y su trayectoria genérica." *Tirant* 19 (2016): 47–56.

Lawrance, Jeremy N. H. "Humanism in the Iberian Peninsula." In *The Impact of Humanism on Western Europe,* edited by Anthony Goodman and Angus Mackay, 220–58. London, 1990.

Pascual-Argente, Clara. "The Survival of Medieval Antiquity: Fifteenth-Century Transformations of the *Roman Antique* Tradition in Castile and Beyond." In *Early Modern Constructions of Europe,* edited by Florian Kläger and Gerd Bayer, 71–89. New York, 2016.

Pinet, Simone. *The Task of the Cleric: Cartography, Translation, and Economics in Thirteenth-Century Iberia.* Toronto, 2016.

Rico, Francisco. "La clerecía del mester." Pts. 1 and 2. *Hispanic Review* 53, no. 1 (1985): 1–23; 53, no. 2 (1985): 127–50.

Surtz, Ronald E. "El héroe intelectual en el mester de clerecía." *La Torre* 1, no. 2 (1987): 264–74.

Weiss, Julian. *The "Mester de clerecía": Intellectuals and Ideologies in Thirteenth-Century Castile.* Woodbridge, 2006.

Index